PRAISE FOR

SAY YOU'LL BE MINE

"I couldn't put down this page-turner. A warm, smart, sexy, and absolutely charming debut with the most important lesson at its center: Real love is built on courage. Meghna and Karthik's happily ever after is the new *When Harry Met Sally*. Naina Kumar's *Say You'll Be Mine* has it all."

—COLLEEN HOOVER

"A fresh and charming story about finding love without losing yourself . . . I rooted for these wonderfully headstrong, big-hearted characters all the way."

—LINDA HOLMES, *New York Times* bestselling author of *Evvie Drake Starts Over*

"Naina Kumar's fresh, compelling voice and lovable characters (including a starchy hero that is now at the very top of my all-time favorites list) made me fall head over heels for *Say You'll Be Mine* from the very first page. This debut about love, culture, family, and friendship is absolutely irresistible—I didn't want to put it down!"

—SARAH ADLER, author of *Mrs. Nash's Ashes*

"Swoony, smart, and charming, *Say You'll Be Mine* is the type of South Asian diaspora romance I've always wished for. Naina Kumar's debut is spectacular."

—NISHA SHARMA, author of *Dating Dr. Dil*

SAY YOU'LL BE MINE

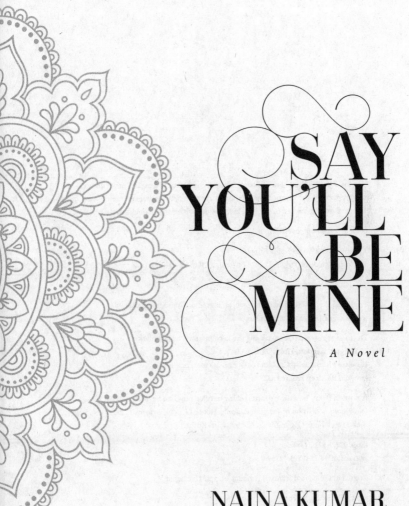

SAY YOU'LL BE MINE

A Novel

NAINA KUMAR

DELL

New York

A Dell Trade Paperback Original

Copyright © 2024 by Naina Kumar
Book club guide copyright © 2024 by Penguin Random House LLC

All rights reserved.

Published in the United States by Dell, an imprint of Random House, a division of Penguin Random House LLC, New York.

Dell is a registered trademark and the D colophon is a trademark of Penguin Random House LLC.
Random House Book Club and colophon are trademarks of Penguin Random House LLC.

A portion from the author's forthcoming untitled novel, to be published by Dell Books, a division of Penguin Random House LLC, New York, in 2025, is excerpted here. Copyright © 2024 by Naina Kumar.

ISBN 978-0-593-72388-3
Ebook ISBN 978-0-593-72389-0

Printed in the United States of America on acid-free paper

randomhousebooks.com

randomhousebookclub.com

9 8 7 6 5 4 3 2 1

Book design by Debbie Glasserman

To my family, who inspire me in so many ways. I love you all so much.

"Ms. Raman, what's an 'arse'?"

Meghna Raman's eyes snapped to her sixth-grade student, Paige, who sat crisscross applesauce on the floor with the others as they went through their scripts, highlighting their respective lines.

"A what?"

"An 'arse,'" Paige replied, pointing at the piece of paper in front of her. "It says it right here. Eliza goes to that horse race and tells the horse to move its 'bloomin' arse.'"

A few of the students snickered, and Meghna let out a sigh. She'd meant to edit that line before passing out the scripts, but it had completely slipped her mind. To be fair, she'd only had three days to prepare for this first day of rehearsal. Only three days to wrap her mind around directing the middle school's fall production of *My Fair Lady*.

"It's 'ass,'" seventh grader Derek told Paige with a smirk. "It's the way English people say 'ass.'"

"Though we'll be using the word 'bum,'" Meghna quickly added.

She didn't want any emails from the parents complaining about this. "I'll send out a new version of the script tomorrow."

"So, now it'll be 'move your bloomin' bum,'" a student whispered loudly, sending the room into another round of giggles.

Meghna shook her head, holding back the grin threatening to break across her face. Teaching wasn't exactly her dream job, but she loved these kids. Even when they drove her up the wall. She checked the clock, wrapped up rehearsal, and headed home to a thrilling night of grading papers.

But before she had even set foot inside her apartment, her phone rang. She blew out a breath and answered without even checking to see who it was. She knew exactly who was calling.

"Hi, Mom," she said as she unlocked the front door.

Her mother greeted her enthusiastically, asked about her day, then launched into a recitation of everything that had happened during Meghna's brother's visit last weekend.

"Beta, he wanted to cook dinner on Saturday and he made macaroni and cheese. *Macaroni and cheese*," her mother repeated incredulously. "It tasted like nothing. Like air. I tried to mix in a little mango achar to give it *some* flavor, but—"

Meghna shuddered at the thought of what that would taste like. "I'm guessing that didn't work?"

"Not at all."

Meghna chucked off her shoes and headed toward the kitchen. "Well, I'm glad Samir was able to visit you and Dad this time. Even if it resulted in *mac and cheese*." She infused the words with all the horror and melodrama her mother had. "I know you've both been missing him."

"We were happy to see him," her mother said. "He's very busy, but we understand. Being an engineer takes a lot of hard work."

Meghna grimaced, dropped a stack of mail on her kitchen counter, and settled in. She knew the exact speech her mother was about to deliver. She'd heard it so many times over the years. She'd even given it a few titles: "The Difficult but Satisfying Life of an Engineer" or "Why Engineering Is the Only Meaningful Profession" or "Meghna, It's Not Too Late to Quit Your Job and Become an Engineer." Though her mother would never put it that bluntly, Meghna knew that was what she really meant.

As if on cue, her mom launched into describing all the difficult and rewarding aspects of engineering, things she had experienced firsthand, she reminded Meghna. After all, she had placed first in engineering college back in India, beating out Meghna's father, who had placed only sixth. But somehow, her mother said, she had fallen in love with him anyway. Their families had considered their relationship scandalous at first, especially since her mother's family was North Indian and her father's South Indian, but they eventually came around, and Meghna's parents had ended up with the first "love marriage" in their family.

Meghna put her phone on speaker, tuning out her mother's familiar words. As a kid, she'd loved listening to her parents' great love story. She'd asked to hear it again and again, dreaming about finding that kind of love for herself one day. She still hoped for it. Even though she had no clear prospects in sight. Even though it felt less and less likely every day.

She sighed and opened her mail. She read a few bills, set aside a couple flyers, and saved a stationery supply catalog she had never ordered from, but loved to look through. And that's when she saw it. A deceptively simple-looking white envelope. It wouldn't have stood out to her, but the address on the front was written in a style of calligraphy she knew all too well.

A wedding invitation.

She frowned. Most of her close friends were already married. And the few who were single wouldn't be getting married anytime soon. Slightly puzzled, she took out the invitation. Two names in large, bold italic sprawled across the middle of the page: *Seth Mitchell and Julie Cox.*

Meghna's stomach dropped.

She hadn't counted Seth in her mental tally of close friends. Seth was in a different category altogether. And even though she'd known he was dating someone, he'd never referred to that person as his girlfriend. Let alone mentioned that the two of them were thinking about *marriage*.

Meghna had met Seth as a college freshman when they'd been assigned as partners in Intro to Creative Writing. She had been smitten when she saw his lanky build, dark-green eyes, and blond hair that he left a little too long.

They'd both wanted to major in creative writing, but Meghna had declared an education major instead. Seth had constantly tried to change her mind.

"It's not that complicated. If you want to write plays, you should write them," he had told her, his voice full of conviction. He hadn't understood why she couldn't pursue writing full-time, but that wasn't his fault. Seth wasn't like her. He never doubted his abilities. Never doubted that he would become a successful songwriter. She'd envied his certainty, his optimism, his lack of fear.

When they'd started dating their junior year, she thought it was the beginning of her own great love story. Seth had been kind, funny, and honest to a fault. "This entire section has to go, Meg," he'd told her as he reviewed her latest draft. "It doesn't add anything." His comments had stung at first, but she soon got used to his direct feedback. She'd started to appreciate the way he couldn't help but tell the truth. It had made his praise even more meaningful. When he'd told her that her character work was stunning, she believed him fully. When he'd called her beautiful, she didn't doubt that he meant it. And when he'd broken up with her after graduation, she knew he meant that too.

"We're friends, Meg," he'd said. "You think so too, right? That we're better off as friends?"

To save face, she'd forced a smile and lied. "Of course, Seth. We'll always be friends."

Surprisingly, their friendship and writing partnership continued. Seth still called or emailed every week. He sent lyrics and voice memos of his songs, and she sent him pieces of the play she had started in college and was still working on. No matter what she was going through, Seth was always willing to listen, to hear her out, to encourage her, or to distract her by making her laugh.

But despite all their conversations, they somehow never ended up talking about their months of dating in college. He never brought it up, and she was too scared to mention it. She still had so many questions. Did he regret ending things? Did he ever think about that time? Had he ever felt anything for her at all?

Meghna swallowed hard, setting the invitation facedown on the counter and pushing all thoughts of Seth out of her mind.

Her mother was still talking to her over the phone. "And before you say anything, let me just tell you about him," her mother said. "His name is Karthik. He comes from a good family. Well educated. Very tall. *And* he's an engineer."

Meghna's prediction about her mother's speech had been completely wrong. This wasn't a talk about it not being too late for Meghna to become an engineer. This was a brand-new speech. One titled, "Meghna, It's Not Too Late for You to *Marry* an Engineer."

"You don't have to promise anything," her mother said. "Just meet him. Once. That's all."

Meghna blinked, completely stunned. She'd never agreed to anything like this before. In fact, it was rare that her parents ever brought up the topic of arranged marriage. They'd found love on their own and expected that she'd do the same. But after she'd turned twenty-eight earlier this year, they'd begun to dial up the pressure. Making comments about her dating life that they probably thought were subtle, but were just hurtful reminders that even though she wanted to find the right person, she hadn't managed it yet. But those small comments and hints were usually as far as her parents went. They had never seriously brought a rishta, a potential marriage proposal, to her.

And they'd never really talked with her about what the arranged marriage process looked like, though Ankita, her closest friend from childhood, had gone through it and had recently gotten engaged to someone her parents had introduced to her. She'd said the initial introduction was awkward, but that it felt like normal dating after that. "Think of it like Tinder," she'd said. "Except your parents are the algorithm, and they're only showing you people they've already swiped right on." She'd thought for a moment, then added, "And both parties are looking for a lifelong commitment. Not just, you know, a one-night stand."

Meghna had laughed, but hadn't thought about it any further. She certainly hadn't thought about going through the process herself. She didn't have anything against it, but it all sounded pretty . . . inorganic. Unromantic. She wanted to meet someone who would sweep her off her feet. Someone who could rival those initial butterflies and swoon-inducing moments she'd experienced with Seth. And she found it hard to believe that she would meet that person through her parents.

But she did want to get married one day. And when she thought about it, she'd tried everything else: blind dates, dating apps, physically bumping into cute strangers at bars. Maybe, in the back of her mind, she'd thought that Seth was out there. That one day, he'd wonder why they hadn't worked out, and they could just try to pick up where they'd left off.

Clearly, that wasn't a possibility anymore.

The back of Meghna's neck warmed, and her hands involuntarily clenched into fists. If Seth could let go of their past and move on, so could she. Maybe getting back out there would help.

"Okay," she told her mom.

The line went quiet. Her mother's stunned silence was somehow louder than anything she could have said.

"Mom, did you hear me? I said 'okay.'"

"Oh. Great, beta. Good. That's good. Leave it to me. I'll arrange everything." She paused, then continued, a faint panic in her voice. "Not your marriage. When I said 'everything,' I didn't mean your marriage. It's just a meeting. An introduction. That I'm arranging. That's it."

Meghna smothered a laugh.

"So, I'll let you know. About the meeting. Soon. But I have to go now. Okay. So. Bye." The call beeped, signaling that her mother had hung up.

Meghna shook her head. She knew her mom had ended the call on purpose, likely fearing that Meghna would change her mind or try to back out, but she had no intention of getting out of this. After all, what did she have to lose?

2

In life and in engineering, Karthik Murthy found that keeping and following a clear set of principles made everything a lot easier. The rules of engineering had come to him naturally. They were sharp and sure. Specific and defined. Life, however, tended to be more complicated. The real world presented too many variables. Too many outcomes he couldn't predict. And unfortunately, he was once again stuck in a situation with no clear path forward.

He stood outside a modest, two-story redbrick home in suburban Dallas. A home that his mother believed was the home of his future bride. Of course, she had thought that about the last seven homes they had visited over the past month. But this time, she said, she was absolutely sure they were about to meet her soon-to-be daughter-in-law. Guilt singed his conscience, but he just nodded and rang the door-bell. There was no way this woman, or any woman, would ever become her daughter-in-law, but he couldn't say that. He had no choice but to play along and hope this would all be over as quickly as possible.

He pasted on a smile as the door unlocked with a mechanical

click. An older woman in a cotton mint-green kurti and jeans waved them inside.

"Welcome, welcome. I'm Radhika."

She hugged his mother, shook his hand, and led them straight to the living room, where several cups of tea and an assortment of snacks waited for them on the coffee table. He scanned the food quickly, pleased to see that the samosas were smaller than normal, the way he preferred. It meant a better fried-pastry-to-vegetable-stuffing ratio than the larger ones he'd had at yesterday's meeting.

He was wondering how many he could take while still being polite, when an amused snort broke his train of thought.

"You hungry?"

Karthik flushed. "Sorry, I—" He looked up at the woman standing in front of him, and whatever he'd been about to say left his mind.

She was stunning. With her long, curly hair and big brown eyes, he thought her objectively beautiful, but it was her wide, uninhibited smile that made him pause. She was vibrant. Brilliant. He felt dull by comparison.

"No, it's fine," she said, waving a hand dismissively. "I was just joking. Go ahead and start."

Karthik shook his head. These meetings followed a very rigid agenda. They weren't supposed to go this way. "No, we can only eat after the introductions."

She raised an eyebrow. "Why?"

Why? "That's how it's usually done."

She shrugged, then gestured toward the entrance of the room, where her parents were greeting his mother. "My parents really won't care," she said, handing him a plate. He took it automatically.

She looked at him expectantly, then frowned. "Really, go ahead." She grabbed a plate of her own and started adding samosas to it. "I'll join you, if you want. The only thing you can't have is—"

"You must be Meghna," his mother said. "I'm Shanti. Karthik's mom."

Meghna. Her name was Meghna. Karthik was sure his mother had told him that before. She had probably shared the woman's biodata or a résumé, but Karthik never paid much attention to the emails his mother sent about these meetings. He wouldn't be marrying any of these women, so there wasn't any point.

"Nice to meet you, Aunty," Meghna said as she handed his mother a cup of tea. The two of them took a seat on the opposite couch, and Karthik sat down as well. He grabbed his own cup and blew across the surface.

So far, none of this was going the way he'd expected. His mother was supposed to introduce him to Meghna. Before he had tea. Or the snacks. She wasn't supposed to assume they had already introduced themselves. He frowned. Should he have introduced himself?

Meghna's parents joined them, her father greeting Karthik with a firm handshake before sitting down next to his daughter. He whispered something that made Meghna laugh, then passed a cup of tea to his wife.

The conversation quickly shifted into familiar territory, and Karthik breathed a sigh of relief. It was time for the parents' small talk, which meant he wasn't required to participate. He filled his plate as the parents talked about what part of India they were from, why they had come to the United States, and how difficult it was to care for their aging relatives while living halfway around the world.

His mother then provided a truncated version of his résumé: where he had gone to school, what he did for work, where he lived. Meghna's parents quickly did the same.

He learned that Meghna worked as a middle school English teacher. Her parents said it matter-of-factly, but he knew the subtle signs of parental disappointment well. Even if he hadn't, Meghna's body grew tense when her parents talked about her job.

It wasn't easy facing that kind of pressure. Those expectations. And it was even harder to not let the desire to please them, to make them proud, affect your decisions. To choose what you wanted, knowing that doing so would result in their disapproval. Or, as had been the case with Karthik's father, his disinterest. His neglect.

"I'm sorry your husband had to stay back in New York," Meghna's mother suddenly said. "We would have loved to meet him."

Karthik's mother smiled, but the strain on her face was obvious. At least to him.

"He really wanted to come," she said. "But unfortunately, he had to stay back for work."

As his mother absently twisted the thin gold band on her ring finger, Karthik wondered whether she had just told the truth. Prioritizing work over family was par for the course with his father, but he wasn't sure if his dad had asked to stay home in New York or if his mother had asked him not to come. Either way, it was for the best. His father had a way of bringing out the worst in him.

Karthik turned his attention back to the snacks on the table, ready to sample some more. He grabbed a jalebi and a couple mini samosas, but when he reached for the pani puri, Meghna shook her head. She checked to make sure their parents weren't looking, then ran her finger quickly across her throat in a *you're dead* gesture. He retracted his arm immediately and took a second look at the pani puri, trying to figure out what was wrong with them.

"Meghna, why don't you show Karthik the study?" her mother said. "There's such interesting art on the walls there. Isn't that right, Akshay?"

"I don't know what you—" Meghna's father started, but Karthik's mother quickly interrupted.

"I'm sure you'd love to see it," she told Karthik.

Meghna's mother nodded her head so emphatically, Karthik worried her earrings might fly clear across the room.

"Oh, right," Meghna said after a moment, looking as if she was barely holding back a laugh. "The paintings in the study. They're *really* something." She got up and gestured for him to follow.

Ah, yes. This phase of the meeting. The one-on-one conversation.

He always felt bad about this part. Well, really, he felt bad about the whole thing. Wasting her time. Her family's time. Disappointing them. And his mother. But he didn't know what else to do. How else to go about it. Or get out of it.

He joined her, walking the short distance across the hall to her parents' study. Once there, they stood silently at the entrance, looking at the three framed print copies of Monet's *Water Lilies* arranged on the opposite wall.

"So, this is it," he said.

"Yeah, that's it." Meghna shrugged. "I'm pretty sure they came with the house, but I guess they had to make up some reason for us to talk alone. At least that's how I've heard these things are supposed to go."

He nodded. She was right. This was exactly how it was supposed to go. They were finally back on track. And that meant it was time to break the news. After seven meetings, he'd figured out a pretty reliable script. Reactions had been mixed, but he'd learned it was best to do it right at the beginning. To just get it out there and . . . What had she just said? That's how she'd *heard* this was supposed to go? She couldn't mean—

"Is this the first time you've done this?"

She let out a small laugh, then lifted a shoulder. "That obvious, huh?"

"No, it's just . . . You've really never done this before?"

"Nope. Never. Have you?"

"This is my eighth meeting this month," he said.

Her eyebrows rose. "Eighth?" She walked over to a pair of brown overstuffed chairs, sat down, and crossed her legs. "So, you're an old pro, then," she said, her voice light and airy. "You'll have to tell me what usually happens next."

He took the seat across from her. He could do that. By now, he could recite the normal agenda in his sleep. "We get about twenty minutes alone. Then our parents come by with some excuse to call us back. They have a few more minutes of small talk and then it's time for my mother and I to leave."

"But eight meetings in a month?" she asked. "That can't be what people normally do. It sounds like a lot."

"I don't really know." He didn't have anything to measure it against. "How many do you have next month?"

"None. This is the first time my parents have ever asked me to meet anyone. They haven't set up any others." She scrunched up her nose. "At least, I don't think they have. They haven't mentioned any others."

His curiosity was piqued. "Would you go on more, if they asked you to?"

"Maybe. I think so," she said.

He frowned. None of this was adding up. Most of the other women he'd met had understood the process. Been invested. But Meghna . . . It was almost as if she'd shown up today just for the hell of it. To see what would happen.

He froze. Had she even agreed to this? Maybe her parents had just sprung it on her. He considered for a moment, then nodded. That was more likely. She didn't seem like the kind of person who would want, or need, her parents to set her up.

To confirm his new hypothesis, he asked, "Why would you say yes to any of this in the first place?"

"Why would *you* say yes?" she parroted back.

"I have a good reason," he said. "But if you wanted to get married, I wouldn't think you'd need to . . . I mean, you seem like you have . . . like you could . . ."

"Are you saying I look like I date around a lot?"

Karthik's cheeks warmed. "That's not what I meant."

"No, it's fine." She leaned back in her chair. "Suffice it to say whatever I've been doing hasn't been working. And you don't know me—maybe I'm incredibly traditional."

He looked at her skeptically. She grinned.

"What? You don't think I'm very traditional?" she asked.

"You could be," he admitted. "But if you were, this wouldn't be your first meeting. You'd have started years ago."

"Wow. You're calling me old now?"

What? A bead of sweat formed on his forehead. "No. Definitely not. That's not what I said."

Meghna crossed her arms. "It's what you meant, though."

He shook his head, but couldn't figure out how to respond. Should he apologize? Yes. That was a good idea. He'd apologize and then he'd find a way to get back to his script. He could still salvage this. He could still— *Was she smiling?*

"You were joking," he said carefully. Slowly. Just in case he was wrong.

"Yes," she said with a laugh. "I'm just giving you a hard time. You're right. I'm not super traditional. But you don't seem that traditional, either. At least, your family can't be *that* traditional if they're fine with the idea of you marrying someone who's only half-Tamil." She pointed at herself.

He shrugged. He knew that some of the more traditional families preferred, sometimes required, that their kids marry someone within their same ethnic group, but his mother had never placed much emphasis on that. And his father . . . Well, Karthik didn't particularly care what his father thought.

"At this point I think my mother would be happy if I married anyone," he said. "And if I was marrying someone Indian, that would just be a bonus."

"I've never asked my parents about it, but I think they see it that way too. But back to you, what's your 'good reason' for agreeing to meet eight women in one month?"

He grimaced. "Okay, maybe calling it a 'good reason' was going too far, but my mother asked me to and I—"

"Couldn't say no?"

"Yes. No. It's—" He ran a hand through his hair in frustration.

"The last few years, all my mother has wanted to talk about is when I'll get married. Every time she sees me. It's the only topic of conversation. And I know she means well, but I don't plan on getting married."

Meghna cocked her head to the side, studying him closely. As if he were a slide under a microscope. He resisted the urge to fidget.

"You don't want to get married?" she finally asked.

"No."

"Ever?"

"No." He swallowed. He wished he'd been able to bring this up at the beginning. Now he was so off-kilter he couldn't remember what he usually said. How he usually explained this.

"Oh," she said. "Okay. Does your mother know that?"

He held back a sigh. "I don't know how to tell her," he said. "The way she talks about it sometimes, it seems like my future marriage is the only thing she's excited about, the only thing she's looking forward to. I don't want to take that away from her." His father had taken enough. Not to mention that the last time Karthik had tried to have this conversation with her, it hadn't . . . It hadn't gone well.

"I love her," he said. "But I wish we were able to talk about something else. Anything else."

Meghna nodded, listening intently.

"Last month, she told me that if I agreed to meet a few of the women she had selected, she'd never bring up the topic of marriage again. So, I said yes. I told her I'd meet anyone she wanted for a year."

"A year? That's so long."

"It is, but I negotiated her down from three. In the end, it seemed like a small price to pay to never have to hear about it again. I just didn't realize how efficient she would be. She's set up two meetings a week for the next few months. And they're all over the country. I don't know when I'll get a weekend to myself again," he said.

"Can't you back out?"

"I can. But I won't. I told her I would do this and I'm not going to go back on my word." Growing up, he'd watched his father make all kinds of promises to his mom and then break nearly every one of them. Karthik refused to do anything that would make his mother think he had turned out anything like his dad. He had promised himself years ago that he would do his best to be honest. Patient. That he'd try to always be there for his mother. To listen to her. Make her laugh. Do anything that would bring her the tiniest bit of happiness.

"So, you're going to do this every weekend for the next year?" Meghna asked incredulously.

"I have to keep my end of the bargain."

"What if you meet someone you actually like?"

"That won't happen."

"How can you be so sure?"

"Because I don't want it to happen," he said sharply.

"Really?" she asked, her voice dripping with doubt. "You're saying you can just will it? Just decide to control your feelings?"

"Yes." He didn't understand how it was even a question. Of course he could. He always had.

"Haven't you ever felt something for someone you weren't supposed to?" she asked. "Accidentally fallen in love with someone completely wrong for you?"

No. He'd never been in love. And to feel that way accidentally? Absurd.

"No one falls in love by accident," he said bitingly. "Love takes time. Intention. Commitment. It doesn't just happen."

"I think you're wrong," she said.

He scoffed. "Why? Because you've *accidentally* fallen in love before?"

A hurt expression briefly flashed across Meghna's face. Then she lifted her chin and met his gaze. "Yes," she said.

Huh. He wondered who she had been in love with. And why it hadn't worked out. Karthik waited for her to elaborate but was met with only silence.

"Well, I haven't," he finally said. They looked at each other for a few moments and the silence resumed.

"Well," she said. "It's probably time for us to head back."

He glanced at his watch. "I don't think so. They usually come get us when it's time."

Meghna let out a loud sigh. "What else do we really have to talk about? You don't want to ever get married. I do. Besides, isn't this what usually happens next?" She extended her arm for a handshake and gave him a tight, forced smile. "It was nice meeting you."

Karthik automatically reached out to shake her hand, but he felt unsteady. Like he'd been walking down a flight of stairs and accidentally missed a step. His mind whirred, trying to come up with something to say. She started to walk past him.

"Wait," he said, putting a hand on her arm. She glanced at him over her shoulder. "What was wrong with the pani puri?"

Her eyebrows knit in confusion.

"The pani puri?" he asked again. "The ones you warned me not to eat?"

"Oh," she said. "Nothing. There just weren't that many left and I wanted to have them later."

"They're my favorite," he said. It was true, but he didn't know why he had felt the need to tell her that.

"Mine too," she said coolly. She shook his hand off her arm and continued walking to the living room, leaving him to follow her.

Later, after he'd said his goodbyes and stepped out into the oppressive Texas heat, he wondered if she was sitting inside, eating the pani puri now. He shook the thought from his mind and climbed into the rental car, trying to avoid the eager glances from his mother. She was wearing the same nervous-but-hopeful expression she wore after every one of these meetings. He hated that look. He hated letting her down. But no matter what, when she asked what he thought, he would respond, like he always did, "I'm sorry, Amma. I don't think it'll work out."

So, it shocked the hell out of him when she asked the question this time and he heard himself say, "I need some time to think about it." He had barely even processed his own words when his mother's arms came around him, wrapping him in a hug.

"That's good," she said excitedly. "That's all I wanted." She continued, saying she would call Meghna's mother and exchange phone numbers, so he could call Meghna whenever he wanted. *If* he wanted, she quickly amended. There was no pressure, she said. But he barely heard any of that. His mind was stuck in a constant refrain: *What did I just do?*

3

"So, the guy was a bust, huh," Ankita said, her voice sounding a bit muffled as it came through Meghna's car speakers.

"Yeah. I mean, the whole thing was weird. He was so . . . I don't know. Uptight? And kind of rude? Or maybe just blunt? Sometimes it's hard to tell."

Meghna had been thinking it over all day and she wasn't able to make up her mind. Wasn't able to make sense of him. All she knew was that after a long day of work, after-school rehearsals, and an internal replaying of everything Karthik had said to her, she was mentally exhausted. She'd called Ankita the second she got into her car, needing to get an unbiased opinion and to vent to her friend.

"Please," Ankita said. "You're always giving people the benefit of the doubt. If you think he was rude, he was rude."

She made a good point. "Fine. *Maybe*. Maybe he was rude," Meghna said as she changed lanes toward the exit that would take her home. "It doesn't matter anyway. He was very clear that he never wants to get married."

Her friend groaned. "What a waste of time. Like you need to go through your parents to find another terrified-of-marriage, commitment-phobic wastrel."

"Wastrel?"

"I've been reading a lot of regency romance. Was he cute at least?"

Hot, Meghna thought. *He was hot.* He'd been tall, with a sharp jaw and a neatly trimmed beard. His hair had seemed to naturally fall perfectly, as if not a single hair dared to be out of place. He'd been solemn, but she'd thought his demeanor and unintended insults were just nerves at the beginning. She had found it endearing. Until the very end.

Her phone rang with an incoming call. Adrenaline spiked through her when Seth's name flashed across the screen. "Ankita, I'm sorry, I'm getting another call. I promise I'll call you right back." She quickly hung up and answered.

"Meg! How are you?" The warmth in Seth's voice immediately lifted her spirits. She hadn't realized how much she'd been wanting to talk to him.

"Good! But first, I have to know how your pitch went!" After years of trying to break out as a songwriter in Nashville, Seth had finally made a name for himself in the country-pop crossover scene. Just this week, a major recording artist—who happened to be an ex-boybander that Meghna *may* have had a poster of in her childhood bedroom—had requested a meeting with Seth, wanting to hear any ideas he might have for his new album.

"It was amazing," Seth said. "I played him the opening of that song I told you about last week and he loved it. He wants to hear the rest." He laughed. "I didn't tell him I haven't finished it, though. Or that I'm really stuck on the third verse."

"Send it over," Meghna said easily. "I'll take a look tonight."

"Really? You're truly the best, you know that, right?"

"Yeah, yeah. I know. By the way, I heard 'Angel in Red' on the radio the other day. It was surreal. I had no idea you were going to go with those lines I sent."

"Well, when they were *that* good, how could I not?"

Meghna's chest warmed.

"How's your work going?" he asked. "Wait, you sent me a text, I think. That they signed off on the play or something?"

"They did," she said, touched that he'd remembered. She'd been fighting for her school to have a theater program since her first day on the job. When the school board had unexpectedly granted her request this semester, she'd been overjoyed, then immediately overwhelmed at the idea of teaching both English and theater and putting a full production together on such short notice.

"I have no idea how it'll turn out. We barely had any surplus in our budget, so we're really stretching to make ends meet, but I'm just happy they didn't give the extra to athletics again this year."

"Well, it'll be nice for you to get back to your roots," Seth said. "Just like old times. You basically played the starring role in every production in college."

Meghna laughed at the exaggeration. "I remember it differently . . ."

"Well, theater was always where your heart was at."

"It still is," Meghna insisted. "Actually, I just sent you a revised version of my second act. I tightened up the part you mentioned, and I think it's really coming along. Have you had a chance to look at it?"

He blew out a loud breath, a *whoosh*ing sound traveling through her car speakers. "No. I'm so sorry. I've been under a lot of stress. So much has been happening. That's what I was calling about, really. I wanted to see if you'd gotten the invitation."

Meghna's smile slipped off her face. Her good mood was snuffed out immediately. "Yes. Yes, I did. Congratulations!" she said, forcing herself to sound happy. "I, umm, I had no idea you and Julie had gotten so serious." Seth had barely even brought up Julie's name around Meghna. And when he had, he'd always made it sound so casual. Seth flitted in and out of "situationships" all the time. She'd just assumed this was another one.

"I really meant to call you before the invitations went out," he said apologetically. "But this all happened so much faster than we planned. Julie had her heart set on this particular venue and they had a surprise cancellation and things really snowballed from there. We've booked the caterers and she's found the dress and there are only a few things left to do."

He paused and took a deep breath. "You know, you've been my closest friend since college. You supported my songwriting dreams in those early days when no one else believed in me. And even though I have an entire team now, you're still the first person I want to send every first bad draft to. Your feedback means more to me than anyone else's. There's no one I trust more. No one whose input matters more. You just . . . you mean the world to me, Meg."

"Thanks, Seth," she said. Even though his words were incredibly kind, a vague sense of dread started growing in the pit of her stomach. "You mean a lot to me too."

"So, I guess what I'm trying to ask is . . . will you be my best man?"

Shock turned her blood to ice. She could barely process what she'd just heard. *His best man? His best* man?

"Wow," she said, a bit numbly. "I don't know what to say."

"Say yes. Please. I can't imagine doing this with anyone else. Plus, think how adorable you'll look in a tux."

Adorable? Like she was a baby or a small woodland animal. *Ugh.*

"And think about how much fun we'll have at the bachelor party!" he said.

She would have to go to his bachelor party? No, she quickly realized. She would have to *organize* the bachelor party. She couldn't do this. She couldn't stand next to him as he vowed to love and cherish someone else. She had to come up with some excuse. Anything.

"You know I'd love to and I'm so honored you asked me, but . . ." Her mind went blank. She couldn't think of a single reason to say no.

"But nothing," he said. "I get why you're hesitating. I know it's not exactly conventional and people might think we're weird, but you've been there for me. For so many years. This is the most important day of my life and I need you. I need you to be there. Please?"

How could she refuse that? "Of course, Seth," she found herself saying. "Of course, I'll be there."

"Thank you," he said, his relief evident in his voice. "It'll be fun, Meg. Really. We can talk about all of the details later, but I'm so excited."

"Me too," she said, trying to infuse her voice with as much enthusiasm as she could muster. "I can't wait. Congratulations again, Seth. I really am happy for you."

The second the call ended, a dull, throbbing pain started in her chest. Her mind went back to Karthik's words. *No one falls in love by accident.* She could almost hear his dry tone. His disbelief. The way he'd spat out the word *love* like it was poison.

But he was wrong. And she had been wrong too. She hadn't just accidentally fallen in love with Seth all those years ago. She may have accidentally stayed in it. She wanted to scream.

Karthik's voice rang in her head again. *Why? Because you've accidentally fallen in love before?* She wasn't sure why those words had hurt so much in the moment. She didn't think it was the question itself, but the way he'd said it. Like she was some unrealistic, naïve Pollyanna.

So, she had accidentally fallen for her best friend. That was normal. And they'd ended up dating. Also normal. And maybe she still had feelings for him. Years later. Even though he was about to get married. While she stood next to him as his "best man." But that didn't matter. Who was Karthik to judge her? Her hands tightened around the steering wheel in anger. Thank God she never had to see him again.

Karthik had made up his mind. He had to see her again. He didn't have much of a choice. He couldn't see any other way out of the mess he was in. Granted, it was a mess of his own making, but he didn't know how he had let it get this out of hand.

He had only been back in Manhattan a few days when he received a calendar invite that made him groan. Today was his father's birthday. It had completely slipped his mind. Thankfully, his family didn't do large birthday celebrations. It would just be him, his parents, and the gulab jamuns they always picked up from their favorite sweet shop in Jackson Heights.

He spent that day at work mentally preparing himself to see his father. He couldn't remember the last time they had been in the same room together. Sure, he made weekly visits to his parents' house in Queens to see his mother, but he always chose times he knew his father would be away. He was tempted to skip tonight, but he knew how much his absence would hurt his mom.

So, he showed up at his parents' house promptly at six-thirty, with a birthday card he had picked up at the corner store around the block. His mother, as always, was glad to see him. His father was curt but cordial. The dinner progressed without incident and Karthik thought he might be able to escape the night unscathed. He should have known something would happen to break the peace. Something always did.

"Karthik told me last week that Marianne might be retiring," his mother said, facing his father.

"Hmmph." His father gave the barest of acknowledgments, not even glancing in Karthik's direction.

A few seconds of silence passed.

"That's right, isn't it, Karthik?" his mother asked. "Marianne's retiring?"

Karthik nodded in confirmation, though his father missed the gesture. His eyes were elsewhere, probably glued to the phone he was doing a poor job of hiding under the table.

Not that it mattered. His father wouldn't care that Marianne Tharp, the senior vice president of Karthik's department, was retiring. And he wouldn't care that Karthik was thinking of putting his name in for the job. Not that Karthik would *actually* be considered for an executive position like that. There were too many rungs on the ladder between his position and Marianne's. Still, it was incredibly rare for their company to have this kind of opening. The least he could do was try.

The room returned to its earlier silence. After a moment, his mother tried to jump-start the conversation again.

"I was wondering, Karthik, what would you think about canceling our next trip?"

Hope flared within him, but it quickly burned out. His mom had arranged three meetings in Ohio next weekend, and she would never give up on her plans so easily.

"I don't know," he said carefully. "Is there a reason you want to?"

"No, I don't want to," she said. "I just thought you might want a break. Some time to think about things . . . about Meghna . . ."

He mentally kicked himself. He knew his thoughtless comment after meeting Meghna would come back to haunt him.

"I emailed her number to you," she continued. "I thought you might want to call her. Maybe talk to her before meeting anyone else . . ."

"You're wasting your time, Shanti," his dad interjected. "Calling everyone you know. Flying all over the country. Setting up all of this for him. He's not even grateful."

"That's not true," his mother said softly. "He's thinking about it. He's—"

"He's said no to eight women. Eight!" His father shot a glare in Karthik's direction. "And he feels no shame about it. He's selfish, Shanti. It's all about him. All about what he wants."

Karthik's temperature rose, but he took a deep breath, letting his father's words roll off his back.

"He doesn't care about what's right for this family," his father continued. "He doesn't care what you want."

Karthik didn't care what his mom wanted? He cared so much that he had disrupted his entire life for her. When had his father ever sacrificed anything for his mother? When had he even *tried* to find out what she wanted? When had he ever cared about her happiness? Or Karthik's?

"I think it's time for me to leave," Karthik said evenly. He folded his napkin underneath the table and set it down on his chair. He knew proper etiquette demanded that he leave it on the table, but his hands were shaking with barely suppressed anger. He couldn't let his father see. Couldn't let him know how badly his words had affected him.

He gave his mother a quick hug goodbye. "I think you're right, Amma. We should cancel the trip next weekend."

"What a surprise," his father muttered.

A streak of rage shot through Karthik's body. Before he could help himself, he added, "Because I called Meghna. Today." The lie tasted acrid on his tongue.

"Really?" his mother asked. Her entire face brightened, only to quickly dampen when his father spoke.

"Wow. Congratulations." His father's voice dripped with sarcasm. "Did you hear that, Shanti? Our son, after meeting eight different women, finally called one of them. What do you think? Should we bring the sweets back out to celebrate?"

The rage within Karthik grew, but he refused to let it show. "Maybe we should. I'm going to ask her to marry me," he said calmly. The words echoed in the room.

"What?" his father croaked.

"I'm going to ask her to marry me," he said again. A sense of rightness settled over him. He headed to leave, but took a final look back at his parents. "Happy birthday," he said with a smile, enjoying the dumbfounded look on his father's face and the joyful look on his mother's. It wasn't until later, when he was halfway back to his apartment, that he realized this meant he'd really have to propose.

He waited for the idea to fill him with horror, but the more he thought about it, the more he wondered whether it was *that* bad of an idea. After all, people broke engagements all the time. And while he was engaged, he wouldn't be expected to travel and meet all these women. The meetings were starting to take a toll on him, and he couldn't imagine lasting the rest of the year at this pace. Of course, going through with this would mean that he'd actually have to call Meghna and talk to her again, but for some reason, that didn't seem like such a bad idea, either.

That night, just as he was about to fall asleep, he reached for his phone, scrolling until he found it: the email his mother had sent him with Meghna's number. He flagged it and set a reminder to call her the next morning before work. He closed his eyes, feeling at peace about his plan. For the first time in the past month, he slept soundly through the entire night.

Meghna lay in bed, eyes wide, staring at the ceiling. Best man? *Best man?* What had Seth been thinking? And what had *she* been thinking? How could she have agreed to it?

She tossed back and forth, finally finding a comfortable position on her side. Per the neon lights of the digital clock on the nightstand, it was five in the morning. And by her count, this was the third time she'd woken up tonight. She closed her eyes, hoping to squeeze in an hour or two more of sleep, but nervous energy hummed through her body.

It would have been hard enough going to Seth's wedding in the first place. Watching him marry someone he considered the love of his life when she'd once imagined the two of them finding their way back to each other. When she'd once thought of him as the one that got away. But this was so much worse. She'd have to smile and pretend to be happy for him. Stand by his side as it all happened and act as if nothing was wrong.

Meghna groaned, reaching for her phone and finally admitting defeat. As much as she wanted to get a bit more sleep, she was awake for good now. She scrolled through her texts and snorted as she reread an earlier conversation with Ankita.

Meghna: So, that call? It was Seth. He's getting married.

Ankita: What??

Meghna: And he asked me to be his best man.

Ankita: WHAT?!

Meghna: And I said yes.

Ankita: . . .

Ankita: I'm coming over.

Just twelve minutes after that text, Ankita had burst through Meghna's door, rushing into the living room, slightly out of breath.

"Are you kidding me? You're going to be his best man? What does that even mean? What will you have to do?"

Meghna had shrugged, trying to keep a veneer of calm. "I'll have to do the same stuff as any other best man." She hadn't mentioned that she had very little idea of what that usually entailed.

"But how could Seth ask that of you? Doesn't he know . . . He has to know that it's weird to ask you. That it would be hard for you and . . ."

Meghna had blown out a breath. "How would he know that? We're friends. We've always been friends. Even when we dated, he didn't really see me as anything beyond that." She had forced her lips into a smile, but the movement was brittle. Stiff. "He's made that very clear."

Ankita's arms had immediately come around her, and Meghna relaxed into the embrace. Maybe Ankita was right. Maybe Seth should have realized that asking her to do this would be hard or weird, but Meghna had never given him any reason to think that their breakup back in college had hurt her. Or that she still harbored feelings for him. She'd always played it cool.

Not that she'd really had any other choice. At their college graduation, Meghna had felt so secure, so safe in their relationship. She and Seth had been going to different cities, but she had never doubted that they could make it work. Never doubted that Seth was just as committed to their future as she was.

When he'd broken up with her, she'd realized how delusional she'd been. Seth had wanted to go back to being friends. Just friends. And the way he'd said it, he'd made it sound like that was all they'd ever been. Like they'd only dated because it had been convenient. Because they'd been in the same class and lived in the same dorm. And now that they were going their separate ways, this was the only thing that made sense.

She'd been crushed, but with time she'd realized it wasn't Seth's fault that she'd gotten carried away. That she'd developed stronger feelings for him than he had for her. She was the one who'd let her expectations get out of control. Who'd dreamed of a future he hadn't promised her. A future he couldn't give her.

She should have learned from that experience. Should have stopped dreaming of an impossible future with him. Instead, she'd made the same mistake again.

After releasing her from the hug, Ankita had entered distract-my-best-friend-so-they-don't-feel-sorrow mode. She'd ordered a pizza, extra cheesy, and found a made-for-Netflix rom-com that was somehow even cheesier.

Both had soothed Meghna's worries and taken her mind off things until the end of the movie, when the main character walked down the aisle in a big, poofy white dress. Ankita had shot her an apologetic glance, but Meghna had barely noticed, her anxiety returning as bright and hot as a flame.

That would soon be Julie. Walking down the aisle to Seth. And Meghna would have to watch it all happen. Just a few steps away. Right up in the action. In front of a crowd. She'd have to compose herself. Monitor her expressions. She wouldn't even be able to look away.

And then she'd have to go to the reception all alone. Sure, she could bring Ankita. Or find some guy on Bumble to take. But she couldn't imagine that would be any better than going alone. Seth would probably know it wasn't a real date. Wasn't a real relationship. He'd figure it was just some plus-one who'd shown up to keep her company. After all, *he* hadn't loved or cared about her that way. Why would anyone else?

Meghna tossed her phone back on the nightstand and turned on the lights. If she was going to be up this early, she might as well try to do something productive with the time. She brewed a cup of coffee, grabbed her laptop from the couch, and climbed back into bed, propping an absurd number of pillows behind her.

Time passed quickly, and an hour and a half later she found herself engaged in one of her favorite pastimes: perusing WikiHow articles for wisdom. She was currently in the middle of one titled "How to Plan a Bachelor Party." She had started with "How to Stop a Wedding" and "How to Tell Your Ex You Still Have Feelings for Them," but had quickly dismissed the advice there. They all started with the recommendation that she speak with Seth about her feelings. And if she was brave enough to do that, she would have done it years ago. Besides, he seemed happy. She wouldn't be the one to ruin that for him.

No, she was resigned to her current situation. The wedding was only three months away, and if she was going to do this, she needed to get started. She pulled up "How to Be the *Best* Best Man" and read through the list:

1. Select location and activities for bachelor party
2. Get fitted for a suit or tux
3. Write and deliver the best man's speech

She stopped reading and dropped her head back with a groan. She hadn't even thought about giving a toast. She opened a new tab in her browser and was about to search "How to Write a Best Man Speech" when the top right corner of her screen flashed with an incoming FaceTime call. She didn't recognize the number and she couldn't imagine that anyone she knew would try to call her at six-thirty in the morning. She ignored it and went back to her search.

She had just started skimming a sample wedding toast when her phone dinged with a text message.

Hello Meghna,

This is Karthik. I hope you are doing well. I'm sorry I called so early, but I have an urgent matter to discuss with you and would prefer to do it face-to-face. Please call me back if you are free or let me know some other times you would be available for a video call.

She read the message. Then read it again. She couldn't believe *Karthik* had been the one calling. But the message sounded just like him: cold, to the point, and exacting. She was tempted to ignore him. It would serve him right. After all, she didn't owe him a conversation. She pulled the speech back up and tried to read it, but her mind wandered. Why had he reached out? What could possibly be so urgent? Why did it have to be face-to-face?

She thought it over for a second, then reached up to wipe the remnants of last night's acne cream off her chin. She wouldn't be able to relax until she found out what he wanted. She shook her hair out of the bun she'd slept in and checked her appearance with the computer camera. Passable. She'd looked better, but it was too early for her to get out of bed for any reason. She smoothed the worst of the frizz with her hands and tucked her curls behind her ears. Before she could think too much more about it, she called him back.

He answered immediately, his face filling the screen.

"Meghna," he said. "Thanks for returning my call."

She blinked. When they'd met in person there had been a normal amount of distance between them, but now they were eye-to-eye, just inches apart. Only separated by a screen. She hadn't mentally prepared for this. And how was it possible that he looked even better than she had remembered?

She forced her gaze away from his face, trying to focus on something other than his warm brown eyes, the sharpness of his jaw, the surprising fullness of his lips. She took in the diplomas hanging on the wall. His white button-down shirt. The large windows that showed a hint of the skyscrapers behind him.

She frowned. "Are you already at work?"

"It's an hour later over here," he replied.

"Right," she said. "An hour later. So, it's seven-thirty?"

"Yes," he said.

"Do you normally start work at seven-thirty?"

"Sometimes," he said. He seemed to notice where she was for the first time. "You're in bed."

"Yeah. A normal place to be this early. At least for some of us . . ."

His mouth tightened. "I'm sorry. I didn't mean to wake you up."

"No, it's fine. I've actually been up for a while. And I live close to work so I am not in any rush. Besides, you said it was urgent."

He straightened. "Yes, it is." He cleared his throat. "I should start by saying that everything I said last weekend is still true. I don't plan on ever getting married."

"Okay," she said slowly.

"That said, I see some benefit to being engaged and wanted to know whether you felt the same way. I think we could reach a mutually beneficial agreement, so we should discuss your interest and possibly negotiate some terms."

He paused, as if waiting for her to respond, but Meghna couldn't make heads or tails out of what he was saying. What agreement? What could they have to negotiate?

"Karthik, I'm not following," she said.

"I'm proposing," he said.

"Proposing what?"

He exhaled loudly. "I'm asking you to marry me."

"What?" Was he joking? Mr. I'll-Never-Get-Married was proposing? To *her?*

"Not really marry me," he quickly added. "Just to say you'll marry me. And to tell other people that you'll marry me."

That confirmed it. He was joking. Or the lack of sleep was giving her hallucinations. It had to be one or the other.

She stared at him for a moment, waiting for the punch line. But he didn't add anything further. He just looked at her expectantly, waiting for an answer.

"You're proposing to me?"

"Yes," he said.

"But you don't want to marry me."

"No, of course not."

She gave a humorless laugh and rubbed her forehead. "Right, of course. How silly of me to think you'd want to marry me when you're asking to marry me."

He winced. "I'm sorry. I'm not explaining this well."

"You're not explaining it at all!"

"I want us to be engaged, but not actually get married," he said.

Like that makes any more sense. "Why?" she asked. "Why would we do that?"

"That's why I was calling. To see if there's any reason that would appeal to you. You already know what I promised my mother. I've been thinking that if I was engaged, I wouldn't have to go to these meetings anymore. I wouldn't have to travel every weekend. And I could save myself some stress."

She took in what he was saying. "You want a fake engagement?"

"Yes, exactly," he said, a note of relief in his voice.

"To get you out of the promise to your mom?"

"Yes."

Her head spun. "But what would I. . . . Why would I agree to that?"

He paused. "I was hoping there might be something you would want. Something you could get out of it. Maybe it would get your family off your back? Take away some of their pressure to get married?"

She considered it for a moment. Her parents would like to see her married, but they'd never really *pressured* her. They just wanted her to be happy. Wanted her to find love.

Of course, they wanted a lot of things for her. And so far, she'd done nothing but let them down. Not like her brother, Samir. He'd followed in their footsteps. Fulfilled their dreams by becoming an engineer. Made them proud.

But *this* . . . For the first time there was something she could do that Samir hadn't managed to yet. By getting engaged, she could finally make her parents happy. What would it be like to see them actually be pleased with her choices instead of disappointed?

She let herself imagine it before her daydream came grinding to a sudden halt. What had she been thinking? She wouldn't *actually* be making them proud. None of it would be real. It'd all be a lie. And when the fake engagement ended, or even worse, if they found out the truth, they'd be just as disappointed in her as they'd always been.

She shook her head. "I don't think so."

"Look, I know it's a lot. But all I'm asking is that you consider it. And not just as a favor to me. I'm willing to be flexible. To make sure you get whatever it is you want. Or need. Please. Just think about it for a little longer," he pleaded.

In the very short amount of time she'd known Karthik, this was the most emotion he had shown. He sounded desperate. Despite her better judgment, she started to think about it. Could she have any use for a fake fiancé? She was pulling up her web browser, about to search for any advice articles on pretend engagements, when the last item she had been reading snagged her attention. The sample best man speech.

It *would* be nice if she didn't have to go to Seth's wedding alone. Even nicer if she could bring a "fiancé" with her.

"I do need a plus-one for a wedding," she said slowly.

"Done. Absolutely. What else?"

Meghna paused. She hadn't expected Karthik to agree that quickly. Without asking any questions at all. It made her stop and think about whether she should be asking any questions of her own.

"Why can't we just say we're dating?" she asked a moment later. "Isn't that what people normally do now?" She didn't think anyone got engaged right after these arranged meetings anymore. At least, Ankita and Rishi had dated for a while before he'd proposed. Meghna had assumed that was the norm.

Karthik opened his mouth, then closed it. He was quiet for a moment, then shook his head.

"That won't work for me. It needs to be an engagement."

"Why?"

"It just does," he said with a stubborn lift of his chin.

She shook her head. "I don't think my parents are going to buy that I'm getting engaged to someone I just met." Not to mention she wasn't entirely sure how she felt about lying to them about something this serious.

"Tell them we're doing a long engagement. Really long. Just say that my family is more traditional but that we'll basically be dating and getting to know each other while we plan the wedding."

"Is that why we can't just date? Because of your family?"

He blinked, then nodded. "Yes. Because of my family."

Meghna sighed. The whole thing seemed incredibly messy.

"Is there anything else you'd want? Anything else I could do? Something I could help you with?" Karthik asked, seeming to sense the hesitancy on her end.

She thought it over for a second. "Just the wedding, really. Well, I'm part of the wedding party, so there may be some other events you'd have to go to."

"Not a problem," he said. He waited a beat. "So, you're saying yes?"

She paused as she imagined showing up to Seth's wedding with this incredibly handsome man on her arm. Introducing him to everyone as her fiancé. Introducing him to Seth. The thought of going to this wedding alone *had* been killing her, and bringing a *fiancé* was a lot better than bringing some random plus-one. It would communicate that she was completely over Seth. That she had someone who loved her. Who wanted to marry her. Even if Seth didn't.

Plus, Karthik would be in New York the whole time so it wasn't like they'd really get in each other's way. They wouldn't have to keep up appearances constantly.

"How long would we be doing this for?" she asked.

"What do you mean?"

"Well, we're not going to actually get married, right? So, I'm thinking we need an end date."

"Right," he said slowly. "That makes sense." He took a deep breath. "Well, the deal with my mother was for a year, so . . ."

Yeah, no. "I'm not doing this for a year." She chewed her lip as she thought it over. "Three months," she said. "Until my friend's wedding. Then we're done."

"That's not enough time. My mom will just restart the meetings and I'll be back to square one."

Meghna's eyebrows rose. "You really think she'll make you do more meetings after the engagement ends?"

"Why wouldn't she? I promised her—"

"A year. I know. But with the broken engagement . . . I mean, it'd be believable if you were heartbroken. If you told her you needed time. And space. If you said you weren't ready to meet anyone new."

A few seconds of silence passed. Then he nodded crisply. "Okay. Three months. Do we have a deal?"

He sat very still, waiting for her answer. No hint of emotion on his face. He was stoic. Calm. Composed. And his arms were crossed, making the muscles there more visible. God, even his *forearms* were hot.

"Yes," she said. "We do."

Surprise, or something like it, flashed across his face, but he quickly masked it. "Good," he said with another nod. "I think this will work out very well for the both of us. I haven't drafted any terms yet, but I could send something around by the end of the week."

"What kind of terms?"

He shifted in his seat. "I . . . I'm not sure," he said. "But I'm sure we'll need more. Beyond what we just discussed. Eventually."

She grinned. "I'm sure we will." And to her surprise, he smiled back.

"Nice shirt," he said.

"Thanks," she said instinctively. She glanced down and almost laughed. She had forgotten she'd slept in this. It was one of her favorites: bright blue with two cartoon bananas talking to each other.

"Can you even read it?" she asked.

"I can make some of it out," he said. "Just enough to get the joke."

"You know Hindi?" she asked with some surprise. She wouldn't have expected Karthik to know any Hindi at all. His family was Tamil, just like her father's side of the family, so if they spoke anything besides English at home, it would be Tamil. Meghna only knew Hindi because it was her mother's native language, and even then, she could only understand some of it. She had grown up speaking mostly English, since that was the only language her parents had in common.

"I only know a few words," he said. "But I've heard this one before."

On the shirt, one banana asked, "Why am I always alone?," and the other answered, "Because you are a kela." "Kela" was Hindi for "banana" and "akela" meant "alone." It was a silly play on words, but it had been a gag gift from her brother. And it had started a fun tradition.

"My brother and I have a bunch of these," she explained. "He found one and thought it would be funny to give it to me for my birthday, so I found another one and sent it to him. Now we can't stop. We've even started designing our own. I'm thinking about making one with two glasses of milk and some joke involving "doodh" and "dude," but I haven't figured it out yet."

The corners of Karthik's mouth tilted up, and the tension in Meghna's shoulders started to fade. Maybe this *would* work out for both of them. Maybe somewhere beneath that yummy, stern, Captain Von Trapp-esque exterior, there was some warmth. Maybe he actually had a sense of humor. Maybe . . .

"Well, I'll let you go, Meghna. I appreciate you taking the time to speak with me. We can circle back on those terms this weekend and discuss how we want to inform our families. Talk to you soon." The call abruptly ended, and his face disappeared from the screen.

Or maybe not.

Karthik buried his head in his hands. That had been a train wreck. His carefully prepared script had gone out the window the moment the call began. He'd tried to recover, but his brain had switched into auto-pilot once he'd noticed she was calling from bed. In her pajamas. He couldn't even remember half of what he'd said. Though he did remember lying to her. Well, half lying.

The reason he needed to be engaged *was* because of his family. Maybe it wasn't due to tradition like he'd said, but he'd already told his dad he was getting engaged to Meghna and he couldn't take it back now. Not without seeing some smug, superior look on his father's face.

At least it had all worked out in the end. He just hoped she wouldn't change her mind.

"You all right, man?"

Karthik lifted his head as Paul, one of this semester's college interns, entered his office and placed Karthik's usual coffee order on his desk. Paul had started at the engineering firm just a few weeks ago, but after his fourth day on the job, he'd dropped his major. Apparently, that was all the time he needed to be sure that he never wanted to be an engineer. But since it had been too late for him to find another internship, he'd asked to stick around. He'd been relegated to lunch orders and coffee runs but didn't seem to mind. As long as his paycheck cleared every week, he was fine doing whatever they asked of him.

Karthik picked up the steaming-hot lavender latte in front of him and took a sip. He closed his eyes briefly, the tense muscles in his shoulders relaxing as the lavender scent calmed his earlier anxiety. He wouldn't have ever thought to try this flavor on his own, but Paul had mixed up the drink orders last week, and instead of his normal black coffee, he'd gotten this instead. Now Karthik looked forward to the subtle, floral flavor every morning.

He took another sip, then answered Paul's question.

"I just got engaged," he said.

"That's awesome," Paul said, balancing a drink carrier with the remaining orders in one hand and raising his other for a high five. He quickly withdrew it. "It *is* awesome, right? You don't look like you think it's awesome."

Great. If the office intern could already see through his fake engagement, he didn't have any hope of convincing his mother.

"No, it's really wonderful," Karthik said. "I'm very happy."

"Uh-huh," Paul responded, clearly unconvinced. He set the drink carrier on the floor and plopped into one of the chairs in front of Karthik's desk.

"May I?" he asked.

Karthik nodded, a bit bemused.

"This happened to a buddy of mine," Paul said. "He was obsessed with this girl in our Advanced Calculus class. He asked her for help with homework, made up excuses to study with her, went to office hours just because she did. Finally, on the last day of class, he just went for it and asked her out. She immediately said yes, and a few days later, he realized he wasn't even that into her. Said it felt like buying the latest DLC and realizing it didn't live up to the hype."

"DLC?"

"You know, downloadable content."

Karthik frowned.

"Like in *Call of Duty*," Paul explained. "You know how you can download extension packs that get you extra items or characters . . ."

Paul continued, going into details that Karthik could barely follow, but from what he understood, he didn't care for the comparison. "She's my fiancée," he said, cutting Paul off. "Not a . . . a . . . video game."

Paul lifted his hands in surrender. "Hey, man, I agree with you. That's just the way he put it."

"Well, I don't feel that way. I'm glad she said yes. Actually, I *needed* her to say yes."

Paul cocked his head to the side. "That's pretty romantic, actually."

Karthik resisted the urge to roll his eyes. His "proposal" had been far from romantic. But it wasn't supposed to be. This was a logical, mutually beneficial agreement between two adults. Nothing more.

"I mean, I'd want to feel that way if I was asking someone to marry me," Paul continued. "I definitely don't feel like that now. If my girlfriend said she wanted to get married, I don't know how I'd respond." He swallowed, unease settling across his features. "I'd probably throw up."

"You're young," Karthik said. "It'll feel different when you're older." Unless Paul was anything like him, in which case the idea of marriage would always result in nausea.

"Maybe," Paul said, picking the tray of coffee back up. "Anyway, good for you, dude. Glad it was good news. I thought someone had died or something." He left to drop off the rest of the coffees, and Karthik slouched down in his chair.

He'd always had a reliable poker face, but it seemed like selling "happy" and "in love" required a different skill set. Luckily, his morning provided multiple opportunities to practice the role of enthused fiancé, as co-workers stopped in to congratulate him, having heard the news from their talkative intern.

The word must have spread all the way to his boss because Marianne showed up at his office that afternoon.

"I hear congratulations are in order," Marianne said, regarding him warmly. She shook Karthik's hand firmly and took a seat. "Actually, I had been planning to stop by anyway. I was hoping to congratulate you on something else, but it looks like there are a few more hurdles before that one's final."

"Oh?" he asked, doing his best to sound casual.

"I'm sure it's no surprise to you that I've been thinking about retirement. And I've been considering who might replace me."

He sat up straighter.

"I don't have final say on decisions like that," she said. "But I can make a recommendation. The C-suite folks seem determined to bring in an outside candidate, but I want to recommend you."

"Me?" Not much surprised him, but he was stunned. Yes, he'd considered applying for the position, but he'd always thought it would be a long shot. He'd been moving up the ranks slowly, steadily, but he didn't have the decades of experience a job like this would require. He couldn't believe that she was actually considering him.

"I think you can do the job, Karthik. I've seen how much you've grown, how much you've matured in this role."

Pride swelled in his chest. Marianne had really taken a chance on him when he'd first started here straight out of college, and her mentorship over the years had meant the world to him.

"My only concern for the longest time was your lack of commitment," she said.

His heart sank.

"You seemed to flit from project to project, trying different things on for size and then dropping them."

He held back a wince. Everything she'd said was true. In school he'd chosen mechanical engineering because it meant he could design . . . anything. But when he'd joined the company, he'd found himself overwhelmed by the options. He'd rotated through most of the groups and experimented with everything, working on turbines, HVAC systems, and pieces and parts for factories. But he'd always stayed far, far away from one team: biomedical.

At first, he'd been enamored of the field. Had been tempted by the idea of creating artificial limbs, pacemakers, even robotic medical assistants. But he hadn't been able to stop imagining what his father would say. How he might react to Karthik choosing something so close to his own career. How he might take pride in it. Approve of it. Think that Karthik wanted to follow in his footsteps.

So, Karthik had ended up selecting at random, ultimately joining the HVAC design team. Sure, some people considered the work bland, but Karthik didn't mind. At least his father couldn't gloat about his decision.

"But in the last few years," Marianne continued, "you've really shown great dedication and follow-through. With impressive results. And what greater sign of commitment is there than marriage?"

Karthik's palms started to sweat.

"I was already going to recommend you for the position," she said. "But when I heard the news this morning, it just confirmed for me that you are the right person for the job. To see you commit to something like this . . . It's what I've been wanting to see from you for so long."

She got up and wrapped her gray shawl around her shoulders. "We'll see what the people upstairs think, and you'll probably have to interview alongside a number of candidates, but I think you have a great shot at this."

He swallowed. "Thank you, Marianne," he said. "I appreciate your faith in me. And your recommendation."

"You deserve it," she said. "Just don't let me down." She wagged her finger at him playfully.

He gave a nervous laugh. "Of course not. I won't."

She headed to leave, then turned around. "By the way, Jim's going to throw a retirement party for me. A small thing, just a couple folks from the office, some friends and family. But you should definitely come. I know a bunch of the executives are going and it'd be a good time for you to mingle with them."

"I'll be there," he said immediately. He was willing to do anything possible to get an edge over the competition. Unlike him, the other candidates would probably be well qualified for the position. He needed all the help he could get.

"Great. Invitations should be going out soon. I look forward to seeing you there," she said over her shoulder as she left his office.

Karthik turned back to his computer, his brain already buzzing with ideas and plans and projects he could pitch. This promotion could change the entire trajectory of his career. But even more important, Marianne had taken a chance on him. Had shown her faith in him by putting his name up for the job. He'd need to bring his A game. He couldn't afford to make any missteps. He couldn't let her down.

He opened a blank document and was brainstorming, typing every idea that came to mind, when a sharp knock disrupted his focus.

"Hey," Marianne said, her head peeking around his office door. "I forgot to mention this earlier, but please be sure to bring your bride-to-be to the party. We all really want to meet her." She punctuated the words with a smile and a quick wave goodbye.

Karthik stared after her, frozen in place. She wanted him to bring his bride-to-be to her retirement party? His *fake* bride-to-be? He dropped his head into his hands and groaned.

"You're engaged?" Ankita asked, her slice of pizza suspended in the air, frozen halfway on the journey to her mouth. "How did that happen? I thought you hated him."

"I never hated him. I just thought he was . . . kind of rude."

"And now?"

"I still think he's kind of rude."

Ankita stared at her in confusion, but Meghna just reached for the remote, avoiding her gaze. She turned on the television, the light casting Ankita's apartment in a soft glow. On the screen, a beautiful woman in a sparkly dress greeted the twenty-three men she would be dating that season. On the living room floor, a box of pizza and an open bottle of Malbec lay between them.

"I don't understand," Ankita said. "Do you like Karthik at all?"

"I like how he looks," Meghna joked. "He's tall. And he's got a really sharp jaw. And this kind of stern, serious look in his eyes. Really, he's a dead ringer for Fawad Khan in *Khoobsurat*."

Ankita's eyebrows rose. "Damn."

"I know!"

"That still doesn't explain why you're engaged."

"Doesn't it?" Meghna teased with an exaggerated wink.

Ankita made a sound of exasperation.

Meghna grinned. She'd never had any intention of keeping the truth from her best friend, but she hadn't been able to resist giving her a hard time. "Look, I'll explain. But you can't tell anyone. Not your parents, not Rishi, not . . ."

"Fine! Just tell me."

"We're not really engaged. We're just sort of engaged. Fake-engaged."

"Fake-engaged," Ankita repeated dully. "And that means . . ."

"That we're not going to actually get married. We're just pretending."

"Riiiiight. Sure. Of course. Makes perfect sense. A totally normal thing to do. No need to explain any further."

"Glad you get it."

"Meghna!" Ankita grappled for the remote and muted the show, frustration clear on her face. "Tell me what's going on."

Meghna sighed and tossed her pizza slice back into the box. She wouldn't be able to finish it while they were discussing this.

"So, remember how Seth asked me to be his best man?"

"Yes, but . . . Oh," Ankita said, realization dawning on her face. "*Oh no*. No, no, no. Seth never should have asked that of you, and you never should have agreed to it, but *this* is not the answer. I mean, does he know?"

"Seth? No, I haven't told him that I'm engaged yet."

"No. Karthik. Does Karthik know you're using him?"

"I'm not using him!" Meghna said indignantly. "And if I am, he's using me too. It's mutual. We're using each other. And this was all his idea."

"Of course. That makes it all just fine then. I'm sure you won't have any issues keeping the truth from Seth. Or from Karthik's parents. Or from yours."

Meghna swallowed, pushing down a twinge of discomfort. She'd tried not to think about this part too hard. Sure, she and her parents didn't see eye to eye on everything, but she loved them. And she didn't *want* to lie to them. But pretending to be engaged for a little while would make her life so much easier. And if everything worked the way it was supposed to, her parents would be none the wiser. They wouldn't discover that any of it was a lie. They wouldn't have a reason to be disappointed in her. Again.

Meghna shrugged, trying to adopt a nonchalant air. "I told my parents last night. They're happy for me."

Ankita frowned. "You don't think they'll be hurt when they find out?"

"They're not going to find out. At least not from me."

"And not from me, either. But how far are y'all going to take this? Won't they get suspicious when you keep putting off the wedding?"

"We're not going to let it get that far. We'll tell them that we're doing a long engagement. That we're still getting to know each other. And after Seth's wedding we're going to break it off." Meghna lifted a shoulder. "They'll feel bad for me, but they'll be fine."

Ankita slowly shook her head. "I don't think you've fully thought this through. And I can't keep secrets from my fiancé. I have to at least tell Rishi."

Meghna groaned. "I really wish you wouldn't. I don't want him to act all weird around Karthik at your party."

"He's coming to our engagement party?"

"I haven't asked him yet, but I think he has to come. Our families will think it's weird if I show up without my fiancé."

Ankita picked up her wineglass and took a long sip. She was quiet for a while, but Meghna knew she wasn't done just yet.

"This is a lot to digest," Ankita finally said, an amused glint in her eye. "We can probably stop watching *The Bachelorette* now since your life has more than enough drama to entertain us."

"Ha. Very funny."

"I'm serious."

"Well, I'm sorry. Not all of us can have lives as drama-free as yours."

Ankita laughed. "You make me sound so boring, but it's kind of true. Since Rishi and I met, the only drama has been whether we want peonies or garden roses at the wedding. And honestly, they look the same to me. It's just fun to have something to argue about. We agree on everything else. A house near our parents, three children, a dog, et cetera, et cetera. He makes life so easy."

"I'm happy for you," Meghna said. And she meant it. Ankita had been wanting a partner for so long, and Meghna was so glad she had found one in Rishi. She felt only the smallest amount of envy. "So, I take it all the planning for your engagement party has been drama-free as well?"

Ankita grimaced. "I wouldn't exactly say that. Mom wants to do a big song-and-dance number, and we're trying to convince her to save it for the sangeet. Hopefully we'll come up with some kind of plan to prevent it by then."

Meghna sat up straight, suddenly remembering she had more news to share. "I know my parents already RSVP'd for him, but I don't know if you saw it."

"Saw what?"

"That Samir's coming to your party!"

Ankita blinked. "Samir? Your brother?"

"Yeah, my brother. I mean, it's not like we know another Samir."

"Right, of course. I . . . I just thought he was still in India."

"He is, but he's been thinking about moving back for a long time. He hasn't decided, but he's going to be in town for a few job interviews. Just to see what's out there. My parents are over the moon."

Ankita looked a bit queasy.

"Are you okay?" Meghna asked.

"Yeah," Ankita said, putting a hand on her stomach. "I think I ate too fast."

"Oh. I think I have Tums in my purse. Give me a second."

"No, no. Don't worry about it. I'm fine."

Meghna paused. "It's okay if Samir comes to the party, right?"

"Yeah, of course," Ankita said, waving her hand in the air. "He's practically family."

"I know. I swear he thinks of you like a second sister. You should have heard him when Mom and Dad brought up your engagement party. He immediately said he wanted to be there for you."

Ankita smiled weakly. "That's great."

"Are you sure you're okay? I can run out and get you something."

"Nope. I'm fine. So, how's this arrangement with Karthik supposed to work out?"

Meghna stretched her legs out in front of her. "Well, he's working on a list of terms, but I have no idea what they'll be."

"Are you going to date other people?" Ankita asked.

Meghna was about to say no, but realized she didn't know the answer. "We haven't really talked about it."

"And I'm guessing you're not going to tell Seth the truth."

"No. That would kind of defeat the whole point of everything."

"What about Samir? Are you going to tell him?"

Meghna brushed a crumb off her jeans. "I don't know. Probably. But I don't want him to leak it to Mom and Dad."

"You might as well tell him. He's going to figure it out anyway. He always knows the truth."

"Yeah, he does have a weird sixth sense about things like this."

"He really does," Ankita said. "He'll know." She closed her eyes and lay flat on the floor.

Meghna cast a worried glance in her direction. "Maybe you should go to bed early. Do you want me to leave?"

"No, don't be silly." Ankita propped her head on a pillow and turned the volume up on the television. "It looks like Matthew B. is about to confess his love on night one. You won't want to miss that. Besides"—she smiled slyly—"you might learn a thing or two about faking your feelings."

Meghna laughed and let herself get swept up in the artificial drama on-screen. She'd deal with the real drama in her life tomorrow.

Meghna checked her reflection in the bathroom mirror, turning and straining her neck so she could see the back of her salwar kameez. Convinced that everything looked the way it should, she twirled back around, holding on to her sky-blue dupatta so it wouldn't slip off her shoulder. She adjusted it one last time, then secured it with a safety pin. There. Now it wouldn't budge even if she got a little wild on the dance floor tonight.

Her phone buzzed, and she swiped it open, surprised at the flurry of notifications on her screen.

> Samir: Are you kidding me?
> Samir: Mom said you're engaged?
> Samir: To who?
> Samir: Call me.

Meghna rolled her eyes.

> Meghna: This is what you get for choosing to live so far away!
> Meghna: But relax. I'll tell you all about it tonight. At Ankita's party.

Samir: Fine.

Samir: But you should have told me.

Samir: What's he like?

Samir: And what's this Rishi guy like?

Meghna hesitated for a second, not sure how much she should tell him.

Meghna: They're nice. But you can tell me what you think after you meet them.

Samir: I can't believe you and Ankita are both engaged.

Samir: Mom's going to be after me next . . .

Meghna snorted.

Meghna: No need to worry. I think Mom knows it would be hopeless.

Meghna: Who'd want to marry you??

Samir: Ouch!

Meghna: Kidding!

Well, she was mostly kidding. She and Samir had been incredibly close when they were little, but the distance over the last few years had made it harder for them to connect. Every time they reunited, Meghna had a harder time understanding him. Still, she was glad he was in town. Hopefully they'd be able to spend some quality time together during his visit. Maybe they could make an effort to repair everything between them.

Meghna: But really, Mom's probably got a future bride picked out for you already.

Samir: Don't even joke about that.

Samir: Seriously. I'll stay in India for good then.

Meghna laughed.

Meghna: Right. Like we don't have any family members there who'd love to make you a match.

Samir: Well, I'll just tell those Yente-wannabes that I'm not interested. No need to find me a find. Catch me a catch.

Meghna grinned at the reference to *Fiddler on the Roof*. Samir may not have willingly shared her love of musicals, but he'd watched all the classics with her when they were children. She sent him a laughing face emoji and told him she'd see him in an hour.

The reminder of the time sent a nervous flutter through her stomach. Karthik would be here soon. He'd been incredibly gracious about coming down to Dallas to attend Ankita's engagement party. He said he'd been about to ask her to attend an event with him in New York, so it felt like an even trade.

Meghna pursed her lips in the mirror, then grabbed a tissue, wiping her lipstick off. It didn't seem like the right color anymore. She searched for a more muted shade of pink and had just put it on when the doorbell rang.

She took a deep breath and shook out her shoulders before opening the door.

Karthik stood outside, his form flickering in shadows until she turned the pale porch light on. He blinked against the sudden brightness, and her mouth went dry. He was all crisp lines and sharp edges contained in the best-fitted suit she'd ever seen. Sophisticated. Sleek. Slate gray. It was like he'd stepped off a Tom Ford runway and walked straight to her apartment.

"Hey," he said, his forehead creased in obvious confusion.

Warmth crept across Meghna's cheeks. She'd been staring. Like she'd never seen a handsome man before. Like she'd never seen *a man* before. She mentally slapped herself across the face and joined him outside.

She could handle this. She could be normal. She . . . she still hadn't responded to his greeting. She lifted her arms to give him a hug, but dropped them immediately, reaching out to shake his hand instead.

"Thanks for coming," she said, pumping his hand up and down. Firmly. Then she broke the contact to scan the street in front of them. She'd called a car a few minutes ago and the app said it was almost there.

"Thanks for agreeing to come to New York next week," he said, shifting his weight from foot to foot. "I know it's more than we initially talked about."

"No worries. Neither of us planned for these things to happen."

His lips twitched, the smallest beginnings of a wry smile. "Maybe we should have come up with some real terms after all."

Her instinct was to return the smile, but for some reason she couldn't get the muscles in her face to cooperate. "Maybe."

They turned back toward the street, the warm night air thick and heavy between them. She snuck a look at him out of the corner of her eye, but any trace of his earlier smile had disappeared. His mouth was firm. Hard. Set in a stern, straight line.

"Let's talk about some terms, then," she said.

He nodded and put his hands in his pockets, slowly returning his gaze to her. "Okay."

She ran through the list of questions Ankita had asked her, trying to select the best one to start with, but when she opened her mouth, the question that came out was "Are we dating other people?"

Karthik started. "No," he said. He paused, then continued. "I don't think we need to complicate this more. And what if our families heard something about it? It just feels like too big of a risk."

"Okay," she said.

"Why?" he asked. "Do you want to? Are you dating someone?"

"No, no. I just wasn't sure."

He nodded thoughtfully, and they fell into a silence that felt more strained than companionable. The car arrived, and they climbed in. The backseat seemed smaller than usual, and Meghna held herself as still as possible, not wanting to accidentally brush up against him. She couldn't remember the last time she'd been this uncomfortable around someone.

Karthik cleared his throat. "So, tell me about your friend. This is her party, right?"

Meghna breathed a sigh of relief. She seized onto the lifeline and immediately launched into a summary of her friendship with Ankita. They'd been friends since they were little, carpooling together every day to school and spending most of their summers at Meghna's house, where they followed Samir around until he was forced to hang out with them. Samir pretended that he hated playing with them and insisted that he was only there because Mom forced him to be, but they all knew he was actually happy to be a part of their little trio.

"That's great you were all so close," Karthik said. "I'm an only child, but I always thought it would have been nice to have a sibling."

"Nice? Sometimes. Samir and I fought constantly. We still do."

"Still, it seems like it would be nice to have someone to fight *with*. And play with. And share things with. My house was so quiet."

"Weren't there kids in the neighborhood? Or cousins?"

"I had friends at school, but they didn't really come over. And all of my cousins are in India. My parents are the only ones here."

"That sounds lonely."

He gave her a look she couldn't quite read. "It wasn't," he said stiffly. "I had plenty to keep me occupied." His tone stung, but she wanted to know what he meant by that. She almost asked, but something stopped her. A sense of foreboding. Like she was about to cross some invisible trip wire. She decided to change the subject.

"I think you'll like my brother," she said. "He's a little wild, but hilarious. Way more outgoing than me."

"I'm looking forward to meeting him," he said politely.

The car came to a stop, breaking the tension that had been growing between them, though a different sort of tension was building in Meghna's chest. This was their first outing as an engaged couple.

Their first time seeing whether they had any chance of pulling this off. She waited a second, took a deep, fortifying breath, then followed Karthik out of the car.

Karthik pulled at his collar, trying to subtly loosen his tie. He felt like it was closing in on his neck. At least, that's what he told himself. His difficulty breathing had to be from the tie. It had nothing to do with the fact that he was attending a large party with all of Meghna's friends and family. There was no logical reason why that should make him nervous.

He opened the heavy door to the building, holding it in place so Meghna could enter. He followed her, taking a few steps inside before coming to a sudden stop, his senses overloaded by their surroundings. Silks in bright pink and yellow and orange covered the walls. Flower garlands were strung up in the entryway and along the ceiling, perfuming the room with the scent of jasmine. Ornate mirrors made the room seem never-ending, and the loud, pulsing beat of Bollywood music filled the air. To his right a group of uncles was already gathered on the dance floor, shaking their shoulders and pointing their fingers toward the ceiling. He watched everything, a bit stunned, until a hand wrapped around his arm.

"Let's find Ankita and Rishi," Meghna yelled over the music. "Do you want a drink?" A waiter passed by at that moment, holding a tray of brightly colored cocktails, and Karthik grabbed one, still gawking at everything around him. He'd attended lavish and elaborate Desi weddings in the past, but nothing like this. This seemed more like a Mumbai nightclub than the reserved, stately functions he'd gone to before. And it wasn't even the wedding.

"What is this place?" he shouted, completely bewildered.

"Ankita's parents' restaurant. They tend to go a bit overboard," she said, still holding on to his arm as she expertly navigated them through the crowd. People called out greetings as they passed, and though Meghna stopped to give a hug or two, she neatly evaded their efforts to draw her into conversation, promising that she would return in a moment. He followed her blindly through the maze until they stopped in front of a woman in a bright red, heavily jeweled outfit and a gangly man with glasses. Meghna threw her arms around the woman and hugged her fiercely.

"Everything looks beautiful," Meghna said loudly.

The woman, who must have been Ankita, laughed and shook her head. "It looks gaudy. We tried to rein Mom in, but . . ." She gestured wildly at the room around them. "It was just easier to let her do what she wanted."

Karthik shook Rishi's hand. "Congratulations," he said. "I'm Meghna's fiancé." As the words came out, he realized it was the first time he'd ever said that out loud. A strange rush of warmth spread through his chest. Rishi congratulated him in return and Karthik turned to greet Ankita, surprised to see a wary, almost hostile expression on her face.

He stretched out an arm to shake her hand as well, but she enveloped him in a hug.

"I know everything," she whispered. A jolt of surprise went through him. "If this ends up hurting her, I'm going to blame you." She ended the hug and shot him a look before returning to her conversation with Meghna. Just a moment later, the two of them were speaking rapidly to each other, and it was clear he and Rishi were not invited to participate.

"They're always like this," Rishi told him. "Sometimes it feels like they're speaking their own language."

Karthik chuckled. Though Rishi sounded put out, he was watching Ankita with a fond expression, clearly not upset at all. Karthik asked the standard, obligatory, polite questions that were expected in situations like this. Where did Rishi work? How did he meet Ankita? How was wedding planning going?

Once they'd exhausted all suitable topics of conversation, Karthik glanced at Meghna and Ankita, checking to see whether they were almost finished. Unfortunately for him, they were still going and didn't seem close to running out of fuel. Thankfully, one of his many efforts to catch Meghna's eye was successful, and she turned to him with a warm smile.

"Do you want to go get something to eat?" she asked.

"Yes. Let's do that."

They said their goodbyes to Ankita and Rishi and walked toward the buffet.

"I'm sorry, I know we can get carried away," Meghna said as she grabbed a clean plate and handed it to him. "And you're probably tired. We can just meet my family quickly, finish dinner, and leave after that."

It was kind of her to offer to leave early, and he wanted nothing more than to escape to his quiet hotel room, but he reassured her that they should stay. She and Ankita were obviously close, and he didn't want Meghna to have to leave the party early just for him.

After they filled their plates, they spotted her family sitting at the table farthest from the dance floor and went over to join them. Karthik greeted Meghna's parents and met her brother, Samir, for the first time. He looked a lot like Meghna, except Samir wore his curly hair cropped short, and his wide smile was slightly crooked compared to hers.

"Mom says you're an engineer?" Samir asked.

"I am," Karthik replied.

"What kind?"

"Mechanical."

"Nice!" Samir said with genuine excitement. "I studied computer engineering, but I'm mostly doing programming these days." He clasped a hand on Karthik's shoulder. "It's great to have another person in the family business."

Meghna coughed, half choking on the mouthful of rice she'd just swallowed.

"You okay?" Karthik asked quietly, his hand reaching out to pat her on the back. But she waved his efforts away, taking a sip of her water and turning to talk to her mother.

"Mom and Dad are engineers too," Samir continued.

"I didn't know that," Karthik replied. They continued their small talk over the course of the meal until their conversation was cut off by the sound of an incoming phone call.

"Sorry," Meghna said, fishing her phone out of her purse. "That's mine." She checked the screen, and a small smile crossed her face. "I have to take this, but you guys keep talking, I'll just step outside. Be right back."

As she walked away, Samir's face darkened.

"I bet it's Seth," he said conspiratorially. "She always gets that goofy look whenever he calls. Man, that guy is *such* a prick."

"Seth?"

Samir's eyebrows jumped. "You don't know Seth?"

Karthik shook his head. "Who is he?"

"I'm sorry. I shouldn't have said anything. He's just an old friend of hers. From college. Speaking of which, where did you go to school?"

Karthik narrowed his eyes at the deflection, but answered, "Berkeley."

Meghna's mother must have overheard because she looked over with a smile. "Isn't that impressive, Samir?"

"Very. But West Coast, huh? Must have been an adjustment for you after growing up in New York."

It had been. But the distance had been the point. Karthik had wanted to be as far away from his father as possible.

"I bet living in India after growing up here has been an adjustment for you as well."

Samir shrugged. "It's been a few years now, so I've gotten used to it. Honestly, both places feel like home."

Meghna's father leaned forward. "But you're planning on moving back soon, right?"

"Maybe," Samir said distractedly, his eyes scanning the room. "Depends on a few things."

Meghna's mother frowned.

"Aunty, Uncle," a high voice called from behind Karthik. "Have you seen Meghna? I needed to ask her—"

Karthik turned around and saw Ankita, her heavy earrings swinging in the air and her mouth open in shock.

"Hi, Ankita. It's good to see you," Samir said, his eyes fixed on her. "Congratulations."

"Thanks," she squeaked. She cleared her throat, then addressed the group. "I was looking for Meghna, but I couldn't find her anywhere. Do you know where she is?"

Karthik stood up from the table. "I'll go get her." She'd been gone awhile. And this seemed like the kind of thing a fiancé was supposed to do.

He followed the path Meghna had taken, but without her to guide him through the crowd, it took longer than before to get through the room. After a few sidesteps and swerves to avoid crashing into strangers, he made it to the door and found her outside, standing on the sidewalk, talking animatedly into her phone.

"Miami's a great idea!" she said. "Much better than Vegas. I'll look up tickets when I get home and start doing some research on things to do." She looked up and saw Karthik standing there, waiting for her. She grinned apologetically. "I have to run," she said into the phone. "But we'll talk soon."

She's planning a trip? With Seth? He frowned. *Is he her boyfriend?* He resisted the urge to ask her about it. It was none of his business. And she'd told him earlier that she wasn't dating anyone.

"Coming back inside?" he asked.

"Yeah, I'm sorry about that. It was just a friend of mine."

Karthik nodded but didn't say anything in response.

"Actually, that wedding I need a plus-one for?" Meghna continued. "It's his."

So, not a boyfriend, then. Something odd rushed through his body. It felt a lot like . . . relief? He rubbed his chest absently. It couldn't be that. Maybe it was indigestion.

"Okay," he said. "You still need to send me the date for that."

"I do," she replied. "I'll send it tomorrow." She smiled, slightly hesitant.

"I like your brother," he said.

Her smile grew. "He's a brat. But I love him," she said. "It seemed like he liked you too."

"I take it you haven't told him about us? The truth, I mean."

"No, but I will. Soon." A determined look settled over her face.

"I know you told Ankita," he said.

"How?"

"She threatened me."

"What?" she exclaimed.

"It was a kind threat," he reassured her. "As far as threats go."

She breathed out a laugh. "That sounds like her."

"She was looking for you, by the way," he said.

She nodded, and they went back inside, the loud music immediately enveloping them. She moved in a hurry, but he placed a hand on her arm to catch her attention.

"I'm going to grab a drink and meet up with you in a bit," he said. He didn't know what Ankita wanted to discuss with Meghna, but he doubted she wanted him to tag along. "Want me to get you anything?"

She declined, and they parted ways. Karthik headed in the direction of the bar, hoping he'd be able to navigate his way there and back in one piece.

Meghna stepped back into the chaos of the room, slightly unsettled, though she couldn't figure out why. The pulsing lights and overwhelming music did little to help her introspection. She scanned the room for

Ankita, but she could only find her parents sitting where she'd left them.

"Mom, do you know where Ankita is?"

Her mother stood up and grasped Meghna's hands. "Beta, we love Karthik. He seems so smart." She waggled her eyebrows. "And looks it too."

"Yes, he's great. But did you see where Ankita went?"

"And it was nice of him to come *all the way* from New York."

"So nice," Meghna said. "But I was asking . . ."

"You're lucky, you know? Not everyone can find someone like that."

Meghna grimaced. She hadn't really found someone. She was still all alone.

"But I found your dad. And you found Karthik," her mother continued. "With our help, of course." She let out a tinkling laugh, her eyes filled with genuine warmth. "We're both so happy for you."

Meghna took a deep breath. "Thanks, Mom. But I was just looking for Ankita. Have you seen her?"

Meghna's mother opened her mouth, but her father quickly interjected. "She was looking for you. I think she said she was going to get dessert."

Meghna gave her father a look of gratitude, and he winked back at her. Her mother frowned, clearly about to say something else, but before she could, Meghna's father turned and kissed her mother on the cheek. Her mother laughed, and then her father whispered something that made her mom blush.

Meghna had no desire to know what had been said, but she was thankful for the distraction, using it to slip away and head toward the dessert table. She couldn't see Ankita standing anywhere near there, but she decided that she needed some ras malai anyway. After that conversation, she was certainly entitled to it. She may have even earned a gulab jamun or two.

She spooned a ras malai into her bowl but was interrupted by the voice of a man behind her.

"Beautiful jewelry," he said. She turned around. The man was older, clearly an uncle, but she couldn't remember if they had met. If they had, she couldn't recall his name.

"Thank you," she said politely.

His gaze crawled over her, starting at her necklace, then roaming over her chest.

"Our women look best in Indian clothes," he said. "I've always thought so."

Gross. Meghna was looking around for an exit strategy when a warm hand suddenly closed around hers.

"I've been looking for you," Karthik said.

She relaxed at the sound of his voice, soft and somehow already familiar.

"Are you her husband?" the uncle asked.

"Fiancé," Karthik bit out.

An oily smile came over the uncle's face. "You're a lucky man."

"I know," Karthik said firmly. He nodded curtly and tugged on Meghna's hand, gently pulling her with him. Once they were a safe distance away, he stopped and faced her.

"You okay?"

"Yeah. No. I'm fine."

"You sure?"

She lifted a shoulder. "Yeah, it's nothing. That guy was just being a creep."

Karthik frowned. "Well, that's not nothing, then." He looked away for a second, then back at her. He blew out a loud breath. "I'm sorry."

She scrunched her nose, confused by his apology. "For what?"

"I shouldn't have cut in like that. I'm sure you could have handled it. It's just . . . I was coming to see if you were done talking with An-kita, and then I saw you there and you looked uncomfortable and . . ."

She shook her head. "Don't worry about it. I wanted to get out of there. Actually, it's probably time for both of us to get out of here. I promised we could try and head out after dinner. I still need to find Ankita, but after that we can call it a night."

Karthik inclined his head toward the dance floor. "Are you sure you don't want to stay longer? Just for one dance?"

She started to laugh at his obvious joke, but stopped when she realized there was no hint of humor on his face. He was serious. She tried to picture him dancing but couldn't conjure an image of it. She was almost tempted to say yes, but the night had worn her out and she was more than ready to go home.

"No, I'm sorry. I'm just too tired. Let's find Ankita and then we can go. All right?"

He nodded and joined her, walking around the room, searching the crowd for her friend. Finally, they spotted Rishi on a corner of the dance floor. He was dancing by himself, his hands in the air, his body swaying from side to side.

"Where's Ankita?" Meghna shouted at him.

Rishi's eyes popped open. "Bathroom," he yelled back.

She flashed him a thumbs up, and he went back to his solo, getting lost in the music.

"Okay, I'm glad we skipped that dance now," Karthik said flatly. Meghna laughed, happy that someone else was there to share in the absurdity of this night.

When they made their way to the restrooms, Karthik leaned against the wall in the hallway and crossed his arms, indicating that he'd wait for her out there. Meghna pulled the door to the women's restroom open and called out, "Ankita?"

She took a step inside and immediately froze. She couldn't process what she was seeing. She blinked, trying to clear her vision, but everything stayed exactly the same.

Ankita, her best friend—her *engaged* best friend—was standing with an arm draped around a man's neck. Her hand was tangled up in his hair, and her lips were locked against his.

Meghna could only see the back of the man's head, but she knew exactly who he was. And it wasn't Rishi. She'd seen Rishi on the dance floor just a few seconds ago, and even if she hadn't, she would have recognized this man's curly head of hair anywhere. Especially since his curls so closely resembled her own.

Ankita was making out with Samir. Meghna's brother.

The door behind Meghna swung shut with a loud *bang*, and the couple in front of her jumped apart.

"Oh my God!" Meghna yelled.

The door flew back open.

"Are you okay?" Karthik asked, rushing inside. "I heard some-one scream . . ." He trailed off, taking in the scene in front of them. "Oh."

Ankita wore a guilty expression, and Samir's eyes were wide with shock, but Meghna could barely think beyond the questions running through her head.

She turned on her heel and left.

"Wait," Ankita called after her, but Meghna kept going, uninter-ested in hearing any explanations.

Her best friend and her brother. How could she not have seen this coming?

Ankita had always had a bit of a crush on Samir, but Meghna had thought she'd outgrown it. In high school, they'd made fun of the girls he dated. And one summer in college, when Samir had kept sneaking out of the house to hook up with some mystery girl, Meghna had jokingly asked Ankita if she was the girl he was going off to meet. Ankita had gagged, thoroughly disgusted by the idea. She'd said she would never in a million years ever, *ever* hook up with Meghna's brother. And Meghna had believed her.

But if that was true, what was going on? Why had she been kiss-ing Samir? He'd *just* gotten back in town. And she was engaged! When had this started? And why had neither of them talked to her about this? Why hadn't they told her the truth?

Hurt and confusion swirled in Meghna's chest, and she picked up the pace, moving as quickly as possible toward the exit.

Between the call from Seth, Samir's comment about "the family business," her mom gushing over Karthik, and *this,* she was done. She had reached her limit on what she could handle tonight.

Heavy steps sounded behind her, but she ignored them, stepping outside and pulling her phone out to get a car.

"Are you okay?" Karthik asked, catching up with her.

"No," she said, not looking up from the screen. "I need to go home." The night had been so much worse than she'd anticipated, and she wanted to crawl into bed and forget all about it.

He was silent for a moment. "Okay. I'll call us a car."

"No," she said, embarrassed to find herself on the verge of tears. "I've got it."

He hummed in acknowledgment but didn't say anything further.

"You know," he said, after a minute or two had passed, "if you want to go home, that's fine, but I think we should get ice cream."

"Ice cream?" She looked up, not sure if she had heard him properly.

He nodded once, his honey-brown eyes meeting hers. "Yes. I think we both need to go and get some ice cream."

"Why?"

He watched her for a moment, then shrugged. "Because it's too warm to get hot chocolate."

That didn't make any sense, and she was too exhausted to try to figure it out. She wasn't sure if Karthik was mocking her or making fun of the situation or if he was simply clueless as to how she felt, but she wasn't interested in prolonging this night. She just wanted to leave. She told him as much, and he thankfully didn't push the matter further. They called for separate cars: one to take her to her house and the other to take him to his hotel.

As Meghna climbed into bed that night, a number of texts and missed calls from Ankita and Samir popped up on her phone.

It's not what it looked like.

I'm so sorry.

That wasn't supposed to happen.

Please talk to me.

I need to talk to you.

She ignored them and switched off her bedside light. She knew she'd have to deal with her brother and her best friend eventually, but she didn't have the energy to sort it all out tonight. She was closing her eyes, hoping to fall asleep quickly, when her phone pinged with another text. She reached for it, intending to silence it for the night, but the sender's name took her by surprise.

Karthik: What does one glass of milk say to the other? What's up doodh?

An unexpected laugh burst out of her, but the sudden emotion led to a cascade of others: anger, frustration, confusion, sadness, and above it all, a deep sense of having to face everything, having to figure it all out, alone. And just like that, the tears she'd been holding back finally began to fall. She turned her face into her pillow and cried.

6

Karthik stretched his neck to the side, twisting it back and forth, reveling in the sound of it cracking and popping. His mother had always told him not to bend it like that, saying that those noises meant he would get arthritis. He wasn't that sure about the soundness of her medical advice, but the stretch gave his aching muscles some relief, and he definitely needed that right now. He'd fallen asleep in the wrong position on his early-morning flight home, and his neck and shoulders were still painfully sore.

He pulled his phone out of his pocket for the fifth time since his plane had landed. Not to see if Meghna had responded to his message. He just needed to check his email. Or the time. Or the weather. At least that's what he told himself. But every time he opened the home screen, he looked at the little message icon, disappointed when there wasn't a new notification.

He wondered if the joke hadn't been funny. Or maybe it had been ill-timed. But how was he supposed to know? He didn't make jokes like that. He had no idea how it would be received. For all he knew, he had offended her. He shouldn't have sent it, but he just hadn't been able to stop picturing the way she'd looked last night. The sad, pinched corners of her mouth, so different from her normal wide smile. The light in her eyes, the sparkle of amusement that had been there most of the night, had disappeared. She'd seemed exhausted. Listless.

He'd wanted to change that expression. Do something to wipe it from her face. Unthinkingly, he'd suggested getting ice cream, hoping to take her mind off the events of the night. Now that he was back in his office, it no longer seemed like such a great idea. She'd seen something shocking, had clearly been upset, and he'd suggested getting dessert. She must have thought him so callous.

And then he'd been back in his hotel room, imagining her lying in bed, still wearing that small, pinched expression. He hadn't wanted her to go to sleep like that. Hadn't wanted her to replay everything in her head. So, he'd sent a joke. *That joke.* He ran a hand through his hair and groaned. He was a fool.

"Dude, did you see what they're doing on the fourth floor?" Paul asked, gliding into his office. He handed Karthik his coffee, then sat in the chair in front of his desk. Karthik didn't know how it had happened, but the intern had developed a daily habit of chatting in his office, always lingering for a while after he dropped off coffee or lunch.

"No," Karthik said, removing the lid from his drink and blowing across the surface.

"It's amazing. They have, like, this robotic arm? One of the guys was showing me the controls. It's not working yet or anything, but I think they're getting close."

Karthik let out a noncommittal grunt. Of course the biomedical team was working on something cutting-edge and exciting. They always were. Karthik had stopped paying attention to their projects after a while. He wasn't ever going to work on them, so what was the point?

"Don't you think that's cool? Almost makes me want to give engineering another chance."

Karthik shrugged, rubbing his eye with the back of his hand.

"Rough night?" Paul asked.

"Just an early morning," Karthik said.

"Same." Paul sighed dramatically. "Actually, I barely slept at all. There's a new club that my girlfriend and her friends were dying to go to. We didn't get home until three."

Karthik nodded, turning to his computer screen. He hoped Paul would take the hint that it was time to start the workday, and even more important, time for this conversation to end.

Instead, Paul took a big slurp of his own coffee. "Why were you up so early?" he asked.

Karthik sighed and slowly turned back to face him. "I had an early flight."

"Where'd you go?"

"Dallas."

"Ohh. That's where your fiancée lives, right?" Paul grinned widely and a bit too knowingly. "Nice. No wonder you're so tired."

"It wasn't like that," Karthik said in a clipped tone. "We had to go to a party. It went late and it was . . . well, kind of a disaster."

Paul's grin stayed on his face. "The best parties are."

"Not this one."

"What happened?"

"Honestly, it's too hard to explain."

Paul rolled his eyes. "Couldn't be more complicated than what happened at last year's Sigma Delta homecoming party. My girlfriend wouldn't text me for a week after that one."

"What does it mean . . ." Karthik stopped, surprised he had actually said the question out loud. He almost let it go, but decided to soldier forward. "What does it mean if she's not texting me back?"

Paul leaned back in his chair, adopting the solemn air of an expert. "What did you send her?"

"A joke."

"What kind of joke? Something dirty?"

"No. Just a pun."

"Like a dad joke?" Paul asked, slightly horrified. "No wonder she's not responding."

"She likes jokes like that," he said defensively. "She collects them on T-shirts."

Paul gave him a look. "Sounds like a match made in heaven."

"And she had a rough night," Karthik said, continuing as if Paul hadn't said anything. "It probably has nothing to do with the joke."

"She had a rough night and you decided to send her a joke?"

Paul made an annoyingly good point. But there was nothing Karthik could do about it now. There wasn't any way he could take it back. He would just have to deal with it. At least he had a week before he had to see Meghna again. A week to put some distance between them. Maybe she'd respond by then. Or even better, maybe she'd completely forget he had ever sent that joke at all. He found himself desperately hoping for the latter.

It had been one week since Meghna had caught her best friend and her brother making out in a public restroom, and she was still ignoring their calls. She wasn't ready to face them yet. Wasn't ready to hear their explanations. Thankfully, she had a reason to be out of town for the next few days and would be able to avoid them for a little bit longer. She was almost looking forward to being in New York for the weekend. Her only hesitation was that it meant being around Karthik again.

She wasn't sure what his problem was, but it was clear that there was *some* problem. Or at least some kind of disconnect between them. At Ankita's party, there had been moments when he'd almost been . . . kind. Considerate, even. But then he'd made those comments about ice cream and sent that joke and she just couldn't figure it out. Couldn't figure *him* out. Had he been making light of the situation? Mocking her? Or just trying to make her laugh?

This was the kind of thing she usually discussed with Ankita.

That she *wanted* to discuss with Ankita. But that wasn't a possibility right now. Meghna wasn't ready to wade through her feelings about what she had seen. She loved her best friend. She loved her brother. But the two of them together? When Ankita had seemed so happy with Rishi? She couldn't believe that neither of them had told her. She told Ankita everything. That apparently didn't go both ways.

She shoved her hurt feelings to the side and smoothed her yellow sundress, adjusting the pleats that fell right around her knees. This retirement brunch party was going to be held outdoors, at some rooftop restaurant, and she didn't want to melt in the hot sun. She was used to the boiling temperatures in Texas, but sometimes New York struck her as just as hot. She theorized that it was because the heat soaked into the concrete, making it radiate all around her.

She couldn't vouch for the scientific accuracy of that theory, but as she walked to the restaurant, she became even more convinced she was right. The heat rose from the sidewalk beneath her, as if she were trapped in an oven. She entered the building, strands of her hair sticking to the nape of her neck. She hoped her sweaty appearance could be mistaken for a radiant glow.

She was meeting Karthik an hour early, before the party started, so they could go over their respective stories. Karthik had described his boss as incredibly inquisitive, and he wanted to be sure they had a response to anything she could come up with.

She rode the elevator to the very top and walked onto the roof, thankful for the fans blowing cool air all around her. She spotted Karthik and was walking in his direction when a sudden gust of air swept through her skirt. She grabbed her dress in a hurry before it could fly up, quickly realizing the pose wasn't half as glamorous as Marilyn Monroe had made it look.

Karthik stared at her for a moment, then jumped up and led her over to his table. She shot him a thankful glance and sat down on her dress, finally pinning it in place.

"Tell me about your boss," Meghna said once she was settled.

"She's retiring."

"Well, I guessed that much," she said with a smile.

Karthik ran a hand through his hair. She'd thought his hair had looked so perfect when they had first met, but she was finding that she liked this rumpled, slightly disheveled look even better.

"They're thinking of me for the replacement," he said.

"That's great!"

A wrinkle formed between his eyebrows. "It's a little more complicated than that."

"In what way?"

"Well, she thinks we're engaged."

Meghna couldn't understand how that was a problem. They technically *were* engaged. "What does that have to do with anything?"

"It's part of why she recommended me for the promotion. Apparently, my inability to commit has been an . . . issue. In the past. She thought *this*"—he waved his hand between the two of them—"meant I was serious or stable or something. I really don't know. All I know is she asked to meet you."

Meghna raised her hands in a *ta-da* gesture. "Well, here I am."

"I know. And I appreciate you coming," he said, a worried look still on his face. "I just don't think she'll buy it."

"Everyone else has. My parents. Yours. What are you so worried about?"

He grimaced. "We don't even know anything about each other."

She raised a shoulder nonchalantly. "So, you tell them this was arranged. Big deal. If they ask anything we don't know, we'll say we're still getting to know each other." She took a sip of the ice water in front of her and breathed a sigh of contentment. "Besides," she said, "I know things about you. You know things about me. You're an engineer. I'm a teacher. You live in New York. I live in Dallas." She tried to think of more items to add to the list, but realized she had already laid out everything she knew about him. Maybe he had a point.

"Well, what do you want to know?" she asked.

He took a sip of his own water and adjusted the cuffs of his shirt, his eyes not quite meeting hers. "Where are we going to live?" he finally asked. "After we get married."

She thought it over for a second. "I don't care. You pick. It's not going to be true either way."

"But we should have the same story," he said, being irritatingly reasonable.

"Fine," she said on an exhale. "New York. I'll move up here. I've thought about it before anyway."

"You have?"

"Yeah. Most people interested in theater dream about moving here at some point in their lives."

"I thought you taught English," he said.

"I do. But I used to want to write plays." She frowned as she registered what she'd just said. "Actually, I still write plays. I'm working on one now, but I just haven't made a lot of progress on it lately. Maybe if I moved here, I'd get back to it."

"You could even go back to school," he suggested. "Get an MFA."

Huh. She'd never thought about that before. Her parents had pushed her to consider grad school for years, but their suggestions were usually limited to business or law school. And engineering, of course, but they seemed to have given up on that one, realizing she wasn't cut out for it.

"Maybe," she said hesitantly. "So, what's going on with this promotion? After all, I should know *something* about your job."

"It's not that interesting," he said. "Almost everyone at the company is some kind of mechanical engineer, and we're all specialized in a particular area. I work on a team that designs HVAC systems. Heating, ventilation, air-conditioning. Mostly for commercial buildings. We study the blueprints, design systems, test them out. But my boss's job is a lot more management and supervision. I'd be overseeing the entire team instead of being a part of it if I got Marianne's job."

Meghna set her elbow on the table, propping her chin on her hand. "Is that what you want?"

He moved his head back subtly, as if he was surprised, as if no one had asked him that question before. "What?"

"This job," she said. "That's what you want?"

"It's the next move. It makes sense." He shook his head. "It's actually more than the next move. It's . . . it's the kind of job I'd thought I'd get in ten years. Maybe fifteen. I still can't believe they're really considering me."

Meghna leaned back in her seat. It sounded like a big deal. And even though it sounded incredibly boring to her, it was obviously important to him. No wonder he was so stressed about the party. "Will you miss any of the day-to-day work? If you'll be spending all your time managing?" If her school asked her to be the vice principal, she'd miss being in the classroom.

He blinked. "I won't miss it. I'll still be involved. But this is what I've been working toward. Where everything has been leading."

"All right, then," she said, deciding to drop it. "What do you do for fun?"

He stared at her blankly.

"For fun?" she asked again. "I write plays, like I mentioned earlier. And I swim. I also watch an unhealthy amount of reality television, but everyone has their vices. What about you?"

He looked away for a long moment. "I run," he finally said.

Of course. He just *had* to be one of those people who liked to run. Not that she had anything against people who ran. She did it too, but couldn't imagine describing it as *fun*. Though she had to admit that it suited him. She could almost picture his perfect hair flying in the breeze, his muscles showcased in his tight running clothes. If she saw him jogging past her in the park, she'd definitely take another look. Maybe more than one. She'd probably smile at him, and he'd just stare right back, his eyes dark and intense, just like they were now. And then . . .

Suddenly, his voice cut through, shattering her daydream.

"Who's Seth?" he asked.

Meghna jumped, but tried to hide it by sipping her drink. Unfortunately, in her haste she choked on the water, accidentally swallowing an ice cube. It slid uncomfortably down her throat.

"Who told you about Seth?" she asked once she recovered.

"Your brother," he said, watching her closely. "Seth's the one who called you at the party, right?"

"Right." She mentally added another thing to fight with Samir about whenever she gathered the nerve to confront him. "He's the one getting married."

Karthik leaned forward, his eyes trained on hers. "He must be important to you."

Her heartbeat doubled. What did he know?

"Why would you say that?" she asked as casually as she could manage.

"Well, didn't you say you were part of the wedding party?"

God, did he remember *everything* she said? She couldn't even remember telling him that.

"I am," she said, making an effort to appear composed and collected. "I'm the best man."

She expected some kind of response to that. Raised eyebrows. A shocked exclamation. Maybe even a *You? The best man?* But he did none of that. He just looked at her thoughtfully and took a sip of his water. She found it unnerving.

"Do you have any plans while you're in the city?" he asked after a moment.

"Not really," she said, relieved that any questioning about Seth was over. "I know we have that dinner with your parents tonight, but I don't have anything else figured out. I'll probably just walk around and find a bookstore. Go to the park."

"You're not seeing a show?"

"I looked into it, but didn't buy any tickets." She hadn't been sure of their schedule for the weekend.

"We should go to one," he said.

"You like theater?" For some reason, she hadn't imagined that he was a fan.

He shrugged. "I don't know. I've never been."

"Really? My parents always took me and Samir whenever the shows on tour stopped in Dallas. They were good, but I would have died to have grown up in New York. To see performances with the original casts. I can't believe you live here and have never been."

He let out a harsh laugh. "Yeah, well, I grew up in Queens. We weren't exactly next door to Broadway. My dad would have thought going all that way for some singing and dancing was a waste of time." He shook his head in disgust, making it clear he felt the same way too.

Meghna's shoulders grew tense.

There were times when it almost felt easy to talk to Karthik. To be around him. And then there were times like this. When he was brusque. Dismissive. And rude.

At least she only had to put up with it for the length of the engagement. Then she'd never have to see him again.

A tense silence settled over the two of them, broken only by the sounds of other people stepping onto the roof. A cacophony of voices mid-conversation carried over on the wind. Meghna breathed a sigh of relief. Marianne's retirement party had begun.

Once everyone said their goodbyes and the party came to a close, Karthik realized he'd spent all that time worrying for nothing. Everyone had loved Meghna. Of course they had. She'd been sparkling and funny and kind. He was quickly learning that that was just her natural state of being. And she'd fielded every question about their relationship deftly.

Several of the executives who would be on the selection panel for Marianne's old position had asked how the two of them had met. A simple question, but Karthik had almost sweat through his shirt. Thankfully, Meghna had answered with ease.

"Our parents, if you can believe it," she'd said with a laugh and a wave of her hand. "We didn't even know anything about each other. And neither of us ever thought we'd go for an arranged setup, but you know, arranged introductions like this worked for all my aunts and uncles. I figured it couldn't do any harm." She'd shot Karthik a wide smile, tucking her hand into the crook of his arm.

His skin had sparked at the touch. Like he was a kid again, shuffling across the carpet in socks.

"Little did I know," she'd continued, "that I'd end up meeting the love of my life." Everyone had *awww*'d appropriately in response and left the encounter with her thoroughly charmed.

By the end, no one had any reason to suspect that they were anything but an engaged couple in love. Before leaving, Marianne had even leaned toward him and whispered, "This one's a keeper." And Karthik hadn't been able to do anything but smile and nod in response. Meghna so clearly was. He was the one with the problems. The one who was so decidedly *not* a keeper.

And if Meghna hadn't figured that out by now, she would surely realize it once they were done with dinner at his parents' house. Once she met his father. The spitting image of what Karthik would look like in thirty years.

He was dreading the two of them meeting and had done his best to put it off, but once his mother had learned that Meghna would be in the city, she'd insisted on making them dinner. They'd met only briefly in Dallas, and she wanted to spend more time getting to know her future daughter-in-law. Karthik hadn't seen a way around it.

He sighed and followed Meghna into the elevator, out of the restaurant, and onto the sidewalk. They stood there for a moment, facing each other awkwardly, unsure of what to do next.

Karthik put his hands in his pockets. "I, uh, was checking on my phone earlier. I couldn't find any tickets for something on Broadway, but there's a matinee performance Off-Broadway that we could go to. We'd have to leave straight from there to go to my parents' house, but it might be—"

Meghna shook her head, her smile tight and small. "That's okay. You don't have to do that. I was thinking I'd just go shopping for a bit."

He paused, a little confused. She'd seemed interested when he'd mentioned going to see a show before, but maybe she had changed her mind. He waited a moment to see if she wanted him to come along, but after a few seconds of silence, he could tell no invitation was coming. He cleared his throat, gave her the address for his parents' house, and left, each of them going their separate ways.

When it was time for dinner, they met a block away from his childhood home, just like they had planned, and walked to the house together. As soon as Karthik opened the front door, the most inviting and comforting smell washed over him: basmati rice, curry leaves, turmeric, and fried onions. He could already tell his mother had made mutton biryani. His absolute favorite.

Karthik showed Meghna to the kitchen table. His mother jumped up to hug them, beaming with joy. His father was surprisingly also pleasant, and expressed his congratulations on their engagement. They all took their seats and began serving themselves from the large bowl of steaming rice in the center of the table.

"Everything looks delicious, Shanti Aunty," Meghna said to his mother.

"Thank you. This is Karthik's favorite dish, you know. I'll send you the recipe so you can learn to make it too."

Karthik wanted to groan. "I know how to make it, Amma. If I want it, I can make it for myself."

Meghna smiled and placed her hand on his arm, silently telling him it was fine. "I'd love to have it," she told his mother. "It's different from the kind my family makes. You can never have too many biryani recipes."

His father shot Karthik an approving look, making the hair on the back of Karthik's neck stand up straight. He couldn't remember the last time he'd been on the receiving end of a look like that from his father. He didn't like it.

"My wife told me you're a teacher," Karthik's father said to Meghna. "I am too. I teach at NYCU medical school."

Karthik resisted the urge to roll his eyes. Of course his dad couldn't go a few seconds without bringing up his work.

"That's great," Meghna said warmly.

His father started explaining all the ins and outs of his research, his latest paper, and the grant proposal he was working on. "I always thought Karthik would be a doctor too," he said. "But he just never had the interest. He would have been—"

"You should try some raita," his mother interrupted, passing it along to Meghna. "The biryani can get too spicy on its own."

A muscle twitched near his father's jaw. It was probably imperceptible to Meghna or a stranger, but not to him. Karthik had learned to look for it. In the past that tic would have meant that an angry outburst was imminent, but somewhere along the way his father's temper had mostly dissolved into neglect. Disinterest.

Some of that disinterest had been there even when Karthik was a child. Making his father proud enough to just *notice* him had been the goal of his childhood. But nothing he'd ever been able to do had accomplished that. And the day he'd told his father he was going to be an engineer and not a doctor had been the final nail in the coffin. Any tiny bit of interest his father might have had in him had vanished. It didn't matter that he was good at his job. Or that his colleagues respected him. Or that he was up for this huge promotion. His father didn't care about any of that.

Karthik took the raita from Meghna and added some to his own plate. "Meghna's an excellent teacher," he said, trying to change the subject. "And she's also a playwright."

"Aspiring playwright," she said, slightly flustered. "It's just something I do for fun."

"You teach English, right?" his mother asked softly.

"I do. And theater."

"I didn't know that," Karthik said, turning to look at her.

She gave him a small smile. "It's pretty new. We never really had the budget for a full-time theater program for our kids, but I did musicals all through school and college and wanted my students to have the same experience. The school finally agreed and gave us the funds, but we'll see how it goes. It's our first time putting on a fall play."

They spoke about how rehearsals were going, and she told them her students were performing *My Fair Lady*, which happened to be one of his mother's favorite movies. The two of them started talking about some of the other movies his mother liked, and Karthik snuck a glance at his father.

He sat stoically, his face blank and almost vacant. He'd probably checked out the second they had stopped talking about medicine, which suited Karthik just fine. In his mind, the less his father interacted with Meghna, the better. His mother was still talking, deep in the middle of a detailed plot summary of a classic Tamil film from the eighties, when his father stood up abruptly.

"I have to go check something at the office," he said. "Meghna, it was a pleasure meeting you."

Meghna seemed a little taken aback that his father would be going into work on a Saturday night, but Karthik didn't bat an eye. This was standard operating procedure for his father. Honestly, he was surprised that his father had stuck around this long.

"Are you sure you have to leave now?" his mother asked.

A tense moment of silence followed. Karthik had never heard his mother question his father in this way. His father came when he wanted. And left when he wanted. Karthik and his mother were quite used to it.

"I have to go in to work, Shanti. You know how it is."

His mother's eyes widened, but Karthik saw a determined glint in them that he had never seen before.

"I do. But I think you can wait to have your *meeting* until our dinner is over."

His father's face took on a ruddy complexion. "I'm a mentor, Shanti. The students are busy, and I have to make myself available to help them." He gestured in Meghna's direction. "As a teacher, I'm sure you understand," he told her. "Of course, the stakes here are even higher. These are future doctors. Not children." A smile crept across his face, slightly cold and condescending. "We can't all dress kids in costumes and play make-believe."

The warmth on Meghna's face faded.

"That's enough," Karthik said crisply. "We understand you're in a hurry. We don't want to hold you up." He looked pointedly at the door.

His father left the house without further fanfare. His mother offered quiet apologies, but Meghna waved them away, guiding the conversation back to his mother's excellent food, asking for recipes for everything.

"Just so you know," Meghna told him when they were in the cab on the way back to her hotel. "If I hadn't been playing the role of a dutiful fiancée tonight, I would have ripped your dad apart for saying that."

Karthik almost snorted. Little did she know that he would have paid a good amount of money to see that.

"And he would have deserved it," he said. "In the future, please feel free to tell him whatever you want. Though hopefully you won't have to meet him again."

"Hopefully," she muttered. "Is he always like that?"

Karthik sighed. "He's usually better behaved when guests are around." When they weren't, he could be much, much worse. It used to frighten him as a child. Now it frightened him for a different reason altogether. Karthik had his father's face. His father's temper. And he was sure he had all of his father's other failings too.

He wanted to be different. To be patient and honest and kind, like his mother. To have some control over his emotions so he wouldn't hurt others with his angry, rash words. But despite his best intentions, he ended up hurting people anyway. Becoming like his father felt unavoidable. Inevitable.

Meghna's phone pinged with an incoming text message. Karthik didn't mean to invade her privacy, but her screen was large, and he could read it from his seat right next to hers.

Seth: Call me ASAP. Need to finalize hotel arrangements for Miami!!

Her phone pinged again. Seth had followed up with a string of emojis: confetti, a dancer, the ocean, and a bottle of champagne.

"He seems to call you a lot," Karthik said in a neutral tone, even though a strange streak of hot energy had coursed through his body when he'd read the text. He adjusted the air-conditioning vent in the back of the car. He was probably overheated. This month had been unseasonably warm.

"He doesn't, really," Meghna said. "We're just in the middle of planning his bachelor party."

Huh. "Well, please feel free to call him back."

"Thanks. It won't take long," she promised, dialing the number. Seth immediately answered, and they began discussing logistics. The call was loud enough that Karthik could hear both ends of the conversation. He convinced himself that it wasn't really eavesdropping. He had no choice but to listen.

They talked about the guest list, how many nights they'd be staying, and some of the restaurants and nightclubs they had researched. Seth made some quippy remark that Karthik couldn't quite catch, but it must have been funny because Meghna let out a loud, unrestrained laugh.

That same strange, hot energy from before returned. Before Karthik even knew what he was doing, he opened his mouth. "We're almost at the hotel, Meghna," he said, a little louder than necessary.

"Who's that? Is that a guy?" Seth asked excitedly. "Meg, are you seeing someone?"

"Yeah, I am." She shot Karthik a look, but he stared back at her innocently. "He's, umm, that's actually my fiancé."

"What?" Seth screeched. "When did this happen?"

"Pretty recently."

"That's wonderful! Congratulations!"

"Thanks," she said flatly.

"I had no idea you were seeing anyone," Seth said. "You know, this trip's going to be pretty much all guys. You should bring him! Then you won't have to hang out with just us losers."

"Oh, I don't know," Meghna said, looking at Karthik worriedly. "I'm sure he's busy then."

"When is it?" he mouthed.

She shook her head, her eyes imploring him to say nothing.

A devilish sense of *something* shot through him. "I'd love to come," he said loudly.

Meghna glared at him.

"Wonderful!" Seth said on the other end of the call. "I can't wait to meet him."

They talked through the remaining details before ending the call. As soon as she hung up, Meghna turned to fully face him, her irritation obvious. For some reason, Karthik couldn't wait to hear what she had to say. He was almost . . . giddy. It was a foreign emotion, but he was thoroughly enjoying it.

"Why would you say that?" she asked.

"I was just thinking about our deal," he said calmly. "If I was really your fiancé, wouldn't I come with you?"

She looked at him uncertainly.

"And we could probably sell our relationship better at the wedding," he continued. "This way it's not out of the blue when I show up as your fiancé. Seth and the others will have met me before."

"I guess," she said slowly.

"Really, what's the harm in my going?" he asked, genuinely curious why it was upsetting her so much.

She looked away, tucking a piece of hair behind her ear. "I just think it'll be awkward, that's all."

"Why?" he pressed. "Wouldn't it be more awkward to go alone?"

Her eyes flashed with annoyance. "Why do you want to go so badly?" she asked, sounding more like herself, her voice filled with its usual fire.

He made an effort to appear casual, even though he found his heartbeat increasing.

"Who wouldn't want to make a trip to Miami?" he asked. The answer, of course, was him. Normally, he'd hate the idea of a trip like this. The beach, a rowdy group of guys, clubbing. Truly a nightmare scenario. He couldn't explain why he was so interested in going, but he was invested now. He had to go.

"And Seth already thinks I'm coming," he helpfully reminded her. "You'd have to come up with some excuse about why I couldn't make it. Wouldn't that be a bit suspicious?"

She stared at him until a look of resignation crossed her face. "Fine," she said. "But you're going to do exactly what I say. We're setting real terms this time."

Her words sent a thrill of anticipation down his spine. "Of course," he said. "I completely agree." She pivoted away to face the window, and he did the same, taking in the blur of the city lit up at night. Without fully realizing it, he let out a small smile.

"I t's Monday. The show's about to start. And I have pizza with goat cheese, Kalamata olives, and hot honey," Ankita said from outside Meghna's apartment.

Meghna looked at the door and sighed. She should have suspected something like this was coming. She'd been dodging Ankita's calls for too long. And last week had been the first time one of them had skipped out on their weekly reality show watch night in years. She shot the door another wary glance. She was dreading this confrontation, and part of her was tempted to just pretend she wasn't home.

"You have to let me in," Ankita called out. "The pizza's getting cold."

Meghna was quiet for a second, then shouted back, "I like cold pizza."

"I know. And I think it's disgusting!"

Meghna rolled her eyes, but got up to let her in. Even though she was still upset with Ankita, it was probably time for them to have it out. Besides, Ankita hated olives. Her ordering them for Meghna was a true peace offering.

She swung the door open. Ankita held a large pizza box, a slightly nervous expression on her face. Meghna took the box from her hands and gestured for her to come in.

"I didn't mean to just show up like this, but you weren't returning my calls. Or my texts and—"

"I needed some space."

Ankita swallowed. "Right. Of course."

They stood there for a moment, awkwardly facing each other, until Meghna put the pizza down on the coffee table and spread a blanket on the floor. They sat down, but neither of them moved to turn the television on.

"I don't know what to say. I don't know how to explain what . . ." Ankita stopped, letting out a loud breath.

"How long has this been going on?" Meghna asked. She thought that was as good a place to start as any.

"Nothing's going on. We didn't plan this. I haven't talked to Samir in . . . in years. Not since he moved to India."

"Then how did it happen?"

Ankita shook her head. "I don't even know. I saw him at your parents' table and that was . . . fine. He came up and congratulated me and Rishi on the engagement. I thanked him. Rishi thanked him. It was all very civil. And then I went to the bathroom and he just . . . He followed me inside and said he needed to talk to me. And then . . . I mean, it was *Samir*, and he was kissing me, and so . . . I kissed him back."

Meghna went still. "What do you mean it was *Samir*?"

Ankita shifted uneasily. "You know I've always liked Samir."

"Yeah, sure. But I also thought you were in love with your fiancé. I mean, seriously, Ankita, this is your explanation? You kissed my brother even though you are engaged to someone else because you had a crush on him as a kid?"

"It wasn't a crush. I was in love with him!"

Meghna snorted. "What? When you were five?"

"No. In college. And he said he was too, but he must have been lying because he literally left for India the next week and I—"

"In college?" Surprise jolted through her, and Ankita snapped her mouth shut, guilt spreading across her face.

Meghna closed her eyes, realizing what this meant. Ankita had lied to her. Something *had* happened between Ankita and Samir that summer.

"I wanted to tell you about it," Ankita said. "I wanted to tell you everything, but Samir didn't want anyone to know. And then it was over and it seemed pointless to bring it up. And embarrassing. And too much time had passed and I . . ."

Hurt blossomed in Meghna's chest. They'd both lied to her. For years.

"I'm sorry," Ankita said. "I am. I mean, I could tell you all about it now and we could talk and—"

"Does Rishi know?" Meghna interrupted. "Have you told him?"

"No, I . . . I don't think I'm going to. It was one kiss. And Samir's back in India and we're never going to . . . It's never going to happen again."

Meghna stared at her in disbelief. "So, that's it? You're going to lie to him too?"

"I *love* Rishi. I just . . . lost my head for a moment. It was a mistake."

"Yeah. Obviously. But don't you think keeping all of this a secret from your *fiancé* would be another one?"

Ankita paled, but offered only an anemic shrug.

Meghna sighed, pulling out two slices of pizza and handing one to Ankita. Ankita picked off the olives one by one, tossing them back into the box.

Meghna was still upset, but things between the two of them were tense enough right now. And she was too tired. Too confused. Too hurt. She didn't want to say anything she'd regret later. She needed time to process all of this.

They ate their pizza in silence until Ankita asked about the trip to New York. Meghna filled her in on what had happened and told her about the upcoming bachelor party.

"How is that going to work?" Ankita asked. "He's going to party with you and Seth and the guys?"

"I can't really picture Karthik partying, but yeah, that's the general idea. It's going to be so awkward. I tried to convince him it was a bad idea, but he's right. It'd be weird if he didn't come now, after he told Seth he would."

"Well, just think of it like an opportunity," Ankita said.

"An opportunity for what?"

"I just meant that if you ever wanted to make Seth jealous, now's a good chance."

"I don't see how. He already knows I'm engaged."

"Yeah, but you're going to have to convince him and everyone else that the engagement is *real*."

"Right."

"So that involves stuff like holding hands, being touchy-feely, kissing . . ."

Meghna's brain short-circuited. She hadn't seriously thought about kissing Karthik before, but now a picture of it popped into her head. Him towering over her, his warm hand on her lower back, his other hand cradling her cheek. A wave of heat swept through her body. *Whoa.* She hadn't expected that.

"Seems like it could be fun," Ankita said.

Meghna shot her an annoyed look. They finished eating, but instead of turning on the show, Meghna said she wanted to have an early night. For the first time in her life, she wasn't really in the mood for two hours of reality television. Ankita left quickly, and Meghna shut and locked the door behind her.

She was still so angry. And frustrated. And irritated by what Ankita had done. By what Ankita had said. She thought this trip could be *fun*? Fun for who, exactly? The whole thing sounded stressful. Pretending to be engaged to this confusing and irritating man, convincing her ex and his friends that their relationship was real, all while pretending she didn't have any leftover feelings for Seth? What about that sounded fun?

The image of Karthik kissing her suddenly popped back into her head. His dark eyes staring intently at her, his stubble scratching her cheek, his body flush against hers. Nervous energy fluttered in her stomach, along with something that felt a lot like excitement. Who knew what could happen on this trip? Maybe there was a chance it would end up being a little fun after all.

"That's not right," Meghna said. "I called and confirmed this yesterday. They told me the room had two queen beds."

"I'm sorry," the man behind the front desk said. "Our system shows you booked a king bed suite. But it's a great room. Much nicer than our two-queen standard."

A breeze swept through the hotel lobby, carrying the scent of the beach toward them. Salt water, coconut sunscreen, and something floral. It blew quickly, disturbing Meghna's hair, and Karthik watched with interest as she absently removed a hair tie from around her wrist, gathered her curls, and twisted them in one sharp movement into a bun.

"No. You need to move us back," she told the hotel employee. "We don't want the upgrade." Meghna turned toward Karthik, an uneasy expression on her face. "I booked a room with two beds. I swear."

"I believe you," he said. Her panic seemed too real for it to be fake. He would almost be offended that she was so upset at the thought of sharing a bed with him, except the idea was making him equally panicky. A bead of sweat formed on his forehead. He wiped it away quickly.

"I can sleep on the floor," he told her. "It's not a big deal."

"But you shouldn't have to. Look," she said, facing the front desk again. "You have to have some room with two beds available? Or at least a rollaway cot?"

The man looked at his computer screen and clacked his keyboard for a few seconds. "I'm sorry," he finally said. "We don't have anything else. I can go talk to our manager and see if there's—"

"Please, yes. Anything you can do," Meghna said hurriedly. The man walked away in a huff, and Meghna swiveled back to Karthik.

"Maybe we can get you another room," she said.

He raised an eyebrow. "Wouldn't that defeat the whole purpose of the trip? Convincing them we're a real couple?"

"You're right," she said. "I'm not thinking straight." She shook her head. "Honestly, I'm a little nervous about all of this."

"Really?" he asked, trying to make his voice even more monotone than usual. "I had no idea."

She stared at him for a moment. "Are you *teasing* me?"

The corners of his mouth tilted up.

"You are. You're teasing me." Her mouth stretched into that familiar, wide smile, and pride flared in Karthik's chest. His words had produced that look on her face. She was directing that joy at him and him alone.

"Hello, lovebirds," a voice called out behind them.

Meghna's smile disappeared.

A sandy-haired man in a floral-print shirt, navy swim trunks, and Birkenstocks walked toward them. Once he was in front of Meghna, the man threw his arms around her and hugged her tightly, almost lifting her off the ground. "You're here!" he exclaimed. He held her for what seemed like several minutes before finally letting go and shaking Karthik's hand. "And you must be Karthik. I've heard so much about you."

Can't say the same. "It's nice to meet you, Seth. Congratulations on your upcoming wedding."

Seth grinned. "And same to you." He turned to Meghna. "And you! I can't believe I didn't find out about this sooner."

Meghna snorted. "You're one to talk. I didn't find out until I got your invitation in the mail."

"Well, we always were too similar for our own good," Seth said, his grin taking on a new dimension, almost as if he was referring to some secret or joke between the two of them. Karthik gritted his teeth.

"Have you guys checked in?" Seth asked. "We got here about an hour ago and were thinking of going down to the beach for a bit—"

"I'm sorry about that, ma'am," a voice from the front desk cut in. "We had an issue with our system, but we have a room with two queen beds available for you. I have your room keys ready and—"

"Oh, no," Meghna said quickly. "You must have us confused with somebody else. We have the king suite."

The manager furrowed his eyebrows. "I was told you needed two beds . . ."

Karthik placed an arm around Meghna's shoulders, pulling her into his body. "Nope. Must have been a miscommunication." Meghna's entire face froze except for her eyes, which were growing wider than he'd ever seen them. He squeezed her shoulder.

"You can't keep me away from this one," he said, letting out a louder-than-normal laugh. Meghna seemed to get the hint. Her body relaxed slightly, and she let out a strained laugh of her own.

The manager looked puzzled, but apologized and handed them their room keys. Seth watched them oddly, his eyes glued to Karthik's hand on Meghna's shoulder. Karthik instinctively dropped his hand and tucked it into his pocket, which seemed to shake Seth from his thoughts.

"Glad that all got sorted out. Y'all take your time getting changed and stuff. We'll be at the beach," Seth said. "Text me if you have any problems, okay?"

After promising to meet up with everyone later, Meghna and Karthik headed toward the elevators. As soon as the doors slid shut, Meghna dropped her head into her palms.

"We can't do this," she said, her voice muffled by her hands. "We should just leave."

No. Karthik started, surprised by how strong that thought had been. He didn't even know where it had come from.

"What are you worried about?" he asked.

She lifted her head, disbelief etched across her features. "Are you kidding me? Were you not just there?"

He crossed his arms. "I think we handled that fairly well."

She rolled her eyes.

"And we'll keep getting better," he continued. "This is new right now. We just need . . . practice."

"Practice?" she asked skeptically.

Yes. That's it. He couldn't believe he hadn't thought of it before.

"This is a performance, right? To make it believable, we just need to rehearse."

"Rehearse what?"

His throat went dry as his mind generously provided him with numerous suggestions. "Everything."

She just stared at him.

"Like earlier," he said. "You acted like we had never touched before."

"Because we haven't!"

"I know, but they need to believe we're together, right? You need to act like it's normal."

"None of this is normal," she muttered.

"No, but it's what we agreed to."

Her face remained blank. Inscrutable.

"I'm just being practical," he insisted.

The elevator doors opened and they stepped out onto their floor, walking in silence to their room.

As the silence dragged on, he began to regret his words. Now she probably thought he was some slimeball trying to come on to her. Like that creep who'd approached her at Ankita's party. He frowned.

He should have offered to leave as soon as he'd noticed she was uncomfortable. Maybe that was what she wanted. He was about to suggest some excuse they could give the group about why he had to leave suddenly when her voice cut him off.

"Mind if I use the bathroom?" she asked. She grabbed a handful of things from her suitcase and stepped inside before he could respond.

A few minutes later she walked back out wearing a bright red bikini and a gauzy white cover-up, though Karthik thought the name was a misnomer. It covered nothing. She wasn't particularly tall, but right now all he could see were her legs. Smooth and long, as if they went on forever. *Whoa.* All thoughts of leaving flew out of his head.

He realized he was staring and quickly looked away, fishing his swim trunks out of his bag. "Excuse me," he said, going into the bathroom. He shut the door behind him and turned on the faucet. A faint buzzing rang in his ears.

What she wears is none of my business. I shouldn't care. I shouldn't even be looking. But for whatever reason, the image of her standing there in that swimsuit was burned into his mind.

His temperature skyrocketed. He splashed some water on his face, trying to erase the picture from his head and cool himself down. Maybe he was coming down with something. Maybe he was contagious. If he was, she'd been exposed to it too. To be on the safe side, they probably needed to quarantine. Lock themselves in this room and never leave. Then she wouldn't go down to the beach looking like that with all those bozo groomsmen around.

None of my business, he reminded himself.

She's your fiancée, the dumb half of his brain immediately replied.

She's not. Not really. And even if she was, it still wouldn't be any of my business. He splashed some more water on his face, his body returning to normal, his rationality slowly returning.

He was attracted to her. It was just biology. Inconvenient, but not an insurmountable problem. He would simply push it down. Suppress it. At least he was aware of it now. And thank goodness Meghna had rejected his pathetic idea to "rehearse." If he had been forced to practice certain . . . things with her, well, he didn't know what would happen exactly, but he worried it would jeopardize their deal. And he couldn't allow that to happen. He stared at his reflection, watching his usual cool demeanor fall back into place. He could control this. He had to.

"I think you're right," Meghna said once Karthik walked out of the bathroom.

"About what?"

"About practicing."

Karthik blanched, his face turning ashen.

"Are you okay?"

Karthik coughed. "I'm fine."

He reached for the unopened bottle of water sitting on the dresser and gulped a good chunk of it down.

Meghna's eyebrows rose. "Are you sure you're fine? You just opened a five-dollar bottle of water."

He reared his head back and looked at the bottle, seeing the fancy brand name and the hanging price tag the hotel had added to it. He coughed again.

"Here, come sit down," Meghna said, guiding him to the edge of the bed. He took a seat and she moved to stand in front of him, placing the back of her hand on his forehead.

He shivered.

"Do you have chills? You don't feel warm."

"I'm fine," he said, his eyes glued to the floor. She leaned back and gave him an assessing look. He didn't have a fever, but his face was flushed.

"Are you sure? Maybe it's the weather change. Sometimes the humidity can make it harder to breathe."

"That must be it," he said. "I'll be fine once I get used to the difference." He closed his eyes and took a few deep breaths.

Meghna grabbed the water bottle and handed it back to him. He let out a thankful grunt, but his eyes remained closed. As he drank the water, her thoughts drifted to the conversation she had tried to start earlier.

Ever since Ankita had planted the idea of kissing Karthik in her brain, Meghna hadn't been able to stop thinking about it. Images of "the kiss" kept popping into her head during inopportune times. While she was teaching. Or talking to her mother. Or trying to work on her play. On the flight to Miami, she'd decided that she just needed to get it out of her system. Just one kiss. And once it was over, she'd be able to put it out of her mind and continue her fake engagement in peace.

She'd started brainstorming ways to convince Karthik that a kiss would be necessary to keep up their charade, but she had never imagined that an opportunity would present itself this neatly. That he would be the one to suggest "practicing." But of course, the second she brought it up, he became visibly sick. Her stomach sank. Had the idea of kissing her made him physically ill?

"Let's go down," Karthik suddenly said, standing up and making his way to the door.

"You sure you're feeling up to it?"

"Yeah. Yeah, I'm fine." He glanced back at the bed, his throat moving in a hard swallow. "I think it'll get better once I'm out of this room."

"Sure. I guess the fresh air could help."

They took the elevator back down to the lobby, stopped at the front desk to grab some towels, then followed the signs to the resort beach.

It wasn't too hard to find Seth and the rest of the guys. They had rented a cabana and were playing loud dance music on a portable speaker. She immediately spotted Eric and Mark, two of Seth's groomsmen, playing beach volleyball a few feet away from everyone else. Back in college, everyone had affectionately referred to them as "the twins," even though they weren't related in any way.

The two of them still looked remarkably alike, standing at the same height, with dark-brown hair and deep-set dimples. Almost all of her friends had been in love with them at one point or another, but she'd never considered them anything more than Seth's annoying roommates. She waved at the guys, and they headed over once they spotted her.

"Meghna!" Eric shouted, bumping his fist against hers. "We need to get you a shot. Mark, did you forget the Patrón in the room or did we bring it down with us?"

Meghna laughed. "Okay, guys, it's still bright out. I'm not ready to get wild yet."

Mark grinned goofily. "Hasn't stopped us!"

She shook her head in mock disapproval. "Well, I'm going to need to pace myself." She grabbed a soda out of a nearby cooler, then dropped her bag and towel on an open lounger. Karthik mirrored her movements, dropping his towel onto the lounger beside hers.

"Guys, this is Karthik," she said, grabbing his hand and interlocking their fingers. "My fiancé."

"Nice to meet you, man," Mark said.

Eric groaned. "I can't believe all of you are getting married. We're not old enough for that yet."

"You may have stopped maturing at twenty-one, but that doesn't mean the rest of us did," Mark replied. Eric shoved Mark's shoulder, and the two of them bickered back and forth while Meghna and Karthik went off to greet the rest of the guys. Meghna hadn't met the remaining two groomsmen before: Blake, a friend of Seth's from work, and Seth's cousin, Ralph, who looked up at them over the cover of his book, then went straight back to his reading.

Seth had already gone for a swim and was jogging back from the ocean, his hair flying in the wind like something out of a commercial.

"Hey, glad you guys are here!" he shouted to them. He joined them at the loungers, claiming the one to the right of Meghna, leaving her sandwiched in the middle between him and Karthik. He picked up a tube of sunscreen and started rubbing it onto his shoulders and face, though both had already turned an alarming shade of pink.

"I always forget that I need to reapply," he said. "You want some?" He waved the sunscreen in her direction.

Meghna laughed, stretching her legs out in front of her, fully reclining in her chair. "When have I ever needed sunscreen?"

"You don't wear sunscreen?" Karthik asked.

"Do you? I've never gotten sunburned."

His brows snapped together. "Me either, but sunscreen is recommended even if you have a lot of melanin. You can still get serious skin damage. Even skin cancer. Dermatologists recommend . . ."

Gah. Why was she finding this lecture so cute? It should have been irritating. She didn't understand it, but she couldn't stop the wide smile spreading across her face. His voice suddenly trailed off.

"You . . . you should wear sunscreen," he finished.

She threw her hands up in resignation. "Fine, fine." She grabbed the sunscreen from Seth and started putting it on her arms and legs. Then she handed it to Karthik and turned around in her chair, presenting her back to him.

"Mind getting my back?" He'd made fun of her earlier for acting like they had never touched before, and she was tempted to give him a taste of his own medicine. See how calmly *he* reacted to having to put sunscreen on her bare skin.

Karthik took the sunscreen from her without complaint, poured it into his hands, and started rubbing it on her. Unexpected sparks of pleasure burst across her skin. They followed wherever his hands went: the backs of her arms, down her spine, her lower back. The pleasure grew, and it was almost as if all the bones in her body had disappeared, like she would melt into a puddle right there and then. But *she* wasn't supposed to be the one so affected by this. And with her back to him, she couldn't even see how he was reacting or if he was reacting at all. Her plan had been poorly thought out. Again, he seemed to have the upper hand in whatever strange game the two of them were playing.

His hands suddenly stopped. She turned, and he immediately averted his eyes, looking off toward the ocean.

"All done?" she asked, working hard to make her voice sound light and breezy.

"Yup. Here you go," he said, handing the sunscreen back to her.

"What about you?"

He shook his head, getting up from the lounger. "Put some on earlier. I'm going to go for a swim." He started walking toward the water, but glanced back at her with an odd expression. She frowned, hoping he wasn't still feeling unwell.

"You two make quite the couple," Seth remarked, his eyes following Karthik's path down the beach.

"Thanks. And I know I've only seen pictures, but you and Julie look really great together." As she said the words out loud, she was surprised to realize she actually meant them. She'd scoured their engagement pictures on the wedding website, feeling a bit nauseous as she went through them. Somehow each pose managed to be more lovey-dovey than the one before. But after she had finished her scrolling, she had to admit they looked like they went together. Like one of those couples in the black-and-white stock photos in brand-new picture frames. They seemed to just fit.

Seth put a hand behind his head, turning on his side to face her. "I think you'll really like her." He pulled his phone out and started swiping his finger across the screen. "Actually, I've been meaning to ask your advice about something."

"Go for it."

"I'm working on something to sing for her at the reception, but I'm worried it's a little too sappy," he said.

Meghna's gut twisted, but she tried to ignore it.

"Could I send you the lyrics? Get your thoughts?"

"Sure," she said. "I'd love to take a look."

He smiled, his teeth unnaturally white and gleaming. Had he gotten them bleached recently? Meghna winced. They were almost blinding.

She'd joked once with him, after his first song had sold, about whether he'd have to change up his look. If he'd start wearing designer clothes or get some trendy new hairstyle. If he'd forget all about her once he became rich and famous. He'd laughed and promised he'd never do that. And she'd been pleasantly surprised that he'd meant it. He hadn't forgotten about her. Not after his breakout hit. Or his second. Or his third.

He'd still been there for her. Still read everything she sent him. And he'd continued to send his songs over as well, showing her how much he valued her and her opinion. Even this last year, when he'd started churning out songs at an unprecedented rate, she'd discussed every one with him, making suggestions and workshopping ideas. It was just what they did. How their writing partnership worked. Though now that she thought about it, it had been a while since they'd had a similar conversation about her own words.

Her phone pinged, signaling he had emailed the lyrics over.

"I'll read it this week," she told him.

"Thanks, Meg. Your feedback on my last song is truly the only reason it sold." He shook his head. "It was a mess before you looked at it."

"Really, it's fine. I like to do it." In their college Intro to Creative Writing class, she and Seth had tried a little bit of everything. Poems, short stories, songs, and plays. He'd gravitated to songwriting, and she'd found her niche in theater, but both had dabbled a bit in the other's craft. She'd written a handful of songs back then, and Seth had liked them just fine, but he'd been much more encouraging and supportive of her plays.

She'd secretly written a few more songs over the years, but never shared the new ones with Seth. His songs were amazing. And he was a professional. She was terrified to see what he would think of her amateur efforts. Plays were familiar. Safe. And she already knew he loved them. Something about songwriting felt more . . . intimate. And she wasn't sure she wanted to subject her songs to Seth's usual blunt feedback.

Seth rubbed the back of his neck, a sheepish expression crossing his face. "And I know I'm really behind on responding to that revised draft you sent me a while ago. I'm so sorry."

"That's okay," she said, though she felt a touch of annoyance. He hadn't responded to anything she'd sent in the last few months, and his comments from before then had been vague but critical. She didn't mind criticism, but he hadn't pointed out what he thought could be improved or how. He'd only said it wasn't working. Though his instincts about these things were usually right. Maybe what she'd sent wasn't working at all. Maybe he had meant that she should scrap it all and start over. What she'd written must have been unsalvageable. She made a mental note to go back and consider yet another rewrite.

"It's just that wedding planning has been eating up all of my time," he said, letting out a big sigh.

"Right," she said, traces of annoyance returning. "And I wouldn't know anything about that."

"Hey, I didn't mean it like that. I know you're probably busy with wedding planning too." His eyes traveled over her face. "Hard to believe we're both engaged, huh?"

"I guess," she said in a deliberately casual tone. "Though it was bound to happen sometime."

"You're right." A strange look came over his face. "Did you ever think . . ." His voice trailed off into silence.

"What?" she asked, her heart beating faster than normal.

He shook his head. "Nothing. It's just a little weird for me to think about both of us getting married. You know, I don't think I've ever even met one of your boyfriends before?"

Meghna almost rolled her eyes. Of course he hadn't. She'd ended

SAY YOU'LL BE MINE 103

things with a number of guys over the years, just so she could seem available around Seth.

"It's going to take me a little while to get used to thinking about you as . . . someone's wife," he said.

She scrunched up her nose. "What does that mean?"

"Only that my little Meg is all grown up," he said with a grin.

Okay, she was fully annoyed now. "I'm not your little anything."

His eyebrows jumped. "Meg, what's going on with you? I'm just joking."

She forced out an exhale. This was Seth. He was just teasing her like always. And it *was* his trip. There was no need to fight over something so trivial. Especially when he didn't mean anything by it. "Yeah, I know."

"So," he said, shrugging off their almost-argument. "Where should we go tonight? I've narrowed it down to three places. . . ."

Meghna listened as he described the options, but found her attention wandering. Sometimes her friendship with Seth felt so one-sided. Like he was constantly asking for her advice. Like she was giving and giving and giving without getting anything in return. But he *was* busier than usual right now. And stressed. Planning a *real* wedding had to be a lot more complicated and time-consuming than her fake one.

Things between the two of them would get back to normal after the wedding was over. They had to.

She refocused on their discussion, helping him pick a place for all of them to go tonight. She pasted a smile on her face when he clinked his drink against hers in celebration.

8

Karthik stood in a corner of the hotel lobby, waiting for Meghna to come down. He'd taken only a few minutes to get ready and hadn't wanted to wait in their room one more second. Not when the one king-sized bed seemed to mock him, looking almost cartoonishly large. They hadn't talked about their sleeping arrangements since they checked in, but he knew he'd be sleeping on the floor. He kept reminding himself of that, but images of the two of them on that bed had flashed repeatedly in his head until he'd had no choice but to physically remove himself from the room.

He flexed his fingers out in front of him. They were wrinkled and dry from his time in the ocean, but he could somehow still feel Meghna's smooth, satiny skin beneath them. After the sunscreen incident, he'd stayed in the water for as long as possible, needing the distance, but he had eventually returned to the group. After all, he was there as Meghna's "fiancé," and he figured that meant he needed to be polite and courteous with everyone there. Even Seth.

It wasn't that he disliked Seth. He didn't really know him. But he couldn't understand what Meghna saw in him. Couldn't understand why she would be friends with someone like that. Seth struck him as someone who was a little too convinced of his own "genius." In the short amount of time they'd spoken, Seth had name-dropped several artists who had recorded the songs he'd written. By Seth's preening, Karthik assumed they were all successful or famous singers, but he hadn't recognized a single name. Still, he'd pretended to be impressed. Seth was one of Meghna's best friends and this was his bachelor party. Karthik wanted everything to go well. Wanted Meghna to be happy.

And she *had* seemed happy with his efforts. She'd thought they'd been successful in convincing everyone that they were really together. But the true test, Meghna had said, would be tonight. She had warned him that after dinner, they would all be going dancing. She'd said the words with an apology in her eyes and promised that they wouldn't have to dance for too long. He'd been confused, but had just nodded politely. She seemed to think he hated dancing, and he wasn't sure what had given her that impression.

"Hey! You ready to go?" Meghna's voice called from behind him.

He turned around. Meghna wore something black and slinky and shiny. Her hair was piled high on the top of her head, and she was walking on the kind of spiky, skinny heels that made him wonder how the people who wore them weren't constantly breaking their ankles. She beamed her signature megawatt smile, sending a jolt through his chest. She was gorgeous.

But of course she was. He had already known that. Had already admitted to himself that he was attracted to her. This wasn't anything new. He could push this temporary, nonsensical feeling to the side. He was here for a purpose. And he wouldn't get distracted. He took a deep breath.

"I'm ready," he said.

"Great. Seth texted to let me know the guys are running late." She rolled her eyes. "Typical. Do you want to wait for them?"

"We can. Really, whatever you want to do."

She raised a shoulder. "We can wait, but I'm worried we're going to miss our reservation."

"Let's go, then," he said. His stomach chose that exact second to let out a growl.

She laughed. "And it seems like you're pretty hungry."

He would normally be embarrassed by something like that, but for some reason, he didn't feel embarrassed at all. "I guess I am," he said lightly.

The restaurant was only a short drive away, and they made it there well within their reservation window. When they sat down at their table, Meghna checked her phone and grimaced.

"They haven't even left the hotel yet," she said. "Should we just go ahead and order a couple things?"

"That's fine."

Their server stopped by a few moments later, and Meghna confidently ordered a slew of appetizers and drinks for the table. Karthik stared at her, slightly dumbfounded.

"How did you know what they'll want?" he asked.

She shrugged. "I've known most of them forever."

"Right," he said. "I forgot you've known Seth since college."

Her eyes darted to his. "How did you know that?"

"Your brother mentioned it."

The corners of her mouth pulled tight. "My brother has a big mouth. But yes, I met Seth in college. And Eric and Mark. They were his roommates."

"How did you guys become friends?"

She waved a hand dismissively. "It's a boring story."

"I'm sure it's not," he said politely, trying not to seem too curious. But he was. He still couldn't figure out how the two could be friends. Why she'd bother putting up with someone like Seth.

"We met in a class," Meghna said. "A writing class. And just kind of clicked."

"Clicked?"

"Yeah." She drummed her fingers on the table. "He was kind of the first person I ever shared my writing with. The first person who ever believed in it. He's a writer too, so he just . . . got it."

Karthik inwardly rolled his eyes, but maintained his usual neutral façade. "Right. He was telling me earlier all about the songs he's written."

Meghna's eyes brightened. "He's a really talented songwriter."

"So it seems," he said evenly.

"I'm sure you've heard something of his."

"I don't think so. I didn't recognize any of the ones he mentioned."

"Really? Not even 'Into the Desert'? That one's really famous. It's on the radio all the time. He used to write these serious, moody ballads in college, but his first song that really sold was kind of this country-pop crossover, so that's what he mostly puts out now."

A spark of irritation flared beneath his breastbone. "I've never heard it."

"Huh. Okay. I'll send it to you later. It's pretty good. And it took him forever to write it. We went back and forth on that one for months."

" 'We'?"

"What?" she asked, her brows knit in confusion.

"You said 'we.' "

"Oh. Well, he wrote it. I just gave him my thoughts. Sent some edits."

"Hmm." Karthik frowned. He still couldn't understand why she would waste her time, let alone her talent, on Seth. Some of his thoughts must have shown on his face, because Meghna responded as if she could hear them.

"I do the same thing," she said, a defensive note in her voice. "I send him my writing too. He gives great feedback."

"That's nice," he said, though he didn't think it was nice at all.

"It *is* nice."

They looked at each other for a moment, the air thick with sudden tension.

"Sorry we're late, Meg," Seth said, finally joining them. The other guys followed him and sat down at the table.

Meg? Did he call her Meg? Karthik had never heard anyone refer to her by that nickname before. Is that what she liked to be called? She'd never told him to call her that. He took a sip of his water, trying to suppress another twinge of annoyance.

"That's fine," Meghna said, turning to Seth with a warm smile. "I ordered all your favorites."

Seth shot her a grin, and that twinge grew into something more. Something hot and dark and bitter. During the rest of the dinner, Karthik tried to ignore it. He enjoyed the food, forced a laugh at all the appropriate times, and even managed to engage Seth's reclusive cousin in a conversation about the high-fantasy, multi-book series he'd been reading on the beach. But that feeling lingered, burning brighter whenever Meghna and Seth shared an inside joke or laughed at Eric and Mark's stories about their wild days in college.

"Enough," Meghna told Eric, shaking her head and holding on to her stomach. "I can't take any more."

"But that wasn't even the best one. Seth, remember that night we—"

"I have no clue where this is going, but I don't think it's anywhere good," Seth cut in with an easy smile. He looked over at Meghna and slung an arm across the back of her chair. "So, best man, where to next?"

That burning sensation in Karthik's stomach flared, but he took a deep breath and pushed it to the side. He listened as Meghna explained their plans for the night, anticipation quickly replacing the irritation that had been growing within him. They were about to go dancing, and he honestly could not wait.

Meghna blinked, the flashing lights in the club making her feel like she'd stepped into the middle of a lightning storm. She wasn't a huge fan of the ambiance, but she and Seth had picked this place for the DJ, and she couldn't deny that the music was good. The electronic sound flowed through her, her shoulders involuntarily shaking to the beat.

Their group split in two, half heading to the bar to get a round of shots and the others heading straight to the dance floor.

She was tempted to get right to the dancing, but waited, waving at Karthik to lower his head so he could hear her over the music.

"Hey, you don't have to dance for long if you don't want to. Or at all. I bet Seth's cousin won't." She pointed toward the bar, where Seth's cousin sat, using his phone as a flashlight to read his book. "You can sit over there and I'll come find you when we're ready to head out."

Karthik straightened, his forehead creasing. "You don't want me to dance with you?"

"No. No, it's not that. I just don't want you to feel like you have to." Meghna tilted her head to the side. "Do you want to? Dance, I mean. With me?"

He nodded once, the movement sharp and pointed.

Surprised delight hummed through her veins.

Well, she definitely wasn't going to turn down a chance to feel his arms around her. Even if he was only being kind. Or doing it for the sake of their arrangement. She encircled his wrist with one hand, pulling him toward an open spot on the floor.

Once there, she turned to face him.

And her jaw dropped.

Karthik always moved in such a . . . controlled manner. Back straight, arms at his sides, chin up. She'd imagined that his dancing would be similar. Stiff. Robotic.

She couldn't have been more wrong.

An ease settled over his shoulders the moment he stepped on the dance floor. He extended a hand to her, and before she could even take in what was happening, he twirled her. The room spun. Then he moved in a series of twists and turns that she normally wouldn't have been able to follow, but his hands on her waist guided her, expertly moving her through them.

She gaped up at him. Who was this man? His eyes shone with amusement, and he quirked a brow at her.

It was like she didn't know him at all.

"You never told me you could dance!"

"You never asked." He tightened the arm behind her back and dipped her. Her vision briefly turned upside down, and then she was back, safely right side up, his arms holding her firmly and securely.

"Besides," he whispered, his breath hot on her ear, "you could have known sooner." He slowed their movements, gradually making their steps smaller. "I asked you to dance at Ankita's party." He took hold of both her hands and placed them behind his neck. "You said no."

And boy, was she regretting that decision.

"Where did you learn all this?" she asked, wonder in her voice.

"I took classes." A litany of questions filled her head, but his hands slid from the sides of her waist to her lower back, and she found herself unable to vocalize them. Unable to vocalize anything at all.

"Speaking of Ankita's party," he said, leaning his head down toward hers. "You never told me what happened after."

"After?" she asked, looking up at him, a bit dazed.

"After they kissed."

The word "kissed" zipped down her body like an electric shock. Her eyes involuntarily went to his lips. His full, soft, utterly kissable lips.

"Kissed?" she asked.

The hands on her lower back tightened slightly, almost bunching the silky material of her dress.

"Yes," he said, his voice lower than it was before. "After Ankita and Samir kissed."

"Oh." Her brother's name was like a splash of cool water. "Things are fine." She smiled wanly. "They're figuring things out."

He nodded, watching her closely. "That's good." They swayed for a moment, looking at each other, not saying anything at all.

"Are you good?" he asked softly. "With Ankita and Samir, I mean."

No. She wasn't good. Her friendship with Ankita felt so fragile. Like the slightest blow would send the whole thing tumbling down. And Samir . . . She hadn't spoken to him since he'd gone back to India.

"I think so," she hedged.

He didn't say anything, but one of his hands slid up her spine, rubbing her back in small circles. She relaxed, leaning farther into his body until she was so close that it just made sense to rest her head against his chest. His hand stopped for a second, then continued moving in slow, lazy patterns. She stayed there for a while, enjoying the sound of his steady heartbeat against her ear.

"Meghna."

"Hmm." She reluctantly lifted her face up to his.

"Are you feeling sleepy?" he asked gently.

"No," she said stubbornly, dropping her head back onto his chest. Truthfully, she was tired, but she didn't want to leave this moment. It was like they were inside a bubble. Inside something magical and wonderful and outside of time. Somehow, she knew it would all burst the second they left.

He let out a loud breath that sounded suspiciously like a laugh. "I think you are," he said. He waited a moment or two, then lifted her chin. "Do you want to go back?"

Meghna barely heard the question. His face was hovering right over hers, his lips so close to her own. If she stood on her tiptoes, she'd be able to kiss him.

"No." The drowsiness from earlier disappeared. "I want to stay." She bit her bottom lip, running her teeth over it before releasing it.

His eyes blazed with something bright and intense, traveling quickly over her face before stopping at her mouth. He stared for a moment and swallowed, his Adam's apple bobbing up and down in the most bewitching way.

And then, to Meghna's extreme disappointment, he looked away, his gaze flickering around until it fixed on a spot above her shoulder. The brightness in his eyes dimmed, and she was tempted to wrap her hands around his jaw. To physically turn him back to her. To force that focused, intense, intoxicating expression back onto his face.

But before she could act on the impulse, his hand curled against the small of her back, drawing her in until her chest was flush against his. His eyes shot toward her lips, then back up. Determination was written across his face. Her heart pounded. He moved a millimeter closer.

"Is this okay?" he asked, so close that their breath intermingled.

"Yes," she said, lifting slightly onto her toes.

Their lips met. But it wasn't the passionate kiss that had been haunting Meghna's thoughts for the last few days. Karthik merely brushed his lips against hers, held for a second, then pulled back. It was over before she could even register that it had begun.

"I'm sorry," he said quietly. "Seth was looking over."

His words were like a punch to the stomach. It wasn't real. Of course it wasn't real.

"Right," she said. "That's what I assumed." She flashed him a perfunctory smile. "Quick thinking."

He watched her, but didn't say anything. His eyes darted to her lips again.

She licked them nervously. "Guess we didn't need to practice after all," she said, trying to lighten the mood. And hide the fact that she had thought, just for a moment, that he had actually wanted to kiss her.

But he didn't laugh at her joke. Instead, he lifted his hand and placed it on the curve of her cheek. Meghna froze.

"I don't know," he said. "Maybe we should rehearse it a few more times." He tucked a loose piece of hair behind her ear.

She swallowed. "I guess practice makes perfect."

He leaned his face back down, erasing the little distance between them. "Exactly." He cradled her jaw with his hand and tilted her head. And then he kissed her. Actually kissed her.

Meghna parted her lips, instinctively tightening her arms around his neck and dragging him closer. He let out a sound of approval, and his lips moved against hers with new intensity. This was more than she had imagined it would be. All-consuming in a way she hadn't expected. There was nothing beyond the feel of his stubble, rough and coarse against her skin. His lips, somehow both firm and soft, pressing against her temple, her cheek, her jaw. The hard plane of his chest crushing against hers. His harsh breaths as they broke for a second, then came back for more. She loved it. She never wanted it to stop.

But it did. It had to. Karthik brushed his lips once, twice, and a third time against hers, then pulled back slowly. Her mind spun and she took a moment to catch her breath. Once she was slightly in control of herself, she glanced at Karthik, trying to gauge what he was thinking, but she couldn't read him. His face was shuttered. It was the way he usually looked, but now it was jarring. So cold. And hard. And distant. She removed her arms from his neck and took a step back.

Whatever fluidity Karthik's body had contained during their dancing had disappeared. His usual posture had returned: his shoulders tight, arms at his sides, chin up. The bubble had popped and there was no getting it back. She felt a sudden sense of loss.

"I'm sorry," Karthik said.

"For what?"

He shook his head. "We shouldn't have done that."

He regretted it? Regretted kissing her? Meghna's cheeks flushed with embarrassment, but she was determined not to let it show.

"Why? It was all just practice, right? It didn't mean anything." She patted his arm. "There's nothing to feel sorry about."

He looked away, not meeting her eyes. "No, I took it too far."

"You didn't," she said firmly.

"We shouldn't do it again."

"Fine." She was exasperated at the turn the conversation had taken. "We won't. Now, are you ready to go back?"

He nodded, and they headed for the door, stopping to say good-bye to Seth and Eric on their way out. The rest of the group had left a while ago, but Seth and Eric had plans to stay out the rest of the night.

"Stay, Meg," Seth told her tipsily. "It's my bachelor party." He gave her sad, puppy-dog eyes, and she couldn't help but laugh.

"It's so late, Seth. The party's over. They're going to close the place soon."

His mouth twisted into a sloppy frown, and she laughed again. She kissed him quickly on the cheek. "Drink lots of water, okay?" She turned to Eric. "Keep an eye on him?"

Eric winked and saluted. "Aye, aye, captain."

She rolled her eyes. Even though Eric was goofy and a bit of a loose cannon, she trusted him and knew he would make sure the two of them got back safely.

She waved a final goodbye and left with Karthik, her good humor quickly fading once she took in the stony, expressionless look on his face. They went back to the hotel in silence, and she was both physi-cally and emotionally exhausted by the time they entered their room. She grabbed her pajamas and changed in the bathroom, growing more and more agitated as she brushed her teeth and got ready for bed. Why had he apologized? He'd regretted the kiss that much? Had found it so distasteful that he never wanted to do it again? How could he be so warm and inviting and intoxicating in one moment and so harsh in the next?

When she came back into the room, she saw that he must have asked for an extra comforter because he had spread one out on the floor, forming a makeshift pallet to sleep on. He must have asked for extra pillows too because he had propped several between him and the wall and was leaning against them. He had a book open on his lap, and his brows were furrowed in concentration. And to top it all off he was wearing thin, wire-framed glasses. Glasses. The sexiest accessory known to humankind. They made him look a thousand times hotter than normal, and Meghna couldn't stand it. Her temper shot through the roof.

"What is your problem?"

9

His *problem?* Karthik set his book down and removed his reading glasses so he could see Meghna more clearly.

"What do you mean?" he asked, puzzled at the anger on her face. Was she still mad about the kiss? If so, she had every right to be. They had a deal and he had pushed and pushed at the bounds of it. Inviting himself on the trip. Suggesting that they "practice." And then kissing her thoroughly, even though she was only kissing him back out of obligation. To keep up appearances. To pretend. He had taken advantage of the situation. Shame and self-loathing washed over him. He deserved every ounce of her anger.

"I'm sorry," he said sincerely. "I'm really sorry. I know I shouldn't have kissed you like that."

But instead of calming Meghna down, his words seemed to only increase her anger. "Are you . . . You think . . . you think that's what this is about?" she sputtered. "That I'm upset because you *kissed me?*"

He had clearly miscalculated. "No?" he asked hesitantly.

She shook her head in frustration. "Forget it." She climbed into bed and switched off the lights, sending the room into darkness. He inwardly sighed and lay down. He tried to fall asleep, but his mind wouldn't let him. It kept replaying their kiss. Over and over again. And it didn't help that Meghna was *right there*. In her pajamas. On that large, inviting king-sized bed. Not that she was in a particularly amorous mood. She was furious at him. He huffed out a breath. He had no one to blame for that but himself.

"Do you want the lights back on?" Meghna asked, her voice traveling through the pitch-black darkness. "I should have asked before. I know you were reading."

"No. I'm ready to go to sleep," he said from his spot on the floor.

They lay there in silence for a few moments.

"I really am sorry about what happened," he said.

Meghna groaned. "Stop apologizing."

"But I took advantage . . ."

"It was a good kiss, Karthik. I liked it."

What? Warring sensations of pride and disbelief swelled in his chest.

"But I agree that it's best we don't do it again," she continued. "We shouldn't confuse this for something it isn't."

She was right, but he still felt a strange shot of disappointment at her words.

"We barely even get along," she added.

"I think we get along fine," he said stiffly.

Meghna scoffed. "Karthik, we're completely different people. Besides, you never want to get married. And I . . . I want what my parents have. A partner and a friend and . . ."

"Love," he said bitterly.

"Yes, love."

"Not every marriage has love."

"I know that," she said. "But mine will."

Silence descended again, and her words echoed in his head. She'd said them with such finality. Such certainty. He turned to his side, wincing at the feeling of the hard floor beneath his rib cage. He'd thought the pillow and comforter would help, but they didn't provide as much cushion as he'd hoped.

"You think your parents still love each other?" he asked.

"Yes, they're . . ." Meghna laughed. "They're almost obnoxious about it. Constantly flirting. Hovering around each other. Samir and I used to be so embarrassed."

"And now?"

"Well, it's still embarrassing sometimes, but it's also . . . sweet. And it's not just them acting lovey-dovey all the time. I've seen them go through hard things. Through loss and grief. And I've watched them support each other. Rely on each other to make it through. What they have is real. A real partnership."

He digested that. He could understand why that sounded appealing, but he couldn't stop himself from comparing it to the example of marriage he had seen in his parents.

"Do you think your parents love—"

"No," Karthik interrupted. He let out a harsh exhale. "I don't think they were ever in love."

He waited a few seconds, then continued. "My dad wasn't exactly . . . present when I was younger. He still isn't, but . . . well, you've met him."

"I have."

"I can't imagine that my mother ever loved him. Or that he ever loved her, but maybe they did. Once. I don't know."

"Were they arranged?"

"They were."

"Is that why you're so against getting an arranged marriage?"

"I'm not opposed to getting an arranged marriage. I'm opposed to getting married. Any kind of married."

"But why? I know your parents' marriage may not have been . . . what you want, exactly, but that doesn't mean you have to write it off completely."

But it did. How could he explain that it wasn't the concept of *mar-*

riage that he necessarily had a problem with? The problem was with him. And his father. He'd neglected Karthik's mother. Neglected both of them. And during the few moments his father had been home, he had been harsh with them. His temper was so fragile and unpredictable. The smallest comment would make him blow up.

Karthik had sworn he would never be like him. And he had worked to undo his damage. He learned how to make his mother laugh. How to lift her moods. How to listen to her when she needed a friend. But his efforts always seemed to be in vain. She'd smile and seem happy around him, but it all disappeared when his father got home. In his presence, she almost appeared smaller. Softer. Quieter. Like she was shrinking herself down. Karthik had promised he would never do that to anyone. Would never belittle or diminish anyone in that way.

But as he'd gotten older, he'd found himself snapping at people. Blowing up at the slightest thing. And every year, the mirror revealed the growing resemblance between him and his father. It was like he couldn't help it. No matter what he did, he was slowly morphing into him. Karthik had been desperate to control his temper, but no matter what he tried, he was unable to stop it. And then, one day, he'd blown up at his mother.

Like always, he felt a bitter sense of shame as he remembered that fight.

She'd mentioned the idea of Karthik having an arranged marriage for the first time, and his anger had exploded. Like some pressure valve within him had finally opened. He'd said things he could never take back. Like, how could she want that for him when it had worked out like *this* for her? How could she stay in such a horrible marriage? How could she think he would ever want a marriage like hers? He had apologized almost immediately. Deeply regretted all of it. And she'd quietly accepted. She didn't bring up the topic of arranged marriage again for years. But the next time she did, he played along, desperate not to wound her again. Even though his feelings about marriage hadn't changed.

After that, everything had shifted for him. He learned how to bury those feelings of rage. Learned to push them down, further and further, until it became second nature to suppress that anger. To suppress all of it. And he'd known that he could never put himself in a position where he could hurt someone like that again. Never put himself in a position where he might repeat his father's behavior.

"I'll never get married," he told Meghna icily. "You should stop trying to change my mind."

"I'm not trying to change it. I'm just trying to better understand . . ." She let out a loud breath. "Never mind. Good night."

"Good night," he replied, relieved that she was finally dropping it. He closed his eyes. He was incredibly tired, but something wouldn't allow him to fall asleep. The minutes passed and he realized he didn't want to end their conversation on this uncomfortable note. The mattress creaked as she shifted on the bed.

"Are you asleep?" he whispered.

"Not yet," she said with a sigh.

"How's your play going?"

She was silent for a moment. "The one I'm writing or the one my students are doing?"

"Both."

"Well, the performance is in a few weeks and we're nowhere near ready. I'm hoping it all comes together, but I'm nervous. I've never done anything like this before. But the kids are working really hard and they seem to be having fun."

"That's good."

"And the one I'm writing . . . well, it's slow going. I've been working on it for years."

"Really?"

"Yeah. Since college."

Ah. "This is the one Seth's been giving feedback on?"

"Yes. He has. Although . . ."

"Although what?"

"Nothing. He just hasn't . . . It's been a busy time for him."

"I'm sure," he said. "What kind of feedback do you guys give each other?"

"Oh, just notes on what we like. What we don't like. Suggestions on what might work better."

"Hmm." He rolled to his back, placing a hand under his head.

"It's really helpful. I've reworked so much and made it all so much better thanks to Seth's comments. Honestly, I don't know if I'd still be writing if it wasn't for Seth. There have been so many times that I've thought about quitting. That I've almost given up. But he's always been there for me. Always encouraged me to keep going."

Karthik felt a pinch beneath his sternum. He ran his fingers over the spot, not sure what had caused it. "I'm sure his songs have benefited from your help too."

"Oh, I don't know. I only make small tweaks. Or suggest changes. Seth's the real creative genius."

Karthik sincerely doubted that, but didn't argue the point. "He made it sound like you'd done more than that. That you'd written the bridge on his last song?" Karthik didn't know music well enough to know what the "bridge" was, but Seth had acted like it had made the song what it was.

"Kind of. I just texted a few lines. But it was only a suggestion. I had no idea he'd actually use it."

"Well, it sounded like he used it. And that it was a success."

"I guess so."

"Do you ever get songwriting credit?"

"No. That wouldn't be . . . I'm not a songwriter."

"But it sounds like you've written parts of songs."

"It's not the same thing. They're Seth's songs."

Karthik was starting to doubt that also, but he didn't want to push it. He had wanted to end the night on a better note, and he wasn't about to start a fight over whether Seth was undervaluing her. Though he so clearly was.

"Well, I'm looking forward to listening to them." His comforter rustled as he shifted again, still unable to find a good position.

"You are?" She sounded surprised, but he couldn't quite tell. Her normally expressive face was shrouded in darkness.

"Yes. Didn't you say you'd send me some?"

"Yeah, I did. I'll send them tomorrow." She was quiet for a moment. "Are you . . . are you okay over there?"

He frowned. "What do you mean?"

"It just sounded like you were moving around a lot." She cleared her throat. "And we never talked about who would sleep on the floor. I mean, it was nice of you to offer, but you don't seem . . . It doesn't sound like it's that comfortable."

He held his breath.

"You could, uh, sleep here. If you wanted. I mean, the bed is huge. We could just, you know, stick to our sides of it." The mattress creaked again, as if she was moving over to give him space.

This was a bad idea. A very bad idea. But he wasn't able to think rationally anymore. He was so tired. And there was a warm, large bed in the room. A warm, large bed with Meghna in it. And if she was fine with him sleeping there, who was he to fight it?

"Okay." He picked up his pillow and fumbled around in the darkness.

"Should I switch on the lights?"

"No, it's fine. I got it," he said as his hand brushed against the edge of the bed, the comforter, and then a soft shape underneath it.

"Sorry," he said automatically, pulling his hand back like he'd been burned.

"For what?" her voice called from the opposite side of the bed.

His gaze swung wildly in the dark. That hadn't been her? He tentatively reached out to touch the soft shape again, only to discover it was a stack of pillows, lying exactly where a body would be.

"Why are the pillows like this?"

"They're a barricade. You know, to split the bed in half."

"They're all the way on my side," he said.

"Well, push them into the middle, then."

He did, pushing them over and climbing into bed. Once he lay down, he began to understand the wisdom of the pillow barrier. Her breaths were so loud, just inches away from him. His mind filled with thoughts of reaching over. Closing the scant distance between them. Kissing her again. Finishing what they'd started.

The pillows were a helpful reminder that nothing would happen. That nothing *could* happen. A physical line in the sand between them.

"Is this better?" she asked, and he almost groaned. This was better. And worse. More comfortable than the ground, but torturous in an entirely different way.

"Yes," he said through his teeth. "Much better." He stretched his body, making sure to stay on his side. The soft mattress enveloped him, and he relaxed, allowing himself to sink farther into it.

She let out a loud yawn, and some of the tension within him eased at the sound. "Good night, Meghna."

"Good night, Karthik."

After a few minutes, sleep finally caught up with him. He shut his eyes and didn't wake up until morning.

The next morning Meghna discovered, to her absolute horror, that she was sleeping on top of something soft. And warm. And cuddly.

She hoped for a second that she was just lying on top of the pillow barricade, but suddenly the soft, warm, cuddly *thing* beneath her moved, and she realized it couldn't have been the pillows. It was Karthik.

She opened her eyes slowly and tilted her head up, relieved to see that his eyes were still shut. His breathing was slow and even. She did a mental assessment of the situation, trying to determine the best way to get out of bed without waking him up and alerting him to their accidental cuddling.

Her upper body lay across his torso, and he had one arm wrapped around her, his hand resting against her lower back. Their legs were tangled together, with his thigh firmly between her legs. She shifted backward slightly, but his body followed with her, his arm tightening and his thigh somehow pressing even closer. She held back an involuntary moan.

She had to get out of here. Now. She turned her head to the side, scowling when she saw the stack of pillows behind her. Traitors. They had absolutely let her down. Her brain took that moment to inform her that if the pillows were behind her that meant *she* had been the one to roll over and invade Karthik's side of the bed, but she refused to accept that. It was too early for logic.

She tried to scoot backward again, but her back pressed up against the pillows, giving her nowhere to go. Another betrayal!

She made a noise of frustration, and Karthik's eyes shot open. *Great.* She steeled herself for what was to come.

"Hey," he said, his voice gravelly and rough.

"Uh, hi."

He blinked, took stock of their position, then scrambled out from under her. "I'm so sorry."

She squeezed her eyes shut, then opened them. "No, I'm sorry. I'm the one who, uh, rolled over in the night. It was my fault."

He cleared his throat, getting out of bed. "It's fine." He walked over to his suitcase, then gestured toward the bathroom without looking in her direction. "I'm just going to take a shower. I'll, uh, be right back."

When the bathroom door closed, Meghna jumped out of bed, rushing to change out of her pajamas. She didn't want to look all disheveled when he emerged from the shower looking fresh and put together and . . . She started to sweat. Why did he have to be so good-looking? She was shucking off her pajama shorts and searching for her jeans when the bathroom door opened.

"I just wanted to say—" Karthik stopped, his eyes growing wide, and Meghna shrieked.

"Turn around!"

He slapped a hand over his eyes. "Why are you in your underwear?"

"I'm changing! Why weren't you in the shower?"

"I was just going to say, umm, that it wasn't your fault. It was nice of you to share the bed. So, thank you. And uh, it's fine that you . . . that we . . ."

"Oh my God," she groaned.

"Okay. I'm going back in." He shut the door behind him.

She sat back down on the bed, punching the pillows. It was all their fault.

Ten minutes later, Karthik opened the bathroom door, clearing his throat loudly before stepping outside. Meghna rolled her eyes.

"I'm decent," she called, zipping her suitcase closed.

He finished packing, and they left the room with their luggage in tow. They met up with Seth and the rest of the guys for a quick breakfast, but avoided making eye contact with each other. Thankfully, no one else seemed to sense anything was off. Seth monopolized her time with questions about a song he was working on, and Meghna appreciated the distraction. This was probably the last time she'd see him before the wedding. Her chest constricted but she pushed the thought to the side, trying to soak up every minute of his attention. The way he listened to her. Responded to her feedback. Asked for her opinion like he really cared what she thought.

He tried out a new line and it was so bad it made her laugh. She shook her head, grinning widely, and caught Karthik looking at her, his eyes dark and focused. Her mouth went dry. She couldn't help but remember the way he'd looked first thing in the morning. That moment his eyes had snapped open. The way his arm had tightened around her before he'd jumped away like she was on fire.

She sipped her orange juice. It tasted acidic and bitter as it traveled down her throat. He probably regretted everything about this morning. The same way he had regretted their kiss.

She'd been flustered. Mortified. But she didn't regret it. In another set of circumstances, in some imaginary fantasy where they wanted the same things, she would have loved to have woken up to Karthik's arms around her. To his scratchy stubble against her cheek. To a good-morning kiss. Maybe more.

The waiter came by with everyone's checks, dragging her back to reality. She reached for her purse but caught Karthik out of the corner of her eye, dropping a credit card to cover his bill and hers. She gave him a quizzical look, and he subtly nodded toward Seth.

She flushed. Of course. He was just keeping up appearances. Behaving like her fiancé. She took a deep breath and straightened in her seat. It didn't matter that she found him wildly attractive. Didn't matter that she had wanted the kiss to be real. They had an agreement, and she couldn't lose sight of that. If Karthik could push past the lingering embarrassment and stick to the plan, so could she.

They said their goodbyes to everyone, Seth swept her up in one last hug, and then she and Karthik shared a cab to the airport.

"So . . ." he started, once the two of them were alone in the car.

"So," she said, doing her best to sound calm. "We're going to pretend like none of that happened."

He gave her a sidelong glance. "If that's what you want."

"It is."

He nodded. "Okay, then."

They were silent for the rest of the drive. And when they parted ways for their separate flights, Meghna stuck out her hand.

Karthik reached out to shake it, a bemused expression on his face.

"See you at the wedding," she said firmly.

"Right. I guess that's the next time we'll see each other."

"It is."

He rocked back on his heels. "Well, have a safe flight."

"You too." She waved a final goodbye, then turned and headed for her gate. The back of her neck warmed, and she was tempted to take one last look at him over her shoulder. To see if he was watching her. To try to catch some unguarded, genuine expression on his face.

But she resisted, keeping her eyes firmly locked ahead. Looking back was pointless. There was nothing between the two of them. Nothing at all.

10

Meghna was sure that every profession had its challenges, but at the moment she couldn't imagine anything harder than teaching middle schoolers to sing in a Cockney accent. Especially when some of her students had a deep Texan drawl. A pang of affection shot through her as seventh grader Blake M. screwed up his face in concentration as he sang "Wouldn't It Be Loverly" with the rest of the class. They were all trying so hard.

She sat back in her chair. Even if they didn't nail the accent, the performance would turn out okay. They knew their lines. They knew the songs. The costumes were almost done. And their Eliza Doolittle happened to be an eighth-grade prodigy who would be attending a special performing arts high school next year. Things would be fine. Meghna closed her eyes and listened to the girl as she sang about how "loverly" it would be to have someone's head resting on her knee. Someone who was warm and tender. And took good care of her.

Meghna thought back to the conversation she'd had with Karthik two weeks ago in Miami. Something about being in the dark and not being able to see his face had made her more vulnerable than she normally would have been. She was a little embarrassed by how much she had shared, and even more embarrassed by what had happened afterward. But she wasn't ashamed of what she wanted. Wasn't ashamed of wanting to get married. Of wanting a partner. She just hadn't planned on laying it all out for him like that.

But maybe it had been a good thing. It had reminded her that they wanted different things. That they would never be compatible. That this was just a pretend engagement, and it couldn't be anything more.

Her phone pinged with an incoming text message.

Seth: Hey! Have you had a chance to review that song I sent you? The one for the reception?

Meghna grimaced. She'd looked at the lyrics. She wasn't sure if she was unable to be objective about his love song for another woman or if the song was really as horrible as she thought it was. The lyrics struck her as . . . trite, filled with clichés and over-the-top language about how Seth would love Julie until the stars fell from the sky. *Blech*. Still, she needed to send him something in response.

Meghna: Sorry, haven't gotten to it yet. Will try to respond by the end of the week.

She put her phone away and wrapped up rehearsal, reminding the students that their first and only performance was only a week away. She waited as the parents picked them up and chatted with the ones she knew. They were all excited about the performance, and their comments helped dampen some of the nerves she felt about it being so soon.

After her last student left, she got in her car and made the short drive over to her parents' house. She normally had dinner with her parents once a week, but she hadn't been by in a while. She had told them she was busy with rehearsals and her recent travels, but really, she was avoiding them because she felt guilty about lying to them.

She had told herself that the fake engagement was harmless. That it wouldn't go too far. But she worried that her parents were becoming a bit too invested in her fake relationship. Her mother kept sending her names of wedding planners and emailing different websites for possible venues. Her father was less forceful, but had mentioned on more than one occasion that he found it odd that he hadn't met Karthik's dad yet. He felt it was important for the families to get along, and he wanted to know when they could hold a formal engagement party.

Meghna pulled up to the driveway and went to the back door, stepping into the warmth of the kitchen. Her father stood at the stovetop, stirring a pot of dal. The fragrant scent washed over her. Cumin and ghee and home.

"Meghna," her father exclaimed. "We weren't expecting you tonight. What a surprise!" He turned down the flame and swept her up in a hug.

"A good surprise, I hope."

"Always." A large smile grew on his face. "Radhika, guess who's here?"

"Well, it's about time," her mother said, her voice carrying from the other room before she even entered the kitchen. "You owe me twenty dollars, Akshay."

Meghna's gaze snapped back to her father. "You made bets on me!"

He winked. "I thought you'd be busy until the play was over, but your mother guessed you'd stop by this week."

"And as usual, I was right," her mother said, walking into the room with a triumphant look on her face. She hugged Meghna, then stepped back. "You shouldn't stay away this long, beta. Your father misses you too much."

Her father let out a booming laugh. "We both missed you."

"Of course," her mother said, turning to face him. "Now, pay up, jaan."

grace ̶ ̶eve ̶ ̶out ̶ ̶way ̶ ̶wi ̶ ̶ou ̶ smarted him.

Meghna smiled as they bickered, but something heavy ̶d hard grew in her chest. Some of that must have shown through h ̶ cheery expression because her father frowned in her direction.

"Is everything okay?" he asked, perceptive as always. "What's going on?"

"Nothing," she said lightly. She reached up into the cabinet and pulled out three bowls for their dal chawal.

Her mother gave her an assessing look. "It's not nothing." She took the bowls from Meghna's hands and started filling them up with rice. "That's the same face you made when you changed your major and didn't tell us."

Meghna went still. She hadn't needed that reminder. Hadn't needed to remember how difficult it had been to explain that she had applied and been accepted to her dream university as an education major and not as an engineering major like they had discussed. Like Samir had been, making her parents proud beyond belief. But her mother continued, blithely unaware that her words had poked at something raw and sensitive.

"Is there anything you need to let us know?" her mother asked.

Meghna's heart pounded. There was, but she couldn't tell them like this. Couldn't tell them that the engagement they were so excited about was a fraud. That she had tricked them. Lied to them. Just like she had before. Just like Ankita and Samir had done to her. She swallowed.

They would be so disappointed. She had finally done something that seemed to make them happy. If they knew the truth, they'd know that she had failed to live up to their expectations yet again.

He mock-grumbled as he fished out his wallet, but her father was clearly amused at the glee on his wife's face. Her mother was the most competitive person she knew, and Meghna's father was her perfect match. He was always willing to put up a good fight, but he lost with

"Jaan," her father said gently. "I'm sure it's nothing like that. Meghna, you're probably just nervous about the play next week, right?"

She nodded, thankful for the out her father had so conveniently provided. "Yes, that's it. I can't believe it's so soon."

Her father poured a generous amount of hot dal over each bowl of rice, and they carried their food to the kitchen table. After they sat down and began eating, Meghna distracted her parents with story after story from this week's rehearsals. They laughed with her about the various antics her students had gotten up to and didn't ask any further questions about her earlier discomfort. Meghna was thankful for the reprieve, but her guilt lingered, bubbling beneath the surface.

Still, it wasn't like her fake engagement would hurt them. Or anyone. It wasn't anything like what Ankita and Samir had done. In fact, telling her parents the truth would likely hurt them more. And that pain was unnecessary. The engagement would come to an end after the wedding, and everything would go back to the way it had been before.

She ate a forkful of the warm, comforting meal in front of her, slightly reassured. There was no need to tell her parents about any of it. She just had to keep putting off their wedding planning efforts until she and Karthik were ready to call things off. That wouldn't be too difficult. She ate another forkful and smiled. She was feeling better and better with each passing minute.

Karthik had never felt this confident in his entire life. He'd studied the numbers backward and forward. He could recite facts about any project the HVAC team had worked on in the last five years. And it didn't hurt that Marianne had privately shared the recommendation she had written for him, and it had been full of glowing praise.

Today's interview couldn't have come at a better time. He'd been out of sorts ever since that trip to Miami. He couldn't get Meghna out of his head. The way she'd felt that morning, her body splayed on top of his. The taste of her lips. That wide smile that always sent an electric shock coursing through his body.

Preparing for the interview had been a welcome distraction. He just needed to focus. Get the job, go to the wedding, and then it would all be over. No more obligation to his mother. No more strange pull toward Meghna. Everything in his life would return to normal.

"Hey, can I talk to you for a sec?" Paul asked, his head peeking around the corner.

"Sure, come in." Paul had just been in his office to drop off lunch, and Karthik was confused that the intern would be back again so soon. He did a quick sweep of the room. "Did you forget something in here?"

"No," Paul said, sitting in his usual chair across from Karthik's desk. "I actually had to ask you something."

"Okay. Sure. What's going on?"

Paul looked at him for a few seconds and then heaved a big sigh. "You wouldn't happen to be related to Dr. Murthy, would you?" He asked the question so quickly that the words blended together. "I know there's probably a ton of Dr. Murthys out there," he continued. "But he's a professor at NYCU medical school? And you know that's where I'm an undergrad and . . ."

Of course. Paul was probably applying to medical school, and he wanted to be introduced to Karthik's esteemed and highly regarded father. Karthik was about to tell Paul that he and his father weren't close and that his dad was unlikely to do him any favors, but Paul kept going.

"I wouldn't just assume you were related to him because you have the same name, you know? But my girlfriend's premed and she was telling me about him and showed me his faculty page and it's just . . . You look a lot like him, so I thought I'd ask."

So, it was the *girlfriend* who wanted the introduction. Karthik shook his head. If anything, that would only make his dad less inclined to help.

"Yes, we're related," he said. "He's my father."

Paul paled. "Shit. Oh, okay. So, umm . . . Are you doing okay? With everything?"

Karthik's eyebrows knit together. "With what?"

Paul's eyes went wide. "There was an article about your dad in our campus newspaper and I just thought . . . You haven't seen it?"

Karthik shook his head. His father's research often resulted in articles and press releases. Karthik never looked at any of them.

"Well, uh, my girlfriend has this mentor and they're really close. She's a student at the med school. And she had been telling us about this professor." Paul shifted in his chair. "Maybe it's easier if you read the article."

Karthik pulled up a search engine on his computer, but waved at Paul to continue.

"Just tell me."

"He's being sued."

What? "Who's suing him?"

"A group of students. Including my girlfriend's mentor. The, um . . . article explains it, but they're suing him for discrimination and some other things."

Karthik found the article and couldn't believe the headline: AWARD-WINNING NYCU MEDICAL PROFESSOR ACCUSED OF DISCRIMINATION, HARASSMENT, AND UNPROFESSIONAL CONDUCT. He scanned the first paragraph, read it again, then leaned back in his chair.

Nine students, all women, had filed internal complaints about his father with the university. After a yearlong investigation, the university had sided with his father, and now the students were suing the school for failing to properly investigate and respond to their complaints.

Karthik continued skimming the article. There were allegations of sexist behavior, derogatory comments about women, preferential treatment for male students, and borderline sexual harassment. Karthik's stomach turned as he read one student's complaint that his ale stu...nts.

Karthik clos...is ey... fa... ad... his ...er... badly. Karthik had even su...cted ...hes...is ...mi...ve been cheating on her, but he'd never imagine anythi... like th...

"I'm sorry, man. I had no idea he was your dad. My girlfriend had actually mentioned him a bunch before. Her mentor was always complaining about him. She said it was kind of an open secret among the med students and they all talked about it, but I didn't think anything of it until I saw his picture and . . ."

Paul's voice faded to a dull buzz as Karthik's thoughts turned inward. He didn't feel an ounce of sympathy for his father. Only a perverse sort of joy that his father's true nature had been exposed. That his precious career and reputation would be forever marred by his actions. But what was his mother going to do?

A wave of nausea rolled through Karthik's body. She would be devastated. The community was small, and word would get around soon. They would ostracize his father and whisper about him behind his back. His father deserved their scorn, but the gossip would extend to his mother too. It was utterly unfair. Over the years, she'd endured his father's neglect, his harsh words and taunts, and somehow, she had borne it all with dignity, even managing to spare Karthik from as much of it as possible. And now she would be subjected to ridicule. Karthik thought he might actually be sick.

"Hey. Karthik. Are you okay?" Karthik opened his eyes. Paul's face was lined with worry. "I'm sorry. Maybe I shouldn't have brought it up. I just thought that it was too much of a coincidence and . . . Dude, you do not look good. Can I get you some water?"

father had rubbed her knee during office hours and commented on the length of her dress. Others complained that his father made frequent comments in class that women made excellent physicians . . . until they got married or had children. Numerous women said they had applied for research positions with his lab, but his father hired only m ·der

h·   ed h   es. His ·ther h l always treated · ; moth
    l ι   ιspeς   at tin ː that h· father   ght ha·
            ·ir   ·d ·   ng¹   ·is.

Karthik swallowed. "No, I'm fine. I'm okay." He closed out of the article on his computer. The time in the corner of his screen spiked his body with adrenaline. He had only five minutes until his interview.

He stood up quickly, but swayed for a second, the ground suddenly seeming uneven.

"Hold on," Paul said, jumping up and grabbing his arm. "You should sit back down. I'll run and get some water. . . ."

"No," Karthik said. "I have to go. I'm late for something. Let me just . . ." Karthik tasted bile in his mouth and made a beeline to the restroom. He reached it just in time and promptly threw up. Afterward, he rinsed his mouth out with water, staring at his sweaty complexion in the mirror. He'd deal with all of this later. He grabbed a paper towel and dabbed at his face. Right now, he had an interview. He was probably only a few minutes late. He could still do this.

He walked deliberately out of the restroom to the elevator, breathing calmly and reciting in his head all the facts and figures he had studied so carefully. Somehow, he managed to get off on the right floor and entered the conference room, where the panel of interviewers was already seated.

"I'm sorry," Karthik said, taking the open seat in front of the panel. "I know I'm running a little behind. I promise that's not how I usually operate."

Several of the interviewers smiled, and Jim Gray, the COO and Marianne's former boss, chuckled. "We know that about you," he said. "Marianne once said you were the most punctual person at the company."

"Oh, I don't know about that," Karthik said.

"Well, I trust her judgment. That's why you're sitting in front of us today."

"And I'm glad to be here." The air was so stuffy. And humid. They needed to fix the AC. Or open a window.

"We've all reviewed your résumé," Jim said. "And we know all the great work you've done here, but tell me this. Why would a born-and-raised New Yorker go out of the city for college?" Jim said the words with a smile and was clearly joking. Karthik's pulse returned to normal. He was about to offer a lighthearted comment in return when Jim continued.

"Don't worry. I know how it is," he said in a teasing voice. "My daughter's about to go to college and all she talks about is getting away from home. Her mother and I keep hoping she'll change her mind and follow in our footsteps instead. We both went to NYCU. But I doubt we'll be able to convince her. She has her heart set on the West Coast . . ."

Karthik's stomach dropped. Just hearing the name of his father's university brought up everything he had been working so hard to put out of his mind. His nausea returned. His hands were somehow both dry and clammy. But none of the panelists seemed to notice his discomfort.

"Anyway," Jim said. "We've all read Marianne's recommendation, we think your work is phenomenal, and we really just wanted to meet and hear from you today. So, what makes you interested in this position?"

"I . . . I was very fortunate to work under Marianne. I learned a lot from her." Karthik swallowed. "I've led a number of teams during my time here and I'm ready to assume greater responsibility. I'm confident I can do the job."

"That's great." Jim smiled warmly. "Truthfully, we all agree. We think you're more than qualified for the position. But why do you *want* the job?"

Why did he want the job? Hadn't Meghna asked him a similar question once? He closed his eyes and tried to remember what he'd said. Something about how this promotion was what he had been working for. How it was the next logical step for him. How it would advance his career dramatically. Those answers seemed woefully inadequate now. A fresh wave of nausea rolled through him.

"I don't know," Karthik said, his voice breaking. "I really don't know."

The other interviewers' faces were a blur, but Jim's was crystal clear. His eyebrows drawn together, mouth parted in shock.

"What do you mean you don't know?" Jim asked.

Karthik shook his head. "I shouldn't be here. I shouldn't. I'm not even er~~~red."

Engaged?"

"You met her. At Marianne's party? Except she's not really my fiancée."

Jim's eyes went round. "What does that have to do with anything?"

"That's the only reason Marianne recommended me for the job. You shouldn't be interviewing me. I'm a fraud." Just like his father. Karthik took a deep, ragged breath. Then another. Something heavy pressed on his chest, preventing him from getting enough oxygen to his lungs.

"Karthik, are you . . . are you okay? If you're not feeling well, we can reschedule. Or we can take a short break and reconvene . . ."

Karthik stood up. "I'm sorry. Please excuse me." He walked out of the conference room, out of the elevator, out of the building, and into a cab. Before he fully knew what he was doing, he was on his way to LaGuardia Airport.

A swarm of butterflies rushed through Meghna's stomach. Tonight was her students' first (and only) performance, and she was so proud of how hard they had worked to get here. Sure, the costumes were repurposed from last year's show, and the set did little to disguise the fact that they were performing in the cafeteria, but she was excited. And the students were too. They were taking selfies in their costumes, wishing each other good luck, and buzzing around with that pre-show energy that Meghna loved so much. She hadn't been backstage before a performance since she was in college, and she hadn't realized how much she'd missed it.

"Everyone, we have thirty minutes," she called out. "Time to circle up."

The students huddled together, forming a ring around her. She walked them through the warm-up exercises they started every rehearsal with: tongue twisters and silly faces and jumping up and down to shake out all the nerves. She gave a modified version of her high school theater teacher's standard pep talk, then sent them on their way, reminding them to use the restroom now before going to their places.

They scrambled away, and she took a deep breath, peeking out from behind the curtain to look at the audience. It was still early, but some parents and teachers were already out in the crowd. Her parents had promised to come too, but they'd probably get there right before showtime. They always seemed to run about fifteen minutes behind everyone else. Her phone beeped, and she pulled it out, expecting to see an ETA from them. Instead, it was a text from Karthik.

Karthik: Hey, can you come out to the parking lot?

That was strange. What parking lot was he talking about? Did he think she was in New York?

Meghna: ?? Did you mean to send this to me?
Karthik: I'm here. In the middle school parking lot.

He was here? At *her* school?

She checked in with a parent volunteer, who promised to keep an eye on things, then rushed outside. It was getting dark. A silhouette of a man standing a short distance away caught her eye. She walked toward him.

"Karthik, what are you doing here? I can't believe . . ." Her voice trailed off when she saw a bouquet of flowers in his hand. "Are those for me?"

He nodded. "Yes. Congratulations on your performance."

Something gooey and hot melted inside her. "Thanks. That's so sweet of you." She took the bouquet from his hands and smelled it. The gesture was kind, but she was still confused about why he was here. They hadn't talked since they parted ways at the airport. Since all that awkwardness between them.

"What are you doing in Dallas?"

He looked away, his eyes not meeting hers.

She searched his face, but the parking lot was poorly lit. She couldn't make out much through the shadows. "Is everything okay?"

"No," he said, but he choked on the word. Almost as if . . . as if he had held back a sob.

Concern grew within her. "Karthik, what's going on?"

He shook his head and wiped a hand over his face, but the noises he made were unmistakable. He was crying.

Her chest cracked open. "Karthik," she said softly, lifting her arms and wrapping them around him. He didn't move for several seconds, his body stiff. Frozen. But then his arms came around her, gently drawing her closer. The sobs wracked his body. His chest heaved against hers. She tightened her arms around him, silently telling him that it was okay. That she was here. They stood there for several moments, arms entwined around each other, until his cries softened and his breathing became more even.

He dropped his chin onto the top of her head and inhaled deeply. "Thank you," he said, his voice scratchy and raw.

He stepped back, and she immediately dropped her arms.

"It's fine," she said, watching him closely. His retreat placed his face under one of the few light poles, and the traces of tears left on his cheek glistened. She took a small step toward him, lifting her hand to his jaw, wiping a tear away with her thumb.

"Do you want to talk about it?" she asked softly.

A breeze swept through the parking lot, and it ran through his hair, scattering it in every direction. She watched it in fascination, absentmindedly moving her thumb back and forth across his cheek. He cleared his throat, and she withdrew her hand, placing it back at her side.

His face had returned to its usual stoic and cold expression, though there might have been a new tenderness and vulnerability in his eyes. "No," he said, a bit hoarsely. "I don't want to talk about it."

She could understand that. She didn't know what had happened, but she couldn't imagine that Karthik cried easily. And certainly not in front of people. She'd let it go for now, give him some space, and check back in with him later.

"Okay," she said, giving him a small smile. "Do you want to come inside? I can't promise the show will be amazing, but you'll get to watch middle schoolers sing in horrible Cockney accents about the rain in Spain."

He let out a short, dry laugh. It sounded forced to her ears, but she was still relieved to hear it.

"Absolutely," he said.

She wrapped a hand around his elbow and led him to the cafeteria. She was about to take him to a seat in the audience, but stopped, suddenly remembering.

"My parents are coming tonight," she told Karthik. "Is that okay?"

She scanned his face. Besides a bit of redness near his eyes, he didn't look like he had been crying. Most people would probably chalk it up to allergies. Still, she didn't want him to be uncomfortable. He hadn't responded to her question yet, but the uncertainty on his face made it clear that he hadn't expected her parents would be there.

"You could come hang out with me backstage," Meghna offered before he could say anything. "It'll be chaotic and you won't be able to see the performance as well as you would from the audience, but . . ."

"That sounds perfect," he said.

She took him to their makeshift "backstage" area and found a chair for him. She'd be running around for most of the show, but he'd be able to watch some of it from this spot in the wings.

"Oi. Ms. Raman, is this yer boyfriend?"

Meghna turned, following the sound of sixth grader Aidan's voice. A few students had gathered around them and were watching Karthik curiously.

"Great job aying in haracter, Aidan," Meghna replied. " nd yes he's   oyfr   "

my b riend.

"Fiancé," Karthik interjected.

"Right. That's what I meant. He's my fiancé."

Her students grinned at them, their teeth bright and white against their faces, which were streaked in stage makeup that resembled soot.

She clapped her hands. "Okay, guys. That's enough gawking. Karthik's going to be sitting here all night, but don't bother him until *after* the show's over."

He raised an eyebrow at that, and she returned the gesture with a wink. Not waiting for his reaction, she took off, corralling her straggling students into their starting places. She managed to get everyone where they needed to be in record time and did a final check with the parent volunteers who were standing by to assist with costume changes and props. Right as she finished, the lights in the cafeteria dimmed, and the beginnings of the overture played. She took a deep breath and crossed her fingers.

Showtime.

eghna had never experienced this exact combination of exhilaration and exhaustion. She simultaneously felt like she could fly and like she might pass out at any moment. But the night had been a success. Numerous parents had congratulated her, and the principal had pulled her aside, saying she wanted to ask the school board for funds to put on another performance next semester. Meghna wasn't ready to think about all the work that would take, but she was excited that the school was finally seeing the value of having a theater program.

The kids were all accounted for and were beginning to leave, so Meghna was finally free to go out and greet her parents. She walked into the audience alone, having previously decided it was best to leave Karthik backstage. He looked more like himself now, but she didn't want her parents asking questions about why he was here. Not that she really knew what he was doing here, either. Beyond a quick "congratulations," Karthik hadn't said anything to her since the performance began. She hoped she'd get some answers from him later tonight.

"Great job, Meghna," her father said, wrapping her up in a hug.

"Thanks, Dad. And thanks for coming." Part of her hadn't been sure if her parents would show up at all. They said they were proud of her, but she couldn't help but compare the way they talked about her job to the way they talked about Samir's career. There was a certain amount of respect in their voices when they talked about Samir that just wasn't present when they talked about her. They had initially been disappointed when she'd decided to become a teacher, but her father had gotten on board fairly quickly. It was her mother who still couldn't understand why she would choose to be anything other than an engineer. But she'd never have her mother's approval. She had learned to accept that a long time ago.

As predicted, her mother offered some half-hearted words of praise and a reminder that Meghna still needed to respond to her email about venue options for the wedding. After promising to do so and to stop by the house for dinner next week, her parents said their goodbyes and Meghna went backstage one last time to collect Karthik. He was still sitting on the same stool where she'd left him, looking out at the stage with an unfocused expression.

"Hey, you ready to go?"

Karthik's attention snapped to her, and he shook himself out of whatever trance he'd been in. "That was incredible."

"Thanks."

"No, really, Meghna. That was . . . I've never seen anything like that before."

Meghna let out a self-deprecating laugh, though inside her something soft and tender bloomed. A little pea shoot pushing its way through the dirt, seeking out the sunlight.

"That's really nice," she said. "But you don't have to exaggerate. I mean, they did a great job, but I'm just glad they got through it."

Karthik frowned. "I'm not exaggerating. I mean it. I had no idea that musicals could be like this."

"Like what?"

He was silent for a few seconds, then shook his head. "I don't know."

Meghna suddenly remembered something Karthik had told her a while ago.

"When you said you'd never seen a show before, I thought you meant you'd never seen a *real* show. Like a professional one. I didn't think . . ."

"No. I've never been to any kind of performance. Except for to-night."

She smiled softly. "Well, I'm glad you liked it."

He looked off at the stage again and then back at her. "How are you so . . ." He waved his hand in her direction. "So unaffected."

Meghna smothered a laugh. Karthik was accusing *her* of being unaffected? Oh, the irony. But she just pursed her lips and asked, in as neutral a tone as she could manage, "Unaffected?"

"Wasn't that just as . . . moving for you? Sweeping and . . . Never mind." He sighed. "I've had a strange day."

Meghna's curiosity was at an all-time high. She desperately wanted to know what had happened, but this wasn't the time to delve into it.

"No, I know what you mean. Musicals can be moving and sweep-ing and . . . all-encompassing. It's just, well, we've been working on this one for a long time. It's different when you experience it brand-new."

"Right. Of course." He stood up, took a step toward her, then stopped. He looked a little lost, as if he didn't know what he should do next. She felt a tug on her heartstrings.

"Do you want to go get dinner?" she asked.

Karthik agreed, following her out to her car, the only one left in the parking lot.

She drove him to one of her favorite spots. It was small and unas-suming, located in a somewhat deserted strip mall, but the family who ran it made the best food and it was always quiet. She figured it would provide enough privacy for whatever conversation they so obviously needed to have.

Once inside, Meghna was relieved to see there was only one other couple there tonight. She waved at Annie, the owner's high school daughter and one of her former students, who was studying at one of the booths in the back. Meghna pointed to indicate that she and Karthik would sit at a table on the other side of the room, and Annie came by a few minutes later to take their order. Karthik deferred to Meghna, so she asked for her usual: fresh spring rolls, green curry, and a pad kee mao to share. Annie slipped away to the kitchen, leaving Meghna and Karthik alone.

Meghna waited a few seconds, then looked at Karthik expectantly. Surely now he would explain what he was doing here.

But he didn't. He took a sip of his water. He looked around the room. And then he pulled the menu back out and began reading it, even though they'd already ordered. Questions bubbled up inside Meghna, but she pushed them down. He was upset and she didn't know why, but earlier it had seemed like he needed space. She could resist invading his privacy, but she needed to talk about *something*. She could only take the silence for so long. She wracked her brain for something neutral to talk about and finally landed on a topic.

"When did you take dance lessons?" she asked.

"Hmm," Karthik responded distractedly, lifting his eyes from the menu.

"In Miami, you said you took dance lessons."

"Oh." He folded the menu and placed it back on the table. "A few years ago. Someone gifted my parents with ballroom dancing classes and, well, they were about to expire, so I went with my mom." He shrugged as if it wasn't a big deal. As if it wasn't the most endearing thing Meghna had ever heard.

"That was nice of you."

"Not really. I just didn't want her to have to go alone." His expression softened for a moment, and he almost looked . . . concerned.

"Karthik," Meghna said gently. "What happened?"

He broke eye contact, looking down at his plate for a moment. "I had my interview today. For the promotion."

Oh. For some reason, that wasn't what Meghna had been expecting.

"I take it that it didn't go well?"

He let out a humorless laugh. "No, it didn't go well." He picked up his fork and put it back down, straightening it so that it was perfectly aligned. He stared at it for a moment, then lifted his head, meeting her eyes directly.

"My dad's an ass," he said.

A surprised laugh almost escaped Meghna's mouth, but she held it in.

"I won't argue with you there," she said.

A ghost of a smile touched his lips, but quickly disappeared. "I thought he was cheating on my mom. Honestly, I've thought that for a long time."

Without thinking, Meghna lifted her hand and placed it over his. His hand immediately became tense. *Right.* He wasn't the touchy-feely type. Just as she was about to take her hand back, he flipped his over so that his palm was touching hers. Then he wrapped his fingers around the back of her hand, holding her in place.

The small touch made her heart soar, but she ignored it, returning her focus to their conversation. "Were you right?" she asked. "About him cheating?"

"Yes." He shook his head. "No. I don't know."

She squeezed his hand lightly and almost melted when he squeezed hers back.

"I don't know how bad it got, or if he did anything that could be considered cheating, but he . . . A group of students sued him. For a lot of things. But mostly for the way he treated women. Unfair treatment and discrimination, but it sounded like there was also harassment and . . ." He stopped talking.

"You don't have to go into the details if you don't want to," she said.

He shot her a look of gratitude. "Thanks. But honestly, that's all I know. That's all the article said."

He went quiet as Annie came back, dropping off the food. Meghna thanked her and waited until she was out of earshot before asking, "That's how you found out? An article?"

"Yes. It was only the campus newspaper, but I'm sure word will spread fast."

Sympathy welled up inside her. She couldn't imagine how awful she would feel if she was in his position.

"I guess there's a chance it's not true," he continued. "But I believe it. All of it."

"Is your father denying it?"

"Maybe. Probably. I haven't talked to him about it yet. And I don't want to talk to him. Really, I'm only worried about my mother. I don't know how she'll take this. I don't even know if she knows. I should have made sure she was okay first, but I wasn't thinking. I just came here."

To Dallas. To see me. Whatever had been growing, that tiny little pea shoot, that promise of *something*, shot up three inches.

They moved on to lighter topics—his thoughts on the lead performer in the musical and questions about how she'd rehearsed with the kids to get them ready—but they mostly ate in silence. It was surprisingly comfortable. Natural.

"Where are you staying tonight?" Meghna asked as she finished off the last spring roll.

Karthik's face reverted to that vulnerable, slightly lost expression. "I don't know."

Annie came by a few minutes later, clearing the plates and dropping off the bill. Meghna grabbed it and paid before Karthik could say anything. He looked adorably grumpy and put out about it, and in that moment Meghna made up her mind.

"Come on," she said, getting up and gesturing for him to follow.

"Where are we going?"

"Back to my place."

As soon as Karthik entered Meghna's apartment, the strangest tune entered his head. It wasn't a song he knew well. In fact, he was pretty sure he had heard it for the first time that night, but he couldn't remember any of the words.

"Ice cream or wine?" Meghna asked over her shoulder as she walked into the kitchen.

"Umm, ice cream's fine," he called back.

A few minutes later she returned with a quart of strawberry ice cream in one hand and a bottle of red wine in the other. "I figured we needed both," Meghna said. "Comfort food."

She set them down on the coffee table in the living room, and he just stood there awkwardly, not sure what to do. There was something odd about being in the place where she lived. The tune from before popped back into his head.

"Sit down," she said, gesturing toward the couch. "I'll be right back. I'm just going to change." She took a step toward her bedroom, then stopped. "Did you pack pajamas? Or anything?"

He shook his head.

"That's fine. I'll see if I can find something for you to sleep in."

She disappeared into her room, and he let his composure drop. His tense muscles relaxed as he sank deep into the sofa. *What am I doing here?* Karthik rubbed a hand over his face. This wasn't like him at all. And he didn't just mean his impromptu trip to Dallas. That he could almost understand. People made out-of-character decisions during a crisis, but he wasn't in crisis mode anymore. His breathing was fine. He wasn't feeling sick. He was almost back to normal. So, why hadn't he done the sensible thing and checked into a hotel? What was he doing in Meghna's apartment?

"You know what I was thinking about?" Meghna asked loudly from her bedroom.

"No. What?"

"That was basically our first date." Some rustling and the creaks and bangs of drawers opening and shutting accompanied her words. "I don't think we'd ever had a meal together before."

"We've had several meals together."

"Yeah, but it's never been just the two of us."

He thought it over for a moment. "I guess you're right," he said.

She walked back into the living room, and he couldn't stop himself from staring. Her hair was pulled back with a cotton headband, and her face had a bright, freshly washed glow. The emerald-green color of her pajamas made her skin appear almost golden. *How does she keep becoming more beautiful?* He swallowed and looked away.

She thankfully didn't notice his gawking as she made her way over to the couch and tossed something at him. He reflexively caught it. He shook out the folded piece of clothing, an oversized dark-gray T-shirt. At least, it would have been oversized on Meghna. It would probably fit him fine.

"Sorry, I didn't have a ton of options," Meghna said as she sat down on the couch next to him. "But I think that should work."

A thought struck him, and something hot and dangerous flooded his body.

"Whose shirt is this?" he asked carefully.

"Oh. Just mine," she said quickly. She grabbed the throw pillow that had been propped behind her and placed it on her lap. She stared down at it, her fingers playing distractedly with one of the tassels.

Realization dawned on him. She was lying.

"Meghna, whose is it?"

She breathed out a sigh. "Fine. You'd have guessed when you saw the front anyway."

Puzzled, he flipped the shirt over. Two cartoon glasses of milk with googly eyes stared back at him. One had a speech bubble on top of it, and he went still as he read what it said.

"That's my joke," he said.

"I know."

"You liked my joke?"

She grinned. "Yeah, of course I did."

He read the shirt again, running a hand over it. "You never responded. I didn't know." He shook his head. "You made this? For Samir?"

"No, dummy. I made it for you."

Startled, he lifted his head. Her face was right in front of his, her eyes shining with barely contained laughter. He leaned toward her instinctively.

But Meghna pulled back, abruptly standing up.

"We should build a pillow fort."

"What?" he asked, trying to make sense of her words.

"Have you ever made a pillow fort?" She grabbed a blanket that had been folded under the coffee table.

"Last time Ankita got dumped, we stayed in one for a whole weekend. We stocked up on ice cream and binge-watched old episodes of *The Bachelor*."

Is that why she'd brought out the wine and ice cream? A flush of embarrassment swept through him. "You don't need to treat me like one of your friends. I'm not Ankita going through a breakup."

"I know that." She frowned. "You don't want to be friends?"

No, I don't. The sudden burst of clarity shocked him, but it led to a series of other revelations. He didn't want to be friends with Meghna. Didn't want to be just friends with his fiancée. He knew their relationship wasn't real and that it couldn't ever be real, but he also knew without a shadow of a doubt that he wanted more than friendship from her.

"I don't know," he told her, his throat suddenly dry. He didn't know exactly what he was doing, but he decided to put it all on the table. To just say what he wanted and let the chips fall where they may. The mask of indifference slipped off his face, and he looked at her the way he had wanted to since that night in Miami. He took a step toward her.

"Can friends kiss?" he asked.

She stood stock-still, an incredulous expression on her face.

"Kiss?" she croaked.

"Yes." He walked closer until they were no more than a few inches apart.

She inhaled shakily. "I don't kiss my friends."

"Okay," he whispered. "Then let's not be friends."

Her gaze flickered to his lips, and something like panic flared in her eyes. He immediately took a step back.

"No," she said, her hand reaching out to grab his. "Stay. I just . . ." She stopped and took a deep breath.

He ran his thumb over the back of her hand.

"I don't want you to kiss me for practice," she said hurriedly. "I don't want you to apologize afterward or regret this one. Like you did last time."

"Regret?" He stared in disbelief. She thought he had *regretted* kissing her? How could she possibly think that? It had been one of the best kisses of his life. One of the best *moments* of his life. He shook his head and took a tiny step closer, looking directly into her dark-brown eyes.

"I didn't regret it. I don't regret it. And I won't regret this."

He didn't know which one of them moved first, but suddenly his mouth was on hers. And it was nothing like their last kiss. All the hesitancy and awkwardness from before vanished. They met with open mouths and roving hands, secure in the knowledge that there was no one around. That there was no need to put on a performance. It was just them.

They broke for a moment, and Karthik trailed kisses from her lips across her cheek, all the way to the sensitive spot right behind her ear. Meghna gasped, and his lips curved into a smile against her skin.

"You like that," he murmured. He continued a path of kisses down her neck. "Let's find out what else you like." His hands traveled from her waist to the hem of her shirt, but she beat him to it, sliding it over her head before he could. She dropped the satiny material on the floor and took a step back, her smile wide and brazen.

His breath caught. She hadn't been wearing a bra. His gaze latched onto her breasts, small and round and utterly perfect. He moved to mold one in the palm of his hand, but she stepped out of reach, shaking her head.

"Your turn," she said, gesturing to the button-down shirt he still wore. With a huff, he started slipping the buttons free, but his hands were shaking so badly that he wasn't able to make much progress.

"If you have scissors I'll just cut the damn thing off," he muttered.

"Language!" Meghna laughed, then cocked her head to the side. "You know, I don't think I've ever heard you curse before."

He fumbled with a button, then threw his hands up in frustration. "Well, you're about to hear a whole lot more in a minute."

"Here, let me," she said, taking a step toward him.

He almost stopped breathing as her fingers came to his chest, slowly undoing one button after another. She trailed lower, the backs of her fingers brushing against his abdomen. He hissed.

"Sorry," she said with a mischievous grin and another brush of her hand. "Complete accident."

"I'm sure." He'd intended to say the words sarcastically, but they came out pleading and desperate instead.

She continued her progress, and after what felt like an eternity his shirt was finally off, lying on the floor next to hers.

"Meghna?"

"Hmm," she said, her eyes slightly glazed over as they traveled across his body.

But he barely registered her blatant appreciation. He couldn't think straight. He couldn't think at all.

"Can I touch you?" he asked hoarsely.

"Yes," she breathed.

He gently, almost reverently, cupped his hand over her breast. She immediately arched her back, pressing farther into him. He brushed his thumb over her nipple, bent his head, and took it into his mouth.

Meghna moaned, her hands moving at once, her fingers getting tangled up in his hair.

"Don't stop."

"I'm not," he whispered, blowing against her nipple, then moved across her chest to pay the same attention to the other one.

How is he so good at this? Meghna tightened her fingers, holding his head against her. He swirled his tongue, and her body grew weak. Karthik's arms suddenly came around her waist as he half caught her and half joined her in her tumble to the floor.

Her back pressed into the carpet. His face hovered over hers. She'd never seen so much emotion in his eyes: a mixture of laughter and admiration and raw need. She wrapped her hand around the back of his neck and dragged his mouth down, kissing him more softly than before, a lazy exploration of lips and tongues. And then the pace increased. Quicker. Faster. Frantic. He settled his weight on top of her, and it was like something clicked into place. Like she'd been waiting for this moment, and now it was finally here.

He reached for the top of her pajama shorts and held his hands at the waistband, ostensibly waiting for permission to push them down. She wanted to say yes. She wanted to say yes so badly, but she hesitated. She'd never been good at casual sex. She tended to catch feelings even when she didn't want them. *Especially* when she didn't want them. She wasn't sure if she could go down this path with Karthik and not get hurt. She'd fallen for the wrong person once before, and those feelings still haunted her. She didn't want to go through that again.

He sensed her hesitation and moved one of his hands to the top of her head, tucking an errant curl back behind her headband.

"We don't have to do anything. We can just go to sleep."

Her heart squeezed, but she didn't say anything. That also wasn't a good idea, given what had happened last time they'd shared a bed. She couldn't allow herself to grow too attached to him. None of this was real. Not when they had an expiration date.

He waited a moment, but didn't protest or argue any further. He got up, extending a hand to lift her to her feet.

"I can sleep on the couch," he said. He propped one of the throw pillows against the arm of the sofa, then toed his shoes off, one after the other.

Something about his response softened her resolve. She wanted to sleep beside him without a pillow barricade in the way. Wanted to know what it would be like to tuck into his warmth in the middle of the night. To wake up beside him without any panic or worry. Even if this was the only time she'd ever experience it.

She picked her top up from the floor, slipping it over her head before walking to stand in front of him.

"Karthik, come to bed."

His head shot up. Surprise was written across his face. "Are you sure?"

She nodded, offering him her hand.

"Just to sleep?" he asked.

She paused. "Yes. Just to sleep."

"Okay." He slipped his hand into hers and followed her to the bedroom.

He changed into his new shirt and took off his pants, leaving him in black boxer briefs that made Meghna immediately regret her decision. She wanted him. And he wanted her. Clearly. Just a few moments ago, when they'd been lying on the floor, she had felt how much. There had been nothing subtle about it. It had been . . . impressive. She shook her head, stopping the direction of her thoughts.

Karthik seemed unaware of her inner struggle as he slid under the covers, dropping his head onto the pillow. She stood still, watching him, taking in the sight of him in her bed. A little strange, but also somehow . . . right.

"Are you coming?"

I wish. A nervous giggle rose in the back of her throat, but she held it in. *Get it together, Meghna.* She switched off the light and climbed into her usual side of the bed. Her body was awkward and stiff. Her limbs were too heavy to move. She kept still, staring at the ceiling, all too aware of the mouthwatering man beside her.

"Meghna?"

"Hmm?"

"Should I go back to the couch?"

She turned onto her side, but she couldn't make out his face in the darkness. "Why?"

"I . . . You seem uncomfortable with my being here. And that's fine. Completely. I'll be okay on the couch." Some of the pressure lifted off the mattress. Almost as if he was getting up. She flung her arm out, meaning to stop him, but in the dark, she couldn't gauge the distance. Her arm swung wildly, hitting him hard in the stomach.

"Oof."

She winced at the sound. "I'm sorry. Are you okay?"

"Yeah," he said, a little breathless, as if she'd knocked the wind right out of him. "I'm fine. I'll move to the couch." He took in a large, gasping breath. "In a moment."

"No, stay. I'm fine with you . . . in my bed." She let out the laugh she'd been trying to suppress. "I'm sorry. I'm not laughing at you. I'm . . ." Another laugh bubbled out of her mouth. The situation just felt too odd to be real. Her very attractive not-real, normally closed-off fiancé had unexpectedly come to Dallas, showed up at her play, shared incredibly personal news with her, and was now lying next to her in her bed. And she'd hit him. She gained control over the laughter and was about to explain when, to her surprise, Karthik let out a chuckle of his own.

He lay back down beside her, his head hitting the pillow with a soft thud.

"It's fine," he said. "I'm fine." His hand touched her shoulder, trailed down her arm, then closed around hers. "Face the other way," he said, squeezing her hand.

She turned onto her side, facing away from him, her heart beating loudly. His arm came around her waist, pulling her back into his chest as he curled his body around hers.

"This okay?"

"Yes," she whispered. It was more than okay. She felt cherished, taken care of, understood.

"You sure? If I do anything you don't like, feel free to take another swing at me."

She laughed, her insides warming at his teasing. "Oh, you know I will."

He laughed in return, the vibrations rumbling through his chest. She closed her eyes, soaking in the sound and feel of that laugh. Rough and gravelly and genuine. She loved it. She wanted to hear it again and again.

She relaxed into his embrace and quickly fell into a dreamlike state, not quite awake, but not quite asleep. He murmured something, and she stirred slightly in response.

"Shhh." The arm around her waist tightened, and she thought she felt his lips skate over the top of her head. "Go back to sleep," he whispered gently.

And she did.

12

The next morning, Karthik woke up to a warm, shapely leg wrapped around his torso. Meghna was half lying across his body, clinging to him like a koala. He smiled and placed a kiss on her forehead before carefully extricating himself from her embrace. He would have loved to linger for a few moments, but he didn't want her to feel awkward or uncomfortable. Especially after the way things had gone last time.

He left the room quietly and went to her kitchen to turn on the coffee maker. As it brewed, he leaned against the counter, his elbow bumping against a messy pile of papers. Curious, he picked up a page, a good portion of which was marked up and crossed out with red ink. He read the first few sentences and raised his eyebrows at a handwritten comment that just said: *HORRIBLE*. He read the line it was referring to and agreed with the assessment. "Your eyes as deep as the ocean blue / You know I'll always love you"? *Yikes*.

Meghna had sent him a number of Seth's songs, and he had to admit that he'd actually enjoyed most of them. But if this was what they were like before Meghna got to them, Seth owed her a great deal.

Karthik dropped the papers, opening the refrigerator to grab eggs, milk, and bread. Then he started cooking breakfast.

"You're making Bombay toast?"

Meghna stood in the entranceway. He held back a grin as her mouth stretched into a large yawn. Her hair was delightfully mussed, and he was struck by the temptation to walk over and mess it up further, to run his fingers through her soft curls and kiss her good morning. But he wasn't sure where they stood after last night.

"You call it that too?" he asked instead.

"Yeah, that's what my dad always calls it." She poured herself a cup of coffee, then pulled out two plates from the cabinet. "So that's always the name that comes to mind. And it's not like it's really French anyway."

"Makes sense to me."

She held the plates out to him, and he put a few slices on each of them. She didn't have a kitchen table, so they ate standing up, their plates on the counter, facing each other. He thought for a moment about how nice it would be to start every day this way.

Every day? He mentally shook himself. He wasn't thinking clearly. Yesterday's events had obviously taken a toll on him.

"So . . ." she said.

He steeled himself, thinking she wanted to talk about how far they had gone last night. And what it meant for their fake relationship going forward. He'd been thinking about it too, but had no answers.

"So . . ." he replied.

"When are you going back to New York?"

Her words were like a slap across the face. A harsh but much-needed reminder of reality. He had to go back. How had he forgotten that? He had to figure out what to do about his job. How to explain things to Jim. God, he needed to talk to his mother. He closed his eyes. He still didn't know how she was doing. If she'd found out yet. If she needed anything.

"I don't know," he said. "Soon." He needed to check what flights were available for later that day. In his rush to get here, he hadn't booked a return flight.

"Oh. Okay. I was just wondering how much time we had—" She stopped, seeing the mess of papers near the coffee maker. "You read that?"

He cringed. "Was I not supposed to? Sorry, they were lying right there. I only read a bit of it."

She grabbed a bottle of maple syrup from the fridge, pouring a generous amount on her plate, then offering it to him. "No, it's fine," she said. "I'm just curious what you thought."

He declined the maple syrup and took a bite of his breakfast. "I'm no expert, but if you made those comments in red, I agree with you."

"Right?" She let out an exhale. "I'm glad it wasn't just me. I don't even know where to start on it. I've been putting off responding to Seth, but the wedding's coming up and he wants to sing it at the reception." She shook her head. "I'm sorry. I shouldn't be complaining about this. I know you have a lot on your plate."

"It's okay." Honestly, he was thankful for the distraction. "Why don't you tell Seth to start over? To try writing a new song?"

"I don't know. I've never told him anything like that before." She blew across the surface of her coffee before taking a sip.

"Has he ever told you anything like that?"

"Anything like what?"

"That you needed to start something over. Start from scratch."

"Oh. Well, yes. A bunch of times. But he's usually right."

"And aren't you right?"

She looked away, but not before Karthik saw a flicker of self-doubt in her eyes. He paused. Meghna had always struck him as sure and confident. Every time he talked with her, she spoke her mind freely and never seemed to hold anything back. Why wouldn't she tell Seth what she actually thought?

She shrugged, but didn't respond. They finished eating in silence, and Karthik grabbed both of their plates, rinsing them in the sink.

"Did he give you that feedback you've been waiting for? On your play?"

"No, but I'm sure he will soon. He has a lot to do before the wedding."

"Including rewriting this song." He picked up a kitchen towel and started drying the plates.

"I guess." She looked a bit distracted, her eyes zeroed in on his hands.

"Because it *is* bad. You're right, Meghna."

She shrugged again, and Karthik felt a twinge of annoyance. Who had made her this unsure of herself?

"Would you ever let me read your play?"

Meghna's eyes shot to his. "No. I mean, maybe. Once it's done. But it's not done."

"What's the play about?"

She crossed her arms defensively. "What's with all the questions?"

"I'm just curious." And he was. He could tell Meghna's writing was a sensitive topic, but he couldn't understand why. He was about to ask more, but the expression on her face twisted his heart. She looked like a cornered animal: nervous, uncomfortable, and a little afraid.

"What are your plans for the rest of the weekend?" he asked instead.

Meghna visibly relaxed.

"Just lunch with Ankita. And an appointment this afternoon. But I can ask her to get lunch another day if you want to do something instead."

"No, that's okay. I should head to the airport before then." He refilled his coffee. "What's the appointment for?"

"A tux fitting."

"For you?"

She nodded.

"You're wearing a tux to Seth's wedding?"

"Yeah. We debated the options, but we landed on a tux so I'll match the rest of the guys. But they said they'll be styling it differently? I don't know. I guess we'll see how it turns out."

An image of Meghna in a tuxedo popped into his head, and he hid a smile. She'd look so cute. He was suddenly tempted to see it for himself.

"What time's your appointment?"

"Around one."

Karthik pulled out his phone and checked the flight schedule. There were several flights with vacant seats in the afternoon, but he really didn't *have* to get back right away. It was only Saturday. Even if he took the last flight of the day, he'd still have all of Sunday to figure things out at home.

He thought it over for a minute, but as much as he wanted to, he couldn't hide out in Dallas forever. He pressed a few buttons, booking himself on the next available flight.

"Yeah," he said, somewhat reluctantly. "My flight takes off right around that time. So I'm going to go shower, unless you want to go first."

She waved her hand dismissively. "No, go ahead."

He made it to the bathroom, hesitated for a second, then back-pedaled. Meghna had already moved from the kitchen and was sitting on the couch in the living room, a copy of Seth's song on her lap and a look of extreme concentration on her face. He watched her for a moment as she crossed something out, mouthed a few words to herself, then pursed her lips. He was again struck by the temptation to delay his flight, just so he could sit here, spend more time with her, and watch her mind at work.

Instead, he walked toward the couch. Her head swung up at the sound of his footsteps.

"Do you need something?" she asked. "There should be new towels in there."

"I'm sure there are," he said. He sat down on the arm of the sofa.

"But I need something else." He looked at her lips, doing his best to be as obvious as possible.

Her eyes lit with comprehension. And maybe it was only wishful thinking on his part, but he thought he saw a flicker of interest in them as well.

"Yeah? Hmm. I wonder what that could be." She smiled and started ticking items off on her fingers. "I have shampoo in there. And conditioner."

The corners of his mouth tilted up. "It's not that."

"Soap? Face wash? A razor?"

"Meghna," he said chidingly.

"What?" she asked, a look of pure innocence on her face.

"Can I kiss you good morning?"

She sighed dramatically. "Well, if you insist." Then she sat up on her knees, put a hand on his jaw, and pulled him down for a kiss.

The moment their mouths met, Meghna wondered why they hadn't been doing this all morning. They'd wasted valuable minutes on food and talking when they should have just stayed in bed the whole time.

"We should have," Karthik said, and Meghna realized she'd said that part out loud. She was about to reply when Karthik's mouth came back to hers. She was rendered speechless, unable to do anything but match his movements with her own. Push when he pulled, retreat when he pressed, part her mouth when he parted his. She ran her hand up and down the scratchy stubble on his jaw, loving the feel of it against her palm. She used that hand to tilt his head at exactly the right angle, and he moaned in appreciation.

"You taste like maple syrup," Karthik said. His tongue touched the corner of her mouth, picking up a leftover drop of it. He withdrew, then came back, planting a soft kiss on that same spot. "So sweet." He leaned back, his face warm and tender. "I love your hair like this."

Meghna let out a surprised laugh. "Like this?" She lifted a handful of the frizzy, messy curls.

"Yes. It makes me imagine messing it up even more." Karthik's eyes filled with heat, and Meghna's stomach twisted in response. He ran his fingers lightly over a curl, twisting it around his finger, then letting it go.

They stayed like that for a minute, just watching each other, until Karthik left to go take his shower. The bathroom door shut behind him, and Meghna stared at it for a moment in confusion.

She'd loved waking up to see Karthik in her kitchen. Making her coffee. Cooking for her. Doing the dishes. He'd looked unbelievably hot while doing it. The way his forearms had flexed when he'd washed the plates? She had wanted to fan herself.

But she didn't understand what any of this meant for their relationship. Their fake relationship, that was. Karthik had been very clear about two things: 1) that he never wanted to get married and 2) that he wasn't interested in being her friend. But where did that leave them? She walked into her bedroom, changing out of her pajamas and into a pair of jeans and a white cotton top.

She sent a quick text to Ankita. *I'm not going to make lunch today, but I'll see you at the fitting.*

Ankita replied quickly.

Ankita: Okay
Ankita: We'll need to talk at the fitting then.
Ankita: I think I'm going to tell Rishi what happened.

Meghna's eyebrows shot up. Since their first conversation about it, she and Ankita had avoided this topic. Ankita knew where Meghna stood, and Meghna hadn't felt the need to bring it up again. At first, she hadn't wanted to rock the boat. Hadn't wanted to make things worse. But then . . . Meghna had started to realize that she wasn't entirely in a position to judge. Not when she was keeping the truth about her own engagement a secret from her parents. And Samir. And Seth.

Ankita: But I'm really scared. I don't know if I can do it.
Ankita: Will you have time to talk about it?

Compassion rose within her, knocking aside the pent-up bitterness that had been brewing toward her friend.

Meghna: I love you.
Meghna: I'll always have time for you.
Meghna: We'll talk about it as much as you want.
Meghna: See you soon. <3

Meghna slipped her phone into a bag and tied her hair into a ponytail. She and Ankita would sort all of this out later. Right now, she wanted to make sure she was ready by the time Karthik was done with his shower. They had a lot to talk about, but not a lot of time left. If she drove him to the airport, they'd have a chance to talk in the car, and she'd hopefully still make it back in time for her appointment.

She needed to know where this was going, or even *if* it was going. She needed to know if last night had changed anything for him. The way he'd opened up and shared his fears. The way he'd laughed and teased her. The way he'd quite literally rolled with the punches. That was a man she could very easily fall in love with. But she wasn't the same girl she'd been in college. She wouldn't allow herself to develop feelings for Karthik if there wasn't a possibility of those feelings being returned. If there wasn't a possibility of a *real* relationship between them.

Karthik stepped out of the bathroom, his hair damp and pushed back from his face. He wore the same suit and shirt he had worn yesterday, but now they were a little rumpled. He tucked his shirt in and frowned at it, as if the wrinkles had personally offended him. Meghna resisted the urge to laugh.

"I have an iron you can use, but I don't think we have the time."

Karthik checked the time on his phone and grimaced. "You're right. I need to leave now." He sighed, swiping and tapping the screen. "I'll get a car."

Meghna jangled her keys. "No need. I'll drive you."

He looked up. "You sure? Don't you have a lunch?"

She shrugged, walking toward the door. "Ankita and I can do lunch another day."

He followed her out, and she locked up behind them.

When she got into the car, a whiff of tea tree oil and lemon wafted in her direction from the passenger seat. "You used my shampoo?" she asked.

"You said I could."

"Yeah, I know, I just . . ." She pulled out of the apartment complex and entered the address for the airport into her GPS. "I didn't realize that meant you'd smell like me."

He frowned. "Do you . . . not like it?"

"No, I mean, I picked out that shampoo. I like the smell. I just like the way you normally smell."

He was quiet for a moment, but when he spoke his voice was pitched lower than normal. "What do I smell like?"

She got on the highway and answered distractedly. "You know, woodsy. Earthy. Like . . . petrichor."

"Petrichor?"

"Yeah. It's that smell when rain hits the pavement."

He didn't say anything in response, so she glanced over at him, only to see a self-satisfied look on his face.

"Don't be weird about this," she warned.

"I'm not," he said smugly. "I just didn't realize you *loved* the way I smell."

"I said 'like.' Not 'love.'"

"Sounds like you love it, though."

She let out a noncommittal sound, but hid the smile that threatened to break out on her face.

"Just for the record," Karthik said. "I like the way you smell too."

"Thanks."

The car went quiet, and for the first time Meghna didn't feel like she had to say anything to break the silence. She almost enjoyed it. There was something new in the air between them. Something almost . . . comfortable. She wanted to continue sitting in this feeling, but it was time to bring up the elephant in the room.

"You want to talk about the kiss, right?"

Meghna's mouth opened in surprise. "How did you know?"

"I've been watching you for the last five minutes. You seemed to be working up the courage to bring it up, so I thought I'd help you out."

"Well, thanks for that, but we both know it wasn't just one kiss." She let out a long breath and kept her eyes on the road. She didn't want to see his reaction to what she was about to say.

"Karthik, what are we doing?"

The car went quiet again, but this silence felt thick and tense and heavy. A few seconds passed.

"What do you think we're doing?" he finally asked. His tone was plain and even, neither harsh nor soft. Just neutral.

"I don't know," she said. "I know it's more than practice."

"It's definitely not practice," he said firmly.

"But it's also not fully real, right?"

He paused. "Why do you say that?"

"Because none of this can be real. Unless you've changed your mind about marriage?"

"I haven't," he said quickly.

"So where could this possibly go?"

He opened his mouth, then closed it. Then opened it again. "There are options between nothing and marriage. It doesn't have to be all or nothing."

"I know that. But for me it does." She winced. "That's not what I meant. I'm not saying we have to know right this second whether we want to get married to each other or not. But I need to know that marriage is on the table. As a possibility. At some point. I mean, I don't even know what you really mean when you say you never want to get married. Are you saying you never want a legal marriage or are you saying you never want a partner?"

He didn't respond for a few moments, and Meghna risked a look over at him. His face was deadly serious, his expression still and pensive.

"Both," he replied.

"Okay," she said, pushing aside the disappointment she felt. "That's fine. I get it. You've said that before, but where does that leave us?"

He went quiet again, then finally let out a sigh. "I don't know."

"Well, I don't want to be friends with benefits."

"I don't want that, either."

"Then what do you want?"

Meghna had been driving as if she were on autopilot. She only now registered that they were at the airport. She pulled into a curbside parking spot in the drop-off zone, switched off the car, and turned in her seat so she could fully face Karthik.

"Well?" she asked.

"I want to be around you." His hands lifted, and he held her face gently.

Some of Meghna's frustration softened when she saw the genuine conflict in his eyes.

"I want to kiss you," he continued. "And talk to you. And . . ." He shook his head. "Why can't that be enough?"

She gave him a small smile. "I want those things too," she said. "But I want more."

"I can't give you anything more," he said with a note of desperation in his voice.

"I know."

Panic flared across his face. "You said you didn't want me to regret anything. And I don't. But I don't want you regretting this, either."

"I don't. I don't regret it. But I also don't think we can repeat it."

He dropped his hands and moved back suddenly. Meghna wasn't sure, but she thought she saw him flinch.

"We need to stick to the original plan. Go back to just being engaged." She let out a short, humorless laugh. "Fake-engaged, I mean. Nothing . . . physical unless it's necessary."

"Makes sense."

Meghna searched his face and saw that the Karthik who had made her Bombay toast this morning was completely gone. In his place sat the man she had much more experience with: the cold, closed-off, shut-down Karthik.

She wished she could turn the clock back. If only she had known that her time with *that* Karthik would be so fleeting.

"You're right," he told her. "We shouldn't lose sight of our original plan. You still need a date for the wedding, and I still need your help. I don't want to do anything that could disrupt our arrangement."

"Okay," she said cautiously. "So, we're on the same page?"

He gave a brisk nod. "Absolutely."

He stepped out of the car, and she was turning the engine on and preparing to pull out of her spot when she heard a knock on the passenger-side window. Karthik stood there, watching her. She rolled down the window so he could speak.

"Send me a picture from your fitting, okay? Of the tux?"

She found herself agreeing, even though she was incredibly confused. Why did he want it? But before she could ask the question, Karthik turned away and walked into the airport. Meghna sat there for a few seconds until the car behind her honked, shaking her out of her thoughts and forcing her on her way.

.   .   .

"Karthik is going to lose his mind when he sees you in this."

Meghna snorted, turning a bit to the side to get a better view of her reflection in the mirror. "Yeah, right."

"I'm serious," Ankita insisted. "You're an absolute bombshell. He's not going to know what hit him."

"As my best friend you're required to say that." Meghna lifted her arms, the movement constrained by the pins the seamstress had just placed, indicating where some last-minute alterations were needed.

Ankita shook her head. "Nope. Once you see these pictures, you'll understand what I'm talking about. You look amazing."

Meghna rolled her eyes, stepping behind the dressing room curtain to change. "Enough about me," she called as she carefully removed the tux, making sure the pins stayed in place. "We need to talk about you." She pulled on her jeans and threw her shirt over her head before coming back out. "Last time we talked, you had a pretty . . . different approach to how you wanted to handle things."

Ankita flinched, and Meghna immediately felt guilty. "I didn't mean that in a judgmental way. I promise. I just meant that, you know, you were pretty adamant about not telling Rishi before."

Ankita rubbed her forehead, letting out a sigh. "Yeah. Well, before I thought it was only one kiss. A mistake made in the moment. Really, I think I was trying to convince myself that was all it was. But then Samir called me." She paused. "He called a couple times."

Meghna's eyebrows rose. She hadn't realized that her brother had been trying to get in touch with Ankita. Meghna hadn't spoken to Samir since the engagement party. Since he'd gone back to India. He'd called and texted, saying he wanted to explain, but Meghna hadn't been ready to hear his excuses.

"I didn't pick up at first," Ankita said. "I thought I could just avoid him. But Rishi started noticing that I'd jump when the phone rang. That I'd send calls straight to voicemail. And he was so sweet. He never asked questions about it. He never pushed to find out what was going on. And that just made me feel even worse. Like I was some horrible person, keeping this big, dirty secret. It didn't seem like one small kiss anymore. It felt like something more.

"So, I called Samir back, thinking I could get clarity. Closure. And move on. But talking to him made me realize that there's still . . . something between us. I don't know what it is exactly or whether there's a future there, but I can't be engaged to someone when I feel like this. It's not right. Or fair to Rishi." She met Meghna's gaze, pain in her eyes. "I love Rishi. I love him. But I don't think I'm *in* love with him. I don't know if I ever was."

Ankita's face crumpled, and Meghna drew her close, pulling her into a hug. "It's okay," Meghna said. "It'll be okay." She held her best friend for a few moments until Ankita pulled back, wiping her tears away.

"Rishi's such a good person," she said. "He's so kind. And when we met, I knew I didn't feel the way I should, but I'd hoped those feelings could grow. And I just . . . I wanted not to be alone anymore. I'm so tired of being lonely."

Meghna knew exactly how she felt. She'd been lonely for a long time too.

"I don't know if things will work out with Samir. I don't even know what he wants, or if *he* even knows what he wants. But I need to tell Rishi. About everything."

"I'll be there," Meghna said. "Before. After. Whenever. Whatever you need."

"Thank you," Ankita said, her eyes shining. "And I'm so sorry. For keeping all of it from you. For not telling you the truth. I was confused. And hurt. And embarrassed. I didn't know how to tell you back then. I didn't know what to say. But I don't want to make that mistake again. You deserved the truth. And so does Rishi."

"I'm sorry too. For not being willing to hear you out. For not trying to see your side of things. I should have tried harder. I should have tried to be there for you." Meghna hesitated. "And I haven't exactly been honest about everything, either. I've been lying to everyone about Karthik. And I've been keeping things from you too." She squeezed her eyes shut. "Karthik and I . . . We kissed."

"You what?" Ankita exclaimed.

"More than once," Meghna admitted. "A couple times. But it's over. Not that it ever really started. He doesn't want anything real. Anything serious. And . . . I don't want to get hurt again."

Ankita nodded in sympathy. "I can understand that."

"But I don't know what to do now. How to be around him. We still have to go to Seth's wedding and pretend like everything's fine, like we're together and in love and . . ." She shook her head. "I have no idea how we're going to do that."

Ankita let out a watery laugh. "We're a real mess, huh? The two of us."

"We are, but at least we're going through it together."

Ankita wrapped her in a quick, fierce hug, and something tight and heavy in Meghna's chest eased during the embrace. She felt lighter. Like she'd let go of something that had only been dragging her down.

"So, what now?" Meghna asked as they left the store.

Ankita linked her arm through Meghna's. "Well, I have ice cream at my place. And we've missed quite a few episodes of our favorite show."

Meghna smiled. "As long as we can build a pillow fort, I'm in."

They headed to Ankita's house, catching each other up on all the small things that had happened in the last few weeks, sharing the details they'd been keeping from each other. Meghna had missed confiding in Ankita, and though they wouldn't be able to resolve everything in one day, it felt like a step in the right direction.

Karthik called his mother the moment he landed and went directly to the house. His father, unsurprisingly, was out of town at a conference, so Karthik was able to discuss everything with his mother alone. She'd heard about the article, though his father hadn't told her any details about the university investigation or the lawsuit. She had about as much information as Karthik did.

She wasn't surprised or shocked when they discussed the news. Just quiet, an inscrutable expression on her face. Karthik told her that he was there for her and asked if there was anything she wanted him to do, but she only said that she didn't want to talk about it anymore. She got up and served dinner, and they ate in silence, like they had so many nights before.

Though she seemed fine, when it was time for Karthik to go back to his apartment, he found that he didn't want to leave her in the house alone. He told his mom that he'd be staying the night in his old room, and she distractedly acknowledged his words before going to bed.

After Karthik had gone to college, his childhood bedroom had been converted into a home office/guest bedroom. The changes caught him off guard every time he entered. Something inside him expected to see pale-blue walls, his twin-sized bed, and glow-in-the-dark stars on the ceiling, but he was greeted instead by a cherrywood desk, a large computer monitor, and a dark-gray couch that pulled out into a bed.

He took a seat and remotely logged into his office email. He had resisted checking it while in Dallas, unsure what he'd find. Unsure if he'd be able to handle it. The promotion was likely out of reach now; he'd basically abandoned his job by walking out without telling anyone. Bile rose in his throat. He'd never done anything like that before. He had no idea what to expect. He might be disciplined, perhaps even terminated for acting so unprofessionally.

Taking a deep breath, he scanned his inbox, surprised to see that there were only a few emails and that the first one was from Paul.

From: Paul
To: Karthik
Subject: ???
Hey, was waiting for you to come back. Hope ur ok. Call me if you want to talk.

Paul had included his personal cell phone number at the end of the email, and Karthik couldn't help but feel touched. Karthik shot back a quick response saying he was fine and that he'd see him at work on Monday. He scrolled further, his blood freezing when he saw that the next message was from Jim.

From: Jim
To: Karthik
Subject: Yesterday

Karthik,

I'm unsure what happened yesterday. I went to your office later and your intern told me you were feeling unwell and were taking a sick day. I hope you're getting some rest and feeling better, but I'm very concerned by all of this. Please give me a call on Monday or whenever you are back to work so we can discuss.

Jim

Karthik blinked. Then read the email again. As far as responses went, this was better than expected. He could talk to Jim. Explain the situation. Or at least explain that he had gotten sick very suddenly that afternoon. That had the added benefit of being technically true. And then he could ask for another chance.

He swallowed. He might still have a shot at the promotion. Karthik texted the number that Paul had sent.

Karthik: This is Karthik. Thanks for covering for me and thanks for the email. I really appreciate it. See you on Monday.

He almost set the phone down, but it beeped before it even reached the desk.

Paul: Np, man. They seemed pretty mad, but hope it works out. Glad ur good.

The phone beeped again. Paul had sent a fist bump emoji. Karthik shook his head with a small smile and sent one back.

He typed a short response to Jim, apologizing for the inconvenience, promising that he had an explanation for his behavior, and thanking him for understanding.

Karthik would have to fight for a second chance, but he could do that. He'd make plans. Prepare for Monday. Look at everything again. And he'd definitely come up with better answers to the panel's questions this time. He did a quick scan through the remaining emails before reaching for his phone again.

He needed to tell someone about this. He pulled up Meghna's number, but before he could share the news, he realized something.

Karthik: I never got a picture of the tux?

Karthik put his phone down and continued reading the emails, his foot absently tapping against the floor. Three minutes later, his phone beeped.

Meghna: Why do you need it?

Astute as always. He thought for a moment. He couldn't say that he wanted a picture because he'd been tempted to go to the fitting with her. That he was desperate to see if she looked as cute as he'd been imagining. They didn't have that kind of relationship. Meghna had been firm in the boundaries she had set for them going forward, and he wanted to respect them. This was the only way for their arrangement to work, and he wasn't ready for it to be over.

Karthik: How else can I coordinate what I'm going to wear to the wedding?

He waited, watching the screen, growing a little nervous when the speech bubbles popped up, indicating that she was typing, then disappeared. They popped back up. Then went away again. Finally, a response came through.

Meghna: Ugh, fine.

A few seconds later, she sent the picture. Karthik tapped on it so it filled the screen of his phone.

The picture was full length and showed Meghna in a tight-fitting, perfectly cut tux. Her hair was pulled back from her face, and she was smiling at the camera, her lips dark red and sinful. This was so far from the image he'd created in his head. Meghna in a tux wasn't cute or wholesome. She was downright sexy.

Without thinking, he replied.

Karthik: You look beautiful.

He waited half a second, then quickly typed on his phone.

Karthik: But now I have to buy a new tux. We can't show up to the wedding in identical outfits.

A few seconds later, Meghna responded.

Meghna: Ha. I'd love to see you rock cropped suit pants.

He breathed a sigh of relief.

Karthik: First of all, on men they're called high waters.
Meghna: It's terrifying that you know that.
Karthik: And second, I look good as hell in them. I have killer ankles.
Meghna: Sure you do.

Karthik looked down at his feet, took a quick picture of them, and sent it to Meghna.

Karthik: See? Proof.
Meghna: Hmm. They're okay, I guess. Nothing like these.

Karthik stared at his phone, thinking Meghna would be following up with a picture of her feet, but nothing came through. He exited the app and came back, but he still didn't see a new message from her.

Karthik: Did you send me a picture? I didn't get one.
Meghna: Because I'm not going to actually send you a picture of my feet, you creep!

Karthik let out a loud laugh.

Karthik: Fair enough.
Meghna: ;)
Meghna: I'm going to get ready for bed. Good night, Karthik.
Karthik: Good night, Meghna.

Karthik turned back to the computer. He pulled up the documents and spreadsheets he had initially gathered to prepare for his interview. He needed to review everything again before his meeting with Jim on Monday. He skimmed for a while, but his attention wandered until he finally opened the web browser and entered something in the search bar: "mechanical engineering positions in Dallas."

Out of all the results, only a few caught his eye. He emailed the links to those open positions to himself, then went back to reviewing his materials for the interview. He wasn't seriously looking at other jobs. He just did this every now and then. The way people searched for homes on real estate websites and saved their favorites without any intention of ever buying them. It was good to know what was out there. To have an idea of what the market looked like.

After reviewing the spreadsheets for an hour, he closed out of them. Relief rolled through him as he realized all the facts and figures he'd studied the first time were still in his memory. He was about to shut down the computer and go to sleep when a thought took him by surprise.

He didn't know why he hadn't thought about it sooner. It was a serious oversight. If he and Meghna wanted to really make people believe their engagement was real, they had to take care of this. People were bound to ask about it eventually.

He opened the browser back up and did one final search before going to bed: "what to look for when buying an engagement ring."

M eghna's thumb hovered over Seth's contact in her phone. She'd started and deleted several emails and text messages over the past few days, but hadn't been able to properly put what she had to tell him into words. After struggling to come up with some kind of feedback for Seth, Meghna had finally reached the conclusion that Karthik had been right. Seth's song was unsalvageable.

She just wasn't sure how to tell him that. He'd never had this issue before. Sure, not everything he'd written had been perfect from the first draft, but none of them had ever been *this* horrible. Meghna took a deep breath and pressed the call button before she could change her mind. He answered almost immediately.

"Meg? Hey! We were just talking about you."

"You were?"

"Yeah, Jules is here too. I'm passing the phone to her. Say hi, Julie!"

"Hi, Meghna!" Julie's voice, bright and clear, came over the line. "It's nice to meet you. Well, meet you over the phone. But I'm excited to meet you in person soon. Seth's told me so much about you!"

Meghna paused, her stomach twisting. She hadn't expected to have to talk to Julie until the wedding. Besides the picture and meet-cute story on their wedding website, she didn't know much about her.

According to the story, Seth and Julie had met at an industry party in Nashville. Julie was an up-and-coming singer-songwriter new to the city, and Seth had promised to show her around. A few months later, Julie's profile skyrocketed after a single she released online went viral. She was still pretty new on the scene, but everyone recognized that she was a star on the rise. Some major outlets had even drawn comparisons between her and Taylor Swift. Shortly after Julie's viral success, Seth had proposed to her in Centennial Park, and now they were getting married there.

"Hey, Julie, it's nice to meet you too."

"My maid of honor and I were just talking about how good everyone's dresses turned out, but then Seth sent us that picture of your tux and we were floored. Beth—that's my maid of honor—is so mad at me now. She thinks she should get to wear one too, and honestly, I have to agree with her. It looks incredible. But we've already ordered her dress, so she's stuck with it! But really, it looks so good on you."

"Thanks," Meghna said, pinching the bridge of her nose. She appreciated Julie's kind words, but couldn't help but feel awkward. "I'm happy with how it turned out too."

"Anyway, I have to run so I'll hop off now, but just wanted to say hello!"

"Bye, Julie. Look forward to meeting you soon."

There was a quiet shuffling noise as the phone was passed to Seth. His voice came on the line, giving Meghna a sudden pulse of anxiety.

"Okay, I'm back," he said.

"Great. Umm, Julie seems really nice."

"She's wonderful. You guys will totally get along. She reminds me a lot of you, actually."

Ouch. His words stung, but Meghna tried to move forward. "Anyway, I know I owe you some feedback on the song. Sorry it's taken me so long."

"No problem. I mean, I've been taking forever with your stuff too. It's just this one has a tight deadline, you know." He barked out a short laugh, and Meghna gritted her teeth.

"Right. Well, I had a chance to read through it, and it's . . . different from your usual songs."

The line was quiet for a few seconds. "Different in a good way or . . ."

"Umm. Just different." Meghna decided to change tack. "What parts of the song are you most looking forward to singing to Julie?"

He asked for a moment so he could pull up the lyrics, then went quiet as he presumably read through it. "All of it, I guess."

Meghna closed her eyes. "I think it might be worth thinking through exactly what you want to tell her with this song and then maybe taking another stab at it."

"You want me to start over?" he asked, genuine surprise in his voice.

"Not necessarily," she hedged. "Maybe just reflect for a bit before revising. Or start over if you think that's easier." He had given her similar advice over the years. Whenever a scene wasn't working and she just couldn't figure out why, it often helped to start from scratch, to go back to a clean slate. But though she'd benefited from that advice, she'd never suggested that he do the same. She'd never thought his songs had needed it.

"So, you hate it," he said flatly.

"No, not at all. I just . . . You're a great writer, Seth. And I think you're capable of more."

He was silent for a bit. Then a loud huff of breath traveled through the phone. "Okay. Well, thanks. And thanks for the feedback."

The call clicked, signaling it was over, and Meghna stared at her phone in confusion. Had he just hung up on her?

He'd never done that before. He'd never responded to feedback from her that way. He tended to be a little sensitive, to pout a bit when she delivered constructive criticism, but she'd never seen him truly get upset. Or react like this. Maybe she'd been too blunt. Maybe she'd hurt his feelings. She felt an overwhelming urge to call him back and apologize, but resisted, thinking it over for a moment. Seth had asked her for her opinion, and she'd given it. Nicely. Far more nicely than he had given feedback to her over the years.

Still, she couldn't shake the feeling that she had done something wrong. She almost called Seth back, but changed her mind at the last second, scrolling to a different name in her phone. It rang a few times, and her heart thudded for a moment. Then Karthik answered.

His voice was deep and urgent. "Meghna, what's wrong?"

"Wrong? Nothing. Why?"

"I wasn't expecting a call from you. Sorry, I just assumed it was an emergency or . . ." Karthik cleared his throat. "How are you doing?"

"Fine. I'm fine."

"Good. Me too."

She waited a second, then blurted it out in a rush. "I told Seth."

"Told him . . ."

"About the song."

"Ah." There was some rustling, as if he was moving around, then the creak and click of a door closing. "How did it go?"

"Not great. He . . ." She let out a small, disbelieving laugh. "He hung up on me."

"He *what*?" The words were harsh. And a bit angry?

"Yeah. It could have been an accident, but—"

"I doubt that."

"I think I hurt his feelings."

He exhaled a loud breath. "What did you tell him?"

"That he should think through some things and try revising. Or starting over."

"And that's it?"

She thought back to the call and ran it over in her head. "Yeah, pretty much."

He was quiet for a moment. "Did you yell at him?"

"No."

"Call him names?"

"No."

"Really?" Then he muttered something that sounded a lot like, *I would have.*

"I feel bad about it," she said. "I almost called him back, but . . ."

"But what?"

"I called you instead."

He sighed loudly, but now his voice sounded softer.

"Meghna, do your feelings ever get hurt when Seth gives you feedback?"

Yes. Meghna stopped, surprised by how quickly that response had come. Seth's feedback had hurt her feelings before. Honestly, most of his feedback hurt her feelings. He was blunt and direct, but that was just the way he was. The way he'd always been.

"Yes, but that's different."

"Why?"

She thought about it, but struggled to put it into words. "It just is."

"Look, I don't know anything about this process other than what you've told me, but it sounds like you did what you were supposed to do. And maybe his feelings were hurt, but that probably comes with the territory. You didn't do anything wrong."

"I guess."

A beat passed. "You doing okay otherwise?"

"Yeah, yeah, I'm fine. You okay?" She'd been wanting to ask that since he'd returned to New York. She had no idea how he was doing with the news of his father, or if he'd talked to his mother. But she didn't want to pry. Or pressure him to share.

"I'm doing okay." He paused. "Can I call you back tonight? And talk some more then? I stepped out of a meeting, but I should get back now."

"Oh, I'm sorry. I should have checked to see if you were—"

"Don't worry about it. I decided to take the call. You have nothing to be sorry about. And you don't need to apologize to Seth, either, okay?"

"Okay. But I really am sorry—I mean, I didn't want to disturb your workday. I should have checked the time, but I—"

"Meghna?"

"Yes?"

"Call me any time you want."

A nervous but giddy sensation swept through her. "Okay. I'll talk to you tonight, then."

"Okay."

He hung up, and Meghna sat there for some time. Processing.

She'd once believed that Karthik was cold. Robotic. Even rude. But she was starting to think that he never intended to be that way. Seth, on the other hand, had always been warm. Bright. Silly. Fun. He'd understood her and her writing, which she'd never shared with anyone else before. She'd felt supported by him. Safe.

But recently, talking to Seth felt a lot like walking on eggshells. Or a game of the-floor-is-lava. Hopping from topic to topic, trying to stick to the safe areas, hoping not to get burned.

Meghna ran her fingers over her phone, thinking again about calling Seth. Karthik was right. She hadn't done anything wrong. She didn't need to apologize, but maybe she could try to smooth things over. Unruffle some feathers. Make things return to the way they had been.

She almost dialed the number, then stopped, setting the phone down and walking away. Maybe she'd try to talk to him another time, but she wouldn't be doing it today.

"My apologies," Karthik said as he stepped back into his meeting with Jim. "I thought it was an emergency."

"You seem to be having a lot of those," Jim said, his tone even, though not entirely unkind.

Karthik held back a wince. "I really am sorry about that. I was unwell that day, but that's no excuse. I should have explained myself. Or at least tried to before walking out. I've never done anything like that before and I *never* will again."

Jim nodded, his face open and thoughtful.

"I'm prepared for this position, Jim. I'm a hard worker. I'm dedicated to this company. And my team. And I have so many ideas I'd like to share with you. I know I'm asking for a lot, but you won't regret giving me another chance."

Jim blew out a breath. "People get sick. It happens. I just wish you would have told us what was going on. But I take Marianne's recommendation seriously, and you've never given us a reason to doubt you before." He paused. "I'll talk to the panel, but I can't make any promises. If they agree to redo the interview, just know that I won't be able to do it again."

"I understand," Karthik replied solemnly.

The atmosphere in the room relaxed a degree, and Karthik segued into a discussion about last year's most successful projects. The conversation somehow went well, and when it was over, Karthik felt confident things were back on track. Jim had seemed impressed and had casually mentioned that Karthik should block out some dates to meet with the rest of the panel.

Karthik headed back to his office, passing by Paul's cubicle on the way. Paul stuck his head out and raised his eyebrows as if to ask how the meeting had gone. Karthik flashed him a thumbs-up, and Paul mimed fist-pumping the air in celebration. The silly action brought a reluctant grin to Karthik's face.

As he settled back at his desk, Karthik's phone chimed with an incoming text message.

Paul: Drinks later? To celebrate??

Karthik stared at the screen in confusion. Paul wanted to get drinks? Outside the office? With *him*? Karthik's first instinct was to politely decline. To say no. But as he debated how to phrase it, another message popped up.

Paul: And I could use your help with something. If you have time to talk

Karthik's brows knit. Well, that changed things. He wasn't sure what the intern wanted, but after everything Paul had done for him, the least Karthik could do was hear him out.

Karthik: Sure. We can go after work.
Karthik: Wait . . . are you even 21?
Paul:. . . . .
Paul: Coffee. I meant we can go get coffee. And I know just the place!

Paul sent some kind of emoji that made confetti burst across Karthik's phone screen, and Karthik shook his head, not sure what he'd just agreed to.

Later, after the workday was over, Karthik arrived at the address Paul had texted. It was exactly the sort of place he'd imagined. A new, trendy spot manufactured to look as if it were run-down, with exposed brick and Edison bulbs hanging from the ceiling.

"Over here," Paul called from a spot in the corner. Karthik headed toward him, perking up when he saw two lattes already on the table, each with a sprig of lavender floating on top.

"So, this is where the coffee comes from," Karthik said as he took a seat.

"Yeah. It's right down the street. Makes it easy." Paul lifted his mug, clinking it against Karthik's. "And cheers, man. I'm glad everything went well today."

"Yeah, me too."

"And everything else is good now, right? With the job? And, uh, your dad?" Paul swallowed, his expression turning somewhat nervous. "I mean, you don't have to answer that. Or say anything. It's just . . . About what happened before, I shouldn't have brought up the whole situation with your dad. I wasn't even really sure he was your dad and I had no idea your interview was supposed to be that day, but still, it wasn't any of my business and I'm so sorry. Though I guess it sounds like it's all working out, but I still shouldn't have—"

"Paul," Karthik interrupted, his voice a shade louder than usual. "It's fine." Paul's mouth slammed shut, and Karthik felt the need to clarify. "You have nothing to apologize for," he said. "But I appreciate you saying that."

"Yeah. Yeah, of course." Paul hesitated, as if he was about to say something more, but he seemed to change his mind, glancing away instead.

Karthik waited, but Paul remained silent, forcing Karthik to continue the conversation. "And are you . . . doing well? With school and stuff?"

Paul gave Karthik a look he couldn't quite decipher. "Uh, yeah. Things are fine. I mean, this semester's kicking my ass, but that's what happens when we get closer to finals."

"When are they?"

"In a few weeks."

"Good. Well, umm, study hard." Karthik cleared his throat. "Is that what you wanted help with? Because it's been a while since I was in school, but I could probably . . ."

Paul let out a rough laugh, shaking his head. "No. No. It's nothing like that." He looked down at the ground, his foot tapping rapidly against the floor. He seemed nervous for some reason, and Karthik couldn't figure out why.

"Paul, are you . . . okay? Is everything all right?"

"Yeah, yeah, I'm fine. I just wanted to ask you . . ." Paul reached for his drink, taking a long sip of his coffee, as if he needed it to gain courage. To give him the strength to say what he needed to say.

Karthik raised his mug to take a sip of his own. He was still swallowing when Paul finally asked his question.

"I, uh, wanted to ask you . . . How do you know if you're in love?"

Karthik choked, coffee gurgling in the back of his throat. He grabbed a paper napkin, but managed to gain control of himself, narrowly avoiding sputtering his drink across the table.

"What?" he croaked once he'd recovered.

Paul groaned. "God, I knew this would be embarrassing. I'm sorry. It's just . . . I didn't know who else to ask. My parents aren't together anymore and none of my friends are in serious relationships. And I really like my girlfriend. Like, a lot, but I'm not sure if . . . if it's love."

"And you decided to ask me because . . ."

"Because you've got it all figured out. With your fiancée, I mean. You seem so happy."

Karthik's surprise almost made him choke again. He must have gotten better at faking it than he'd thought.

"Well," he started, unsure how to even begin to answer Paul's question. "That's because Meghna is . . . special. She's, uh, the one."

"Right," Paul said impatiently. "But how did you *know*? How did you know that she was the one?"

"I just . . . did."

Paul looked at him skeptically, and Karthik scrambled to come up with something more believable. "Love can't be explained, Paul. It's just . . . It's wanting to be around the other person. And . . . wanting to talk to them. It's wanting to hear about their day and tell them about yours. It's doing everything in your power to make them happy, even if it comes at a cost. Even if it means denying yourself or sacrificing something so that they can be happy. So that they can get what they want. It's caring about them more than you care about yourself and showing them how much you care. Every day."

Karthik stopped, taking a deep breath. He'd probably just bumbled the whole thing. Just made it clear that he knew nothing about love. That his entire relationship was a fraud. But Paul didn't seem to be calling his bluff. He was just watching him, quiet and thoughtful.

"Is that how you feel?" Karthik asked. "About your girlfriend?"

Paul waited a moment, then sighed. "I don't know, man. That all sounds a little too intense for me."

Karthik shrugged, relieved as the conversation drifted on to lighter topics. Paul regaled him with bits of office gossip and rumors, then shocked Karthik when he got up and gave him a quick hug and slap on the shoulder before saying goodbye.

Karthik walked back to his apartment a bit bemused by the whole experience. He wasn't sure what to make of it. He was just thankful he'd been able to come up with something on the fly when Paul had asked that absurd question. He put the strange conversation out of his mind as he unlocked his door and grabbed some leftover takeout from the fridge. Then he dialed Meghna's number, making good on his earlier promise to call her back.

She answered, and his shoulders relaxed at the sound of her voice. She asked about his day, and Karthik filled her in on the conversation with Jim.

"So, you feel like you got the job?"

"It's way too early to tell," he said. "But I'm still in the running. At least, Jim made it sound like I was. Fingers crossed I'll get another interview with the panel."

"Well, that's still great news."

"Thanks." He cleared his throat.

"How's, uh, everything else? Everything with your family?"

Karthik sank a bit farther into the couch. "I don't know. I talked with my mom."

"How'd it go?"

"She didn't react at all."

"I— I don't . . . What do you mean?"

He closed his eyes. "She didn't want to talk about it. I asked if there was anything she needed, anything I could do, but she said no, and I just felt so . . . so . . . useless." He took a deep breath. "I don't know what else to do."

"I'm sorry."

"It's not your fault," he said immediately.

"I know. But I'm still sorry." She exhaled softly. "I don't think there *is* anything else for you to do. Other than be there for her. And it sounds like you're doing that."

"But it doesn't feel—" A lump rose in his throat. He tried to swallow the uncomfortable sensation down. "It doesn't feel like enough."

She didn't say anything, but her gentle breathing told him she was still on the line. The quiet companionship made him feel a little less alone.

"Thanks," he said.

"For what?"

"For listening."

"Anytime."

He sat there for a moment, looking down at the plate on his lap. His food had gotten cold. He went to stick the plate back in the microwave.

"Hey. Can I ask you something?"

"Of course," she replied.

"Why does Seth call you 'Meg'?"

She didn't respond for a second, so Karthik continued. "Is that what you prefer to be called? Would you want me to call you that?"

"No. I mean . . . It's just . . . Seth's the only one who calls me that."

Karthik's chest tightened. "Oh. Okay."

She sighed. "It wasn't my idea. He had a hard time pronouncing my name at first, so he shortened it."

Karthik paused, then scoffed. "How hard did he try? Your name's pretty easy."

"I know."

"Two syllables. It doesn't get much easier than that."

"Yeah."

"You should tell him to say your name properly."

"Maybe. But it's been so long. And I've gotten used to it at this point."

"But do you like it?"

She was quiet for a second. "It's fine."

"All right, *Meg*."

"*Ugh*. No. Don't you dare call me that."

Karthik laughed. "Fine. I won't. But you know, you can tell Seth exactly what you just told me."

"Maybe," she said hesitantly.

He took his plate out of the microwave and headed back to the couch. "Are there nicknames you do like? Or does everyone call you Meghna?"

"Pretty much. I mean, Mom calls me 'beta,' but that's it."

"Really?" He brought a forkful of lo mein to his mouth. "You and Ankita don't have special names for each other?"

"No. Do you have any nicknames?" she asked.

"Nope."

"Well, then, I think we should give each other some."

Karthik paused, his fork mid-twirl in the noodles. "Like what?"

"Hmm. Kar? Karth?"

No way. He hated both of them. They sounded . . . fine, but they weren't him.

"Yeah, no," he said. "I think we're both on the same page about not liking shortened versions of our names."

She snorted, and he smiled at the sound. He took a bite of his food and suddenly thought of something.

"Since we're engaged, shouldn't our nicknames be more like terms of endearment? We can use them when we're at Seth's wedding. Just to convince people, I mean."

"I guess . . ." she said slowly. "Do you have any ideas?"

" 'Honey'?"

"Yuck."

He laughed. "Okay, so not that. 'Dear'? 'Babe'?"

"'Babe'? Karthik, please be serious."

"You try coming up with some, then!"

"Fine! Umm, my parents call each other 'jaan,' but I don't think we should use that one."

He tried to place the word, but his Hindi was extremely limited. "What does it mean?"

"Life. Like the other person is their life."

He considered it for a moment. He couldn't imagine calling someone else his life. Couldn't imagine someone else being so vital, so necessary, so . . .

"What about 'darling'?" she asked.

He made a face. "Too cowboy."

"What?" She laughed, and the sound of it warmed him from the inside out. "What does that mean?"

"Can't you hear it? You're the Texan. It sounds like something a cowboy would say with a piece of straw in his mouth." He did his best imitation of a southern drawl. "Howdy, darlin'."

Peals of laughter burst on the other end of the call. "Please say that again," she said in between breaths. "You have to."

"Never. Once-in-a-lifetime experience."

She let out one final laugh. "Okay. Fine. No 'darling.'"

"Sweetheart" and "love" popped into his head. He was about to mention them, but stopped himself. They both felt too intimate. Too real.

"Maybe we should just let one come up organically," he suggested.

"Maybe."

They said nothing for a few seconds until Meghna indicated she needed to hop off the call. After hanging up, Karthik finished his dinner by himself, like he had so many nights in the past, but for some reason, the act felt so much lonelier than it ever had before.

. . .

Three days later, an email from Seth arrived in Meghna's inbox. It contained no apology or explanation for why he had hung up on her before. In fact, the email contained nothing in the subject line or body of the message. Just an attached document with brand-new lyrics for her review. She scanned the song quickly. It was completely different and at first glance, much better than the old one.

She closed her laptop, stretching her legs out on her couch. It had been a long day at work, and she'd planned to watch some mindless television, but reached for her phone instead.

"Hey. Is this a good time?" she asked.

"Yeah," Karthik said, slightly out of breath. "I'm just at the gym."

"Oh. I can call you back later if that's—"

"No." Some electronic beeps played in her ear. "It's fine. I'm slowing down the treadmill. What's up?"

"Nothing really. Seth sent me a new song to look at."

"Yeah? Is it any good?"

"I can't tell yet, but so far it seems better than the last one."

"Good. That's good." He wasn't quite panting, but his breaths were loud and harsh and quick.

"How was your day?" she asked.

"Fine," he said. "Jim told me I'll get that re-interview with the panel. It's good news, but they're asking for more this time. A big presentation. A final pitch on why I should get the job and what my vision for the HVAC department is going forward."

"Congrats! How are you feeling?"

He blew out a breath. "Good, I think. Nervous, but good. It'll be a lot of work, but I have some ideas already. Some projects I've had in mind for a while. There's a new method of computer modeling I want the company to implement. I think it'll help us better analyze whether the ventilation system we've designed has any flaws that need to be addressed. But there are a couple different softwares out there and I want to test them out before pitching one to the company. I was going to start working on it this afternoon, but I got distracted. My, uh, dad called me."

"Oh. What did . . . What did he say?"

He sighed loudly. "I didn't answer. I got angry just seeing his name on the screen and didn't think it was a good idea to talk to him in that state. But I called my mom, just to check in on her."

"Yeah? Is she doing okay?"

"Fine. Or at least she's acting like everything's normal and fine. But it's obviously not. I mean, my dad never calls me, so something must have happened. I asked if he'd told her anything, but she changed the subject."

"Maybe . . . Maybe it's worth calling him back?" she asked hesitantly. "To see what he wanted?"

"Maybe. At the very least, I should stop by the house. Just to make sure Amma's okay. I don't know if she's in denial or what, but she didn't sound like herself."

"It's probably a lot for her to process."

"You're right. I guess I just wanted something . . . more from her. Shock. Anger. Rage. Something." A frustrated sound escaped him. "But it's not like she's ever really reacted to his behavior before. She's always accepted it. Put up with it."

"It's hard for me to imagine that," Meghna said. "I obviously don't know her very well, but at that dinner at your house she seemed to speak her mind. Especially when your dad left early."

"Yeah. But he's always doing things like that. Leaving early. Not showing up at all. I think she only said something because you were there." He laughed humorlessly. "Not a good look for the daughter-in-law, you know? Appearances and all that."

Meghna didn't think that was the only reason. His mother didn't seem like the type to care too much about what others thought. And from the way Karthik had described her, she was quite resilient.

"I'm worried about her," he continued, somewhat quietly. "And I don't know what to do to make things better."

"I know," she said softly.

They were quiet for a moment until Karthik asked her how her work was going.

"It's going okay," she said. "The board's signed off on a larger budget for the spring play. And they've asked me to put it together."

"Of course they did," he said. "How could they not after your last success?" His praise traveled through her, warm and shimmery, sparking little bursts of pleasure. "Are you going to do it?"

"I don't know. I love the kids. And I had fun working with them, but I need to think about it a bit more. The principal's really trying to convince me, though. She said I could get more volunteer help from the parents this time so I won't have to do it all alone, and she's letting me choose the musical."

"Anything you'd want to pick?"

"I'm not sure." She hadn't really thought about it yet.

"What's your favorite?"

Ugh. Such a hard question. A few contenders came to mind, but *Fiddler on the Roof* jumped to the very top. He wasn't familiar with it, so she described the plot, and it reminded her why she loved that musical so much in the first place. It wrestled with themes that were all too familiar to her own life. Family and tradition and the conflict that came with changing ideas about marriage and love.

"I think I'd like that one," he said.

"You should go see it. Or watch the movie."

"Maybe," he said.

They talked for a few more minutes until his workout was done and he said he was leaving the gym. She expected him to hang up, but he stayed on the line as he walked back to his apartment. He continued asking her about different plays and musicals until Meghna found herself yawning and growing sleepy. She kept her phone on speaker as she got ready for bed, discussing her favorite plays and why he needed to see them. When she climbed under the covers, she placed the phone next to her pillow, keeping it in speaker mode, and they continued talking late into the night.

After that, they somehow ended up talking almost every day for the next two weeks. One time, Karthik saw someone walking down the street in a silly, punny T-shirt and just had to tell her about it. Another night, Meghna read an article about the most popular terms of endearment and called him to discuss. They still couldn't settle on ones to use for each other, but they'd laughed over the silliest ones on the list.

Over the weekend, Karthik looked up last-minute tickets for Broadway shows and went by himself to see *Les Misérables*. He called her the moment he walked out of the theater, his voice full of excitement as he described the performance as "gripping" and "gritty" and "breathtaking." As Meghna listened to him, something soft and tender swept through her. They chatted for his entire walk home about their favorite moments and songs.

He called one night after he went by his parents' house to check on his mother. They'd played a round of cards and his mother had ended up winning, like she always did. The two of them had spent a lot of weeknights in his childhood that way. After he'd left for college, his mother had joined a local group of women who played twenty-eight, the popular Indian card game. She'd only gotten better and better over the years.

Karthik had tried to press her, tried to bring up his dad, but his mother refused to give him any insight into how she was feeling. She just said everything would work out and that Karthik didn't need to worry about it. Meghna expressed her sympathy and shared his frustration that his mother still didn't seem to care about what had happened with his father at all.

Meghna called him after she finished reviewing and editing Seth's song, saying it was one of his best yet. And it truly was. She didn't know what had happened with the last one, but Seth's new song was somehow sweet without being saccharine, and reading it had honestly given her goose bumps.

Karthik said he was glad the new song was better, then asked her how her own play was going. She evaded his questions, saying she had been too busy to work on it, but he kept digging.

"Does your play have songs in it?" he asked.

"No. It's not a musical."

"You know, I've only ever seen musicals."

"Yeah. Two whole musicals," she teased.

He snorted. "Fair enough. But I should go see a play soon."

"I think you'd like it."

"But there aren't any dance numbers."

She laughed. "No. No dance numbers."

"I think I'd miss it. Being raised on Tamil movies has made me expect people to break out into song and dance every once in a while," he said.

"Hindi movies are the same way, though I never made that connection before. Maybe that's why I love musicals so much."

"Could be," he said. "You know, with all your songwriting experience, maybe you should try writing a few. You could add them to your play. Turn it into a musical."

She rolled her eyes. *Please.* "I don't really have that much songwriting experience. I mean, I've written a few things here and there, but nothing seriously."

"Come on. I don't believe that. I bet you've written half of Seth's songs. At least."

"I haven't," she said, her voice tight and tense. She didn't understand why he kept insinuating things like this. Why couldn't he understand that she and Seth were just writing partners? Providing feedback and helping each other out was just what they did. She'd never take credit for his work, just like he'd never take credit for hers.

"Sorry, I just meant you've obviously helped him a lot. He's said that too, you know."

"I guess."

He cleared his throat. "So, you're all ready for the wedding? The song's done. Your tux is finished. Is there anything else you're in charge of?"

"Not really. Honestly this best man thing is so much easier than being maid of honor. No floral arrangements or bridal shower or—"

"Or?"

"Shoot. I completely forgot about the toast."

"Well, you still have two weeks, right? That's plenty of time."

She let out a loud breath. "It seems so much sooner than that."

"I'm happy to read it after you're done or help you with it."

"Thanks, but I think that would make me a little nervous. It'll be fine. I just need to get started on it."

"Okay. I'll talk to you later, then."

Meghna paused. She hadn't meant that she'd start writing it right this second, but she might as well try to work on it some tonight. After they said their goodbyes, Meghna pulled out her laptop, but something made her click on a different folder on her desktop. One she hadn't touched in a long time. She scanned the familiar pages and thought over what Karthik had said. What if she could add songs to her play? Was there a chance the whole thing might work better as a musical? She opened a blank page, and instead of typing a speech for Seth, she tried, for the first time in years, to write a song.

K arthik had never been to Nashville before. He knew people often referred to it as "Music City," but he hadn't expected to hear live country crooning just minutes after he landed. On his way to the baggage claim, a man in one of the restaurants had sung into a microphone in a distinctive southern twang. There hadn't been a lot of people in the post-lunch, late-afternoon crowd, but the singer hadn't seemed to mind. He'd given it his all, singing with depth and emotion and intensity. Not holding anything back.

Karthik had watched him for a while, then made his way to the baggage carousel, where he now stood, waiting for his luggage.

"Hey!" a familiar voice called. Meghna walked in his direction, pulling a suitcase behind her. She greeted him with a wide smile, and it took the air right out of him. Though they had talked quite a bit over the last few weeks, he hadn't realized how much he had missed seeing her face.

The realization caught him off guard, and he struggled for a moment to breathe normally. He hadn't felt this winded since that night she'd accidentally socked him in the stomach. The thought made him want to laugh, but because he was already out of air, he was only able to wheeze.

"I'm glad we timed our flights this way," Meghna said. "Once you get your stuff, we can . . ." She stared at him. "Are you okay?"

"Yeah," he said with some difficulty. "I'm fine. Just a little out of breath. Give me a second."

Her beautiful lips twisted into a frown. "Didn't you have a problem breathing in Miami too? Do you have an inhaler? Do you need one? Maybe we should see a doctor."

Something in him rejoiced at the idea that she was concerned about him, but he shook his head. "I'm good."

He thought for a moment about telling her that *she* was the reason he was having difficulty breathing, but decided against it. She had been clear that nothing could ever happen between the two of them again. And he couldn't imagine how cheesy it would sound. *Meghna, I don't need to see a doctor. It's you. You literally take my breath away*. Ridiculous.

He snorted, and her eyes widened in concern.

"Sorry," he said. "Travel makes me a little loopy."

"And out of breath?"

"That too." He spotted his bag and pulled it off the carousel in one move.

"Are you sure you're okay?"

"Yes. Really. I'm fine. We can get going."

She nodded, somewhat skeptically, but followed his lead as they got into a cab and headed to their hotel. They had a few hours to kill until tonight's rehearsal dinner, but Karthik wasn't sure if Meghna had planned anything or if she needed to be there early.

"You think we have time for any sightseeing before tonight?"

"Sightseeing?" Her brows jumped in surprise. "You want to go sightseeing?"

"Why not? I've never been here before. Have you?"

"Yeah. A few times. To visit Seth."

Of course. "Well, if we have time, I'd like to look around. Do you have a lot to do before the rehearsal dinner?"

"Not really. I'll need some time to get dressed, but that's it. Where would you want to go?"

He shrugged. "Anywhere." He didn't care where they went. He was just hoping to spend some time with Meghna before she got swept up in the wedding festivities.

"What about the Parthenon?" Meghna asked. "It's in the same park where the wedding's taking place, and I think we could walk to it from the hotel. I've seen it from a distance, but I've never gone inside."

"Sounds great."

They arrived at the hotel and quickly checked in at the front desk.

"I booked two rooms this time," Meghna told him as they waited for their room keys. "Didn't want to repeat that mistake."

Karthik smiled tightly, even though his stomach sank. She left it unsaid, but he knew she had booked two rooms to ensure that they wouldn't repeat any other "mistakes," either.

"And there's no reason to share," she continued. "Julie's family is from here, so almost everyone's staying at her parents' place. And the rest are at a different hotel, so we won't be running into anyone we know."

"Great." He should have been happy at the news. He'd always preferred having his own space. But he'd anticipated sharing a room this weekend. Just to keep up appearances. He swallowed down his disappointment and grabbed his key.

They put their bags away in their respective rooms, then met back in the lobby to walk the short distance to Centennial Park.

Karthik shivered, pulling his coat tighter around him. The leaves in bright reds and yellows made it still feel like fall, but the crisp air and chilly breeze hinted that winter was almost here. He stuck his hand in his pocket, running his fingers across the velvet of the small box he had put there.

He'd conducted thorough research on the ring, telling himself that he was only doing it for the sake of their deal. To convince everyone that they were really engaged.

But buying the ring had been an impulsive decision. He'd stopped by a jewelry store one day after work, and the moment he saw the ring in the tray, he knew. He hadn't thought about their fake arrangement or whether it would help them pull it off. He'd only thought about Meghna. About whether she would like it. About how it would look on her hand.

"How's the preparation for the interview going?" she asked, her voice cutting through his thoughts.

"Fine," he said. "I'd collected most of the data points already, so it's just a matter of organizing them and putting it all into a presentation format. I'll have a few days to get it finalized when I get back."

He removed his hand from his pocket and cleared his throat.

"And your job?" he asked. "Have you picked out what you're going to do for the spring play?"

"I have." She walked quietly beside him for a few seconds. "But I think it's going to be my last one."

"Really?" He looked over at her in surprise.

"Yeah. I think I'm . . . Well, it was your idea, actually."

"What do you mean?"

"I took your advice and tried writing a few songs, and . . . it works, I think."

"What works?" he asked, still not understanding.

"The play I'm writing. It's working a lot better as a musical." She let out a small laugh. "I honestly haven't written like this in so long. It just feels . . . fun. And I think I want to focus on that for a while."

"You sure you won't miss rehearsing with the kids?"

"Not one bit." She laughed again. "I love them, but I never wanted to teach theater. I'm excited to see what we can put together next semester, though."

"Me too," he said.

She shot him a sideways glance.

"I mean—" He stopped. He almost took it back or tried to explain it away, but it was true. He wanted to be there in the spring. He wanted to watch them perform. From that same spot backstage. Or from the audience. Really, he just wanted to sit wherever Meghna was. Wherever she happened to be.

He took a deep breath and put his hand back in his pocket, wrapping his fingers firmly around the ring box. It suddenly seemed simple. He wanted to be wherever Meghna was. He didn't know much more than that, but he needed to tell her the truth: that somehow, without him even realizing it, this arrangement had morphed into something more. Something real. He didn't know what it would mean for their fake engagement. Or how it would work with him in New York and her in Dallas. Or if he'd be able to give her everything she wanted. But he had to tell her. And find out if she possibly felt the same way.

"We should probably talk about this," Meghna said.

Karthik's breath caught. Had she somehow read his mind?

"About what?"

"About our end date."

He halted mid-step. "What do you mean?"

"Well, you just made it sound like you'd be in Dallas in the spring." She paused beside him, glancing up quizzically. "And I don't know. I mean, this was supposed to be our end date. The wedding. Are you . . . Are you saying you want to keep this going?"

His blood raced. Was she open to that? Continuing their engagement? He swallowed. "Would you want that?" he asked.

"I . . ." She shook her head. "I don't know. I don't think so."

A sharp pain went through Karthik's chest.

"I mean, I can't keep lying to my parents about this. I've only felt okay because I knew it would be over soon." She frowned. "Has something changed? With your mom? Because if you need more time, we can talk about it, but—"

"No," he said, cutting her off. "I misspoke earlier. About Dallas.

Wasn't thinking." He gave her a strained smile. "Ending it after the wedding is fine."

They continued their walk, moving closer and closer to the Parthenon, but Karthik hardly noticed. He was hot. And sweaty. And his stomach . . . He took a deep breath, trying to ignore the twisting in his gut.

He hadn't been thinking straight. He couldn't tell Meghna how he felt. Not now. Not when he'd been thinking about how to confess his feelings and she'd been wanting to know when they could call the whole thing off.

Not that he could blame her. She was being reasonable. More than reasonable. She was sticking to their plan. Their rational agreement. He was the one who couldn't get a handle on himself.

The ring burned hot and heavy in his coat pocket. He was tempted to get rid of it, to chuck it as far as he could throw, but he curbed the childish impulse. He needed the ring. He needed to fulfill his obligations. He'd promised Meghna that he'd be her "fiancé" for this wedding, and that was exactly what he was going to do.

"I got something for you," he said, as casually as he could manage. "Just for the wedding. I'll return it after."

"Yeah?"

He pulled the small box out of his pocket, opened it quickly, and held it out in front of his body.

The blood rushed from Meghna's head.

He bought a ring? And not just any ring. A dream ring. Thin gold band. Sparkling oval diamond. She swallowed. A huge diamond.

"Is this real?" she asked, her eyes glued to the ring.

"No. Of course not."

She breathed a sigh of relief.

"Why would you ask that?" His tone was sharp. Hard.

She snapped her head up.

A strange expression crossed his face. His brows furrowed, and he almost looked . . . guilty. Like a kid who'd been caught with their hand in the cookie jar.

"I think it's a normal question," she said.

"Well, I'd never propose to you," he said forcefully.

What? She bristled. Karthik hadn't been like this around her in a really long time. He'd been almost . . . sweet. But now, it was like the past few months hadn't even happened. He was back to being brusque and unfeeling and . . . What was he even talking about?

"I mean, I'd never propose to *anyone,*" he continued. "You know that."

Her confusion faded. He'd misunderstood her question. "The ring, Karthik. I was asking about the ring."

"Oh, that." His face cleared. "Yes, that's real."

"What?" she exclaimed. "Why wouldn't you just buy something fake?"

Karthik shrugged. "I didn't think about that."

She shook her head. "I guess it doesn't matter anyway. Since you're returning it."

"I guess so."

She looked back at the ring. Honestly, it *was* perfect. Exactly what she'd pick out for herself. If this was real.

"Did you say yes?" someone yelled. Meghna looked up. A small number of people were watching them from a distance. A man pushing a stroller. College students sitting on a blanket. A runner who'd stopped to stretch.

They didn't need to perform for these strangers, but what else could she do? Shout back that none of this was real? Meghna pasted on a big smile and thrust her left hand toward Karthik.

"I did!" she said loudly.

Karthik stared at her hand like he'd never seen it before. Like he didn't know what she wanted him to do with it.

"Put the ring on my finger," she said through her teeth.

He did, his hand shaking a bit as he took the ring out of the box and slid it into place.

It fit perfectly.

Some of the college students let out a whoop, and the runner came by and offered to take their picture.

They didn't really need a picture, and honestly Meghna didn't really *want* a picture of this moment, but it felt too awkward to refuse. She handed her phone over, posed with Karthik, and took it back without even checking to see how the picture had turned out.

They continued to their destination and paid to get inside the building, but once there, she didn't enjoy any of it. She kept getting distracted by the new weight on her hand. By the way it caught the light and cast sparkles on the floor. After a few minutes, they went back to the hotel to get ready for the rehearsal dinner.

Once dressed, she pulled up the wedding website to check the address for tonight, freezing when pictures of Seth and Julie filled her screen. She dropped onto the edge of the bed. She'd remembered that Seth had proposed to Julie in that park, but now that she'd been there herself, she recognized the background of these pictures.

Seth had proposed on the steps of the Parthenon. Very close to the spot where Karthik had given her the ring.

She zoomed in. Seth knelt in front of Julie, a large grin on his face. Julie's hands were plastered against her cheeks in surprise. The light hit both of them just right, illuminating their skin, setting them aglow.

Meghna continued scrolling. Seth must have hidden some photographer right before he popped the question because all of these pictures looked professional. Like something out of a magazine. Glossy and bright and perfect.

Nothing like the sad, quick, phone-camera-quality picture she and Karthik had just taken. She left the website, pulling the picture up for the first time. The day had been cloudy, so the image had turned out a little grainy. Shadows played across their bodies. Still, it hadn't come out *that* badly. Karthik's arm was loose around her shoulders, and she leaned into him, looking directly at the camera with a decent smile.

But the expression on Karthik's face took her by surprise. His lips curved up, the gesture small but genuine. As if he was actually happy in that moment. As if he was content. But he wasn't facing the camera. His head was tilted down and to the side. He was looking at her.

She stared at the picture for several more moments. She knew it was fake. That he was just pretending. But for a second, she wished that it could all actually be real.

She imagined that moment as a real proposal. He would be awkward. With shaky hands and uncertainty. And she'd laugh, soaking up every moment. She'd probably stop him mid-speech, making him smile in relief. He'd slide the ring onto her finger and kiss her. A backbending, passionate, straight-out-of-a-movie kiss. And that same stranger would come up and take this grainy, imperfect picture. Karthik would smile down at her, just like he had then, but this smile would be real.

Meghna's phone chimed, disrupting her daydream. Karthik was downstairs waiting for her. She got off the bed, took a final look in the mirror, then went down to meet him.

Karthik pulled at his cuffs, and Meghna drank in one of her favorite sights: Karthik in a suit. He always looked impeccable. Put together in a way she never managed to be. But tonight, she felt an . . . awareness that she never had before.

His gaze tracked over her body, pausing where the ring sat on her finger.

"It looks good on you," he said.

She flushed, glancing down at the ring, then back at him. "Thanks."

They continued to the rehearsal dinner. Meghna had taken only a few steps inside when someone swept her into a hug.

"Hey, girl," the man said warmly, squeezing her tighter.

Meghna pulled herself out of the heavy arms around her and turned to see who it was. "Eric?"

"Who else?"

She laughed. "Hi. You're here early."

He checked his phone and frowned. "I'm right on time."

"Exactly. That's early for you," she teased.

He snorted, then reached a hand toward her, clearly intending to ruffle her hair in retaliation. She took a large step backward, her back bumping against Karthik's chest.

"Don't touch the curls," she said. "Seriously. You know how easily they frizz."

Karthik's arms came around her waist, pulling her firmly against him.

"I like when they frizz," Karthik said into her ear, loud enough to be overheard, making it clear he was only saying it for Eric's benefit.

Still, Meghna's face warmed as she remembered what Karthik had said back in Dallas. How he'd liked the way her hair had looked first thing in the morning. How her frizzy curls had made him imagine messing her hair up even more.

She absently touched a piece of hair, tucking it behind her ear.

"Holy hell," Eric said.

Meghna's hand froze mid-movement. "What?"

"That's some rock. You didn't have that in Miami." He moved closer, taking hold of her hand and examining the ring. "I would have remembered something like that. God, Meghna, it's huge."

"Oh, it's just . . ."

"I should have gotten something sooner," Karthik said. "But I couldn't decide for the longest time. I must have looked at over a hundred different rings before I landed on this one."

He brushed her cheek with a kiss. Her skin tingled. He turned her slightly in his arms so she could meet his eyes.

"Sorry it took so long."

"It's fine," she said softly, more confused than ever. Was anything he'd just said true? Or was it just a story for Eric?

Eric watched both of them, a large grin on his face. "So, when's the big day?"

"Oh . . . I don't . . . We haven't . . ." Meghna stammered.

"Next year," Karthik cut in smoothly. He ran one of his hands up and down Meghna's arm. "We're enjoying this phase and don't want to rush anything, right, Meghna?"

"Right. That's right."

"Well, I'm excited for it," Eric said. "I haven't been to an Indian wedding before, but I imagine the food's a lot better than what we get at these ones."

Meghna shook her head. "Of course the food's the first thing you think about."

"Obviously. What else is there? If I have to sit through another dry chicken or underdressed salad at one of these things . . ." He shuddered dramatically.

Meghna and Karthik both laughed, following him farther into the restaurant. Seth had said they were doing a small, informal rehearsal dinner with just the wedding party and family, and Meghna was happy to see that they'd stuck to that plan. The room was barely half-full, with only a few tables set for dinner.

"Welcome, everyone," a woman with a clipboard and a Britney Spears headset said. "If you're in the wedding party, please join me at the front of the room. If you're not, please find your name card and take a seat. Dinner will be served in just a moment." Meghna headed to the front, greeting Mark and the remaining groomsmen she had met at the bachelor party.

"Meghna!" a voice called out. "I'm so happy to finally meet you in person. I mean, I know we met on the phone, but it's not the same." Meghna turned around, immediately recognizing Julie from the pictures. Before she could say anything, Julie enveloped her in a warm hug. "Seth talks about you *all* the time. I feel like I know you already."

The sentiment was sweet, but Meghna's mouth tasted sour. Julie didn't know her. Not even a little bit. "It's nice to meet you too," Meghna responded. "And congratulations."

Julie smiled, her eyes bright and shining. "Thanks! I can't wait for tomorrow. Seth told me the two of you cooked up something special for the reception and I've been poking around for hints, but he hasn't shared a peep. He usually shares all of his work with me and I get to read through everything, but not this one! Also, I hope you don't mind, but I thought it would be fun for you to get ready with me and the rest of the girls tomorrow. You don't have to, of course, but we'll have someone there to do hair and makeup and there'll be a mimosa bar. It'll probably be a lot more fun than whatever the guys have planned, so please join us. I mean, only if you want."

"Of course," Meghna said. In the face of Julie's warm enthusiasm, she wasn't sure how else she could respond. At that moment, the wedding planner interrupted, separating them and maneuvering the group into pairs.

Meghna was paired to walk down the aisle with Julie's maid of honor, which was quite a relief. She'd been a little concerned about the unconventional arrangement, worried that it meant she'd have to walk alone. The idea of walking by herself down the aisle toward Seth had made her sick a month ago. She hadn't been sure if she'd even be able to do it. But for some reason, the idea didn't make her that nervous anymore.

The wedding planner instructed them about timing and made them walk through the process of going up and down the aisle. After practicing it a few times, and only messing up once due to Eric's constant jokes, the wedding planner let them go, announcing that dinner would start soon.

Before heading back to the table, Meghna approached Seth, hoping to check in and clear the air. Since receiving his last rewritten version of the song, she and Seth had only spoken a few times. She'd told him how much she liked the new song, and he'd apologized for hanging up on her. Meghna had tried not to apologize in return, but ended up doing it anyway. After that, he'd taken her notes with good grace, making several adjustments to the new song. Things seemed to be back to normal between the two of them, though Meghna wasn't sure.

"Hey, everything looks great," she said.

Seth laughed. "Thank our wedding planner. I had nothing to do with it. And nothing to do with the planning." He scanned the room, and Meghna followed his eyes, looking at the neutral-themed space, the tables covered in beige and taupe, with just a hint of dusty rose.

"Well, it turned out well," she said. "It almost looks like something out of a bridal magazine. Casual, but elegant. Rustic, but refined."

He grinned. "I'll tell Julie you said so."

"So . . . How are you feeling about tomorrow?"

"Good. Excited, I think." He lifted a shoulder. "Maybe a bit nervous?"

"I think that's normal."

"Guess you'll find out for yourself soon," he said with a laugh. "I saw Karthik made it, but I haven't gone over and said hi yet. Things all good with you two?"

"Yep. Couldn't be better," she said, lying through her teeth.

"Good, that's good." He put a hand on her shoulder. "I'm really happy you're here, Meg. You've always been someone I can lean on. And I appreciate it. Even if you sometimes are a little too harsh with me." He let out a chuckle, and Meghna frowned.

"Harsh?"

He dropped his hand and shrugged. "You know. You don't really hold back. You can be a little . . . mean at times. But don't worry. I know it comes from a good place."

Was he kidding right now? "I don't think I've been mean, Seth."

"Don't worry about it, Meg," he said with an easy smile. "I forgive you."

She didn't need his forgiveness. She hadn't done anything she needed to be forgiven for.

"If this is about the feedback I gave before, about the song . . ."

He laughed, the sound coarse and brittle. "We don't need to rehash all that. It's in the past now. You just went a little too far and . . ."

But she hadn't. She'd just been honest with him. Had given him the feedback she thought he needed. It might have been the most drastic suggestion she'd ever given him, but her advice to start from scratch had obviously worked. The song was much better than it had been before.

She was tempted to get into it, tempted to push back, to find out what he was really upset about. Seth had always been brutally honest and up-front with her, but now it was like there was a hidden meaning to his words. An extra layer she couldn't understand. She wanted to get to the bottom of it, to find out what had gone so wrong between them and see if she could fix it, but this wasn't the time or place to have that discussion. She pushed down her irritation and wrapped up their conversation, telling him she was excited to hear the song tomorrow. Then she left and joined Karthik at their table.

The groomsmen were seated near him, and Karthik laughed at something Eric had just shared with the group. She sat in the empty chair beside him, and Karthik greeted her with a rare open and relaxed face.

"There you are." He swung an arm over the back of her chair, and the casual gesture made something in her stomach flutter.

"You had a good talk with Seth?" he asked quietly.

"I did."

"He ever say sorry for hanging up on you?"

She nodded.

"Good." His hand hovered dangerously close to her bare shoulder. A ghost of a touch. His thumb barely sliding over her skin. "You ever tell him to stop calling you Meg?"

"No."

He opened his mouth and was clearly about to say something more when Mark interrupted.

"You call her Meg too?" he asked Karthik.

Karthik shook his head. "I don't."

"Oh. Sorry, I thought that's what you said."

"No, I . . . Meghna prefers to go by her whole name," Karthik said.

"Yeah, I knew that," Eric chimed in from across the table.

"You did?" Meghna asked, slightly surprised.

"That was, like, one of the first things you told me," Eric said. "Seth always called you 'Meg,' but when I met you and tried calling you that, you shut it down. I always figured it was only okay for Seth."

Mark nodded. "Me too. Thought it was some special couple thing just for the two of you."

The arm around the back of her chair went stiff.

"Special couple thing?" Karthik asked.

Oh God. Meghna wracked her brain for a way to change the subject. She wasn't interested in reliving her brief experience dating Seth back in college. Not when she was sitting here at his rehearsal dinner, just trying to get through his wedding weekend. And she especially didn't want to discuss it when she was seated next to her fake fiancé. Who didn't even know she had dated Seth at all.

But before Meghna could interrupt and change the topic, Eric answered Karthik's question.

"You know, back in college. When they dated. I mean, it wasn't that long, but they acted like a couple even before that."

Meghna smiled weakly, and Eric went off on a tangent, leading to a funny story about their college days that thankfully had very little to do with either her or Seth. She sipped her wine and hoped Karthik would be distracted by the story. But when she discreetly looked at him out of the corner of her eye, she almost choked.

His expression was neutral. Composed, in his usual manner. But his eyes were dark and intense. Laser-focused on her. They made an unspoken promise that even though they wouldn't discuss any of it now, he would definitely be bringing it up later.

Meghna swallowed nervously as all her hopes of avoiding this particular conversation vanished like smoke.

15

They dated? Karthik shouldn't have been surprised. He'd picked up on *something* strange between the two of them. But he'd never thought for a moment that Meghna would have actually dated Seth. He still had a hard time believing they were even friends.

It wasn't that she owed him this piece of information, but how had it not come up before? Was there a reason she'd want to hide it from him? A wisp of a thought crossed his brain, followed by an intense, almost nauseous feeling. He took a deep breath through his nose. He couldn't allow that thought to fully develop. He had to get through the rest of the night first.

He glanced at Meghna, who was watching him quietly, an uneasy expression on her face. His stomach rolled. He broke eye contact, pretending to listen to another of Eric's silly stories, slipping into a mode of being that was all too familiar. He nodded at the correct moments, laughed politely at others' jokes, and responded to any questions that were asked. The perfect picture of a loving and caring fiancé.

Meghna, on the other hand, wore every emotion on her sleeve.

When the dinner came to an end, the panic that flashed across her face was unmistakable. Karthik's heart jumped in his throat, but he maintained a cool demeanor as they said their goodbyes and went back to the hotel. At the point where they needed to part ways for their separate rooms, Meghna attempted to say good night.

Karthik cut her off. "I'm just going to change into something more comfortable. But we need to talk."

"Oh. I don't know if that's really necessary. I think we can—"

"It's necessary. Your room or mine?"

"Umm. Mine's okay. We can—"

"Great."

He turned on his heel and entered his room, waiting until he'd brushed his teeth, washed his face, and changed into sweats and a T-shirt before allowing himself to think and feel what he'd started to at dinner.

God. It wasn't possible, was it? That she still had feelings for Seth?

The sickening feeling from earlier returned. He didn't want to think it was true, but if it was, it would explain so many of the questions he had about Meghna's odd friendship with Seth.

Like why she put up with his rude comments and feedback. Why she helped him, over and over again, even when she got nothing in return. Why she made herself available for his every phone call and thought he was a "real creative genius." Why she tolerated him calling her a nickname she hated.

He crossed the hallway in a bit of a daze. He must have knocked on Meghna's door, because suddenly she was there, inviting him inside.

"What, um, what did you want to talk about?" she asked, her voice slightly higher than normal.

"You know what." He looked around the room. He didn't want to stand here awkwardly while they talked about this. He moved an armchair from the corner so that it faced one side of the bed and gestured for her to sit. She hesitantly perched on the edge of the bed while he took the chair.

"You and Seth used to date," he said evenly.

"Uh, yes. Years ago. And not for that long."

"Okay." He nodded, but he knew that wasn't the entire story. If it was, she wouldn't be this nervous. And he wouldn't feel this sick to his stomach.

"We've talked about him a lot, but you've never mentioned it." He exhaled loudly. "Was there a reason?"

She shifted on the bed. "A reason?"

"A reason you never brought it up."

Meghna looked away, but didn't respond.

He waited. If there was one thing he was sure about, it was that Meghna wouldn't lie to him. If the relationship had been so insignificant that it had slipped her mind, she would say that. Or maybe it had been so long ago that it wasn't worth mentioning. Or it had been just a silly college fling. Or they had realized they were just good friends and it hadn't been a real relationship after all. Or she didn't even think about Seth that way anymore, so it wasn't worth bringing up.

He waited for her to say something. To give one of the many explanations running through his mind. But she stayed quiet.

That sick, worried feeling faded away, and something hot and angry took its place. It coursed through his veins, raising his body temperature, increasing his pulse. He got up from the chair and started talking before he even realized it.

"He's a dick."

Meghna's jaw dropped. "What?"

"He is. And you know it too. He's constantly ignoring you. And when he's not, he's putting you down."

"That's not true."

He scoffed. "Please. When's the last time the two of you talked about something *you* needed? I bet he still hasn't given you feedback on that piece you sent him months ago."

Her eyes blazed with emotion, but she didn't respond.

"He hasn't, has he?"

"He's been busy."

"Right. And you aren't? You've made time for *him*."

"It's not the same."

"Why?"

"Because it's not," she said loudly, getting up from her spot on the bed. "You don't know the first thing about him."

"Oh? Enlighten me, then." He took a few steps toward her. "Is it because he's such a genius? That's why I couldn't possibly understand? That's why he deserves all your time and effort and work?"

"He *is* good at what he does. Why is that so hard to believe? You said you *liked* his songs."

"Yeah. I did. Because you basically wrote them."

She pointed angrily at him, almost poking him in the chest. "You don't know what you're talking about."

"Really? I don't?" He let out a humorless laugh. "I know more than you think."

"Like what?"

"Like why you're still writing that same play from college. Why you haven't moved on to anything else. He's convinced you that it's not good enough. That *you're* not good enough. And you're willing to believe it."

"You haven't even read it!"

"I would if you let me. But I don't have to. I know you. I've seen your work. I know it's good."

A flicker of doubt crossed her face before her expression hardened. "You don't know me. You don't know anything about me."

"Oh, and Seth does?"

"Yes. He does. And he—"

"He's using you!" he nearly shouted. "He wants you around to pump his ego, to fix his work, to make it better. But what has he given you in return?"

"You're wrong. You couldn't be more wrong. He's supportive and encouraging and . . ."

"He doesn't love you. He's getting married to someone else!"

Meghna inhaled sharply, letting her breath out in an angry huff. "I know that! Don't you think I know that?" She marched even closer. "Why else would I have agreed to this? Why else would I have brought *you*?"

The words were like a dagger to his throat. He almost choked on them, but he managed to spit out a response.

"That's why you agreed to this? That's why you said yes?"

"I told you that. I told you I needed a plus-one to a wedding."

"Yeah, but you didn't tell me that you were *in love with the groom*!"

Meghna's eyes widened, but she didn't deny it. She didn't say anything. She just stood there in front of him, her chest rising and falling rapidly, her eyes bright and furious, her hand clenched into a fist against her side. Almost as if she was preparing to hit him square across the jaw.

His chest tightened.

"You need to leave," she said quietly.

Immediately, like a balloon pricked by a needle, his anger deflated. Remorse, swift and cool and heady, rushed through him. What had he been thinking? He hadn't lost control like this in . . . in years.

"I'm sorry," he said. "I'm sorry."

"For what?" she asked bitingly.

"I shouldn't have raised my voice. Or gotten angry."

"But you're not sorry about what you said."

He wasn't. He had meant every word. Seth was a dick. Anyone who didn't value Meghna was a dick. And he wouldn't apologize for saying that.

He shook his head slowly. "I'm not."

Hurt flashed in her eyes. She took a step back from him. "Then you need to go."

He wanted to stay. He wanted to take back the last few minutes and try it all again. He wanted to tell her that he admired her. That she was talented. And hardworking. And smart. And that she deserved someone who saw all of that. Who saw all of the wonderful things that made her *her*. And that person wasn't Seth. He didn't deserve an ounce of her time. Her attention. Her love.

"I'm sorry," he said again, even though he knew the words weren't enough. There was nothing he could say that would repair the damage he'd done. He walked out the door, and the last thing he saw before it swung shut in his face was Meghna's crumpled expression, her eyes shining with unshed tears.

16

The next morning, Meghna sat patiently as her hair was clamped, pulled, and stretched through a curling iron. She watched in the mirror as the stylist picked up a newly formed curl, turning and twisting it into place. Meghna flinched when yet another bobby pin slid uncomfortably against her scalp.

"Sorry," the stylist said, her voice muffled by the bobby pins between her teeth. "Almost done."

Meghna thanked her, sneaking a peek at the other bridesmaids. All of them were ready and dressed and once Meghna was done, Julie would be the only one left. Though the whole experience could have been awkward, Julie and her friends had welcomed Meghna into the fold, asking her questions about what Seth was like in college, begging for information about the special song he had been working on, and sharing funny stories about their dating lives.

"My lips are sealed," she said when Beth, the maid of honor, asked again for a hint about the song. "I don't want to ruin the surprise."

Julie laughed. "I'm sorry they're bothering you so much about it. But it's shocking that Seth has managed to keep this a secret for so long! He always shows me what he's working on. It's like he can't help it."

"He doesn't just *show* them to you," Beth said. "Remember when he played 'Angel in Red' for us? You told him to change the whole second verse and he listened to you. He basically rewrote it because you said so."

"Not at all," Julie said, waving a hand dismissively. "I just suggested moving it to the end. The real difference happened when he made that key change."

Meghna froze.

"And when he added that new chorus, remember?" Beth added.

"Oh, yeah. That line about how 'her words are like poison and I'm drunk on her lies'? I love that one. I met this girl at the studio the other day and she'd gotten it tattooed on her arm. I took a picture for Seth and he couldn't believe it."

Goose bumps prickled on the back of Meghna's neck. That was *her* line. They were talking about her line. And the key change? That had been her suggestion too.

"Did you . . ." Meghna's voice came out high and squeaky. She cleared her throat. "Did you help him with that second verse at all? The one you told him to change?"

Julie flushed with pleasure. "Did he mention that to you? That's so nice. I mean, we were just messing around with it. I ad-libbed a few lines while he played it and he ended up using a few of them."

Meghna swallowed. He'd never mentioned that. Meghna had seen several drafts of the song. And though the second verse had changed a lot, he'd never said that Julie had helped him with it. He'd let Meghna think those changes were all his.

And the changes Meghna had made? She'd offered those freely. As his writing partner. As his friend. She'd known that the songs were his at the end of the day, but she hadn't realized that he had pretended he'd come up with *everything* on his own. That he'd lied about all the help Meghna had given him. That he'd taken credit for Julie's words.

A lick of anger shot up her spine.

"Julie, can I talk to you for a second? Outside?" The words were out before Meghna could reel them back in.

Julie's eyes lit with surprise. "Yeah, um, sure."

Meghna followed her out of the room, down a hallway. She took a deep breath, trying to calm herself down. She was so angry. At Seth. At Karthik. At herself.

Karthik had been right. Seth *had* been taking advantage of her. He hadn't looked at her own writing for months. And he expected too much from her. Expected that she'd drop everything to answer his questions, take his calls, provide feedback. Their writing partnership had somehow become all about him. Part of her had known that, but it had happened so slowly. She hadn't been able to fully accept it. Especially because . . . it was Seth.

Seth, who'd read her work and encouraged her when no one else would. Who'd listened to her. Who'd made her feel seen and valued. Who'd broken her heart.

And now Karthik knew that too. Her face heated as she remembered the way he had thrown that accusation at her. Like a grenade. And at the time, she hadn't known how to respond. She wasn't sure whether she had ever really been in love with Seth. This . . . this couldn't possibly be love. But she had felt *something* for him, and knowing that Karthik had figured that out . . . She wanted to sink into the floor.

Julie raised an eyebrow, and Meghna hesitated. She didn't want to mess things up for Julie. Not on her wedding day. Maybe she had wanted that a few months ago. Had secretly hoped that the wedding wouldn't happen. But she didn't want that anymore. Meghna faltered for a moment, wondering if she should even bring any of this up. But if she didn't say it now, it'd be too late. Julie was set to marry Seth in a few hours, and she deserved to know the truth before then. She deserved to go into the relationship with her eyes wide open. To not be strung along or used for her talent.

"Julie," she started. "That song you were talking about? I saw what the second verse looked like before. It was . . . It was completely different. If you made those changes, I think you deserve songwriting credit."

Julie laughed lightly. "That's so sweet, but really the lines I gave Seth were lines I cut out of one of my own songs. Lines I hadn't planned on using anyway. I'm glad they worked for him, but it wasn't a big deal."

A sneaking suspicion crept through Meghna's mind. "Did you do that on other songs?"

"Yeah, some. But I mean, Seth's helped me with my music too. He always listens to my stuff and tells me what's working and what's not."

"But Julie, that's not the . . . If you've been writing parts of . . ." Meghna stopped, taking a deep breath. "Those lines you were talking about? Back there? Those lines from 'Angel in Red'? I wrote them."

Shock splashed across Julie's face.

"I know you may not believe me or think I'm just making it up, but . . . I texted those lines to Seth. I meant for them to just be a suggestion. I didn't think he'd actually use them. Though when he did, I mean, it wasn't that surprising. He'd done it before. And it was just a couple lines. He always made it seem like it was no big deal because the rest of the song was his. But if you've been . . . If some of this has been yours . . ."

"Not on that song, but . . ." She bit her lip. "Did you do anything on 'Eyes on You'?"

"Some work on the bridge."

Julie's mouth dropped open. "Me too! He told me he wanted to change the rhyme structure. So, I helped him rewrite it. Except for the last line, but that must have been . . ."

Meghna nodded. "That was mine."

"He never said . . . He never said anything about you writing any of it. I mean, I knew you were writing partners. Seth's always said how thankful he is for you and that you've helped him so much, but he never said . . ." Julie trailed off, her eyes blank and unfocused.

Meghna's mind whirred, pieces of lyrics running through her head. How many of the words she'd once attributed to Seth's "genius" had really come from Julie? How many times had Seth lied to her? Taken credit for something that wasn't his?

Anger churned low and heavy in her gut. She wanted to go find Seth. Confront him. Ask him how he could do this. She almost suggested it, but when she saw the expression on Julie's face, the words died in her throat.

Julie looked so lost, her gaze distant. There was a tiny tremble in her lower lip.

"What do you want to do?" Meghna asked gently. Even though she knew exactly how she wanted to handle things, she wasn't the only one wronged here. And this was still Julie's wedding day.

"I don't know," Julie whispered.

"Okay. That's okay." Julie needed more time. And so did she. Meghna could get in Seth's face and have it out, but then what? She needed to think things through. What could she ask for? And how could she hold him accountable? She needed to make a plan.

"Why don't you finish getting dressed? I'll try to figure something out, but I won't say anything to Seth until you're ready, okay? Want to meet downstairs in an hour?"

Julie sniffed, but nodded, offering a small, sad smile. Then she left, heading back to finish her hair and makeup. And put on her wedding dress.

"Meg, you all done?"

Meghna blinked, looking at the man standing in front of her. The man she'd thought she'd known so well. She blinked again. It was like there were two of them. Seth as he was now, and a holographic image flickering on top of him. The perfect Seth she'd created in her head.

The one who listened to her. And supported her writing. The person she had thought she was supposed to end up with.

And what hurt the most was that she hadn't entirely made that version of Seth up. At one point, Seth really had been her friend. Whenever she'd been tempted to give up on her play, to give up on writing once and for all, he'd encouraged her. Whenever she'd doubted herself, he'd told her how much he believed in her, how talented she was, how one day she'd succeed. At one point, he'd really cared for her. Maybe not in the way she'd wanted, maybe not in the way she'd cared for him, but there had once been something real between them.

Sure, he'd been blunt. And he'd always had a bit of an ego, what she'd once thought was confidence but now recognized as pride. But that Seth never would have claimed someone else's words as his own. Never would have claimed *her* words as his own. Somewhere along the way, he'd changed. Maybe it had happened when he'd gotten a taste of stardom. Or when he'd felt the pressure to keep producing hits, to keep staying on top. Either way, she didn't know who he was anymore.

Loss swept through her as the image of the old Seth flickered once more, then went out entirely. Leaving the real him behind.

"All done getting ready, I mean," he said.

"Yeah, I'm done." She smoothed her hands down the front of her tux. "The rest of the girls are still in there, though."

He invited her into the room designated for the groomsmen, and the next hour passed quickly. A fast catered lunch. Posing for photographs. A quick pep talk from Eric to calm Seth's nerves. A thankful round of hugs that Seth gave all of them afterward.

Meghna flinched the second his arms came around her, but tried to hide it. She smiled and joked with everyone while keeping one eye on her phone. Time was almost up.

She slipped out of the room, heading downstairs, relieved to see Julie was already there. At least she hadn't changed her mind about meeting.

Julie waved, the lace of her dress rustling as she moved. From the firm lift of her chin and the color of her cheeks, she appeared to be in better spirits than earlier.

"I talked to my manager," Julie said. "And my lawyer. To figure out what we can do."

Meghna nodded. In between groomsmen activities, she'd been able to squeeze in some research of her own too. "What did they say?"

"That I have options. That *we* have options." Julie blew out a breath. "They both said I don't have to go through with the wedding if I don't want to, but they made it clear we'd take a pretty big hit if I walked away. 'Runaway bride' may make headlines, but they both assured me that it's not the kind of publicity I want." She sighed. "But I don't know if I can get married to Seth right now, either. I'm not even sure I want to *be* married to him anymore."

Meghna could understand that. If she was in Julie's shoes, she certainly wouldn't want to go through with this wedding, but she also knew how tough this industry could be. How difficult it was to break through and how quickly you could lose it all. Julie had worked so hard on her music and was finally starting to taste success. Meghna could understand why she wasn't ready to let that all slip away.

"Whatever you decide," she told Julie. "Whatever you need, I'll support you."

"Thanks," Julie replied, her forehead creasing with worry. "It's just . . . The idea of being married to Seth, the idea of being stuck with him *forever* . . ."

"It doesn't have to be forever," Meghna said, an idea sparking. "It could be temporary. You could wait it out for a while, then end things."

"I guess."

"And if he doesn't meet the terms you want, the terms you *demand*, you could go public with everything. Tell everyone the truth."

Julie tilted her head. "That . . . That's a really good idea."

The two of them discussed the remaining details, pooling together the information they'd gathered and coordinating a plan.

"So, when should we do this?" Meghna asked a moment later.

"How about now?"

Meghna's eyebrows jumped. She'd hoped they could confront Seth before the wedding, but hadn't imagined that Julie would agree. "I'm fine with that, but . . . Are you sure?"

Julie nodded, already tapping away at her phone. "Absolutely. The sooner we get this over with, the better. I don't think I could stand up there and exchange vows in front of everyone without getting this out first."

A ping sounded a few seconds later, and Julie looked up with a tight smile. "He's on his way."

The sound of heavy footsteps reached them first, then Seth appeared, walking so quickly that his blond hair flapped around him.

"Are you okay?" he asked, looking only at Julie. "Did something happen?"

Julie crossed her arms. "I'm okay. I'm not sure about you."

He took a step back. "What do you mean?"

Julie's eyes glittered, and her face was cold and hard. "Meghna and I were talking earlier. Comparing notes. About your songs."

Seth paled.

"It seems like the two of us may have accidentally co-written a song or two," Julie continued. "Maybe more."

Seth let out a weak laugh, his eyes bouncing between Meghna and Julie. "I think that's overstating things. I mean, you and Meg have both helped me. A lot. But I hardly think—"

"You want to know what I think?" Julie interrupted. "I think if we look back through your emails, we'll find that many of your words came from one of us." She lifted a shoulder casually. "And maybe some other people too."

Guilt flashed across Seth's face, and Meghna realized Julie's guess had been right on the mark.

Julie wilted, her hard expression fading away. "You know, I was going to try to give you the benefit of the doubt. I *wanted* to give you the benefit of the doubt. But—" She shook her head, watching him with a sad, resigned expression.

"Are you . . ." Seth stopped, swallowing nervously. "Are you calling off the wedding?"

Julie laughed, but the sound was hollow. "No, my whole family is here. And my career just started taking off. I can't afford a scandal."

"Oh, thank God. Julie, I love you and—"

Meghna resisted the urge to roll her eyes. Maybe he did love Julie. Maybe he really had meant it when he said Meghna was his best friend. But he had a funny way of showing it.

"I've just been under so much pressure," Seth continued. "Under so much stress. You wouldn't believe it. My agent and the label . . . They expect a lot from me. They basically told me that if I don't send out a song a month, people will forget who I am. And I tried at first. I really tried to keep up, but I couldn't, and then . . . Well, you both were there for me. Supporting me. And . . . you have to understand the position I was in. But it all stops now. I promise. It was just a temporary thing, and—"

Julie held up her hand, stopping him mid-sentence. "I called my lawyer. Here's what's going to happen." She took a deep breath. "You're going to marry me. With a smile on your face. And then you're going to give me and Meghna songwriting credit on every song we contributed to."

"And back pay," Meghna added. "We deserve to be paid retroactively. For all the time we didn't have credit."

Julie nodded in her direction. "Yes. And back pay. Then *after* you've done all that, maybe I won't divorce you."

Seth's eyes widened.

"But we'll have to see," Julie continued. "And if you don't make things right, I'm going public with this story. I'll sue. A divorce may land me in the tabloids and get me some negative press, but suing a man for stealing my words? I think fans will understand that. And stand by me. After all, they stood by Taylor Swift."

Seth's eyebrows knit. "Actually, that's not exactly what happened with her—"

"Close enough," Julie interrupted, and Seth's mouth snapped closed. "Meghna, anything else you want to add?"

Meghna turned toward Seth. He looked at the floor, unable to meet her eyes.

There was so much she wanted to say. That she'd trusted him. Opened herself up. Shared her words and her time and her attention and her love. And he hadn't deserved a single second of it. She'd put him first over and over. Believed him when he belittled her. And he'd barely given anything in return. Instead, he'd taken from her. Even now, he wasn't sorry. He hadn't apologized once.

But she struggled for a moment, unsure how to phrase it. How to put it all into words. At her silence, Seth darted a glance her way. A bit of hope was etched across his face. As if he expected her to back down. To forgive him. To take his side. Again.

Pure rage, all fiery and hot and fierce, swept through her. "You're a dick, Seth. You're a liar and a fraud and I only wish I'd realized it sooner."

"Meg—"

"No. That's not my name and that's the last time you ever call me that." She shook her head. "I should have told you that a long time ago. Back when we were actually friends. Back when you were actually there for me. Back when you valued what I thought and felt and said. But that hasn't been true for a long time. After tonight, I don't want to see you. I don't want to hear from you. No more texts or emails or phone calls. We're not writing partners. We're not friends. We're nothing."

Seth's face fell, and Julie clapped her hands together, watching Meghna with approval. "Well said. So, Seth, just to confirm, you agree to our terms?"

He nodded slowly, reluctantly, just as Julie's phone beeped. She glanced down, then grimaced. "It's the wedding planner. It's time to go."

They left for the venue, and though Seth seemed subdued, no one commented. The rest of the wedding party probably thought it was normal for the groom to have some nerves right about now. Eric clapped him once on the back, then they all separated as the wedding planner lined them up, pairing them off just as she had the night before.

The music started, and Meghna briefly closed her eyes. She'd been dreading this day for so long. But now, as she walked down the aisle with Julie's maid of honor beside her, she didn't feel jealous. Or sad. She was . . . thankful. Thankful that she'd learned the truth. That she wasn't the one marrying him today. That she was finally able to let him go.

She was almost halfway to him, his blond hair shining, his too-white teeth stretched into a wide smile. She looked away, searching the crowd on either side of the aisle. She couldn't see him, but Karthik was sitting out there. Somewhere. She reached the end of the aisle, and Seth's smile fell slightly as she moved to stand beside him.

She ignored him, scanning the room again, trying to find Karthik. Yes, he owed her an apology. And she was still angry about the way he'd spoken to her last night. But at the moment she just wanted to see his face. She wanted to know that he was there. That at the end of this whole ordeal, he'd be waiting for her. And they'd talk through things and everything would go back to the way it had been.

She stopped, frozen at her last thought. She *wanted* things to go back to the way they had been. She wanted him to call her when he saw a new musical and she wanted to tease him when he got too serious. She wanted to wake up to Bombay toast in the kitchen and hear how things were going with his family. She wanted him at her friends' parties and her middle school plays.

Really, she just wanted him.

The music changed, and everyone stood up, turning to face the entrance. To watch the bride appear. Meghna looked at the crowd again, but now Karthik was easy to spot. He was the only one half turned, his body at an odd angle. The only one not looking for Julie. The only one looking right at Meghna.

Meghna's heart pounded. She had been lying to herself. She didn't just want things to go back to the way they had been. She wanted more. She wanted to kiss him whenever she wanted. She wanted to introduce him to others as *hers* and have it actually be true. She wanted . . . She wanted their relationship to be real.

Julie walked down the aisle, and the crowd pivoted, turning to follow her progress. And though Karthik moved in time with everyone else, his eyes never left Meghna's.

His face was neutral, composed, and a bit tense. But his eyes were soft. Apologetic. Tender.

The ceremony started, and Meghna broke eye contact, looking at the couple in front of her. And though she pretended to watch it all happen, she barely heard a word of it.

Maybe Karthik never wanted to get married. Maybe any future between the two of them was impossible. But that look in his eyes had been real. He felt something for her. And she had feelings for him too.

She'd tried to prevent it from happening. She'd put up boundaries. Tried to keep him at a distance. Tried to remind herself that it was all fake. But the truth was, she'd been falling for him for a long time.

Her eyes welled with emotion, and she forced herself to blink the tears away.

She was tempted to look back at Karthik. She was tempted to tell him everything. She knew it was a bit of a gamble. She might have misread that look. She might have been the only one to develop feelings. But it felt like a risk worth taking if it meant there was even the tiniest chance that what she had with Karthik could be real.

The officiant's voice, loud and booming, shook her from her thoughts. And Meghna forced herself to smile, still blinking away a few tears, as Seth and Julie kissed and were pronounced husband and wife.

. . .

For the second time in the last twenty-four hours, Karthik watched Meghna's eyes fill with tears. The sight had been a punch to the gut last night, but it felt even worse now. Because these tears meant that he had been right.

Meghna was in love with Seth.

Karthik's eyes had been trained on her from the very beginning of the ceremony. She'd met his gaze at first, then looked away, watching the happy couple. She'd had a faraway look on her face, as if she'd been thinking about something else, trying to distract herself from what was going on. And then at the end, she'd put on a smile. But he'd seen the truth. Her eyes had been glistening, and she'd blinked repeatedly, as if she was trying not to cry.

His stomach twisted.

The bride and groom walked back up the aisle, and the wedding procession, including Meghna, followed. Finally, it was over. He left with the other guests, moving with the general flow of the crowd from the outdoor ceremony space to the tent that had been set up for the reception. Drinks and little hors d'oeuvres passed by on small trays, and he blindly grabbed the first thing that came his way.

He found a corner and hovered there. For a moment, he thought about leaving. He wasn't sure he could play the loving fiancé now. It felt too close to the truth. Too painful.

But he'd made a promise to her, and he would keep it. He took a sip of his drink. It was bubbly and crisp and light. It wasn't at all what he wanted. It wasn't at all how he felt.

He never should have allowed himself to think that Meghna might care for him. How could she? Especially after the way he'd hurt her last night. After he'd lost his temper. He couldn't get the image of her face out of his mind. The way it had crumpled up. The way she had looked at him. As if she couldn't believe he had hurt her that way.

He'd made a mistake. He'd imagined for a second that things

could be different. That *he* could be different. But last night had proven that wasn't the case. He'd lost control. He'd lashed out at her. He'd acted like an ass. He'd acted just like . . . just like his father.

Karthik set his glass down firmly. It wouldn't have mattered if she was in love with Seth or not. Seth was just an easy target. A place Karthik could throw all the blame. The real issue was with himself.

He wasn't good for her. And neither was Seth, but someday she'd meet the right person. Someone who could love her. Someone who could be the kind of partner she dreamed about. Who could give her the kind of marriage she wanted. Someone who wouldn't hurt her the way he had. Karthik couldn't hold her back from that. And that's all a relationship with him would be doing.

He took one last sip and made up his mind. His promise to Meghna would be over once he got through tonight. And then he would let her go. For good.

"Hey!" Meghna called as she approached his little corner of the room. Her eyes were bright, and her smile stretched wide across her face. If he didn't know better, he would have thought she was happy.

She put a hand on his arm. "I've been looking everywhere for you. I have something I need to tell you."

He tensed, sure he was about to be chewed out for his behavior yesterday.

"Me too," he said before she could continue. "I need to apologize. I shouldn't have spoken to you like that last night. I was angry and I took it out on you. I know you know Seth better than I do, and I had concerns about him, but I shouldn't have brought them up that way. I didn't mean to hurt you and I'm very sorry that I did. I . . . I never want to hurt you. I never want to do *anything* that hurts you."

It was why he needed to end this. If he tried to make things work with her, it was only a matter of time before he hurt her again.

Her hand slid down his arm to grasp his hand.

"I know that," she said. "I was so angry at you, and we'll need to talk about this more, but those things you said about Seth? They're things I've known for a while, but I just refused to acknowledge them. Refused to deal with them."

Right. Because you love him. He winced at the thought.

"And I know that I need to," she continued. "And, well, thanks to Julie, I think I'm starting to. But that's a much longer story. Right now, I need to tell you that—"

"Hey, guys," Mark said as he and Eric joined them. "Nice ceremony, wasn't it?"

"Sure," Eric said. "But I'm ready to eat."

Meghna gave a nervous laugh. "I'm not."

"Right," Eric said, wagging his eyebrows. "Dinner means we're getting closer to your big speech."

Karthik squeezed Meghna's hand. "You're going to do great," he told her.

"Thanks," she replied softly.

He smiled at her, and she smiled in return.

"You guys are unbelievably cute," Eric said. "It's honestly annoying."

Mark laughed. "You need to set Eric up with someone," he told Meghna. "He's been whining all weekend about how he's so tired of showing up to these weddings alone."

"Why don't you set him up with someone?" she asked Mark.

"Please," Eric said. "The last time he tried to do that, he ended up dating her instead."

"It didn't exactly happen that way," Mark said indignantly.

"It totally did," Eric said. "Karthik, what about you? Do you know anybody?"

Karthik shook his head. Out of all of Seth's groomsmen, he liked Eric the best. He wished he knew someone who could match Eric's laid-back energy. Someone who'd enjoy his sense of humor. But no one came to mind.

"No, sorry," he said.

Eric sighed. "It's fine. I'll just be alone forever."

They all laughed, but were interrupted by an announcement that dinner would be served soon. They found their seats, and the meal started with a plate of leafy greens.

Eric took a bite and grimaced.

"What did I say about underdressed salads?" he whispered under his breath, and Karthik chuckled in response.

"You know," Eric said a few seconds later. "I've been meaning to ask you, what's the job market like in New York?"

Karthik frowned. "I'm happy to share anything I know, but I don't know much about the music industry—"

"I don't work in music."

"You don't?"

"No. That's just Seth. I'm an engineer." Eric paused. "Did Meghna not mention that? She's the one who told me to talk to you."

Huh. She'd never brought it up to Karthik. "What field are you in?"

"Biomedical."

Karthik jolted as he felt an unexpected stab of jealousy. Paul had been providing regular updates on the robotics project the biomedical team was working on, and though Karthik had feigned disinterest at first, he hadn't been able to resist the temptation to check it out himself. The robotic arm was impressive. Stunning. And for a second, he had let himself imagine how exciting, how fulfilling, working on a project like that must be.

But those kinds of thoughts were pointless. He would never work in a field so close to his father's.

"We have a great biomedical department at my company," Karthik said. "I can put you in touch with someone."

"That would be great." Eric smiled. "Thanks."

They turned back to their meal, but as the dinner continued, Meghna grew more and more agitated. She fidgeted in her seat and twisted her napkin in her lap until Karthik placed his hand over hers.

"Are you nervous?" he asked quietly.

"Yeah."

"About the speech?"

She swallowed. "Yeah, the speech. But also . . ."

"Also?"

She shook her head. "It's nothing. We'll talk about it later." She flashed a wan smile, then turned to finish her dinner.

He ate the rest of his meal absentmindedly, distracted as he counted down the hours remaining. The night was passing too quickly. Soon their fake engagement would be over. He imagined she'd be relieved. Once Seth's wedding was done, there would be no reason for her to lie to her parents anymore. But for him . . . He looked over at Meghna. This was likely the last meal they'd ever share. The last time he'd sit next to her like this. The last time he'd get to pretend that she was actually his.

The clinking sound of a spoon hitting glass interrupted his thoughts. He squeezed Meghna's hand one more time, and she squeezed back before straightening in her chair. It was time for the toasts.

M eghna stood up, the words from her carefully prepared speech running through her mind. She'd committed it to memory and fully intended to use her theater experience to deliver it. It was perfect. The right blend of humor and sincerity. But none of it seemed right anymore. She caught a glimpse of the "happy couple," and some of the tightness in her chest eased at the encouraging look on Julie's face. Meghna scrapped the speech and just started talking.

"Seth and Julie are an incredible couple," she said. "And being around them, witnessing their relationship, has taught me so much. I used to think that love was about the butterflies. That swooping feeling you get in your stomach. The way your heart floats the first time you see 'the one.' But we all know that those feelings can fade. Sometimes people aren't who you thought they were. Sometimes first impressions are wrong.

"These days, I'm more interested in the quiet kind of love. The kind that takes time. And effort. And patience. The kind that sneaks up on you. Slowly. It builds and builds until you suddenly realize that *this* is the person you want to turn to when things get bad. *This* is the person you want to call when you get good news. They're the one you want to share every high and low with. Even when they frustrate you. Or confuse you. Even when they're nothing like the person you thought you were supposed to end up with. They probably challenge you in ways you never wanted. Or change the way you look at certain things. They might even be the only person in your life who calls you on your shit." She paused as a few couples chuckled, exchanging knowing glances with each other. "And maybe you get angry about it at first. Or defensive. But they so often end up being right in the end. Because they know you. The *real* you. Better than anyone else."

She lifted her drink, turning to face the bride and groom. "So, let's raise a glass to Seth and Julie. Seth, I think we all know you've found that person in Julie. And Julie, I hope you never stop calling Seth on his shit."

The room laughed, and the sound of clinking glasses filled the air. Julie raised her champagne flute toward Meghna, giving her a wide smile and a conspiratorial wink before knocking her glass meaningfully against Seth's. He let out a laugh, but there was a glint of fear in his eyes as he looked at his new wife. It was clear that he'd gotten the message.

She sat back down, and as Julie's maid of honor started her speech, Meghna allowed her thoughts to wander. Though her toast was finished, she had a much more nerve-wracking talk ahead of her. She peeked at Karthik. He was politely listening to the maid of honor, and Meghna took advantage of his distraction, running her eyes over him appreciatively.

He looked . . . dapper. There wasn't any other word for it. With his crisp lines, clipped words, and composed expressions, he appeared almost out of time. Like he'd stepped out of a black-and-white movie. A classy, solemn leading man.

Meghna's hands itched with the urge to run her fingers through that perfect hair. She just wanted to shake him up. Disorient him until she saw a hint of the relaxed Karthik that hid under the surface. Sure, he seemed chic and poised, but he was a pressure cooker, and she wanted to see him let off a little steam. Maybe help him let off a little steam.

A mischievous thought struck her, and she slid her foot out of her shoe, running her toes up the side of his shin.

Karthik jumped, looking over at her with surprise. Meghna hid a smile, smoothing her expression, trying to look as innocent as possible. *Play with me,* she tried to telepathically communicate. She gave him a quick wink to drive the point home.

His brow furrowed in confusion, and a sting of disappointment singed Meghna as he turned away from her and continued listening to the end of the toast. Everyone clinked their glasses for the last time, and Meghna lifted hers toward Karthik.

He raised his glass in return, tapping it against hers, but for some reason he wouldn't meet her gaze. His eyes bounced around, looking anywhere but at her. The disappointment in her stomach grew, but she tried to shrug it off.

"You know you're supposed to make eye contact when cheersing," she told him teasingly.

"Hmm," he replied.

"'Cheersing' is not a word," Eric cut in from across the table.

"Well, it should be," Meghna said. "What would you call it?"

"Oh, I don't know. How about toasting?"

Meghna rolled her eyes. Eric replied by sticking his tongue out at her.

"All right, children. That's enough. But for the record, she's right," Mark said to Karthik. "You're supposed to make eye contact."

"Otherwise it's seven years of bad luck," Meghna said.

"No, it's seven years of bad sex," Mark said.

"So that explains it," Eric muttered loudly.

Meghna laughed, but stopped quickly when Karthik didn't join in. He sat very still with no sign of amusement on his face.

She waited for the conversation to shift to another topic, then dropped her voice.

"Hey, is something wrong?"

Surprise and a touch of guilt crossed his face. "No. Nothing's wrong," he said quickly.

Meghna frowned. "Is this about last night? Because really, it's okay. And I—"

"Do you want to dance?" he asked.

Meghna looked at the dance floor. "Right now?" Seth and Julie were still in the middle of their first dance.

"No. Later. Whenever."

"Umm. Sure. But are you sure you're okay? Because you seem—"

"I'm fine," he said curtly.

The hair on the back of Meghna's neck stood up straight. Something was definitely wrong.

"I think we should talk about whatever's bothering you," she said quietly. "Did you get some news about your parents?"

"No. It's nothing like that."

"Then what is it?"

Applause broke out as Seth and Julie's first dance ended, and Meghna instinctively clapped her hands together. A voice invited everyone onto the dance floor, and Karthik stood up, extending his hand to her.

"You coming?"

She got up, lifting her head so she could look him straight in the eye. "Not until you tell me what's going on."

"Nothing's going on."

"I don't believe that."

He didn't say anything in response. He just stood there. Stubbornly. His hand was still in front of his body, palm up.

"Fine," she said. She put her hand in his. "We'll dance, but we need to talk later."

He led her past the tables to the edge of the dance floor, then held her the same way he had in Miami: his arms around her body, both hands pressed against her lower back, his face right above hers.

But this time his skill on the dance floor wasn't a surprise to Meghna. She wound her arms around his neck and relaxed. Even though something was off between them, being held by Karthik felt natural. Familiar. Safe.

The tempo of the music picked up, and Karthik's hand moved to capture hers from the back of his neck. He held it for half a second, then turned her so fast that Meghna couldn't help but give a surprised laugh. The room spun, then Karthik caught her, holding her for a moment before sending her into another twirl.

When Meghna was firmly in his arms again, she breathed a sigh of relief. Not because she hadn't enjoyed the sudden twists and turns, but because Karthik was finally wearing a genuine smile on his face. The shuttered expression he'd been sporting all night had fallen away.

Meghna's heart squeezed. This was *her* Karthik. She didn't know where he had been earlier or what had been bothering him, but right now, he was fully present. Fully here.

The song ended, and Karthik dipped her, holding her in that pose for a moment longer than normal. His face hovered over hers, his eyes intense and focused. She glanced at his lips, but he didn't move a millimeter closer. It seemed there was something she needed to clear up first. It was only the very beginning of the conversation they needed to have, but she wanted to get this part out of the way now.

"I changed my mind," she whispered.

He tightened his hold, pulling her back upright. The next song started, slow and steady. She wrapped her arms around his neck as they started to sway.

"About what?" he asked, his hands returning to her lower back.

"I'm saying I want you to kiss me."

His hands flexed, digging into the jacket of her tux. "Are you sure?"

She nodded. He leaned toward her, and she tilted her face up.

But at the last second, he pulled away, his eyes averted, looking at a spot behind her shoulder.

"Is this because Seth's looking over?"

Meghna shook her head. She didn't need to turn around. This wasn't a performance anymore. Not to her. And, hopefully, not to him.

Relief flooded Karthik's eyes, and Meghna smiled, rising on her toes to meet him.

"Kiss me?" she asked softly.

He muttered something, and it sounded a lot like "Finally," but Meghna wasn't sure. Still, as his lips came to hers, it felt like the right sentiment. *Finally*. She'd replayed their kisses dozens of times, thinking she'd never get to experience them again, but now here they were. She tightened her arms around his neck and parted her mouth, but it wasn't enough. *More,* she thought as she tilted her head to the side, deepening their kiss. *More*. But even though she was partially lost in the feel of him, she was still aware that they were in public. There were too many people around.

She pulled back. His eyes were bright with emotion, and his gaze didn't waver from her face. The calm, debonair, black-and-white-film actor was gone. He'd been replaced by this fully alive, fully in color, passionate man. And he was all hers.

"Let's go," she told him, slightly out of breath.

"Where?"

"It doesn't matter."

She turned and walked out of the tent. His presence, large and full of promise, followed right on her heels.

"Are we leaving?" he asked, a hopeful note in his voice.

"No. I can't. I have to stay until the end, but we can . . ." She led them away from the glowing light of the tent and into the dark, cool night. Once they'd crossed a safe distance, she turned to face Karthik.

"I just wanted us to have some privacy," she told him.

He took a step toward her, then stopped. "So . . . so we could talk?"

"No."

He closed the remaining space between them, putting his arms around her and pulling her flush against him. "Thank God."

His mouth was back on hers, and this time, there was no need to hold back.

Karthik knew this might be the last chance he'd ever have to kiss her. And he was determined to make the most of it. He cupped Meghna's cheek in his hand, tilted her face, and parted her lips with his own. He almost groaned at the taste of her tongue. He thought he heard a moan in response, but he couldn't fully hear past the blood rushing in his ears.

She tasted like the intense heat of summer and the sparkling sweetness of champagne. How was he supposed to let go of this feeling? Let go of her? He pulled back, but her arms tightened around his neck, preventing his retreat.

"Don't stop," she whispered.

"I'm not." He scanned their surroundings and gently moved her backward, pressing her up against a tree.

She relaxed as she realized what he was doing and leaned her head back, stretching to one side, exposing her neck.

He took the invitation, pressing a kiss to her jaw, then lower, continuing down the curve of her neck. He stopped only when he reached the stiff collar of her shirt.

"I really wish you were wearing a dress right now," he whispered against her skin.

She arched against him. "I thought you liked the tux."

"I do." His hands moved down her back, sliding lower and lower. "But imagine all the things we could do if you weren't wearing pants."

He squeezed. "I'd lift your dress up. Slowly." He kept one hand where it was and let the other one slide up the side of her thigh, mimicking the way he'd lift the edge of her dress.

"I could touch you. Touch your bare skin," he said into her ear.

She shivered in response. "And then?"

He pressed a kiss behind her ear, and she let out a rush of breath.

"What would you want to happen then?" he asked.

"I'd want you to touch me."

"I am touching you." He moved his hand lazily up and down her thigh.

"Not there."

He laughed against her neck. "Hmm. Where, then?"

She moved his hand from her thigh to the exact place she wanted it, over the fabric of her pants. "Here."

He cupped her, and she let out a sound that he knew he'd be hearing later in his dreams. "Right here?" he asked, pressing against her with the heel of his palm.

"Yes," she breathed. He moved in small circles, faster and faster, and she moved in response, showing him what she needed. He knew the exact moment pleasure found her. She tensed against him, and her breath came quickly, and though he could barely see her face in the darkness, he memorized as much of it as he could. He never wanted to forget this expression. Never wanted to forget this look on her face.

Her entire body went slack, and he pulled her firmly against him. She released a shaky breath, leaning her forehead against his shoulder. He moved his hand gently up and down her back.

"I wasn't expecting that," she said.

He smiled into the darkness. "Me either."

She lifted her head and pressed a quick kiss on his chin.

His chest filled with warmth.

That warmth faded when a slightly nervous expression crossed her face. She opened her mouth to say something, and Karthik grew tense.

He didn't want to hear what she had to say. He didn't want to hear that they'd gone too far. That she couldn't be doing this at her ex-boyfriend's wedding. That she was still dealing with her feelings for Seth. He didn't want to be reminded that after tonight, this would all be over. He knew that. But he wasn't ready to hear it. Not yet.

"We should go back," he said.

Her forehead wrinkled. "Is that what you want?"

"No, but that was the deal, right? Being your date tonight?"

She stepped away, and he dropped his arms.

"That's what you'd call this? *Being my date?*"

He moved toward her. "No. Of course not."

"Then what was it?"

He couldn't tell her the truth. He couldn't tell her that he loved her. Not when there was nothing he could promise her. Nothing he could give her. Not when it meant that he'd end up hurting her again.

"We're attracted to each other. We've known that," he said instead.

"Yes, but I thought maybe . . ." She stopped, her chest rising and falling. "Karthik, I—"

"Have you decided how you're going to tell your parents?" he asked quickly.

She blinked. "Tell them what?"

He stuck his hands in his pockets. "You know, that the engagement is over?"

She stared at him, disbelief and confusion on her face. "You still want to . . . I thought . . ."

A lump rose in his throat.

Then she shook her head and looked away. "I'm sorry. I was just confused. When we talked earlier, I thought you said something about extending the engagement. But I remember now. You said we didn't need to do that." She glanced back at him. "Right?"

He was tempted. So tempted. But extending the end date would only put off the inevitable.

"Right," he said.

She nodded. "Then no, I haven't decided how to tell my parents. I guess I'll tell them in person. When I get home."

"I'll do the same."

"Great," she said in a voice he had never heard from her. Flat and even and gray.

He swallowed. "Actually, could we wait until Wednesday? So I can do it after my interview?"

She frowned.

"I just thought we should coordinate," he continued. "You know, tell our parents at the same time? That way they don't call each other and find out before one of us has the chance to speak with them. And I'd like to wait until the interview is over, so—"

"Fine," she said. "We'll tell them Wednesday night."

He nodded nonchalantly. As if none of this bothered him. As if his heart wasn't cracking in his chest.

"How do you think your mom will take it?" she asked.

He sighed. "I don't know. I mean, she's going through a lot right now. But I think it'll be fine."

"You don't think she's going to make you start going to arranged meetings again?"

"No."

Meghna arched an eyebrow. "Why?"

He answered truthfully. "Because I'll be heartbroken."

She scoffed, and the sound pierced through him. "You think she'll buy it?"

"You'd be surprised. I can be a good actor."

Hurt flashed in her eyes, but quickly disappeared. "Yes. I know." She walked back in the direction of the tent, and he followed her.

"What about your parents?" he asked.

"Well, my mom's been emailing me with all kinds of wedding ideas. She's going to need to be let down easy. But at least I won't have to lie to them anymore."

"That's true."

She continued toward the tent, but stopped abruptly before entering.

"Think you can *act* like my fiancé for the rest of the evening? We still need to keep this performance going for a little bit longer."

"I can do that," he replied, his voice slightly hoarse.

"Great." She spun and went back into the reception, but Karthik stayed right where he was.

He dropped his head into his hands and took a few shuddering breaths. He'd made the right decision. He knew that. But it still hurt like hell. He took another deep breath before dropping his hands. He allowed his practiced, controlled expression to fall back into place, then followed Meghna inside.

As Meghna walked over to the bar, she realized she had been wrong. Incredibly wrong. There was no *her* Karthik. He had turned out to be the person she had thought he was from the beginning. Cold. Unfeeling. Self-centered. He'd gotten what he needed out of this arrangement, and now he was done.

She looked around the room. The crowd had thinned since she'd last been in here. People must have started heading home. But even though the reception was winding down, the dance floor had only gotten rowdier. And she wasn't surprised to see that Eric was front and center, leading a conga line around the room.

She asked the bartender for a shot of anything and took out her phone while she waited. She sent a quick text to Ankita.

Meghna: Can we talk later tonight? Karthik dumped me. Fake-dumped me. I don't know.

The response was immediate.

Ankita: Do you need to talk now?

Meghna: No. Still at the wedding. Maybe in an hour?

Ankita: Call any time. I'll be here.

Ankita: Also, he's an ass.

Ankita: A maggot.

Ankita: A first-class buffoon.

Ankita: A wastrel!!

Meghna: Thanks.

Meghna put her phone away and downed the mystery shot in front of her. It tasted like gasoline. She didn't care. She asked for another.

Then she went to join the conga line, forcing a smile onto her face.

Out of the corner of her eye, she saw Karthik. He wasn't dancing. He was standing near the entrance, watching her. It probably looked odd for him to be by himself. To keep up the charade, Meghna probably needed to go over and join him. But right now, she didn't care.

She'd talked a big game earlier about whether he could still pretend for the rest of the night, but she honestly didn't have it in her. She couldn't pretend anymore. She was done.

She was too disappointed. Angry. Upset. At him, but also at herself. Shouldn't she have learned from her experience with Seth? Instead, she'd repeated the exact same mistake. She'd ignored all the things that bothered her, made excuses for his behavior, and created an imaginary version of him in her head. But that version of Karthik hadn't been real.

None of it had been real.

Her stomach sloshed, and she wasn't sure if it was the breakup, the alcohol, or the dancing that had caused it, but she decided cake could only help the situation. Thankfully, while they were outside, they'd missed out on the cake-cutting, the bouquet-tossing, and the garter-throwing, so pre-cut slices were already set out on a table for anyone to take. She picked up a plate, plopped down at the first table she saw, and took a bite. Something lemony and floral burst in her mouth. She wished it was chocolate.

Someone made an announcement that it was time for the bride and groom to go, and she followed everyone outside. Sparklers were passed out. The air was filled with cheers and goodbyes. And then it was done. They had left. The wedding was over.

It was all over.

Karthik appeared at her elbow, and he joined her in saying good-bye to everyone.

"You ready to go?" he asked. And she nodded.

They walked the short distance back to their hotel in silence. Meghna didn't have the energy to discuss anything else tonight. But as they entered the lobby, she felt the weight of Karthik's gaze on her hand. She removed the ring, handing it to him wordlessly.

He took it, somewhat startled.

"I wasn't going to ask for it back," he said.

"Well, I can't keep it."

"But shouldn't you hold on to it? Keep it until after we tell our families? What if you see your parents before Wednesday? Won't they ask questions about it?"

Ugh. Why was he making this so difficult? She didn't want to wear this ring. Didn't want to have to keep track of it. She didn't want the reminder that this diamond was the only thing that had not been fake between them.

"It'll be safer with you."

He put the ring in his pocket. "If that's what you want."

"It is."

A few seconds passed in awkward silence. Meghna wanted to say good night. She wanted to head straight to her room, vent to Ankita for a while, and fall asleep. But for some reason she couldn't make herself do it.

"What time is your flight tomorrow?" she asked instead.

"Early. I'll really only get a few hours of sleep. Yours is in the afternoon?"

"Yeah," she said, not even surprised that Karthik had remembered her flight information. He always seemed to remember everything she told him.

"I guess this is goodbye, then."

"I guess so."

He watched her carefully, almost like he was waiting for an invitation or an opening for a hug, but she made no move to offer one.

"I'll see you . . ." He stopped and let out a short, rough sound. "I don't know when I'll see you next."

"I don't think you will."

"Right." He cleared his throat. "That, uh, makes sense. Would you maybe want to stay up a bit? We could practice how we'll tell our parents? Figure out the best way to do it?"

She shook her head, stifling a yawn. "No. It's too late now."

"Yeah. Yeah, it is." He scratched the back of his neck. "But maybe when we get back? Maybe I could call you and we could . . ."

"Sure. Maybe." Really, she just wanted to go to bed. Put this whole night behind her.

Karthik seemed to get the hint. He gave her a small, sad smile and told her good night. Then she left, heading back to her hotel room. Alone.

Her feet throbbed after spending most of the night dancing, leading to a combination of relief and pain when she finally took her heels off. She quickly changed into pajamas, switched off the lights, and climbed into bed. But just as she was about to drift off, her phone beeped.

Ankita: You alive? Still want to talk?

Shoot. She'd almost forgotten. Meghna pressed Ankita's number and winced when she saw the time on the screen. One-thirty A.M. Ankita had likely stayed up just for this conversation.

"I'm sorry it's so late," she said.

"It's fine. Tell me what happened."

And Meghna did. Ankita listened to everything, talked with Meghna about how she was feeling, then added some news of her own.

"When you get back home, you're coming over," Ankita said. "We'll get ice cream and bring the pillow fort back out."

"That sounds good."

"We'll both need it. Because I'm pretty sure my engagement is over too."

Shock skittered through Meghna's nerves. The last time they'd talked, Ankita had made up her mind to tell Rishi the truth, but hadn't decided when. Meghna had promised to be there before and after for moral support. She felt horrible that she couldn't be there now.

"You told him?"

"Yeah. I did. I told him everything. It all just kind of . . . came out. All at once. He wants some time to think, but I think we both know it's over."

"Are you okay?"

"I don't know. I don't know how to feel about any of this. On top of everything, Samir called again." She let out a long sigh. "He wants to come to Dallas. So we can see each other. Talk things out. But … . I rushed into a relationship with Rishi for all the wrong reasons. I can't rush into one again. Especially since it's been so many years since I really knew Samir. Who knows how much we've both changed. I told him I needed space. I'm sure we'll talk eventually, but I don't think I'm ready for that right now."

"I'm proud of you," Meghna said. Ankita had told the truth even though it was hard. Had set boundaries that she needed. Had refused to rush into anything. Meghna hadn't always made those choices in the past, but she was determined to make them in the future.

"And I know I wasn't willing to hear about things before," Meghna continued. "But I'm here. Anytime. And I promise to not be grossed out about the fact that it's Samir." At least she'd *try* not to be grossed out.

Ankita laughed. "You're allowed to feel however you want about any of this, you know."

"I know. But I want you to be happy. I'll at least try to listen before passing judgment."

"Me too."

"Well, if you promise, then . . . Karthik and I almost had sex in the park."

"You *what?*"

Meghna nearly laughed at the shock in Ankita's voice, but filled her in on all the juicy details she had left out before.

Things were still a mess. For both of them. But together they'd find a way through it.

After they hung up, Meghna closed her eyes and finally fell asleep.

Sometime later, she woke up with a start. Meghna wasn't sure what time it was or how long she'd been asleep, but it had felt like minutes. She fumbled for her phone and saw the time on the screen. 5:03 A.M.

A shuffling, scratching sound came from the hallway, and she immediately shot up straight. Was someone outside? She stayed still, straining her ears to listen, but couldn't hear anything else. Two seconds later, a message appeared on her phone.

Karthik: I'm leaving for the airport. Have a safe flight.

Meghna waited a moment. Maybe there would be another text. A message saying that he wanted to talk. That he was right outside her door. That he'd made a mistake. That he couldn't go back home leaving things this way. But nothing else came.

Meghna switched on the bedside lamp and tiptoed to the door, peering out the peephole, but she didn't see anyone there. She wasn't sure if she'd imagined it or if Karthik really had been out there, but it didn't matter anyway. He was gone. And soon she'd be leaving as well. She quickly went to the bathroom, climbed back into bed, and forced herself to get a few more hours of sleep.

T he following Tuesday, Karthik was at his mother's house for their usual weekly dinner. They exchanged the normal pleasantries and played a few rounds of cards, but the headache roaring through Karthik's brain made it difficult to concentrate. He lost every hand until his mother finally took pity on him and ducked into the kitchen to fetch the food.

Karthik waited until she left the room, then closed his eyes. Meghna had never responded to his text message. He assumed she had gotten home safely after the wedding, but he didn't know. He rubbed his temples.

If she had reached Dallas safely and hadn't said anything, that meant she was avoiding him. He should have expected that. It had only been a few days since he'd broken off their engagement. But it wasn't like their relationship had ever been real. It wasn't like she had ever had feelings for him. Had ever felt half of what he felt for her.

His mother returned with two plates; placing the one with an absurd amount of rice and curry in front of him. He shook his head good-naturedly and was about to take a bite when his mother's voice suddenly pierced the air.

"Dad's moving back to India," she said.

Karthik's gaze snapped to his mother. "What?"

His mother lifted her napkin and dabbed a corner of her mouth. "Dad's decided to move back to India," she repeated calmly.

Karthik set his fork on the table. He couldn't believe what he was hearing.

When his mother had texted him earlier today and asked him to stop by the house, Karthik hadn't thought much about it. He had planned on checking in, hearing how she was doing, and maybe poking around for some news about his dad. He hadn't expected this.

"You're moving to India?" Karthik asked in disbelief.

"No," his mother said. She squinted, staring at his plate. "Do you not like the chicken? I tried Renu Aunty's recipe instead of my normal one, and I think the gravy has too much coconut. I have biryani in the freezer. I could defrost that."

Karthik's brain was buzzing. He could hardly make sense of what his mother was saying. Was she moving to India or wasn't she?

"What do you mean?" he asked.

But instead of helping with his confusion, his mother just looked at him with concern. "I can defrost the biryani," she said slowly. "If you'd rather have that instead."

Karthik shook his head. "No, this is fine, I meant . . . You just said Dad's decided to move."

"Yes. But I'm not moving with him."

Okay. Nothing made sense now. He had thought that the news of his dad would shake her as badly as it had shaken Karthik. But this whole time, she had been calm. Unfazed. Unbothered. Or at least, that was how she had seemed. Now it almost sounded like . . .

"Amma, are you leaving Dad?"

A spark of surprise lit his mother's eyes. "Yes. That's what I was just saying."

A *Why?* almost left his mouth, but he held it in. He knew *why* she would leave his dad. He supported it, even. Had hoped for it. He'd just never thought that his mother would actually do it. That she would actually walk away from the marriage. That she would end things.

And how was this the first time she was bringing it up? He'd had no idea that she'd even thought about this. Not since he'd mentioned it during their fight all those years ago.

"I didn't want to burden you with any of this," his mother said. "But I've been thinking about it for a while. You dad wasn't always like this. Before we moved here, he was different, but then . . . things changed. It was slow. Gradual. I used to think everything might return to the way it had been, but now I know that's not going to happen." His mother paused, then looked at him with an expression Karthik couldn't quite decipher, almost as if she was checking that he was doing okay. Convinced by whatever she must have seen on his face, she continued.

"You know Chandra Aunty's a lawyer? I've been meeting with her to discuss options, and I think . . . Well, she thinks I could keep the house. I don't think your dad would want it anyway, and I could stay here, or sell it and go someplace else, or—"

"If you want the house, we'll make sure you get it," Karthik said. "But if you don't, you can stay with me. For as long as you want."

His mother shook her head. "You say that now, but once you're married, things will change." A small smile crept over her face. "I don't think Meghna would want me around constantly."

"Meghna won't be around." Karthik flinched. He'd planned to break that news to his mother tomorrow night. *After* the most important interview of his career.

"Did . . . did something happen?" his mother asked, concern heavy in her voice.

Karthik held back a sigh. The cat was out of the bag now, so he might as well get it over with. "We broke up," he said flatly.

"What? Why?"

"We just want different things. And I can't . . ." He broke off, his throat suddenly tight. "I can't be what she wants."

His mother frowned. "I don't understand."

Karthik rubbed his forehead. He wished he'd had more time to prepare. To come up with some explanation. Right now, all he could think of was . . . the truth. "Meghna wants a partner. Someone who listens to her. And supports her. And encourages her. And loves her. And . . ."

"And you can't be that person?"

"No," he said hoarsely. "I can't."

Karthik's mother was silent for a moment. She opened her mouth to say something, then subtly shook her head, taking a bite of her food instead. Karthik tentatively picked his fork back up. Was that it? His mother didn't have any more questions for him? She was just going to accept that things between him and Meghna were over? That they were done?

He swallowed, his unease growing. How was his mother so calm? How was she completely *fine* with the fact that he'd never see Meghna again? Never hear her laugh or listen to her describe another musical? Never get to read another one of her ridiculous T-shirts?

He shoveled a spoonful of rice and chicken into his mouth. The flavors burst across his tongue, but he barely registered them. He waited a second, then cleared his throat.

"Could you not talk to Meghna's parents about this? At least, not yet. She's planning on telling them tomorrow and it's probably best if they hear it from her."

His mother looked up, her gaze careful and assessing. "Okay," she finally said. "Meghna's mom called about venues, but I'll just wait a few days before I get back to her."

"Thank you." He took another bite. "When, uh, when is Dad leaving?"

Hurt flashed across his mother's face, and then all trace of emotion was wiped clean. "I . . . I think he's already left. But you'll have to ask him."

Karthik nodded. There was a fat chance of that happening. Everything within him rebelled at the thought of talking to his father, but he'd figure that out later.

After they finished their meal, Karthik excused himself. He still had some last-minute preparation he wanted to finish before his re-interview with the panel tomorrow. He hugged his mother goodbye, but held on a little longer than normal.

"You know I'm here for you," he said. "For whatever you need. I . . . I've wanted this for you for a while, but I never expected . . ."

"I know," his mother said softly. "And I'm sorry. About Meghna."

He smiled ruefully. "Me too." After a shared look of pain and understanding, he left.

After a full day of work, Meghna sat on the couch with her laptop balanced on her knees. She read over everything she had written yesterday, then opened the Excel spreadsheet she'd worked on one afternoon and never opened again.

Months ago, when she'd gone to New York for the retirement party, Karthik had mentioned the idea of getting an MFA. She'd been hesitant. Though her mother may have finally conceded that engineering was out of the picture, she still frequently implored Meghna to consider grad school so that she could do something "professional."

Her mother didn't mean to be hurtful. But a lifetime of hearing those comments had made Meghna tense up at any mention of further education. She'd always dismissed the idea out of hand. She'd never once thought about going back to school to work on her writing. Not until Karthik had brought it up.

Her breath caught, and a sharp pang shot through her. She hadn't allowed herself to think about Karthik. At least not too much. But now she couldn't help but replay that conversation. They'd been talking about where they would live after the wedding. And she'd said

New York. Not that it had been real. They'd just been practicing what they would tell people.

But days later, she'd thought about actually moving to New York. About how she'd always wanted to do it, but never made any real plans. That night, she'd started researching, creating a list of MFA programs in the city.

She read through that list now. Most required that she submit a sizable writing sample, and thankfully, she had one. If she kept working on it at this pace, she'd be able to finish it in time for this year's application cycle. Maybe that was what this play had been meant for all along.

She was opening her calendar to add some deadlines when a knock on the door took her by surprise. She hadn't been expecting anyone, and she was shocked to see her father standing outside, cradling a stack of Tupperware containers in his arms.

She'd purposefully skipped out on last night's family dinner, unsure if she could be around her parents and not spill everything. How she and Karthik were over. How the engagement was through. How she'd failed. And let them down. Again.

"Dad," she said, ushering him inside. "Hi. I wasn't expecting you." She took a few of the containers from him and walked toward the kitchen. He hadn't called or texted. And her parents never showed up out of the blue. "Is everything all right?"

"Fine, beta. Fine." He followed her, opening her fridge and putting everything away. "Your mother's working late tonight and she left me with clear instructions. She made extra food yesterday, thinking you were coming, and I was told to pack it up and bring it here." He smiled. "Between you and me, I was also instructed to phrase it in a way that would make you feel guilty for canceling last minute, but I never promised to do that. I'm sure you were busy. I wouldn't have bothered you at all, but I've learned to always follow your mother's directions." He winked. "And I can never pass up a chance to see my favorite daughter."

Meghna gave him a smile, but despite her father's disclaimer, guilt swirled in her gut. She'd kept so much from her parents. Lied to them repeatedly. And here her father was, being so kind and understanding on top of everything. It was almost too much for her to take. Her eyes pricked, tears beginning to form.

Her father frowned. "Meghna, what happened? What's wrong?"

The tiny bit of control she had over her composure slipped, and a sob escaped before she could help it. "I'm sorry," she said, wiping her eyes with the back of her hand. "I'm sorry. I'm fine."

She wasn't. Clearly. Which her father seemed to understand, though he didn't press. He just waited, his eyebrows knit in concern, as she caught her breath.

"Karthik and I," she started. "We're not, we're . . ." She shook her head, stopping herself before the rest of it came tumbling out. She'd promised Karthik that she wouldn't say anything before his interview. And she didn't want to break her word.

"We're just very different people," she finished.

Her father leaned against the kitchen counter, his mouth twisting into a frown. "In what way?"

Meghna raised her hands, floundering for a moment. "We're not . . . I don't . . . I'm not sure that Karthik . . . I'm not sure he's ready to get married."

She heaved out a deep breath. There. It wasn't the whole truth, but that was as close as she could get to it tonight.

Her father regarded her thoughtfully, his gaze soft. Reflective. He was quiet for a minute, then said, "I know your mother and I have told you the story about how we met."

Despite her poor mood, Meghna almost smiled at that under-statement. Her parents had shared their love story so often that Meghna had almost committed it to memory. Her mother had been the ambitious, loud, high achiever in engineering school and her father the quiet, shy student who'd asked her for help. After many study sessions, and despite their differences in culture and language and background, the two had fallen in love.

"But I don't know if we've ever shared all of it," her father continued. "We've told the short version. The one where everything works out in the end. Because ultimately it did. But when we were in the middle of it . . ." He gave a small shake of his head. "Your mother was always clear about our relationship. About what it was. Where it could go. She told me from the very beginning that we had to end things once we graduated."

Meghna's mouth almost fell open in shock. Her father was right. They'd never told her *this* version of the story.

"Your mother had a lot of dreams. She wanted to move abroad. Attend graduate school in the UK or the States. And she didn't want to get married. She didn't want to account for a husband. She didn't want to factor one in or give up her plans for him." His lips quirked, his expression growing fond. "I understood that. I understood her fears. But I still hoped. I always hoped for more. I tried to show her that I wouldn't hold her back. That marriage may have been like that for so many of the women we knew, for so many of the women in our families, but it didn't have to be like that for *us*.

"I'd secretly hoped that she would change her mind. That she'd be willing to tell our families about us. That she'd take a risk. Give us a chance to make things work. But then graduation came and . . . she was direct. To the point. She ended things the way she'd always said she would. She got into a graduate program in Texas, and I had a job offer close to my family. I moved to Chennai. She moved to the U.S. And I thought that was it."

A small, rueful smile crossed his face. "I cried almost every day for a month. And my parents didn't understand what was happening. They didn't understand why I refused every proposal they had for me. Why I refused to even meet any of them. But the thought of marrying someone else . . . I couldn't fathom it. I was still so in love with your mother.

"And then, months later, on a completely normal Tuesday, your mother showed up at our house. I still remember what she was wearing. A white salwar kameez with bright blue dots. A blue dupatta draped around her shoulders. Her long dark hair in a single braid down her back." He shook his head, his eyes glistening. "This brave, bold woman marched right into my family's household and just said, 'My name is Radhika and I'm in love with your son.'"

Her father's voice was shaky. Rich with emotion. And tears flooded Meghna's vision, making everything a bit blurry. "She looked right at me and said, 'Akshay, I made a mistake. You are my jaan. You are my life, and if you love me too, I need you to move to the U.S. with me.'" He laughed. "Even in the middle of a heartfelt apology, she was demanding. Intense. And I'd never loved her more. She called me 'jaan' for the first time that night. I didn't know what it meant, but then she told me. *Life*."

He shook his head. "It seemed strange to call a person 'life.' But your mother explained that when we were apart, she felt like she was living without a piece of her soul. Something necessary for her to breathe. And she never wanted to feel like that again."

Her father hastily wiped a tear from his eye. "I thought I understood it then, but now, after years of marriage . . . I understand it so much more. When your mother smiles, I can feel it. Deep in my chest. And when she's not happy, when she's hurting, it's like I'm hurting too. We're different from each other. In so many ways. But I would never want to be apart from her. She is my jaan. My life. And when you feel that way about someone, the hard things, the things that make you so different, they're worth working through."

Meghna swallowed, her throat tight with emotion. She so badly wanted to feel this way about someone. And if Karthik had been willing to give their relationship a real chance, if he had been willing to try, maybe they could have worked through things. Put their differences aside. Found a path forward. One day, maybe they would have felt this way about each other. Called each other "jaan."

But Karthik wasn't interested in anything real. He'd made that perfectly clear.

Her father watched her, a faint note of hesitation crossing his face. "And I know your mother can be hard to understand sometimes. She expresses her love differently. We can both see that you're . . . content. With your job. But we want more than that for you. We want you to be excited and passionate about what you do. And while I can see that engineering would never have been that for you, your mother is a little more . . . single-minded. Her work has given her that kind of joy, and she can't imagine that everyone doesn't feel the same. But ultimately, she just wants you to be happy, beta. We both do."

"Thanks, Dad." She gave him a hug, then reheated the leftovers her mother had sent, inviting her dad to stay for dinner. As they ate, Meghna debated whether she would share her news about applying for an MFA. She'd planned on waiting until things were final, until she'd been accepted somewhere. But maybe she could share the news earlier. Maybe her father was right. All this time, she'd thought her parents were unhappy because she'd failed to live up to some unreachable standard, but maybe they just wanted her to be happy. Maybe they'd be excited for and proud of her if they saw she was pursuing something she loved.

After her father left, she turned back to her computer, a small kernel of hope growing as she filled out her first application.

19

Karthik drummed his fingers against his thigh. Jim had just popped out of the conference room to let Karthik know that he and the rest of the interview panel were running a few minutes behind schedule, but they'd be ready for him in a moment.

The delay was unexpected, but not unwelcome. Karthik had been on edge all morning. He was almost grateful to have a few seconds to relax. To calm himself down before going inside.

He'd tried to go through his day like normal. Sipping his lavender latte. Checking his email. Talking with Paul—though that conversation had been far from relaxing.

Paul had barreled into his office early that morning, slightly out of breath. "Dude, I'm so sorry about your engagement."

Karthik had sighed, leaning back in his chair. "How did you even find out?"

"Your mom told me."

Karthik's eyebrows had shot up. "You talked to my mom?"

"Yeah. She left a message with me when you were in that meeting and we got to chatting. She's awesome."

"Yeah. I know," Karthik had replied flatly.

Paul had looked at him in confusion. "What's the matter? I didn't think you'd be mad if I talked with your mom. She's really nice. She asked if I'd had any homemade meals lately and said she'd send something with you next week. I was really looking forward to it, but if it's not okay—"

"No. No, it's fine."

"But what happened? I thought things with you and Meghna were going well. Didn't you just go to a wedding together or something?"

"We did. That's actually where we decided to end things."

"But why?"

Because Karthik was a fool. Because he'd accidentally fallen in love.

"We just wanted different things," Karthik had said evenly.

"Well, I'm sorry, man. Really sorry."

Karthik had told him not to worry about it, then done his best to put it all out of his mind so he could focus on the interview.

When he'd first joined the company straight out of school, he'd been so preoccupied, distracted by worries that his father had been right. That engineering was a mistake and he should have become a doctor. But after some time, he'd realized that going to medical school wouldn't have made a difference. Nothing Karthik did would ever make his father happy.

So, he'd buckled down at his job. Marianne, and others, took notice and rewarded his hard work. He redoubled his efforts, really committed to his team and his clients, and then, he started moving up. With each move came more responsibility, but also recognition. Respect. Appreciation. And today, this final interview, was the culmination of all of it.

He should have been overjoyed. He should have been proud of his hard work and where it had taken him. But for some reason, he just felt . . . off.

His phone beeped. Karthik grimaced when he saw it was a text from his father.

Dad: I received a grant to conduct some research in India. Had to leave very quickly. I'll be here for a while, but will travel back for your wedding.

Karthik resisted the urge to roll his eyes. There was nothing his father cared more about than his job and professional reputation. He wouldn't have wanted anyone to know he'd been terminated.

Maybe he had received some kind of research grant, but that wasn't the full story. There was more to it, but Karthik wasn't sure if he was interested in finding out all of the details. His father had lost his job. He'd moved halfway around the world. And his mother was staying here and seemed to be taking it all in stride. There wasn't really anything else for Karthik to be concerned about.

Of course, he *could* call his father. He could demand answers. Ask his father how he could treat his mother this way. He could yell at him. Tell him how disgusted he was by his behavior. By his choices. But there was no answer his father could give that would change the way Karthik felt. No answer that would fix things. That would justify his behavior. There was no closure at the end of this. Maybe there was just . . . acceptance. This was who his father was. And he wasn't going to change.

Karthik's phone beeped again.

Dad: Also, heard about your promotion. Congratulations. Proud of you.

Karthik's stomach rolled. *Proud of you?* At one time in his life, hearing these words from his father would have meant everything. Now they just made him want to throw up.

He didn't *want* to be the kind of person his father would be proud of. Someone who kept secrets. Who yelled at the people they were supposed to love. Who chose their career over their own family. Who lied. He swallowed, his throat suddenly itchy and dry.

How different was he from his father, really? Hadn't Karthik been lying to his mother for months? Even now, he still hadn't told her the full truth about his engagement. He still hadn't told her it had all been a trick to get out of his promise to her.

He'd been so afraid of hurting her again. Of reliving their past conversation about marriage. He'd thought pretending to go along with her plan would cause her the least amount of pain. But his good intentions didn't cancel out his deception. They didn't make it right.

And Meghna. He'd confronted her about Seth. He'd made her cry. And then, like his father, he'd just . . . left. Ended things and walked away. Like a coward. He should have done more than just say sorry. He should have been honest with her. He should have told her how he felt about her. What she meant to him. And that he didn't want the engagement to end. He should have stayed and fought for her. Showed her how badly he wanted to make things right.

How badly he *still* wanted to make things right. Karthik's pulse jumped. Yes, his father had run. He'd literally fled the country to avoid facing his mistakes, but Karthik didn't have to follow his example. He'd run once, but that didn't mean he had to keep running. He could stop. He could go to Meghna and tell her the truth. Tell her that their engagement, their relationship, none of it had been fake to him. That he . . . he loved her. And that he never should have let her go. Maybe he'd already ruined any possibility of her feeling anything for him, but he had to at least *try*.

Karthik pulled out his phone, his hand slightly shaking. He had to book a flight. He had to see her. Talk to her. Before it was too late.

Jim walked out of the conference room, a large smile on his face. And Karthik froze. He was tempted to leave. To bolt again. To run. But he wasn't his father. He would stay and face things. He would see things through.

He stood up, shaking Jim's hand and following him. As he took a seat in front of the panel, Karthik made a split-second decision. He'd been so desperate to not be like his father that he'd held himself back from happiness. From Meghna. And from a job he could actually love.

He'd thought that his current job was fine. That he could work in HVAC design for the rest of his life. That he could be content doing something he wasn't passionate about. But Meghna had shown him that he was wrong.

Meghna, who'd fought and fought against a school board so her kids would have the opportunity to perform. Meghna, who'd written for years, refining her craft, slowly but steadily working toward her dreams. Meghna, who took risks, even when it was hard. Even when there was no guarantee things would work out.

"Before we start the interview, I wanted to say something," Karthik said. "If it's all right with you, Jim."

Jim waved a hand, gesturing for him to go ahead.

"Thank you. And thank you to everyone, really, for your time and patience and for giving me another opportunity to speak with you. I've been thinking for a long time about a question I was asked the last time I was in front of this panel. About why I want this job. And it made me think about the reasons I became an engineer in the first place.

"I grew up in a house where something was . . . broken. And as a kid, I remember thinking that if I could just figure out what was wrong, the reason why nothing felt right, maybe I could find a way to make it better. I tried so many different things, but no matter what I did, everything stayed the same. Whatever was broken . . . I couldn't fix it."

Karthik took a deep breath. "But in this job, that's exactly what I get to do. Clients come to us, present us with a problem, and we're paid to analyze it. To come up with a solution. To create a device that can solve things."

A few of the panelists nodded.

"And then we test that device. And if it doesn't work, we try again. We try and fail, over and over, until we figure it out. We're constantly inventing and creating solutions out of thin air. And I could tell you that this promotion would allow me to do that work on a broader scale. To oversee multiple projects, to bridge the gap between our team and our clients, to help the company achieve greater success.

"But that wouldn't be the full truth. Because really, until recently, I'd forgotten that this was the reason I'd wanted to be an engineer in the first place. I'd forgotten about that initial passion, that thrill of finding and creating the perfect answer to a problem. And I know that if I was lucky enough to receive this promotion, I could lead the HVAC design team and do the job well, but what I'd really like is an opportunity to be considered for a different area."

Karthik risked a glance at Jim, but Jim's neutral expression gave nothing away. "The biomedical group is working on the projects that I'm most excited about," he continued. "And that's where I want to be. I know it would be a newer area for me, but I wouldn't ask for any favors. I'd be happy to start over, to prove myself all over again. I know I've thrown some curveballs in this process, but I promise, if you're willing to give me this chance, I won't let you down."

Two of the panelists exchanged a bemused glance, and Karthik's stomach dipped. Clearly, this wasn't what they'd been expecting. And he couldn't blame them. Karthik hadn't even expected that he'd say any of this, but he didn't regret it. He'd taken a risk, and even if it didn't pay off, at least he'd tried. Meghna would be proud that he'd tried.

He glanced at the clock, resisting the urge to fidget. He didn't have a lot of time if he wanted to make it onto the next flight to Dallas. Even if he left now, he'd be cutting it close.

Jim tilted his head, drawing Karthik's focus. "So," Jim said slowly, stretching out the vowel as far as it could go. "Just so I have this right, you're telling me that given a choice between an executive position and an entry-level spot on the biomedical team, you'd prefer the entry-level job? All because that's what you're most *passionate* about?"

Karthik held back a wince. "Yes, sir. That is what I'm saying."

None of the panelists said anything. The air was tight and tense, and Karthik braced himself for rejection. But then Jim laughed, the sound like a crack of thunder sending a jolt through the room.

"Okay," he said. "I mean, we'll need to talk about it some more, but if the head of the biomedical group approves, I wouldn't have a problem with it. It would truly be an entry-level position, though. In terms of pay and benefits and—"

Karthik shot to his feet, offering Jim an enthusiastic handshake. "Yes. Yes, I understand. Thank you." Jim gave him a slightly bewildered smile, but clasped his hand firmly and told him they'd make plans to discuss it further next week.

After the panel dismissed him, Karthik calmly walked out, waiting until he was past the glass doors of the conference room before breaking into a run.

He didn't stop until he reached Paul's cubicle, feet almost skidding against the carpet, wheezing and out of breath. "Paul," he said, relieved to see that the intern was there. "I need to go. Can you cancel anything I have for the rest of the day? And I'll need a plane ticket to . . ."

Paul grinned. "Way ahead of you. Check your email."

Karthik pulled out his phone, shocked to see that he was already booked on the next flight to Dallas. "What? But how did you . . ."

"Just go, man. Go get her back."

Karthik stared for a moment, then took three large steps forward, throwing his arms around Paul. "Thank you," he said, barely even registering Paul's slack-jawed expression when he let go and sprinted away.

"You're welcome!" Paul called a few seconds later, his voice carrying as Karthik raced out the door. "Good luck!"

Meghna took a deep breath as she pulled into her parents' driveway. She'd driven here straight from school, but had opted to take the scenic route, forgoing the freeway for the side roads, looping around the neighborhood park, and even driving up and down her parents' street a couple times. But time had run out. She couldn't stall any longer.

It was time to tell her parents that the engagement was done. The plan had been to wait until Karthik's interview, and as far as she knew, that had taken place sometime this morning. She'd been tempted to text him "good luck." To ask him if he was nervous. Or confident. Or worried. To find out how things were going with his dad.

But she'd refrained from sending anything. A little while ago they'd called each other regularly, talking about everything and nothing. But he didn't want that kind of relationship with her anymore.

Just as she'd summoned the strength to switch off the car and open the door, her phone rang. She embraced the opportunity to delay the conversation with her parents and answered immediately, not realizing she'd accepted a video call until Samir's face filled the screen.

She recognized the inside of Samir's Hyderabad apartment and mentally calculated the time difference.

"Samir? Why are you . . . Isn't it the middle of the night for you?"

Samir nodded. He looked far from well rested. Dark-purple shadows lingered under his eyes, and the smile on his face was tight. Tense. "Yeah," he said. "Couldn't sleep."

"Well, you look like shit," Meghna said, the words escaping her mouth before she could help it.

The tight smile on Samir's face relaxed into a genuine one. "Thanks. It's nice to see you too."

Meghna rolled her eyes. "You know what I mean. You look like you haven't slept in days."

"That's not far from the truth." Samir lifted a shoulder, grimacing slightly. "I haven't slept through the night in a while."

"Why?"

"Doesn't matter. I, uh, wanted to talk about something else first."

Meghna knew exactly what he was about to say. It was the conversation she had been avoiding for a while. The apology she had known was coming. The idea of it had made her angry in the past. Had brought up every emotion she had felt the night of Ankita's party. But time had softened those feelings, so she nodded and gestured for him to continue.

"Go ahead."

"Did Ankita . . . did she tell you that it was all my fault? Everything that happened? Because it was. I wasn't thinking straight. I was impulsive. And stupid. And I didn't mean for it . . . I didn't know that—"

Samir stopped, looked down for a moment, then started again. "Mom told me Ankita's not engaged anymore. Is she okay? Have you talked to her?"

Meghna struggled for a second as she thought about how to respond. Ankita was upset. And still processing everything. But she'd asked Samir for space, and Meghna doubted her friend would want him to know every detail about her broken engagement.

"She's okay," she said. "And I'm okay too, by the way. I'm about to tell Mom and Dad this, actually, but you might as well know . . . Karthik ended things."

Samir's eyes widened and continued to widen as Meghna finally told him everything. How the entire engagement had been fake from the beginning, how she'd just wanted a date to Seth's wedding, and how things had changed. At least for her. But obviously not for Karthik.

"So, at least we have each other," Meghna said. "Me and Ankita. Though what she's going through is obviously worse. What she had was actually real."

Samir flinched. Or at least it looked like he'd flinched. It could have just been a glitch on her screen.

"What you felt was real too," he said. "You shouldn't downplay that. You're allowed to feel hurt by all of this."

"I know. But it was my fault. I shouldn't have allowed myself to think it could be real. That he could have actually felt something. I shouldn't have—"

"And I shouldn't have kissed your best friend while she was engaged to someone else. Shit happens."

A laugh flew out of Meghna's mouth, and Samir shot her a grin.

"Not too soon to joke about it, then?" he asked, with a slightly hopeful expression.

"Don't push your luck. But speaking about that . . . Ankita didn't tell me everything, but she made it seem like the two of you had had some sort of . . . something. In the past?"

The grin slipped right off Samir's face. "Yeah," he said, his voice somewhat hollow. "It was a long time ago, but yeah, we, uh, we did."

Meghna swallowed. "Okay. Fine. But I need you to know something. If you hurt her . . . If you ever do something that makes me have to choose between you and Ankita, I'm going to pick her. I'm always going to pick her."

Samir snorted. "I don't blame you. If the choice was between me and Ankita, I'd do the same. I'd pick her every time."

Something inside Meghna softened. She hesitated for a moment, then asked the question that had been hovering in the back of her mind for months. "Samir, are you in love with her?"

He was silent for a few seconds. His eyes conveyed something heavy. Something almost . . . sad.

"I think I was," he said softly. "Once. But now? I . . . I don't know."

"That's not good enough," she said. "You need to figure it out."

"I know."

"Because if you come anywhere *near* her and you don't know for sure—if you actually end up moving back here and you're not sure—"

"I know. I, umm, didn't tell you, but I got a job offer. In Dallas. Last time I was there. I was going to take it. Before the party. But now . . ." He swallowed. "I don't think it's fair to her. To come back like this. I won't move back until I know exactly how I feel. Until I'm sure."

Meghna squashed down the angry words that had been rising within her. She'd been about to threaten all manner of pain on her brother if he ever hurt Ankita the way he had so obviously hurt her before, but the expression on her brother's face made her stop. For once, he wasn't joking. His face was solemn. As serious as she'd ever seen it.

"Okay," she said.

But he didn't seem to think she was buying it. "I mean it," he continued. "Really, I *swear* it. If I move back, it'll be because I'm one hundred percent in. Because I'm ready to convince her that I can be worthy of her. Because I'm ready to do anything, *anything,* to win her back."

He was quiet for a beat, as if he too was surprised by the depth of emotion he'd just displayed. He cleared his throat, then asked, "How are you planning to tell Mom and Dad?"

She accepted the abrupt change in topic for what it was. "About Karthik? I have no idea. But I don't have a ton of time to figure it out."

"You don't think it's worth—" Samir stopped talking and looked at Meghna somewhat warily.

"What?"

Samir raised his hands defensively. "I don't want you to jump down my throat when I say this, but don't you think it's worth maybe . . . telling Karthik how you feel?"

No. No, it certainly wasn't worth it. It sounded like the worst idea Meghna had ever heard.

"He ended things, Samir. Why would I tell him anything? He didn't even want a *fake* relationship with me, let alone a real one."

"You don't know that. There's a chance he could feel the same way."

Meghna was about to disagree, but Samir continued. "And even if he doesn't, you'll feel better knowing for sure. You'll know one way or the other and then you can move forward. Without regrets."

A flush of heat went up the back of Meghna's neck as she thought about having this conversation with Karthik. It would be embarrassing. He'd pity her. He'd say he was sorry that she misunderstood things. She wouldn't be able to handle that.

"Look, I know I'm the last person who should be giving advice about things like this, and that you and I . . . that we aren't as close as we used to be, and a lot of that is my fault. Probably all of it is my fault. And everything I did only made things worse. But I'm just saying . . . That's what I wish I would have done. I wish I'd been honest earlier about how I felt. That's all."

"I'll keep it in mind."

"For what it's worth, I really liked him when I met him. He seemed like a great guy."

Meghna nodded and quickly wrapped up the call, though Samir's words continued to ring in her head.

Samir's assessment might have been based on only a few minutes spent with Karthik, and his judgment was obviously flawed, but even so, Meghna agreed with him. Karthik was a good guy. A great one, even. But no matter how much she wanted it to be different, he just wasn't hers.

Meghna scrubbed her hands over her face and finally exited the car. She unlocked the back door to her parents' house and entered through the kitchen, where the scent of cardamom and ginger perfumed the air. She followed her nose to the large pot still simmering on the stove, inhaling greedily before grabbing a mug and pouring herself a generous amount of chai. Her parents' voices carried from the living room, and she headed toward them.

"Mom? Dad?" she called out. She took a sip of her tea as she rounded the corner, then almost spat it right out.

Karthik . . . was . . . here? Sitting on the couch. In her parents' house. Was she hallucinating? She blinked, but her vision didn't change. He remained firmly in place.

His jaw was hard. His mouth grim. But his eyes were bright and luminous, filled with something she'd never seen before. He looked at her like . . . like they'd never stopped pretending.

Her face flushed under the intensity of his stare. *What is he doing here?* Meghna tore her gaze away and almost jumped when she noticed Karthik's mother was here too. Sitting right beside him.

"Beta!" Meghna's mother got up and gave her a hug. "You're here. Look who's surprised us!"

Meghna forced herself out of her stupor. "Wow," she croaked. "What a . . . nice surprise." She smiled weakly, her movements stiff and mechanical as she hugged Karthik and his mother, then took the open seat on the couch beside him.

Karthik's gaze was a tangible presence on her side profile. His hand lifted off his thigh, hovering uncertainly, then landed back on the tiny sliver of space between them. Was he trying to hold her hand? Were they supposed to be pretending right now?

She turned in his direction, fully prepared to get some answers, to ask if they could speak privately so she could find out what the hell was going on, but before she could get the words out, her mother started talking.

"You didn't know they were coming, right, beta? That's what they told us when they got here a few minutes ago."

"No, Mom," Meghna said. "I had no idea."

"Well, you didn't miss much. We've just been catching up. Though we haven't talked about everything yet." Meghna's mother smiled. "I bet you're excited about the news," she told Karthik. "Though I guess we really have you to thank for it."

Karthik's eyebrows knit in confusion. "Thank me for what?"

"For Meghna deciding to apply for an MFA! She only told us about it recently, though I'm sure you've been talking about it for a while. Meghna said you were the one to bring it up. To suggest it first. We've been wanting her to go to graduate school for so long. Of course, we used to hope it would be engineering, but Meghna was adamant that she didn't want to do that. So, we suggested more laid-back options. Law school. Business school. But she wasn't interested in those, either. But finally, she's applying to graduate school. And we have you to thank."

Meghna's breath caught. When she'd told her parents the news, her father had immediately been supportive. Her mother, on the other hand, had been full of questions. She'd been a bit confused about what it meant to study fine arts and hadn't understood why Meghna would leave a stable job to pursue it. But when Meghna had framed it as "going to graduate school," most of her mother's concerns had evaporated.

The conversation had gone better than Meghna had expected. And this reaction from her mother . . . Well, this was her version of trying to be supportive. But it still hurt to hear her dreams diminished this way. To hear them attributed to someone else. To hear *Karthik* get all the credit.

Meghna's father picked up on something, his face tight with concern as he looked in her direction, but Meghna just shook her head subtly. It wasn't worth getting into. Not now. Maybe she'd try to have a conversation with her mother about this later.

"You shouldn't be thanking me," Karthik said, his voice even and measured. "I had nothing to do with it."

Meghna glanced at him in astonishment. What was even happening right now? She'd never told him that she was applying for an MFA. She'd expected him to be somewhat surprised by the news, but to brush it off. To pretend like he'd known about it all along. She hadn't expected . . . Well, she hadn't expected any of this.

"But I'm incredibly proud of Meghna," Karthik continued. "And I was proud of her before she decided to apply for this too. She's a dedicated teacher. Her students love her. And she single-handedly put together that musical with barely any funds or support from the school board. And I know you saw how much her hard work paid off because you were there. Did you know the principal has been begging Meghna to put together the next one?"

Meghna's mother glanced at Karthik with surprise and shook her head. "I didn't know that."

"Well, she has. They're even setting aside more resources next semester because Meghna convinced them that a theater program was important. She put her heart and soul into helping her students, even though teaching has never been her dream. And now, for the first time, she's pursuing something just for her. Not what you or anyone else wants her to do. She's a gifted writer, you know. And I couldn't be prouder of her for doing this. For going after what she wants. And you should be proud of her too."

"I am," Meghna's father said. "I'm always proud of you, Meghna." He clasped his wife's hand tenderly, giving her a meaningful look. "And we can both do a better job of letting you know that."

Meghna muttered a thank you, but couldn't tear her eyes away from Karthik. When he'd first started talking, she'd been stunned. He'd never read a word she'd written. Hadn't even known until that moment that she wanted to get an MFA. But the second he'd found out about it, he'd understood what it meant. This wasn't for Seth or *his* writing. This wasn't for her parents or their desire for her to go to grad school. This wasn't for her students or her principal or the parents or the school district. This was just for her.

And Karthik *saw* that. He immediately recognized all of it and saw *her*. And he'd been able to put it into words. So simply. So clearly. He'd said the things she'd thought and felt but had never been able to bring up to her parents.

Karthik turned at that moment, and their eyes met.

"We're going to step into the study," Meghna said, her voice high and clear. "Excuse us." She got up from the couch, and Karthik followed her, the sound of his footsteps mimicking the heavy beat of her heart.

They paused at the entrance to the study, looking at the three framed print copies of Monet's *Water Lilies* arranged on the opposite wall.

"They're *really* something," Karthik said, and Meghna hid a smile at his repeating the sarcastic comment she had first made about the art.

"My parents, you mean?" she asked playfully, pretending to misunderstand.

He started. "No. No. Of course not. I meant the paintings. Because of what you said the first time about them. Your parents are great. I shouldn't have said anything back there. I shouldn't have talked to your mom that way. I didn't mean—"

"You didn't mean it?"

"No. I meant what I said. But that doesn't mean I should have said it."

He ran a hand through his hair, frustration evident on his face.

"I was just kidding," she said softly, and he relaxed a fraction.

She wanted to ask what he was doing here, but over the last few minutes she'd come to the conclusion that Samir had been right. If she didn't tell Karthik how she felt, she'd regret it. Maybe not right away, but eventually. In a few days or weeks or months, she'd wonder if the man who saw her so well, who knew her down to her bones, could have possibly loved her, or at least felt the same way about her that she did about him.

Honestly, she wasn't sure if it was love. There was too much unsaid. Too much unknown. Too much and not enough between them. All she knew was that she'd never felt anything like *this* before. And if this wasn't love, then it was something a lot like it. And whatever it was, it was worth the risk of potential embarrassment. She took a deep breath and smiled hesitantly at the man in front of her.

Karthik was worth the risk.

"Have you changed your mind about marriage?" she asked.

Karthik blinked and Meghna inwardly cursed.

None of this was going according to plan. Karthik had come here to tell Meghna he loved her and instead had ended up ranting at her parents. Disrespecting them. He assumed Meghna had called him in here to chastise him. But instead . . . she was asking him about marriage? His heart thudded, hope building dangerously in his chest.

"Don't answer that," Meghna said quickly. "That's not what I meant to say. I wanted to tell you—"

"I don't know," Karthik interrupted. He took a step toward her. "But I'm realizing that I was wrong about a lot of things. And I *want* to be wrong about this too." He lifted a hand in her direction, then dropped it. He wanted to touch her. Her cheek. Her hair. Her arm. Anything. But he had no idea what she was thinking. What she was feeling. He forced himself to continue.

"I want to think that I could get married one day. That I could do it. That we could have a different kind of marriage than my parents, but I'm scared," he admitted. "I don't want to hurt you."

"You won't," Meghna replied immediately, and Karthik swallowed a wave of emotion. He didn't deserve her faith in him. Her trust. But he'd do everything in his power to earn it.

"Karthik, are you saying that . . ." Meghna trailed off into silence, her beautiful eyes wide and searching.

He looked away, his gaze sweeping around the room. He needed a moment to compose himself. To gather his thoughts. To figure out how to say this.

"Remember what you told me?" he finally asked. "The first time we met?"

Meghna huffed out a laugh. "I said a lot of things the first time we met."

Karthik's lips curved into a soft smile. "You did. But this one . . . I thought about it for a long time. You said you'd accidentally fallen in love before. And I thought that was ludicrous. That it was impossible." He shook his head. "But I was wrong."

"What are you saying?"

He leaned toward her, so close that her face took up his entire field of vision.

"I'm saying I accidentally fell in love with you. But I don't want you to feel any pressure. I don't know how you feel, but I'd like us to have more time. We could continue the engagement. Get to know each other more. Give you time to see if you could . . . if you might . . . see a future. With me. I don't know whether I'll ever be able to change my mind about marriage, but I want to. I want to give you everything you want. To be everything you want."

Meghna placed her fingers over Karthik's lips, and he immediately stopped talking.

"You already are everything I want," she said. And then she kissed him.

He froze for a millisecond, shocked over what she'd just said, then moved with fervor. His hand threaded through her hair, and his tongue swept into her mouth. She shivered, then swayed as if the muscles in her legs had gone slack. He pulled back, looked at her for a moment, then maneuvered the two of them so that he sat in one of the brown overstuffed chairs where they'd had their first conversation.

She straddled him, rising onto her knees so that for the first time she was taller than him. She pushed his hair back from his face, and he closed his eyes. Unable to believe this was happening. Unable to believe this was real.

"I wasn't ready to say goodbye," he said, his voice full of emotion.

She smiled and placed a soft kiss on the underside of his jaw. "Me either." She ran her hand over his hair again, and he savored the sensation. "I was planning on telling you I had feelings for you. I've . . . I've had them for a while, but I didn't know how you felt."

He leaned forward to kiss her again, but she pulled back.

"Wait," she said. "I . . . I need you to know that I was wrong too. With what I said before. I never . . . I never accidentally fell in love. I thought I had. Once. But I don't think that was love. Not really. You know, I remember what you said that day too. That love takes time. Intention. Commitment. That it doesn't happen accidentally. And I . . . I think you're right."

Karthik watched her intently, his hand moving up and down her back. Somehow, he understood everything she wasn't quite saying. She wasn't ready to say those words. To return his declaration of love. But that didn't bother him. They both had things to work through. They both needed time.

"Maybe we're both right," he said quietly.

"Maybe."

Their mouths met, and they lost themselves for a while in kisses that made Karthik feel like he didn't know where he ended and Meghna began. They were one unit, hearts beating in unison, their breaths in sync. They were somehow able to anticipate how the other would move and match those movements in time.

"So . . ." Meghna said, once they'd taken a break to come up for air. She was sprawled across his body, her head against his chest, and his arms were wrapped tightly around her.

"So . . ." Karthik replied.

"We're going to have to go back eventually."

Karthik threw back his head and groaned dramatically, making Meghna laugh.

"I'm serious. We've been in here a long time. They're going to think we're—"

"That we're what?"

Meghna's cheeks took on the slightest rosy glow. "You know, that . . . that we're—"

"Oh. I get what you mean." Karthik waggled his eyebrows and tried to give her a suggestive look, which only sent Meghna into a fit of giggles.

Karthik couldn't help but smile, even after Meghna's laughter came to an end.

"What?" Meghna asked after she'd gained control of her breath.

"I love your laugh," he said honestly, his hand lightly playing with the ends of her hair. "I love being the one to make you laugh."

"I like your laugh too."

"Almost as much as you like the way I smell?" Karthik asked, his voice as smug as he could make it.

Just like he'd hoped, Meghna laughed again. "Yes, almost as much as that."

"So, what do you want to tell them?" he asked. "When we go back in?"

"The truth?" she suggested.

Karthik leaned forward and kissed her, and it felt softer and sweeter than any kiss they'd shared before.

"That sounds good to me." They looked at each other for a long moment, discussed the remaining details, and then left the study, walking out hand in hand.

Meghna's mother was the first to notice that he and Meghna were back in the room. She smiled widely, then elbowed her husband in the ribs.

"Jaan, you owe me fifty bucks. They're holding hands."

Meghna's father smirked but shook his head. "We don't know what they're going to say."

"Well, clearly they're still together."

Meghna laughed. "Fifty? You're betting higher than usual, Mom."

"That's how confident I am, beta."

Karthik's mother frowned. "I thought our bets were supposed to be secret."

"Thank you, Shanti," Meghna's father said. "Excellent point. And we definitely weren't supposed to announce them the second the kids came back."

Karthik's eyes widened. "Amma, you're part of this?"

His mother shrugged. "Why not? We had to find some way to pass the time. We thought we'd make our predictions about what you two talked about. But I'm not telling anyone my guess." She waved a small slip of paper in front of her. "They were supposed to be secret. That's why we wrote them down."

"I'm sorry they sucked you into this, Aunty," Meghna said wryly. She took a seat on the couch, and Karthik joined her.

"Don't be," Karthik said. "I shouldn't have been that surprised. Amma's something of a card shark. She's legendary at twenty-eight." His mother denied ever cheating, but somehow she always ended up winning.

Today, though, she had an unfair advantage. Before coming here, he'd called his mother and told her his plan. And the truth. That his engagement to Meghna had been a farce from the beginning, but along the way, he'd fallen for her. His mother had been surprised and hurt, but she had put it aside for now, insisting that she come to Dallas with him.

Meghna's mother's eyes shone with interest. "We should play, Shanti. I've got a set of cards somewhere. We have an uneven number, but we could make it work. Do you usually—"

"Mom," Meghna interrupted. "Can we save that for later? Karthik and I have something to say." She took a deep breath. "We were planning on telling all of you that we had decided to call off the engagement."

A sharp inhale came from Meghna's mother.

"But we spent some time talking and, well, we realized that we really care about each other. And we don't want our relationship to end."

"I knew it," Meghna's mother said triumphantly.

Meghna rolled her eyes and looked over at Karthik, as if to ask whether he'd take the lead. He didn't especially want to, but it was clear she was ready to pass the reins.

"But we're still going to call off our engagement," Karthik said.

"Ha!" Meghna's father said. "Radhika, you didn't guess that."

Karthik's mother leaned over to read Meghna's father's slip of paper, and her lips curled up. "Neither did you, Akshay. You guessed they were breaking up. I'm the only one who got it right." She unfolded her own piece of paper and read, "Meghna and Karthik are going to call off the wedding, but stay together."

The room filled with stunned silence, then Karthik laughed and turned toward Meghna. "Okay, I told Amma some stuff, but *I* didn't even know we were going to do that."

"How could you . . . how did you . . . ?" Radhika sputtered in Shanti's direction.

Karthik's mother delicately raised a shoulder. "It was a calculated guess."

"We're playing twenty-eight when this is over," Radhika said. "I demand a rematch."

Karthik's mother smiled serenely, and Karthik couldn't help but grin. It looked like Meghna's mother had finally met a worthy competitor.

"Congratulations, Shanti, on the well-deserved win," Meghna's father said. "But Meghna, Karthik, can I ask why you're ending the engagement? You said you care about each other, yes?"

"We do," Karthik said, squeezing Meghna's hand slightly. "Very much."

"So, why not stay engaged?"

"We don't want to rush anything. We just want to take it a day at a time," Meghna said. "Without the pressure of a wedding around the corner."

They'd both agreed that ending the engagement was the right call. Karthik was looking forward to just . . . spending time with Meghna. Without any kind of end date. Without having to pretend.

Meghna's mother frowned. "So, that's it? You're both just . . . dating?"

Meghna laughed, and Karthik couldn't help but smile.

"Yeah," she said. "I guess we are."

20

"Well, that went about as well as we could have hoped," Karthik said.

Meghna snorted as she pulled out of her parents' driveway. Everyone had accepted the end of their engagement rather quickly, though Meghna still hadn't told her parents that the engagement had never been real to begin with. She wanted to tell them the truth. She wanted to be more honest with them about a lot of things. But she'd decided she would discuss it with them later. Privately.

Besides, once her mother had confirmed that Meghna and Karthik were happy and were still in a relationship and that nothing seriously bad had caused them to take a step back, she'd dropped it and reissued her challenge to Karthik's mom. In record time, she'd wrangled up a pack of cards and started dealing. And before they knew it, Meghna and Karthik had been roped into their mothers' high-stakes game of twenty-eight.

"This is *not* how you deal," Meghna's mother had said petulantly, after losing a hand. "There are rules for this. Everyone knows that you have to deal—"

"One at time," Karthik had said.

"All at once," Meghna had said at the same time.

They'd turned and looked at each other with surprise.

"No, but you have to deal them all at once," Meghna had said. "Otherwise no one gets dealt a good hand."

"Exactly," Karthik had said. "Some people end up with hands that are too good. They need to be distributed evenly so it's fair."

"But where's the fun in dealing them fairly? You never get half-courts if you deal like that."

Karthik had been about to launch into his next point when they'd been interrupted by the sound of all three parents laughing. They'd finally agreed on a compromise, alternating the dealing style each round, but the fights between the two of them had only gotten more and more ridiculous until the mothers had practically shooed them out the door. They'd insisted they had a real score to settle, and they didn't want Meghna and Karthik interfering.

"How long do you think they're going to keep playing?" Meghna asked, grinning over at Karthik in the passenger seat.

"No idea. But I'm glad we got out of there. I don't want to see what happens when your mom inevitably loses."

Meghna raised an eyebrow. "Are you seriously trash-talking on your mom's behalf?"

Karthik laughed. "I didn't mean to. I was just telling the truth. Amma *never* loses."

"Well, we'll just have to see about that." Meghna slowed down before coming to a complete stop at a red light. She almost turned right, but realized it was pretty presumptuous of her to head straight back to her apartment. She and Karthik had a lot to talk about. A lot to figure out. "Do you want to go get dinner?" she asked.

Karthik shifted uncomfortably in his seat. "Uh, if you want to. Sure. We can."

She peeked at him from the corner of her eye. He was looking straight ahead. Spine straight. Jaw tense. His hand clenched into a fist. Almost as if . . . as if he was restraining himself.

A lick of fire coursed through Meghna's body.

"Or we could go back to my—"

"Your place. Yes. Let's do that."

She almost laughed at his eagerness, but managed to rein it in. Still, she couldn't help but tease him.

"Or . . . I could just pull over?"

Two seconds of silence. Then a loud exhale.

"Yes," Karthik said, his voice gravelly and rough. "Please."

Meghna shivered. She'd meant it as a joke, but she was dead serious about it now. If she didn't get her hands on him soon, she might combust.

She turned onto a quiet street and had barely put the car in park when she felt Karthik's hands on her body, lifting and pulling her over to the passenger seat.

He moved all at once, a blur of motion, capturing her lips with his own. He moaned into her mouth and the sound set her ablaze. God, she'd missed this. The feel of his body against hers. The softness of his lips. The coarse texture of his beard.

The logical side of her mind knew they'd been kissing just a little while ago, but those kisses had been like cotton candy: sweetness that was so fragile, so delicate, that it melted on the tongue. Wonderful. Magical. Tender. Fleeting.

But this kiss? This kiss was a bite of green chili. Scorching heat. The kind that built and built and built, numbing her tongue, her mind, her senses. But she didn't care. She wanted more. She bit down on his lower lip, and he let out a sound that was half-groan, half-growl. She bit down again, gentler this time, then soothed the sting away with her tongue. Quick as lightning, he broke away, moving his mouth along her jawline to her ear, nipping her lobe lightly.

She gasped.

"You like that?" he asked, catching her lobe between his teeth again.

"Yes," she breathed, her hand coming up to grip his shirt collar. She didn't want him to move. She wanted to keep him there. Right there. For as long as possible.

"Good," he said. He planted a soft kiss behind her ear, then trailed more down the line of her neck. "I like it too."

His hands came around her waist, and he gently pushed her toward his knees. He held her there for a few seconds, his breaths loud and harsh. Then he leaned his forehead against hers, almost involuntarily. As if he needed some space to calm himself down, but couldn't help but touch her.

His hands traveled up and down the sides of her body. "I've been thinking about this since the card game. It was torture. Back there. In here. I needed to touch you."

"Me too," she said. "I needed to touch you. I *need* to touch you."

She scooted forward slightly, needing to be closer. To feel him. To press against him. But Karthik's hands tightened around her waist, so she stopped, going still.

"I don't want to—" He broke off with a laugh. "That's not true. I *want* to. So badly. But not like this. Not here. You deserve . . . you deserve better than this. You deserve more. So much more."

She wanted to disagree, to say that she was more than happy to get it on in the car, but his voice held a note of something *else*. Something small and sad and resigned.

He let out a sound of frustration. "You deserve someone who would plan a perfect night. Who'd buy you flowers and arrange some elaborate surprise and sweep you off your feet. Not someone who just . . . just *mauls* you in a car."

Meghna snorted, and Karthik pulled back, looking at her in disbelief.

"Are you laughing?"

"No. Well . . . kind of? Karthik, it was *my* idea to pull over. And if there was any 'mauling' here, it was completely mutual."

She expected him to smile at that, or to at least acknowledge her words, but he just looked away, avoiding her gaze. He took a deep breath, but otherwise remained silent.

"Hey," she said softly. "What's going on?" She placed her hand on his jaw and turned his face back to hers, shocked to see genuine panic in his eyes.

He swallowed. "I . . . I don't want to turn into my father. I remember him always being the way he was, but my mother said he didn't start that way. I want to think that I can choose to be different. That I can choose to be better. But a part of me . . . a part of me thinks I can't stop from becoming more like him. I don't want you to get hurt. I don't want you . . . anyone . . . to go through what my mother did. You deserve better than that. You deserve better than *me*."

Meghna let out a breath, something finally clicking. As if the last puzzle piece had slid into place. She'd been staring at these crooked, jagged, disconnected pieces for so long. Holding them in her hands. Moving them around, lining them up. Trying to make them fit. Trying to make sense of them. But now she could see the full picture. She could finally see him.

"There's no guarantee you won't hurt me," she said. "Or that I won't hurt you. We're not perfect. We're going to hurt each other's feelings. And when we do, we'll apologize. And do our best to not do it again. But I'm not going to hurt you the way your dad hurt you. And you won't hurt me that way, either. You're not your father."

Karthik started to speak, but Meghna placed her fingers over his lips.

"I know you don't believe that. And I don't blame you. After everything you've seen. And experienced. I'm not going to try to convince you otherwise, but let's just take it a day at a time. You don't need to figure all of it out right now. I don't have it all figured out right now. But let's just try. Try to put in the work. With me."

Karthik nodded, his face solemn but tender. He leaned forward and kissed her, brushing his lips lightly against her own. Meghna closed her eyes. This kiss felt like a promise. An intention. A commitment.

Now all they needed was time.

He pulled back, and they looked at each other for several seconds.

"Are you ready to go home?" he asked, his voice cutting through the silence.

She nodded, and Karthik's hands tightened around her waist. Almost as if he wanted to keep her there. As if he didn't want to let her go. But after a moment, he lifted her, helping her scramble back into the driver's seat.

Meghna smiled, then turned the car back on and started driving the two of them home.

As Karthik followed Meghna into her apartment, his mind started playing a tune. He concentrated, but no words popped into his head. Just the same tune. Over and over.

It wasn't an unpleasant feeling. And he recognized the tune as one he'd heard before. It had played in his head the first time he'd visited Meghna's apartment. It was a soft melody. Subtle and sweet. And it made him feel *something*. The way a well-scored scene in a movie brought up all the right emotions. He just couldn't put his finger on what that emotion was. He felt lighter, maybe?

Meghna dropped her purse on the couch, then went into the kitchen. The electric kettle clicked loudly.

"I'm making tea," she called out. "Want any?"

He smiled, unbuttoning his shirt cuffs and rolling the sleeves up slightly. They'd had endless cups of chai at her parents' house when they'd all been playing cards, but obviously that hadn't been enough for Meghna. He tucked that piece of information away, adding to his ever-growing file on Meghna's likes and dislikes, and took a seat on the couch.

"No, I'm fine," he replied. He put his feet up on the ottoman and leaned back. He didn't realize he'd closed his eyes until cool fingers brushed his hair off his forehead.

Meghna stood in front of him, a curious expression on her face and a mug of tea in one hand.

"Hey," she said softly, her fingers still playing in his hair. "You okay?"

He closed his eyes again, enjoying her soothing touch. He felt fine. Ecstatic, really. But the last few hours had been an emotional whirlwind, and he was still taking it all in. He told her as much and she nodded, sitting down next to him.

"I feel the same way." She swung her feet up onto the couch, tucking them beneath her. "It's a little overwhelming. There's so much to talk about. So much to square away. Like, what happens next? I still live in Dallas and your job is—"

"I started job searching in Dallas," Karthik blurted out. "I made a list of jobs I might apply to. I haven't looked at it in a while, but some of them looked pretty interesting, so . . ."

Meghna's eyes went wide. "But what about your promotion? Wasn't your interview supposed to be today? What . . . what happened?"

He shrugged, adopting a casual tone. "I got demoted."

"What?" Meghna's jaw dropped.

Karthik grinned. "I asked for it. I told the panel that I wanted a chance to work on the biomedical team more than I wanted a promotion. I'm not starting from scratch or anything, but it's definitely a step down. But it means I'll get to work on cutting-edge technology. Things that really help people. You know, one of the teams is working on a robotics project? It's designed to assist during surgery, cutting down on errors and bad outcomes. It seems amazing and I . . ." He shook his head, a bit bemused. "Are you laughing?"

Meghna raised a hand over her mouth, but she couldn't quite cover her wide smile. "No, no, I'm not. It's just . . ." She laughed again. "The job sounds incredible. And I'm so happy for you. But . . . you're really going to be working on a robot?"

"Yes," he said, slightly confused. "I mean, I'd phrase it more like I'll be working on robotic technology. Only in the medical context, though with some modifications, I'm sure it would have applications for . . ."

Another laugh flew out of her mouth. "I'm sorry, it's just, when I first met you, I used to think you were a bit . . . well, robotic. And now you're actually going to be working on robots and it's all so . . . surreal. But it's wonderful. I'm so happy for you."

Karthik laughed. "You thought I was a robot?"

"Only because I didn't know you! But now I do, and . . . you have to stay in New York. Look at you! You're actually glowing talking about work. I've never seen you this way."

Karthik smiled. "There are jobs like this in Dallas too. I'm sure I could find one. I actually started looking for jobs closer to you a while ago. Before Seth's wedding. Because somehow, even then, I knew that I wanted to be wherever you are. Maybe that's Dallas. Maybe that's someplace else. But wherever you go, I want to go too. So, what do you want to do? I know your job is here. And your parents and Ankita and—"

Meghna shook her head, watching him with a look that made his heart thud a little faster. "I'm applying to programs in New York. I'm applying other places too, but I searched for options in New York first." She smiled tentatively. "I think I knew then too. Somehow. Before I even knew I knew." She laughed, loud and warm and utterly beautiful. "Does that even make sense?" she asked.

"Yes," he said, moving toward her, almost without meaning to.

He was drawn in. Her presence was magnetic. "I think I fell for you at the beginning. When I first proposed the entire . . . Well, when I first *proposed*. There were other ways to get out of that promise to my mother, but I didn't even try to think about any of them. I just wanted to see you again. I just wanted an excuse to be around you. I didn't really know that was what I was doing then, but—"

Meghna inched closer, rising on her knees so that they were face-to-face.

"I didn't know for sure until the wedding," she said. "But I think it started for me that night in the parking lot. When you surprised me. Standing there with flowers—"

Karthik let out a self-deprecating laugh, thinking about what a mess he'd been that night. "I'm glad I at least brought some flowers," he said, half-jokingly.

But Meghna didn't laugh. She looked as serious as he'd ever seen her.

"I don't care about the flowers. That's not what I . . . That night. It meant everything to me. For the first time, you let me see you. Really see you. I couldn't make sense of you before that. I didn't understand . . . but then you invited me in. And what I saw, what I learned about you . . ." Meghna lifted her hands, reaching out to hold his face. "I don't know exactly when or how it happened, but I started falling for you, Karthik. And I never stopped."

Karthik felt weightless. Like he might float away if it weren't for Meghna's hands on his face. Holding him steady. Anchoring him to the earth.

He placed his hands on top of hers, holding them in place for a moment. Then he lifted one of her hands off his cheek and turned it over, kissing the center of her palm.

Meghna inhaled sharply. Karthik smiled, holding Meghna's gaze as he pressed a kiss to the inside of her wrist.

Something bright and hot flashed in her eyes, and then she moved. He went tumbling, her momentum knocking him flat on his back. He barely had time to recover before her mouth came to his, and then he was lost. In the feel of her body pressed against his. In the softness of her skin. He wanted to feel it everywhere. Needed to feel it everywhere. Needed to—

Meghna rocked against him, and all rational thought left his mind.

"Bedroom. Now." It wasn't the most eloquent seduction, but he wasn't able to manage much more at the moment. All he knew was that he wanted her. More than he'd ever wanted anything.

Meghna pressed her lips to his, hard and fast, but somehow still sweet. And then she climbed off of him. He followed her toward the bedroom, stopping at various times on the short journey there to kiss her, to slide his hands up and down her curves, to push her up against a wall and sweep his tongue against hers.

Meghna lifted her dress over her head, and for a moment Karthik was only able to stare. His mind went blank as he took her in.

"You're beautiful," he said hoarsely.

"So are you," she said, her hand tracing his jaw carefully, as if she held something precious. Something treasured and fragile. Then her hand trailed down his neck, his chest, his stomach, stopping every now and then to undo the buttons of his shirt.

He swallowed as he let his shirt fall to the floor. Then Meghna's fingers curled around one of the loops of his jeans, and she tugged him gently, leading him the last few steps to the bed.

The rest of their clothes came off, fluttering to the floor like pieces of confetti. Meghna's lips curved at the thought. This was a celebration, after all.

And then Karthik's lips were on hers and they were on the bed, and any trace of humor left her mind. Karthik kissed his way down her body almost reverently. Worshipfully. And she had never felt more cherished.

He lingered between her legs, then kissed the very center of her. Meghna gasped. She couldn't see a thing in the darkness of her bedroom, but that only heightened the sensation. Every stroke. Every sweeping movement of his tongue. Again and again and again. She could barely stand it. Could barely think straight. She was falling off the edge and she didn't want to fall like this.

She wanted to fall with him.

She reached down, pulling at him, and he finally got the message. He crawled back up her body, settling on top of her. She almost came apart just from the feel of him.

"I need you," she whispered, bringing his mouth to hers.

"I need you too," he said, his voice strained and raw. He moved, brushing against the most sensitive part of her, and every nerve in her body turned to fire.

"Now," she said, arching against him. "I need you now." She grabbed a foil packet from her nightstand, then reached down, wrapping her hand around him. She brought him right where she wanted and stroked him once, willing him to press forward. Willing him to *move*.

"Wait," he said, his voice harsh, his breathing loud and uneven. "Wait."

Meghna immediately removed her hand.

"What's the matter? Were we . . . were we moving too fast? We can slow down. We can—"

"No," he said, even as she felt his weight lift off her body. She mourned the loss of it, then blinked as the room suddenly filled with light. Her eyes adjusted to the brightness. And Karthik came back to bed, his eyes ablaze.

"I just wanted to see you." He settled back over her and placed his hand on her cheek, moving it up to brush her hair behind her ear. "There. That's better." He stroked his thumb along her bottom lip and smiled.

Her heart squeezed.

And then he was exactly where she wanted, and finally . . . he moved. Wonder and awe played across his face, and then she wasn't able to pay attention any longer. Her brain shut off and her eyes slid shut. He felt so good. So right. She matched his movements, returning them in full, their bodies playing the same song in perfect harmony.

"I love you," he said. And then his mouth was on hers, his tongue entering and retreating in time with him. Meghna moaned, the sound getting lost in their kiss. He pulled her closer against him. Meghna wouldn't have thought it possible, but here they were. Skin to skin. Somehow even closer than before.

"I love you," he said again. Softly, then loudly, as they both came apart.

Meghna let the waves of pleasure wash over her, holding on to them for as long as she could, only opening her eyes when the intensity faded. Karthik's body was slack, his face cradled in the curve of her neck, his breaths harsh and uneven against her skin.

He placed a kiss at the spot where her neck met her shoulder, then rolled away, turning so they both lay on their sides, face-to-face. Meghna smiled drowsily. She felt comfortable. Safe. Elated. But she already missed his touch. She inched closer, pushing slightly so Karthik rolled onto his back, allowing her to put her head on his chest.

Karthik's arm immediately came around her, his hand sliding into her hair. She closed her eyes, enjoying the sensation of his fingers running against her scalp, sifting and playing with her curls.

"I knew I'd enjoy messing up your hair," he said, his voice deep and rough, with a note of humor.

Meghna laughed. "You can mess it up like *that* anytime you want."

She snuggled closer until she was half-sprawled on top of his body. The steady sound of his heartbeat was like a lullaby. She was almost asleep when she froze, hearing an odd noise. It was . . . it was coming from Karthik.

She lifted her head off his chest and frowned, watching him carefully.

"Are you humming?" she asked, a note of surprise in her voice.

"What?" Karthik shook his head, but he wore a slightly sheepish expression. "No. I'm not."

"Yes. Yes, you are," Meghna said with a laugh. "It was really soft, but I could feel your chest vibrating. What were you humming?"

"I don't know."

"Well, do it again."

Karthik sighed, but hummed the same tune as before.

Meghna listened intently, then realization dawned. "I didn't realize you liked that song that much."

Karthik huffed out a sound of frustration. "I don't even know what song it is. But it's been stuck in my head ever since we came back to your place. It happened the first time I came here too."

"The first time you came to my house?"

"Yeah."

A small smile played on Meghna's lips as she reached across his body for her phone. "It's a good song. Here, I'll play it for you." She scrolled through her music app, then pressed play. "It's called 'On the Street Where You Live.' It's from *My Fair Lady*."

Karthik smiled, his eyes growing warm and tender. "I think I remember it now," he said softly. He wrapped his arms around her, and they lay back down. Her head returned to his chest, and they listened silently as the song continued.

Meghna could picture the scene from the musical in her head. The man in the song was absolutely besotted, strolling down the street where his love lived, singing about how being on that street made him feel like he was floating. How he didn't care if people thought him strange, but there was nowhere he'd rather be than on that street. Because she lived there.

The song ended, and Karthik pressed a kiss on the top of her head.

"That's how I feel," he said. "Every time I'm here."

"I didn't know you liked my apartment that much," she joked.

He laughed, and she enjoyed the way it sounded. With her head pressed to his chest, she could feel his laugh move through his entire body. Could feel the joy radiating from within him.

"I like your apartment just fine. But that's how *you* make me feel I don't care where I am. As long as you're with me."

"Me too," she said. And she meant it. Whether they ended up in Dallas or New York or somewhere else entirely, it didn't matter. Somehow, they'd make it work.

She closed her eyes, sleep approaching faster and faster.

"Hey."

"Hmm," she responded, her voice sounding as drowsy as she felt.

"We never really set any terms, did we? For the fake engagement, I mean."

She thought it over for a second. "Well, we said we couldn't date other people."

"Right. We did say that." He ran his hand down her back and pulled her closer against his body. "Well, that's a pretty good term. We should keep that one."

She laughed. "I think so too."

"Okay," he said. "Anything else we should keep? Or start?"

She lifted her head and kissed him.

"How about we talk about it tomorrow? Or the next day. Or the next." She smiled as she lay back down. "We've got all the time in the world."

He hummed his agreement, and Meghna drifted off to sleep, dreaming about a future filled with punny T-shirts and musicals and laughter and love. And Karthik, standing by her side, as they experienced it all. Together.

Epilogue

TWO YEARS LATER

"You're going to be late," a deep voice murmured in her ear.

Meghna scowled. "I'm not going to miss my flight. I've got plenty of time." She looked back at the stage and pursed her lips. "Shruti, could you try that again? Maybe a little angrier?"

The college student nodded, repeating her line a couple times until Meghna stopped her. "That's it. That's perfect." She checked the time on her phone and cursed. "Okay, *now* I've got to get going."

Karthik chuckled, and she shoved him playfully. "That's a wrap on our last rehearsal!" she called out. "See you all next week." She rushed out of the auditorium, pulling her suitcase behind her. She still couldn't believe that these students had volunteered to help with her first ever stage reading. She'd spent the last few years of her MFA program refining and revising her musical, and soon she'd get to sit in the audience and listen to these actors read *her* words. And maybe, one day, if everything kept going according to plan, she'd get to see her entire musical performed.

Karthik caught up with her, swiping her suitcase out of her hands. "I already called you a car," he said as they exited the building. He greeted the driver, then put her bag in the trunk.

He gave her a quick hug goodbye, but she held on a little longer. "Are you sure you can't come with me?" she asked, even though she already knew the answer.

He smiled, leaning down to kiss her. "As much as I'd love to celebrate your dad's birthday, I've got that meeting this afternoon. You'll have to go to Dallas by yourself."

"But it's a Saturday," Meghna whined, but Karthik just shook his head.

"Didn't you just leave rehearsal? Isn't that *your* work?"

"Yeah, but that's different."

"Why?"

Meghna lifted a shoulder. "Well, because my work is fun."

Karthik laughed and helped her into the car. "Well, believe it or not, I think my job is fun too." After one last kiss, he told her to travel safe, closed the door, then waved goodbye.

Meghna waved through the window and smiled. She still didn't see how Karthik managed to find engineering "fun," but she had to admit that he was enjoying his new job a lot more than his old one. Since joining the biomedical team, Karthik had been coming home excited and eager to talk with her about his latest projects. The work was hands-on and creative, and the robotic surgical assistant he'd been working on was in its final stage of beta-testing. If everything went according to plan, it would soon be out in the market.

Meghna loved that he was happier, but she hated that he had to stay back in New York and work this weekend. Thankfully, her flight to Dallas passed quickly, and soon she was exiting the airport, keeping an eye out for her parents' car in the pickup line. She couldn't wait to see them, even though she had to mentally prepare herself for the incoming questions.

Her mother kept asking when she and Karthik would get married, and Meghna was never sure how to answer. Honestly, she had no idea when, or if, she and Karthik would get married.

True to his word, Karthik had been trying to work through his reservations about marriage. Almost eighteen months ago, he'd told Meghna that he wanted to start going to therapy. There was so much unresolved with his father, and though he didn't want to believe it, he still had a lot of fear that he'd turn out like him. Meghna had been supportive of Karthik's decision, and it had helped them have a lot of conversations about marriage and the future, though they rarely discussed anything concrete.

But Meghna wasn't in any kind of rush. She loved Karthik. And their life together. She would love to be married to him one day, but she didn't want to hurry anything along. She wanted to marry him whenever he was ready. And she was more than willing to wait for whenever that was.

"Meghna," her father cried, waving at her from the passenger seat. She went over to greet her parents and climbed into the back. On the drive home, they caught up, talking about their plans for her father's small birthday celebration at home. But for some reason, Meghna's mother was uncharacteristically quiet, leaving Meghna and her father to carry the bulk of the conversation.

It wasn't until they pulled into the driveway that her mother finally started talking.

"You know, I wouldn't normally do this, beta, but is there any chance you'd be interested in a rishta?"

Meghna just stared at her mother, confused by what she was hearing.

"I mean, it's been two years," her mother continued. "And you should know that you have options if Karthik won't propose."

"What are you talking about?"

"Well, a friend's son came to visit and we thought you might like to meet him. He was going to be in town anyway, so what's the harm?"

"The *harm* is that I'm not interested, Mom," Meghna said. "It's a waste of time."

"But how do you know that?" her mother asked. "Without meeting him?"

"Because I'm with Karthik!"

Her mother breathed out a world-weary sigh. As if she was the one with something to complain about.

"Fine," she said. "But he's already here. His mom's an old friend from college. She asked if he could come by for tea, and I said yes. He'll only be here for a short time. But I think he's a great catch, Meghna."

Meghna gritted her teeth, following her parents into the house. She didn't know what her mother was possibly thinking. Sure, her mother made hints and asked questions and pushed every now and then, but she had never done anything like *this*.

"Do you mind getting him?" her mother asked as she poured herself a cup of chai from the teapot on the table. "He's in the study."

Meghna tossed up her hands in frustration, but walked the short distance there. The sooner she got him, the sooner this could all be over.

Karthik ran his fingers over the ring in his pocket as he paced back and forth in the study. The study where he and Meghna had really talked for the first time. Where they'd realized they both had feelings for each other. The study where he was about to propose.

Technically, this would be his third proposal to Meghna, if he included the initial fake one on their first video call and the other fake one in Nashville. But this was the first time he would really mean it. The first time he would propose marriage without any fear. All he felt now when he thought about marrying Meghna was anticipation. Excitement. He couldn't wait to begin this new chapter of their lives, and he wanted to start it now.

The door to the study swung open, and Meghna walked in quickly before coming to a sudden stop.

"Karthik? What are you doing here?"

He didn't say anything. He just smiled, walking toward her eagerly. He'd made plans for what he would say. How he would do this. But he couldn't resist moving closer, drawing her in for a kiss. She responded, moving her mouth against his, but after a moment, she pulled back, her face slightly confused.

"What are you doing here?" she asked again. "I thought you had to stay back in—"

Karthik dropped to one knee, and Meghna stopped talking, her mouth opening slightly in surprise.

"Are you sure?" she asked. "We don't have to . . . You don't have to . . . Karthik, I'm fine waiting. I really am, and—"

"Well, I'm not. Meghna, I love you. And every time I close my eyes and think about the future, you're there. Front and center. The first person I want to see when I wake up and the last person I want to see when I go to sleep. I love being there for you. In the big things. And the small things. And I love that you're there for me too. You're my home. My family. And I don't want to wait. I fell in love with you a long time ago. And I want to keep loving you. Every day. For as long as we both shall live. So if you—"

"Yes," Meghna said, her eyes bright with emotion. "Yes."

Karthik laughed. "You're supposed to wait for me to—"

"I don't care," she said, pulling on his hand, making him stand back up. "I love you. And yes."

He kissed her, and they stayed locked in each other's arms, only breaking apart when sounds of celebration traveled from the hallway. They opened the study door to see Meghna's parents and his mother standing there with glee written across their faces.

Karthik shook his head, but laughed loudly. He should have expected that their parents would try to eavesdrop.

Meghna's mother rushed to hug Meghna, then pulled back.

"You're not the only one who can act, beta," her mother said smugly, making Meghna laugh, then reach back to hug her again.

Meghna's father congratulated them and handed out glasses of champagne, while Karthik's mother watched Karthik with a smile.

"You know, this means I successfully arranged your marriage," she told him.

"Amma, I never doubted you for a second," he replied with a deadpan expression, which got a loud snort from both his mother and Meghna.

His mother wrapped her arms around him, and he used that moment to offer a quiet but sincere "Thank you." For introducing him to Meghna. For loving him so well. For standing up for herself and finding her own happiness.

In the past couple of years, his mother had blossomed, taking control of her life in a way he hadn't anticipated. She'd turned her decades of skill in the kitchen into a flourishing business, running her own catering company. She operated out of the house for now, but had plans to expand, with the hope of opening her own restaurant one day. He couldn't have been prouder.

The doorbell rang, and everyone went to get it, but Karthik put a hand on Meghna's arm, stopping her from following.

"What?" she asked, turning to him with a raised eyebrow.

"It's just Ankita and Samir. I invited them to come over for the celebration."

Meghna smiled. Ankita and Samir had gone through some ups and downs over the last couple of years, but with time and therapy, the two had emerged stronger and more in love than ever. Samir had moved back to Dallas a year ago, and from what he'd told Meghna, he was planning on asking Ankita to move in with him soon.

"We should go say hi—"

"We can go see them in a minute," Karthik said, tugging her back into the study and closing the door.

Meghna looked around in surprise. Then her face split into a wide grin. "Yeah? And what are we going to do in here for a whole minute?"

He moved toward her, putting his hands on her waist, pulling her body flush against his.

"I've got a few ideas," he murmured, and she laughed.

Then he let her go and started unbuttoning his shirt.

Meghna's eyes widened. "Seriously? Right now? I thought you were kidding."

Karthik winked, but kept unbuttoning. "Just wait a second. You didn't let me finish my proposal. I have one more thing to show you."

He pulled his collared shirt off, revealing the T-shirt he wore underneath. It was light gray with a large yellow daisy in the center. Above the daisy was a speech bubble with the words "I'm a phool for you."

Meghna burst out laughing, and Karthik smiled. He'd designed a couple different options, but he was glad he'd gone with this one. "Phool" was Hindi for "flower," and daisies were her absolute favorite. He bought them for her every chance he got.

She threw her arms around his neck. "I'm a fool for you too, you know."

He smiled. "Oh, I know."

She swatted him playfully, then sighed as the voices outside the door grew louder. "We should probably get back out there."

Karthik shook his head, his eyes bright and focused on her. "Not until I get another kiss from my fiancée."

"Your *real* fiancée," she said, pushing up onto her tiptoes.

He smiled, cupping her face in his hands. "You are more than my fiancée. You are my jaan."

She beamed, closing the remaining distance between them. And then their mouths met, sealing their engagement and starting their future with a kiss.

Acknowledgments

I started this book when I was working remotely from my parents' house during the pandemic. Like so many, I was feeling pretty burned out at the time and needed something joyful and fun in my life. Writing this book gave me all that, and so much more.

But I never would have turned that first draft into the book it is today without the help of a lot of people. First, an enormous thank-you to my wonderful agent, Johanna Castillo. I truly don't think anyone could have advocated harder for this book. Thank you for believing in it and in me, and for always patiently answering my endless questions. And thanks to everyone at Writers House, especially Victoria Mallorga Hernandez, Peggy Boulous Smith, and Cecilia de la Campa.

My editor, Kara Cesare: You made a lifelong dream come true for me and I can't thank you enough. Thank you for loving this book and these characters the way you have. I feel so lucky that I get to work with you and the entire team at Dell, including Jesse Shuman, Kara Welsh, Kim Hovey, Jennifer Hershey, Debbie Aroff, Taylor Noel, Corina Diez, Jennifer Garza, and Melissa Folds. And thank you to Elena

Giavaldi for designing such a beautiful cover, and to Debbie Glasserman for making the inside of the book just as beautiful.

Thank you to my UK editor, Vikki Moynes, and the entire team at Viking UK, including Harriet Bourton and Ellie Hudson.

My kind and brilliant friend, Jessica Goudeau, this book wouldn't exist without you. Thank you for telling me that I should write a romance and for giving me my first deadline. I'm so thankful to have you in my corner.

I always thought writing would be a lonely experience, but through this process I met a vibrant community full of the most talented, funny, and wise people. Thanks to SF2.0 and #RevPit, especially Natasha Hanova. To Reapera—Maggie North, Amanda Cianerelli, Tania Lan, and Lavanya Simha—I'm so glad we met. The group chat keeps me smiling all day long. Ellie Palmer, Ava Watson, and Scarlette Tame—I love getting to go through the ups and downs of all of this with you. Your friendship has been such a wonderful gift. And a huge thank-you to everyone else who read an early draft of this book: Michelle Emdin, Christina Arellano, Mae, and Megan Brown.

I'm also so thankful to all the incredible South Asian romance writers who carved a path where there wasn't one before. Your books have meant so much to me and they gave me the courage to write a story of my own. In particular, Nisha Sharma, thank you for being so kind and welcoming and for introducing me to a lovely, supportive community of desi romance writers.

To my parents. My mother, who encouraged my love of reading with weekly trips to the library, and my father, who gave me an unlimited budget for books. Thank you for everything and for letting me live with you during the pandemic. That time was so special and I'll always treasure it. To my siblings, who had to grow up listening to me drone on and on about the latest book I was reading (let's be honest . . . I still do this), thank you for your patience and for not getting too annoyed with me. And an extra thanks to my sister, who read the earliest, roughest draft of this story and told me to keep going.

To my dog, Sylvie, the most faithful and loyal writing companion: Your sweet cuddles and kisses and quiet napping by my side—all of it got me through this.

And lastly to my childhood self, who loved books with all her heart and dreamed of writing her own one day . . . we did it!

SAY YOU'LL BE MINE

A NOVEL

NAINA KUMAR

Random
House
Book Club

Because
Stories Are
Better Shared ™

A BOOK CLUB GUIDE

Dear Reader,

This book feels like a product of my whole life up until this point: my love of romance novels, musical theater, my family, and my internal processing and wrestling with ideas about love and marriage. Like some of the characters in this book, my family is both North and South Indian, and that's because my maternal grandparents fell in love. My Nani was North Indian and she and my Nana, who's South Indian, were teachers at the same school. They always found excuses to be around each other, and after my Nani rejected every arranged match her parents suggested, her father asked if there was anyone special she had in mind. When she relayed this story to me years later, she told me she didn't know where she got the courage from, but she managed to nod her head. Her bravery was rewarded because their families ended up being supportive, and my Nana and Nani had the first love marriage in my family.

My paternal grandparents are South Indian and had an arranged marriage, as did my parents, and I've seen incredible love and partnership in those relationships as well. During the pandemic, I lived with my parents for a time, and when we watched *Indian Matchmaking* together, they brought up the idea of matchmaking on my behalf. It wasn't the first time they brought up the topic (or the last), but it was that conversation that sparked the idea for this book. I wanted to explore a story where a modern, arranged set-up resulted in a joyful, romantic relationship. A blend of tradition and modernity. And I think that's exactly how this story turned out. Meghna and Karthik have a long, windy, nontraditional road, but they start with an arranged meeting and end up in love. On their own terms. In their own way.

Thank you for choosing to read their story. I hope you enjoy it and I hope it brings you joy. And just like Meghna and Karthik, I hope you find and hold on to love in all its forms. Always, on your own terms. In your own way.

Love,

Naina

A Conversation with Naina Kumar

RHBC: Let's go back to the beginning. How did *Say You'll Be Mine* start for you?

NK: I started writing *Say You'll Be Mine* as an exercise for myself, to see if I could actually write a book. I'd wanted to do it for so long, but I'd never been able to write more than a chapter of anything until a dear friend told me that I should write a romance. I'd been trying other genres, but I've always been a romance reader and rom-com fan, and once she pointed that out to me, everything clicked. I sat and outlined *Say You'll Be Mine* and came up with 85 percent of the plot in one sitting. I took my favorite romance tropes and rom-com set-ups, and infused them with the cultural specificity of my experiences, and this was the result! From the very beginning, it felt different from anything else I've ever tried to write and I'm so happy it was the one.

RHBC: You've written a swoon-worthy romance, but it also wrestles with some big questions about family and the expectations that they foist upon us. Why was this important for you to explore?

NK: I wish I could say that it was a truly intentional choice on my part to explore this theme in the book, but really it was a natural extension of my own wrestling with these questions. I'm the oldest child in my family, and my parents certainly have had some expectations for me. Some of those expectations I've met, but others I definitely have not. I was interested in exploring not just the pressure of living under familial expectations, but the result of not meeting those expectations and intentionally choosing something different. Also, as I've gotten older and developed true friendship with my parents, I've come to realize that these expectations are usually well-intentioned, borne out of love and of just wanting the best for their children. That doesn't make the pressure or the struggles that these expectations cause okay, but I do think it offers more nuance to the situation, and Meghna gets to experience some of that nuance with her parents over the course of the book.

RHBC: What's one challenge you had writing this book?

NK: Everything I did with this book was a first! My first time drafting. My first time revising. My first time doing any of it. So, I think that was the biggest challenge. Just figuring everything out from scratch.

But more specifically, figuring out what Karthik *wanted* was a challenge. I knew what he didn't want. He didn't want to get married. He didn't want to hurt people. He didn't want to be like his father. But it took some time to figure out what he actually wanted, in part because he himself doesn't fully realize what he wants until much later in the story.

RHBC: Have your views on love or success changed over time the way that Meghna and Karthik's did? How did they change, and what did you learn?

NK: I think they have. I didn't have the *exact* views that either Meghna or Karthik have about love or success, but similar to Karthik I was pretty plugged in to a climb-the-ladder-of-success mentality for a while, and it took something big to shake me out of it. I've come to find success for me is less about achievement and recognition and more about the actual work I'm doing and whether it brings me joy, and I think I'm much happier for it!

And my view on love is still evolving. Near the beginning of the book, Meghna and Karthik have this conversation about whether love is something you happen to feel or something that takes time and intention and commitment, and at the end Meghna wonders if they're both right, and I do too. In a lot of the arranged matches in my family, the love between the couple grew with time and only came about after they'd made a commitment, after they'd married each other. I don't know if I've always appreciated that, or thought of it as romantic, but now I think it absolutely can be! It's not that dissimilar to Meghna and Karthik agreeing to a pretend engagement and then developing real feelings along the way.

RHBC: Did you learn anything about yourself while writing this book? Is there a message you want readers to take away from it?

NK: A lot of the characters in this book take big risks—for love, for their own happiness, and for their careers: Meghna leaves a stable job to pursue her art full-time, Karthik takes a pay cut to pursue his passion, and Karthik's mother defies cultural norms and divorces her husband. We also learn that in the past, Meghna's mother boldly proclaimed her feelings for Meghna's father in front of his whole family.

Writing their stories made me realize how truly risk-averse I've been in my own life, and made me think about what I've been afraid of and whether there are any risks I want to start taking. I hope readers will resonate with that too!

RHBC: And for the final question, something just for fun! If *Say You'll Be Mine* were to become a movie, who would you want to see cast?

NK: I absolutely loved Simone Ashley and Charithra Chandran in *Bridgerton,* and could see both of them as Meghna! I always envisioned Seth as Chad Michael Murray circa *Freaky Friday*. And if we get to use a time machine, I'd love to see a slightly younger Sendhil Ramamurthy as Karthik!

Questions and Topics for Discussion

1. Why do you think Meghna and Karthik are drawn to each other and agree to the terms of their engagement? If you were in either of their positions, would you have agreed to it? Why or why not?

2. In what ways are Meghna and Karthik different? In what ways are they similar? With whom do you sympathize and identify with more? Did you find yourself taking sides as their story unfolded?

3. Meghna decides to follow her passion for writing over the pragmatic career her parents wanted for her. Discuss one or more choices you've made in love or life that led you to where you are today. Knowing what you know now, would you still make those same choices?

4. At the start of the novel, Meghna and Karthik want nothing more than to get through Seth's wedding and remain firmly in their respective lives. How and why do we see their priorities shift as time goes on? At what moment did you think to yourself, "They might be meant for each other"?

5. Discuss how Meghna and Karthik grapple with their Indian heritage, identity, and cultural expectations. How does gender play into how each of these characters has to navigate marriage?

6. Meghna's unexpected romance with Karthik quickly develops into a passionate love story, changing their lives forever. Along the way, they learn how to open up again. Discuss a time when you had to be vulnerable to develop a new relationship.

7 How does Karthik's view of his parents' marriage inform his own view of marriage? How do our parents and families shape our lives?

8. What did you make of Seth? What role does he play in Meghna's evolution? Do you think he intentionally took advantage of Meghna's feelings for him, or do you sympathize with the pressure he was under?

9. Romantic comedies from the nineties, along with a prolonged stay with her parents during the pandemic, inspired Naina Kumar to write *Say You'll Be Mine*. Did this story remind you of any of your favorite classic rom-coms? Which ones?

10. The author weaves a number of themes throughout *Say You'll Be Mine*, including love, culture, family, passion versus career, and figuring out who you are and who you want to be. What other themes did you see in this novel? Which one resonated the most deeply with you? .

11. How do you picture these characters' lives continuing after the book ends?

12. Did *Say You'll Be Mine* prompt you to question your understandings and definitions of love and marriage? In what ways does the book convey the love one might have for a partner or family member as not static, but fluid or malleable, taking different forms at different moments in time?

Turn the page for a sneak peek at the next

novel from Naina Kumar...

SEVEN YEARS AGO

I open my eyes to a face entirely too close to mine. I can't take in the full picture, but I catalog the features I see. A large nose. Morning stubble. A firm mouth that's partly open, releasing small, warm breaths that puff against my skin.

The room is dark, but there must be light filtering in from somewhere because it's reflecting off of something. Glitter. Specks of gold. Something that sparkles in a streak down the curve of his throat.

A very attractive throat.

I register the too-warm blanket on top of us. Or maybe it's the heat radiating off of him. His leg's thrown over both of mine. And my body's tucked against his, his hand resting on my hip.

I don't want to move. I want to stay here, all wrapped up in him. But my eyes are so dry it hurts to blink. And my mouth tastes like cotton.

Water. I need water.

I squint in the direction of the nightstand, grabbing the half-empty, very crinkled plastic bottle sitting there.

As I reach for it, light bounces off of something else. But it's not glitter. It's . . . a ring. A diamond ring. I pick it up off the table, running my thumb across the solitaire. I suspect it's not real, and when my nail accidentally scrapes the metal, pieces of gold varnish flake off, confirming my suspicion.

Who knows where we got this from? Last night is a blur. Maybe it came out of a slot machine. Maybe it was a prize. Some cheap, plasticky bauble. I set it back down, but at this angle I notice there's a bit of engraving on the inside.

I peer closer, raising it higher to get a better look.

I read it once. Then read it again.

And my stomach turns to lead.

Viva Las Vegas. On their own, those words would be fine. My memory's coming back to me in pieces. I know we're in Vegas. And I know the man beside me is the man I'm falling in love with, but that doesn't mean I'm prepared for the two words that follow.

Wedding Chapel.

Viva Las Vegas Wedding Chapel.

"Nikhil," I whisper, shaking his shoulder gently. "Nikhil."

His eyes are hesitant to open. They flutter a couple of times, his body fighting for more sleep before finally giving in. He blinks in confusion, and then a moment later, recognition sparks.

As he meets my gaze, his mouth curves in a warm, lazy smile, and I feel it low in my stomach. Desire pierces through my panic, curling within me like smoke.

"Good morning," he says, his voice all gruff and hoarse. He always sounds like this when he first wakes up, and it's quickly become my favorite alarm. I love the way he whispers in my ear. The way he follows it by brushing his lips along my cheekbone.

I've never known anyone like Nikhil. I've never *been known* by anyone like Nikhil. I've never had anyone see all the broken, scared, awful parts of me and pick me anyway. This summer should have been the worst of my life with all my anxiety surrounding the bar exam. And there has been plenty of that. Nikhil saw me at my lowest. Crying and stressed and unsure. But somehow, he made it better. Just by being with me. Listening to me. Making me take breaks. Forcing me out of my room and into the sunshine. Cheering me up with his smiles. His jokes. And just . . . his presence.

Being around him makes everything better.

"Morning," I tell him. The panic that disappeared a little while ago has fully returned. I have to know what happened. I have to know if it's true. "Do you . . . do you remember anything about last night?"

His brows crinkle. "Not much. We had dinner with your friends and then . . . I remember saying goodbye to them, and after . . ." He frowns. "Did we come back here? I think that's what we were going to do, but . . . I'm not sure."

"Okay," I say. "Okay. Umm, don't freak out." Really, that message is for me as much as it is for him. "But do you remember anything about this?" I grab the ring, showing it to him.

His eyes grow wide. "Oh my God." His gaze bounces between me and the ring a couple of times. "We actually got married? That . . . that was real?"

We stare at each other for a moment, both of us processing the shock as the news settles in. A vague memory of me wearing a scratchy white veil floats through my brain. It was attached to some kind of firm plastic headband and I remember it really hurt my ears. I rub one of them absently, though there's only a bit of dull pain now. Nikhil was standing in front of me, I think. I don't remember what he was wearing. This foggy image appearing in my mind could easily have just been part of a dream, if not for the ring I'm still grasping tight in my hand.

And then . . . Nikhil does the strangest thing imaginable.

He laughs, all bright and sunny and deep. It sparks something within me, and suddenly, I can't help but laugh in return.

"We're married," he says.

"Yeah."

"You're my wife." Wonder rings loud and clear in his voice, and it washes over me like sunlight. It warms me, scattering the dark and anxious feelings I had moments before.

I'm somebody's wife. I'm *Nikhil's* wife.

I don't fully know how I feel about that yet. But the idea doesn't sound as scary as it did when I first woke up.

He watches me, hesitation creeping through his expression. "Are you . . . are you okay?"

"Yeah," I say, surprised to hear myself say it. Surprised that I mean it. "Yeah. I think I am."

He draws me closer, his arms coming around me, his forehead resting against mine. We stay like that for a while until my entire body relaxes, leaning into his.

"I love you, Meena," he says, and my heart jumps at the words. It's not the first time he's said them, but it still feels unreal. I don't think I've fully wrapped my mind around it. That this kind and patient and wonderful man actually loves *me*.

"I know this is fast," he continues. "And it's not something we planned. And I know how you like your plans."

I laugh, and he leans back to watch, grinning in return.

"But I'm in this. I'm in this with you. Whether there's a signed piece of paper or not. We can get rid of it. We can rip it up and file the proper stuff and go back to the way we were. Or we can keep it. I don't care. None of that changes anything for me. You're it. You're it for me. I'm here. And I'm yours. For as long as you want me."

Something clicks in this moment. Something right and sure slides into place. I want Nikhil. I won't ever stop wanting Nikhil. I won't ever stop wanting to be around him. Whether there's a piece of paper or not.

"You're it for me too," I whisper back.

A bit of hair slips in front of my face, and Nikhil reaches out, tucking it behind my ear.

"I'm guessing we made vows," he says. "But I don't remember any of them. And I don't remember most of the traditional ones either, but I want to make some now." He takes a deep breath, his face growing solemn and tender.

"Meenakshi Nader, I promise to be there for you."

"And I promise to be there for you."

He pauses. "You don't have to—"

"I want to." I want to promise this man everything he's promising me. I want to show him that I mean it. That we may have entered this whole thing accidentally, but I'm choosing to stay in it. I'm choosing him.

"Okay." His hand finds mine, his thumb rubbing over my palm. "What's mine is yours," he continues.

"What's mine is yours."

"In sickness and health, and rain and shine, and bad times and good. I promise to share all of it with you. All of it. For better or worse."

"For better or worse," I repeat.

He smiles, wide and beaming, and I feel it all the way in my chest. "Now, I think this is the part where I get to kiss the bride."

Laughter bursts out of my mouth, and he catches the sound, his lips sliding against mine. His hands come up to cradle my face, and I reach for him in return. My hands travel along his arms, his neck, my fingers sliding into his hair.

What Nikhil said earlier was true. I've never really deviated from my plans before. Never really done anything reckless. But this doesn't feel reckless. This just feels right.

I love him and I don't care what it takes. The two of us are going to be okay. We're going to go back home. To Houston. And we're going to make this marriage work.

1

I step out of Houston's Hobby Airport and walk straight into hell.

Literally. Figuratively. Emotionally. I'm in hell in all ways.

Part of me is tempted to turn right back around. Southwest has a steady handful of flights between here and D.C. I'll just march to the counter, check this bag back in, and be on my way. No one will know about this out-of-character burst of irrationality. No one will know I was ever here, in my hometown, the one place I promised I would never return to. I'll leave the past where it belongs and just . . . move forward.

Except I can't. That's why I'm here in the first place.

I pull out my phone and check the Uber app. The ride I called the second the wheels made contact with the runway is still a good twelve minutes away. *Of course.* The universe knows how much I don't want to be here, how quickly I want to get this all over with. So, it's doing the exact opposite. Slowing things down. With my luck, we'll end up hitting traffic on the way there, dragging things out even more.

I'm moving to slip my phone back into my purse when something sharp collides with the middle of my back. I stumble, my phone falling out of my hand. I wince at the *thwack* it makes as it hits the concrete floor.

"Sorry," a man's voice calls. "Sorry about that." I turn to face the perpetrator, but I only catch a glimpse of a dark-haired man, his hand holding tight to a young girl's. They're navigating through the crowd, walking quickly toward the entrance to the airport, and it's only then that I notice the number of people that are moving alongside them.

Houston's crowded. It's a big city. It's not unusual for the airport to be busy, but still, something feels off in the air. It kind of reminds me of my usual morning commute. People move at a quick clip, a slight frenzied, caffeine-induced adrenaline spurring their steps. But it's not the kind of crowd I expected to find here on a Saturday morning. The energy is strange. Almost . . . frenetic.

I squat down to pick up my phone, dusting it off and grimacing when I flip it over to see the large crack now running across the screen. *Great.* The universe strikes again. Or maybe I really am in hell. The blistering heat from the sun and the slight scent of sulfur invading my nose certainly make it seem that way.

I swipe toward the rideshare app, trying to see how much longer I'll have to wait for my car. The image is all blurry, the screen distorted due to the fall. The phone buzzes in my palm, some kind of notification banner flashing across the top. I squint, but the text is unreadable. I think there's some kind of emoji or icon. Something gray and round. Maybe a cloud? I pull it closer to my face, trying to make it out, but before I can the phone vibrates again, a little green symbol popping up. An incoming call. I answer, even though I can't quite read who it's from.

"Hello?"

"Meena. Hi. Did you make it okay?"

Some of the tension leaves my shoulders. "Yes, I made it," I answer my fiancé. "Just landed and I'm—"

A white Toyota Camry pulls up, and though I can't confirm it in the app, I'm almost certain it's for me.

"Shake, give me just a second," I say. "I think my car's here."

"Wait, Meena, I don't know if you should—"

The driver steps out of the car, and I pull the phone away from my ear, though Shake's voice continues faintly.

"Meena?" the driver asks, and I nod, meeting him near the trunk and handing him my carry-on bag.

I climb into the back seat and place my purse near my feet before I return to the call. Shake's still talking, and though I've missed the last few seconds, I can guess what he's said.

"I know you're worried about this," I interrupt, clicking my seatbelt over my chest. "But it's really not that big a deal. I'll be in and out. Quick and easy. I'll be back home in time for work tomorrow."

I booked the latest flight available for tonight out of Houston. Maybe it was optimistic of me, thinking this would take less than a day to sort out, but I'm a good negotiator. It's a key part of my job. And there's no reason we can't all be professional about this. At the end of the day, this is a deal like any other. There's something I want. And though I don't know what it is, there must be something the other side wants too. And once I figure that out, I'll make him an offer he can't refuse.

I almost smile at the thought. He won't know what hit him. He's never seen this side of me before. Never seen me go all *Godfather* on somebody. He doesn't know what I'm capable of. But after today, he will.

"You . . . you think you'll be back in time for our meeting tomorrow?" Shake asks, the words slow, slightly hesitant. "Because you know how important it is. It's not something I think we should postpone."

"Yeah. I know, but I really don't think this'll take that long."

"But your flight . . ."

I frown. Shake should know this. He has my itinerary. I forwarded it to him before I left. "Yeah, I'm flying back tonight. The plan hasn't changed. Nothing has changed."

"Really?" His voice sounds more normal now. There's a hint of relief in it that wasn't there before. "That's great. So, everything's okay, then? Because it sounded like things were going to be bad. Like, really bad. I wasn't sure if you'd be able to get back tonight. I was almost going to suggest you turn around now and just come home."

My frown deepens. What does he mean by *it sounded like things would be bad*? Has my lawyer been talking to Shake? Sharing information with him? I mean, they are friends. Shake is the one who referred me to him in the first place. But if there is news, neither Shake nor my lawyer have shared it with me. My lawyer only told me that he hadn't heard anything. That there'd been no response. He hadn't given any indication that things would be particularly bad once I got here. Unless . . . is Shake jealous?

We've been engaged for only a couple of weeks. We dated for only a few months before that. But Shake has never once been possessive. Of my time. Of my attention. Of my . . . well, anything, really. We don't have that kind of relationship. In fact, Shake wants to keep things open. He thinks monogamy is antiquated. Outdated. And I don't disagree. We have our own reasons for being together. For getting married. And love isn't one of them.

Maybe I should feel some kind of thrill that my fiancé is feeling jealous. Maybe I should find that exciting. Someone more romantic than me might see it that way. But I don't.

"Shake, you have nothing to worry about. I promise."

"Okay. Good." He clears his throat. "Maybe things were exaggerated. Sensationalized. But still, just . . . be safe. And if things look like they might get worse, get out of there. Just turn around and leave. We can always book you on an earlier flight, okay?"

"Sure," I reply, even though I'm not quite sure what he's talking about. Does he actually think I'm going to be in danger? That the situation might turn violent? I almost scoff at the idea, but then the car turns down a familiar street, and the sound dies in my throat.

The trees are taller. I don't know why that's the first thing I notice, but it is. When we first moved into this neighborhood, everything was new. The sidewalk was freshly paved. Little saplings lined the block, each one spaced out at a perfect distance from the others. And they all had that weird rope situation circling the trunk, connecting each one to a stake in the ground. They must have been there to give the trees support or something. To help them grow.

Whatever it was, it clearly worked, because none of the trees have them anymore. They all stand alone. Strong. With nothing tying them down.

"Shake, I have to go." He responds with a goodbye, but I barely hear him. My mind's too busy playing a weird game of past and present.

Mrs. Patterson used to live in that house. That small, one-story home with the wraparound porch. I used to see her gardening, her gloved hands pulling up weeds, her large hat blocking out the sun. She waved at me every time I walked down this way, which was rare. I was in a strange sort of self-imposed exile those days. I locked myself in my room with my bar prep materials, studying at all hours of the day, fueled by dread and panic that I might fail the bar exam. Again.

Goosebumps prickle up my arms, and I rub them away. She probably doesn't live there anymore. The bushes in the yard are overgrown. Scraggly. She wouldn't have ever let them get that way.

The car turns left, drawing us farther into the maze of this suburban subdivision. Drawing us closer to the cul-de-sac where I once lived.

I was surprised when I found out *he* still lives there. Not just in the same neighborhood, but in the same house. The one he always called a "starter home." I hated that. The way he made it sound temporary from the very beginning. As if it was just a stepping-stone to something bigger and better. I liked our home as it was. At one point, I thought it was perfect.

Warm red brick. A fireplace with a mantle. A backyard with a tall, old tree, Spanish moss dripping from its branches. A tiny kitchen with barely any counter space. A living room with a secondhand couch, and two bedrooms on the second floor. In the guest bedroom, where I spent a great deal of time, there was a large window facing out onto the street. I angled my desk to face it so I could glimpse the outside even if I couldn't be a part of it.

The house was small, but back then it was my whole world. Back then, it was ours.

I blink as that house comes into view now. It takes me a second to recognize it. It's the same shape and size, with the same driveway to the right leading to the garage.

But it's just . . . wrong. It's so wrong.

The car pulls to a stop, and I leap out, barely remembering that I need to grab my bag from the trunk before I storm to the front door.

I rap my knuckles against the hard surface, but no one comes to greet me. Instead, I'm met with the loud creak and screech of the garage door opening around the corner. I walk in that direction, every cell within me thrumming with energy, with the need to confront him.

But that fire slowly dies as I draw closer. He's facing away from me. His form is slightly shadowed in the dim light of the garage, but I can tell he's bending over. He lets out a grunt as he grabs hold of something. A large pallet or crate of some kind.

I'm about to announce myself, but then the back of his shirt rises, exposing a strip of warm, tan skin. My mouth goes dry. Did he always have a lower back like that? With . . . with . . . ridges? Can human beings even form muscles like that there? How can that be possible?

"You painted the house?" I ask. The words rush out quickly, as if my mind's desperate for anything that will change the direction it was heading in just a second ago. "You painted all that red brick white? Why would you do that?"

He turns around immediately, whirling so fast that the pallet of bottled water wobbles in his arms. It tips to the side, almost falling, before he adjusts and catches it.

"Meena?" His voice is hoarse. His eyes are wide with shock. But I don't bask in his surprise the way I thought I would. I don't get to savor it, relish the moment. Because whatever shock he's experiencing, my body seems to be echoing it. My heart is thumping, beating wildly. The sound of blood whooshes fast in my ears.

I didn't properly prepare for this. Sure, I did my research and fine-tuned my negotiation strategy. But I didn't prepare for the full force of him. I didn't let myself imagine what it would be like to see him face to face.

It's been years. And logically, I knew that, but I didn't think about the toll those years would have had on him. In my mind he was preserved in amber. A relic. Static. Unchanging. But he's aged.

And so have I.

I lift a hand to my hair before I realize it and try to play it off by tucking a piece behind my ear. Does he notice the occasional strand of silver sparkling here and there? The sharp cheekbones that were once hidden beneath the fuller, rounder cheeks of my youth? Time has changed me, though it shouldn't matter. I shouldn't care what he thinks. But it's been six years. I'm not the girl he remembers. And for some reason, I care.

"Meena?" he asks again. His brows crease, new lines I've never seen before forming on his forehead. "What . . . what are you doing here?"

When I thought of this moment, I imagined doing something dramatic. Like pulling out the papers and waving them in the air. Telling him he needed to sign on the bottom line or he'd be sorry.

But all of that sounds silly now.

His gaze flickers, flitting down toward my left hand. I'm tempted to curl my fingers into a fist, but I leave them loose, relaxed at my side. As if I don't know what he's doing. What he's checking for.

Thank God the ring Shake bought me is too big. Now there's nothing for Nikhil to stare at. Nothing for him to ask questions about. My engagement ring is safe, out of sight, tucked away in my purse. I put it there so I could stop by the jewelry store on my way to work one day. So I could get it resized. But I keep forgetting.

"Nikhil," I say, and his eyes shoot back to mine. "It's been weeks and you haven't responded to anything. None of my emails. None of my calls."

He scoffs. "Right. *Your* emails. *Your* calls." His words are harsh. Mocking.

"My lawyer's emails," I amend. He rolls his eyes, and I immediately regret my attempt at a conciliatory tone. "You know what I mean."

"I don't," he shoots back. "I never do."

Oh. So, it's going to be like this. I square my shoulders. "You need to sign them, Nikhil. We need to just get this over with."

He shifts his weight to the side, leaning his body against the garage wall.

"What's the rush?" he asks.

I resist the urge to cringe. I'm usually smoother than this. Subtler. I know how to play it cool. To pretend like I don't need anything. To act as if I'm really doing the other side a favor. To make it seem as if they're the ones that want the deal. But all my negotiating tactics, all my skills seem to have vanished. I've let him glimpse the one card I was supposed to hold on to.

It's like being back around Nikhil has reduced me to the age of the person I was back then. Emotional and volatile and so . . . young.

I change the topic. "Why did you paint over the brick?"

He watches me, studying my face for longer than feels comfortable, then shakes his head. "Why do you care?"

"I don't," I reply, but we both know I'm lying. I don't have a better answer to offer though. I care and I don't know why and it's only making me angrier.

"Look, this will only take a few minutes," I say. "You sign it and I promise you'll never have to see me again. I'll head right out of here, go straight back to the airport and—"

A flash of surprise crosses his face, but it quickly vanishes as his mouth sets into a stern, thin line. "You won't," he says. He pushes off the wall and heads toward the door. "Grab a crate, will you?" he calls over his shoulder.

I stare at his retreating form for a second, then scramble after him. "What do you mean I won't?"

He balances the bottled water on his hip, freeing his hand to turn the door handle. When he steps inside, he glances back at me and groans. "You seriously didn't grab anything? We're going to need to bring all of it in."

If this is a delay tactic, it's the strangest one I've experienced yet.

"What are you talking about?" I ask as I follow, jumping when the heavy door swings shut behind me. He still hasn't changed that, then. He always said he would, but it's the same old door that we used to have. Always slamming shut when I least expect it.

He finally puts the water down, dropping the pallet onto a stack of similar crates assembled on the floor. "Don't you read the news?"

My jaw almost drops. Is he kidding me? The man who never wanted to read a newspaper, who never wanted to know what was going on in the world we lived in, is asking *me* if I ever read the news.

"You know I do."

He lifts a shoulder. "Well, things change. People change. It's not like you and I know each other anymore."

Ouch. That hurts. It shouldn't because he's only stating the truth, but it stings. Like a manicurist rubbing acetone over a papercut. "Well, I haven't changed," I say, before I quickly correct myself. "Changed in that way, I mean. Of course I read the news."

A muscle twitches in his jaw. "So, you came here. To my house. Fully knowing what was about to happen."

"Knowing *what* was about to happen?"

His brows snap together. "There's a hurricane in the Gulf, Meena."

"It's hurricane season," I reply. "There's always a storm in the Gulf." But even as I say the words, I know they're coming from a place of denial. *No. No, no, no, no, no.*

I pull out my phone, and the screen is filled from top to bottom with blurry images. Messages I can't read. Notifications I can't make sense of. But I don't have to be able to read them to know what they all say.

I rack my brain, trying to recall whether I read or saw anything about this. Nothing popped up when I booked my flight here. No warning indicating that a storm was on its way. I vaguely recall a headline about a hurricane forming off the coast. I must have read it yesterday or the day before, but I meant what I said earlier. There's always a storm in the Gulf this time of year. After some time, the headlines about these things start to run together. For good reason. Most of these storms don't materialize into anything. They tend to dissipate before reaching the shore. I've learned not to get too worked up about it until there's actual imminent danger.

Still, if something was close to Houston, surely I would have noticed it. Surely someone would have told me.

"Was your flight canceled?"

My eyes dart up. I expect him to look smug or cocky. Like he's had one over on me. Like he's known more than I did all along. But his expression is gentle. Relaxed. Open.

I lift a hand to my forehead, trying to rub the tension out of it. "I don't know. My phone's not working. I can't tell."

"When was it supposed to leave?"

"At ten."

He nods, but from that stiff, stilted movement I can tell he thinks there's no way that plane is leaving tonight.

"But everything was fine," I say. "Earlier. Everything was okay. I . . . no one mentioned anything about a storm when I left—"

"It was veering east," he says. "No one was predicting it would come this way until midmorning." He ducks down, removing a water bottle from the plastic wrapping and handing it to me.

I twist the cap off and gulp it gratefully.

"I had stocked up," Nikhil continues. "At the beginning of the season. Just in case. So, I've got plenty of water and food. And we have hours until it makes landfall. It's supposed to get here late in the night, so we'll have time to board up the windows and move some things up to the second floor . . ."

Oh, no. I'm not staying here. I'm not staying here with *him*. There's no way. We won't survive it. I'd rather take my chances with the hurricane.

I turn back to my phone. Surely I can find a hotel. There must be something available. Somewhere. I press the icon that looks like my travel app, but I know I've tapped the wrong thing when Olivia Rodrigo's last album starts playing instead.

"Shit." I press the same icon, but instead of stopping, the music only seems to grow louder.

"Here, let me," Nikhil says, reaching for it. I yank my arm away, but not before his fingers lightly brush against mine.

It's fleeting. Over in less than a second. But electricity tingles at my fingertips, sending tiny shocks toward my elbow. I shake my hand, trying to get rid of the sensation, which somehow, miraculously, silences my phone. I look down in surprise, then groan when I see that the screen is now pitch-black. This thing is officially broken.

"Maybe I can switch to an earlier flight," I say. "If I could use your phone. Or your computer, I could . . ."

"People are evacuating, Meena. Those flights are going to be booked."

The small hope that had been building within me dies a quick death. He's right. I hate that he's right. I remember what that crowd at the airport looked like when I landed. Now I understand the mad rush everyone was in.

"It'll be okay," he says gently. "We'll get through this. This house is in good condition, and like I said, we have everything we'll need. Flashlights and radios and I even installed a backup generator last year. It doesn't always work, but it should kick in if we lose power."

I nod along as if I'm listening. As if it's the *storm* I'm worried about and not the fact that I'm about to be stuck sharing a house with the man I'm trying to sever ties with once and for all.

Turns out I was right before. I am in hell. But it's worse than I thought. Because now I'm trapped here. With the one person I hoped I'd never have to see again.

My *husband*.

NAINA KUMAR is a lawyer by day and a reader and writer of romance at night. She lives in Texas, close to her family, whose antics provide endless inspiration. When she's not writing, she enjoys taking her rowdy rescue dog on walks, rewatching *Gilmore Girls* on a loop, and shopping at HEB. *Say You'll Be Mine* is her debut novel.

nainakumar.com
Twitter: @nkumarwrites
Instagram: @nkumarwrites